End Papers

A Season in Paradise

Mouroir: Mirrornotes of a novel

The True Confessions
of an Albino Terrorist

End Papers

Essays, Letters, Articles of Faith, Workbook Notes

Breyten Breytenbach

faber and faber

LONDON · BOSTON

First published in 1986 by
Faber and Faber Limited
3 Queen Square London WC1N 3AU

Typeset by Goodfellow & Egan Cambridge
Printed in Great Britain by
Butler and Tanner Frome Somerset

British Library Cataloguing in Publication Data

Breytenbach, Breyten
End Papers
1. South African essays (English)
I. Title
082   PR9367.7

ISBN 0-571-13944-2

Contents

Pretext   page 9

Blind Bird

Boland	37
The Fettered Spirit	40
Cultural Interaction	44
Beda Breyten	49
Vulture Culture	53
The Writer and his Public or Colonialism and its Masks	62
Notes from a Political Discussion Paper Contributing Some Elements Towards a Strategy for Revolution in South Africa	66
Random Remarks on Freedom and Exile	71
Conflict and Literature in South Africa	77

Burnt Bird

Pierre Mesnard's Story	87
Freedom	91
Paris	94
The Writer and Responsibility	98
Keep Clear of the Mad	107
Berlin	111
9 June 1983	116
A Festival of Poetry in Rotterdam	119
My Dear Unlikely Reader	125
Palermo	130
from Notes of Bird	135
Fumbling Reflections on the Freedom of the Word and the Responsibility of the Author	142
Upon Hearing about the Hertzog Prize	147
Dead Locust Rumours and Language as the Random Thoughts of Camels	150
Poetry Is	156

the rabbit hunt, September 1984   158
Letter to a Figure in Manet's *Olympia*   160
Angel   162
A Reading of the Present Situation in South Africa,
    Autumn 1984   167
Desmond Mpilo Tutu   181
On the Ethics of Resistance as a Writer
    in a Totalitarian State   184
I Write   195
Can Reform Still Obviate Revolution?   196
Black on White   201
A Letter from Exile, to Don Espejuelo   207
A Letter to Winnie Mandela   213
Dear David   216
Early Morning   223
Breytenbach by Espejuelo: The Interview   225

End Notes   231

All things are absolutely true at all times.
Some things, however, are more true than others from time to time.

Don Espejuelo

And it must be remembered that at birth the chameleon is transparent.

Ka'afir

In heaven and earth, no ground to plant my single staff,
I delight that man is nothing, all things nothing,
Wonderful, this three-foot sword of the Great Yüan,
Like lightning it flashes through the shadows, severing the spring
wind.

Wu-hsüeh Tsu-yüan

Pretext

In heaven and earth, no ground to plant my single staff,
but I can hide this body where no traces will be found.
At midnight the wooden man mounts his horse of stone,
crashing through a hundred, a thousand folds of encircling iron.

Sesson Yubai

[i]

The stage is bare. The eye opens. The inner space, a hall, is vast and
desolate. A film of grey dust covers and permeates everything. You
can actually write on the floor, or on the walls if you feel like having
the mantle of prophecy descend upon you. EUTHANASIA FOR OLD
ROCKERS. When wind enters the dust rises in whiffs here and there.
Here and now are indicated by whaffs.

When you look (again) there are figures on the raised section,
motionless, locked into their expressions, hearkening to their long-
ings as if to pain. First there is Angel, bent double, meaty wrists
suspended above the keyboard, his eyebrows all tied up, paunch
sitting tight. Praying he must be. Or kipping. He has the head of the
turbit. Facing Una who stands with breath stilled at lips, fingers
fixed in a fondle of flute-holes, long grey hair curl-darkening his
face down to the collar. His reflection is shadowing him in the
black-polished wood of the open-tail piano, lending ears. Behind
Angel Narciso sits, he of the darker countenance, the frowned
forehead tilted to attention, one hand shading the strings and the
other petrified on the precipice of plucking. And next to him again
José Watsenaam, limp the neck and the shoulder, holding his guitar
like the light-dripping shield of some deceased warrior. Breathing

9

as if sucking a seegar. The air is known as *'Una flauta en la noche'*.

Further back in the wings, the wings are scorched, and barely discernible because of a parenthesis of blackness paragraphed there, the Old One has his presence. He has his legs crossed and his lips hovering between smile and sneer, and protruding from the boniness of his fingers a cigarette like some stylus with its vocabulary of ash. Also, above the head, a whooff of cold smoke. Nothing is quite as nightly as ink.

Nearer to you, hard in the foreground, an act has been frozen. Someone has conceivably been shot or knifed or cracked open, it doesn't matter, and some other one is hunkered down, cradling in the lap the head of the recently expired dead. The mourner has shoulders twisted in the mould of lamentation. There is the question of the game. Watch out for the soft signals. You surmise that you recognize the persons to the extent that they make you think of mice or of melons, or that you have witnessed that scene before, or some such parody, or that you identify with the agony, but you cannot be dead certain since it is all too close to you for your perception to focus properly.

When wind enters the windows move.

[ii]

(There is the question of the game. When broaching the subject, that is the Other (the Odder), the means of doing so is the game. Communication is a play – instinctively in that one is sublimating mating, the need to chase to catch to dominate and to devour the Other (the Odder); in an acquired fashion because the game is a social defence, of weaving (ducking and diving) and of remaining out of reach and therefore untamed. The game – the linking of movements, the pirouettes and the arabesques, the looking and the writing – is verbal and gestural. It is the exploration of the contours of the Odder. Through the game you create the chance of risk, of becoming the unknown in new knowledge, of falling headlong through astonishing landscapes, and you establish the possibility of maintaining control. Or at the least of keeping a check. For what it's worth. Of bringing the Odder to heel . . . It is erotic, as testing power always is; it can be an end in itself. The anticipation of eating is more nourishing than food.

What then if the Odder is the I? Does the game become sterile?

No, the feeling of the movements will be more complex and the silences more ambiguous. Not to say pregnant. *Jeux est un autre.*
  Never rape a lady against her wishes.)

[iii]

Death is a trip. Traveller afflicted by *Cacoethes scribendi.*

[iv]

Last night you and people close to you went to eat in a rooftop apartment. Through one slanted window a pale and cold moon could be observed drifting through the skies. Later you wended your way home up the dark hill emerging from the many subdued rumours of the city. ('Squelched' would be closer to the truth. Watch your step! Paris must be the number one European city risking total immersion in dogshit.) And just before retiring to bed your ear picked up the hoo–hoot of the owl. A plaintive sound. It could have been the moon. Your sister remarked upon the strangeness of hearing an owl here in this concrete labyrinth. But there must be trees not far off, she said. In a courtyard or a park. And: the owl is a wonderful bird, it is only a pity one never can see it. And: but it mustn't come and cry here. Not now. Death comes so easy. During the night you dreamed, the dream is the muted remains of the scream, or rather you admonished yourself in nightmurmurs: that you ought to rinse some mice and leave them out on the balcony for the owl. So clean that the ultimate mating would make a squeaky sound. The shivering of tiny but rapid movements bathed in moonlight. The darting across the balcony in the cold. Mice, big as pumping hearts, disputing the protection of pot plants. A shadow will come gliding. The predator will stoop, swoop, thrash, and return to a slightly swaying treetop, or a blocked-off loft some-where. Blood and fur at the beak. The tree will in due time wither from the fumes and the acid rain. Death comes easy, easy. (As to Ethiopia.)

[v]

Your sister had brought riches with her: a land. A land in the sense of roots and rocks and odours and locusts and space and the infinite variations of blue. A slowness in the uptake, a turning over of words in the mouth to reveal other reaches. But a land too in the opening up of nostalgia and myth: that stretch of the tongue which the White writers are now so tempted to traverse. No Man's Land. A country where reality (or history, personal and communal, as perceived or imagined through White eyes) is such a fertile soil for Literature. We bury our history as fast as we can kill it off. Sometimes we dig up the corpse to burn it for good measure. South Africans are learning about rituals, about cartoons, about 'magic realism'.

This land of youth. She brought back to mind the wind-blown family graves crawling with ants. There is famine in Africa. Do you remember the farms in the dunes bordering on the mutter of the sea, the farmsteads with wide verandas cooling the interior, and in the gloom of an empty room, Bahbah, the strange girl, sitting there, plump and white and pasty as a queen bee, dressed in the immaculate manifold folds of a bride? The bridegroom will never put in an appearance. No lover on horseback Saturday night. And the years slipped by. There was Rachel – a living miracle, the people said – born without arms or legs. A cascade of blonde curls. Listen to her thump–thumping on her rump down the corridor. Shiny floor. No flute-playing for her. She married a farmer called Swart. She was bedded and gave birth to twins, who turned out to be angels, and then she died. The coffin no bigger than a travelling trunk. There was the man with the leaking heart who slept in a bed that smelled of ginger. When you put an ear to his chest you could actually hear the gurgling sound of faulty pipes. There were people who went off to war to become POWs so that they could escape like rabbits across frosty potato fields and become heroes and thenceforth drunkards swapping tales for drinks. There were suicides. A bullet through the head without even taking off the hat. Floorboards stained with blood. In the dark you could listen to the shuffling in the loft. There were beautiful widows who left for far-off regions and returned with small children at hand. Three-year-old pregnancies. There was the cousin who walked into the jeweller's down that busy street of that coastal town, you know which one, who sighed and promptly fell down dead. Tch tch. So young still. There was Uncle David who had this wonderful knack of talking to birds, and taming them with a cooing of lips and a cooling of hands. They tailed him everywhere, the cranes and the pigeons and the turkeys and the peacocks screeching like demented Greek goddesses. And Uncle David's wife, harsher even than the climate, used to catch them and twist their necks. She had a thing about birds. Or maybe about Uncle David . . . The ancient country.

And now in turmoil. You are told of how police and military personnel patrol the Black townships, directing searchlights there at night, from a distance, and pulling off shots whenever they detect human movement. A *son-et-lumière* show. You listen to someone who has been to a hospital recently where, among other victims, he came across a young boy deliberately shot in the back while lying on the floor of a police cell, by a Black policeman ordered to do so by the White officer. *Pour l'exemple.* The legs paralysed . . . Cortèges come snaking out of the townships where palls of smoke linger, carrying their dead shoulder high. The lines of heavily armed police are sullen. The journalists, waiting with cocked cameras for scoops, will be stoned. You are told that in some significant ways the revolution has already taken place, from within, and that the Whites don't know about it. The rejection of the White state is total. People are indifferent to overtures for the reform of iniquitous structures emanating from the rulers. Collaborators are slain. The youngsters force their elders to stop drinking. 'You have drowned your humiliation in alcohol. We are through with the ways of the White man!' And then the army surrounds and enters a township, kicking down doors, hauling off school kids who are boycotting classes or staying home out of fear for the boycotters. One grandmother (you are told) stays home with a 9-year-old child, to keep him off the streets. The men in 'bush-war' outfits, with their machine-guns and their yelping curs, drag him away. The grandmother goes berserk with worry. She had been entrusted with the care of the boy. On foot she starts looking, from town to dusty town, from detention centre to police station. Three days later she finds him in a distant place, inchoate with terror, swollen from beatings, crying in pain and bewilderment . . . The White are blind. Like in 'Rhodesia' they will enter the areas they can no longer control, jumpy, at a loss to recognize foe from 'neutral', not being able to distinguish a 'terrorist', who has just buried his armoury of stones, from an innocent bystander or potential informer. Eyes slide off faces. The land has become foreign and hostile. In due time mines will be laid, the country divided in 'operational areas'. It is said that, along sections of the 'Rhodesian'– Mozambique border, the sky used to be black with vultures. Animals would trigger off the booby-trapped frontier fences. The stench of decomposing meat covered vast areas. The gorged birds would flutter, could scarcely hop away.

[vi]

South Africa is a symbol. South Africa is a reality. These two truths are intimately linked, as are the mirror and memory, and both can operate simultaneously. (There is the broken mirror, the wooden object with shards of sun-spewing and image-scattering glass, used to lure larks down to earth, to kill them.) But image changes depending on where you are situated, and so does reality. Listen, South Africa is a running sore on the world's conscience, depicting all the misery and the bitterness and the humiliation within the frontiers of one state where one man squeezes dry and pushes down the other in the name of 'racial superiority', of 'civilization', of 'survival', of 'anti-communism' . . . Listen again: Azania is that part of the world where the magnificent struggle for freedom, for mutual understanding, for justice and for self-respect expressed in the respect of the Odder, refuses to be effaced. Take reality if you wish: the minority hogging power (supported by those who white-wash them abroad, having themselves invested in the blood-sucking) will tell you that their regime is the last rampart against atheism, that they impose peace, that they create prosperity, that they honour the culture and the traditions of the Odder . . . They will dress in the same clothes you do; they will be decent and reasonable and hospitable and well spoken; they will speak to you of the horrors of the Far Right taking over unless you 'understand the situation'; they will tell you how they have reformed iniquitous structures; they will draw you unwittingly on to the ground of shared Whiteness . . . While the Western and Christian values in the name of which they rule are perverted and rotted beyond recognition or revalorization: where the only 'peace' and daily bread given to 73 per cent of the population will be famine and tear gas and buckshot and baton charges and bulldozed shanties and mass removals and hospital beds with chains for the wounded and snarling dogs and treason trials and death squads killing and mutilating the corpses; where culture and traditions are reduced to the harsh reality of living as foreigners, as migrant labourers, as squatters in lean-tos, scrabbling for food on rubbish dumps, going dressed in rags, separated from husband and wife and child – in the land of milk and honey, the land of their birth, potentially the richest land in Africa!

Power always projects its own legitimacy. The questioning of central authority – and of the dogma shoring up that authority – must be seen as 'subversive'. 'Security' is identified with government. 'Peace' is the most terrible status quo that could ever be imposed on South African Blacks.

There is no democracy, ever. There is a power relationship between those who rule, and the others (the odders) – where either party may manipulate for partisan purposes the formal structures that incorporate, more or less, notions of democracy or representativity. (There is an ongoing struggle, always having to be renewed, in some parts of the world, to have the principles of democracy entrenched in such a way that they would supersede the power struggle, and serve as the immutable framework for public life.)

Powermongers recognize each other, even if only in the name of international law and order (except where national interests or ambitions preclude the recognition of the other's legitimacy). There is something universal in the relationship between rulers and subjects, in the acceptance of certain methods to maintain that rule, which is far stronger and more ancient than the differences that may emerge from opposed ideologies like socialism and liberalism, or democracy and totalitarianism. Botha, being a politician in power, ultimately belongs to the same species as Reagan, Thatcher, Lubbers, Mitterrand, Gorbachev, Nakasone, Alfonsín, Kohl, Mengistu, Bongo, Machel . . .[1] The killers of South Africa's DNS, the CIA, the KGB, Mossad and all the other spooks and moral cripples of the world are birds of a feather.

No ground is ever neutral. It is a field of tension, of power. The dissident may attempt to enter that area, to exploit it for his or her purposes, to air alternative positions, principles and options. In South Africa, with starkly opposed cultural centrifugal forces, the only role the dissident can hope to play is that of subversive, culturally and politically – as 'traitor' if judged by the dominant ideology of his group. (Naturally his motivation will not be treachery but exactly the opposite: South Africanness, justice, majority rule, anti-racism, tolerance, decency. He will subscribe to the minimal and non-negotiable demands so bitterly fought for by the majority: one unitary state; the same privileges and responsibilities for all; one citizenship; equality before the law; greater social and economic justice; democracy in the sense that the citizens can and must be involved at all levels of decision-making . . .)

You are a fool, of course. You and others like you (because in a

[1]*Note* Of course I'm not suggesting that all those in power and oppressors. Botha is the pinnacle of a dictatorial regime whereas Mitterrand, Alfonsín and others represent, after democratic elections, the majority of their people.

limited way it will be possible to form groups and organizations of dissidents) will be tolerated to the extent that you do not sensitize too much the severely depoliticized White milieu. You will then have to decide whether your opposition, which you have adapted in order to survive, now permitted to exist, is not just objectively making the totalitarian state stronger by giving it a lark mirror of internal flexibility. You may have to provoke breaks, or go into exile, which ultimately must be silence, at least as concerns the central problems of your country.

You may take some consolation from the fact that you are obliged to become more aware of the peripheral nature of understanding, of the unspoken areas, the un-inked perceptions that define group relations, of the ethics of resistance, of the liberating pain of awareness, of the collapsible contents of identity. You may be freed from your roots. In fact, if you were to move through the experienced understanding of compromises and the liberty and limitations of action, without self-indulgence or complacence whilst retaining the commitment to the cause of liberation – *but knowing that the struggle, like life, is a process never to be completed* – you have a fair chance of being favoured and obliged to become 'cool' like a Jew or a Black American or a Palestinian. A professional survivor.

[vii]

What exactly is it that happens to the prisoner during his stay behind the walls? The first fact to remember will be that he has entered *another world*. He may perhaps come to understand that the prison universe is but the reflection of 'normal' outside society, the earlier life . . . but more lifelike. Because his closed world can be found in the mirrors of that other one of which he is now deprived: like the other it has its conventions, language, history, myths, social organization, hierarchy, cults, rituals. The inmate will, were he to rot there for long enough, start to experience his physical and social environment as being the 'essence' of life, the nitty-gritty of conceivable relations between people, all the while knowing (or imagining) that the essential is elsewhere. For this essential absence one can substitute *woman, money, steak-chips-wine, walks in the mountain* – freedom, if you want to be grandiose. Along this line one can trace the mythification of the notion of 'essential'.

Know that you will learn only one thing in prison; to be a

16

prisoner. To pretend that it is possible to rehabilitate somebody while he is locked up is absolute crap. Nearly all the gaolbirds you'll ever meet are economically weak and marginalized in society. Their incarceration can only accentuate the rifts between them and the world.

When you are imprisoned, and if you were to spend any length of that time in isolation, it is inevitable that your sense of time and space will be altered. To survive you will have to let yourself go – the right way: the attachment to an unchangeable and perhaps immortal ego is necessarily disposed of. You will be conditioned without being ever in the position to measure the extent of the modification. You are forced to share in the evil since it takes place in your presence. You are exposed to the unmasked intimacy of human baseness which can never be justified. There is no antidote to the knowledge of evil.

Because prison, this much at least is true, does not veil the harshness of human relations. Treachery is existential, self-evident, the norm. Besides, we are *we* and they are *they*. No fancy smirks and hoity-toity pretences as with the soft-gloved bourgeoisie. Repression itself becomes a reassuring habit, a reference field enclosing security. And yet, to survive, to create the vital living space, to keep optional the perception of self as something unique – and thus the possibility to live with the self even if you don't much respect it – you will have to keep on inventing yourself. Contradiction! Trap!

But now you are free! You have to get out of the above. No choice. Willy-nilly you enter the bourgeois world, ours, which will henceforth be *other*. And here you are strangely dispensed of a whole set of restrictive notions, such as 'private life' or 'standing' or 'aesthetic norms and scales' or 'truth' or 'initiative' or 'meaning of life'. Only thing is you'll now be lugging along a shrunken horizon, without knowing it. You've been burnt, and the regeneration is going to be searing.

First assessment: there are zones that will remain scorched forever. You have been programmed for self-destruction. Watch it! You are going to learn the ropes of depression. You have lost the sense of measure. Do not underestimate your need to be re-admitted.

You will have to take yourself, and that doesn't follow naturally. In the slammer you invented a you in order to make life bearable, to breastplate yourself with a certain dignity. Outside you will invent yourself as a re-creation, a reincarnation. The invention will no longer be a go-between, but an aperture, a cycle of hops, a verse embroidered with silences. Contradiction! Trap!

And you'll be helped by what prison taught you: a finer feeling for the *framework* within which you travel, of *rhythms* (yours, those of the Odder), of *structures* of *links* and *tensions*. With, let us hope, a sharper sense of the ethical implications of any action, grounded in your weaknesses.

No doubt you'd have lost the intimate and instinctive acceptance of all things, the gift of mindless relaxation. Never again will you let go completely. You will not 'belong'. You'll be – make no mistake, my china – the perennial exile. Just as well, believe you me.

There's no miracle cure-all. Reinsertion will be helped along by those close to you. (And with expert aid!) You will need to integrate and to valorize your experiences. Let time do its nut.

Listen, keep vivid your holy abhorrence of all things unjust leading to human degradation, but wire it to an animal patience. Contradiction? Trap? Look, Freedom is not going to be this flush of blood you dreamed of for so long, but rather a weird enjoyment of the banal and pale-day unexpected, even of greyness, and the skeletons of words.

[viii]

Thus you mumbled away to yourself ... Much turgid water has flowed under the Pont Saint-Michel since that rainy night, 5 December 1982, when you landed at Charles de Gaulle Airport. Two officials forthwith penetrated the aeroplane and kissed you on both cheeks on behalf of the Minister, of France, of freedom. Then you and the lady were piloted to a reception area, the doors were thrown open and in barged the squawking journalists, stretching their scrawny necks, shaking their heavy wings into place, cleaning their strong hooked beaks on the microphones. 'When are you going back?' one of them cawed, looking you over with a beady red eye.

The interminable road ribboning into Paris was soppy-shiny with rain. You had forgotten the directions, and you recognized them all. Dorin, the previous French ambassador to Pretoria, was waiting to welcome you in the lobby of the hotel (Lutetia) where the authorities had kindly offered to put the two of you up for as long as you needed to recuperate. All expenses covered. (Except for what you had from the mini-bar, as you discovered a few days later upon leaving the refuge with tiny bottles of cognac and whisky stuffed in your pockets.)

And the rigmarole started, with your feet hardly touching ground. You remember how the next morning your lady had to lead you by the hand (like a short-sighted bird) across a busy intersection to go and buy some freedom clothes. You could feel the cobblestones of Paname through the thin soles of your African shoes.

During the following weeks and on and off over the two years after your arival, as the horrors of your country kept on spilling in an increasing volume from the media, and particularly after your books were published, you became a soft target for flocks of journalists of many countries. Most of them knew not what they were doing, knew next to nothing of South Africa, knew a few paragraphs less than nothing about your work, and that little had to be squared with preconceptions.

It could not be otherwise. For so many of them journalism is a quick shuffle to find the shortest route to simplification and super-ficiality. They are in fact immune to news – in the sense of news being something new having to be tricked into the treacherous old game of words – let alone perception. Some (such as that little fellow whom you have to think of momentarily, living in a maggoty column of the London *Observer*) are so bloated with prejudices, so stupefied by the putative influence of their dribblings, so mesmerized by the need to be 'original', that they can hardly be restrained from kissing their own claws.

In any event, you soon learned that this exposure was inevitably going to flaw your relationship to and with your own work, and quite soon too you came to the conclusion that you'd have to conclude this in-between slice of your existence – already out of prison but not yet arrived in paradise – that you'd have to back out of the hack standby role of 'Mr Ex-Detainee', 'Mr Anti-Apartheid', Mr Odd(er) Afrikaner' if you wanted to survive at all through creating (which implies crashing, breaking), that above all you'd have to tip a goodbye hat to the personage of 'Mr Exile' and *move forward into new pastures* unrestricted by past and guilt and passport and belonging to death. Except that you're wedded forever to the cause of the South African people. Except that there are many cannibals in the world, and nobody wants to let you go, and you were flattered by notions of self-importance and usefulness, and you anyway had to complete your period of mourning (which is a physical process, the unravelling and the knitting), and the urgently desired *soon* snaked over the horizon like a sentence that just doesn't want to end. Dear you, you sighed. But finally got around to dotting the 'i's, coming to terms with a messy history, putting together this record passing itself off as a book. As now. Here. Laboriously. To get it over and done with. As of now. *The last will and testament of the wandering African.*

(You were starting to enunciate clichés with great gusto. You became an expert of the sincere natter and the spouter of hot 'political' air.)

But butterflying was to be a gradual process and it was to find its juridical embodiment in the changing nature of your paper status. You arrived a South African citizen, became a political refugee (with a sky-blue passport that could not have changed in appearance since the Second World War) and then, in December 1983, a naturalized French citizen. What a difference between the attitudes of the civil servants handling foreigners queueing for residence permits and those dealing with newborn citizens! But, of course, there are vastly more of the one kind than of the other . . . And so you were to become a Frenchman, free at last to travel without forged documents, free eventually to castigate your adopted *patria* if the need arose. (As it would.)

Had Paris changed? Not really – at least not physically. Some old buildings had been transformed from within with every nook cannily exploited. There were new phone booths everywhere, none of which worked. You could now elicit money from slots in walls and these would sometimes devour the plastic card you fed them. On some street corners there were big green containers where you presumably were to leave your rubble, bottles and cadavers. Ashcans were now made from a dove-grey plastic; they had orange lids and wheels and black plastic bags lining their innards. *Concierges* had become *gardiens d'immeuble*. The old wrought-iron and steel-plated *pissoirs* had been uprooted, carted off, melted down, and had been replaced by odd oval-shaped cubicles, perfectly closed in: you were (judging by the printed instructions and colour-coded signals) to slip a coin in the spacelab's maw for an invisible door to slide open and permit entry for you to come and execute your intimacies. Naturally you weren't ever going to be fool enough for such a passage to the nether world. Sometimes you passed by just as the trap closed on a hapless victim and for a mad moment you could actually hear the suave strains of a Strauss waltz and the swishing of many spouts covering the pilgrim's desperate imprecations before he disappeared in a long-drawn-out, claustrophobic, soft sucking sound, as in a sigh – gone forever from the air-, sight-, sound- and smell-tight bubble. (Down the drain?)

But ah, the dogshit! Mounds and smears of it everywhere. There were freshly painted images of dachshunds in the gutters: these must have been secret signals to the dog population of the city to let go with the runs, anywhere, at all times. Again and again you came across owners being led on leashes by their canine overlords and saw the dogs arching their backs and straining their hindlegs to produce kilos of defecation on street and pavement and in doorway and courtyard and garden while their humans picked their noses or scratched their privates and challenged you, high-stepping passerby, with the hostile eye of cooped-up city freaks. Never again would you be able to walk the streets and with impunity watch the world-renowned play of light and clouds (like swans going upstream) in the beautiful Paris sky.

Futuristically-clad fellows with dark-visored helmets mounted the sidewalks with their motorcycles and positioned themselves over an offending dropping. The motorcycles had green box-like contraptions on the back (each topped off with a flashing lamp). These would be lowered over the evidence and remain there, vibrating viciously like you-know-whats for the lonely. For a very long time. It is believed that these lowered boxes were fitted, underneath, with brushes swiftly rotating in opposite directions. After the very long time had passed the Martian would stop the shaking, jack up the box, squint down at the object of the exercise, get off his machine, open the box, peer some more (the smoked visor no doubt obstructing the vision), take out a scoop and a small broom, sweep up the matter and deposit same with implements in the box. They were referred to, you learned, as 'the mayor's dung beetles'.

The nature of graffiti – always the pauper's encyclopedia and wisdom – had changed too. Most of it was now just visual pollution, unintelligible drivel to you: small ads for rock groups written in punk. Here and there some spirit survived. *L'anarchie est dans la rue;* underneath which some sad drifter had added: *moi aussi* Or: *Mangez-vous les uns les autres.* Or again (political?): *Les cocos sont comme les poils, on en a plein le cul!* Sometimes, rarely, you would come across an expression of fey charm: *Having nothing to say is no reason for not saying it.* Municipal workers did their best to clean façades and public pedestals. On one huge recently whitewashed square of wall, barely covering the wall-writings underneath, someone had freshly printed in small, precise letters: *This one is too beautiful to pass up.* And elsewhere you saw: *Euthanasia for old rockers and other stallions.*

And you were ill at ease in the country you found. Your peevishness probably had more to do with your state of mind than with the surroundings. Yet, despite the multiplication of means and the obvious release of freedom enjoyed by the media, and despite the praiseworthy acts of some militants using their powerful new positions literally to save the lives of an endangered species – the

21

revolutionary, particularly of the Latin-American variety – you were to learn that Europe's outward-looking *élan* of generosity had been broken, that the perfidious blabmouths (otherwise known as the Parisian intelligentsia) had swung right in a typically bourgeois reaction against Lenin the Father and Sartre the Holy Ghost, that there was no more student activism (except of the Fascist kind), no more trade unionism worth admiring, that public life had become corporatist, that unpunished racism (showing its purulence in acts called *bavures*, or 'incidents') was on the increase, that the Social Democrats in power ultimately had preciously little in common with Socialism. You met and admired some officials, a few outstanding public servants and a remarkable minister or two, and you tried to support them in some specific ventures. What could be done was done. But it was an erratic dance. The Left refused to trust and to mobilize the people. The trappings of power rapidly crushed the representatives. They were finally just common or garden politicians – avid for the preservation of their power and influence and privileges. Although some of those you got to know were steering French society (never say *'la France!'*: there can be no other country in the world where every upstart scoundrel and his mate so easily boom inanities in the name and on behalf of *'la France!'*) with great courage and dexterity through the inevitable troubles of an economic mutation, against the dead weight of 'progressive' and 'workers'' mythology.

The people of Paname hadn't changed much. The shy old man diffidently hawking *Le Monde* was greyer and walking with greater difficulty, but still as philosophical when sitting down to rest his feet and have a coffee with you. The Auvergnat patron of the corner *bistrot* had lost his hair but managed to be recompensed by a waist-tube of flesh. He still uttered the same racist and xenophobic commonplaces while polishing his glasses.

The demographic make-up of the city had however changed somewhat. You now saw far more Third World people, particularly on certain lines of the underground transport. Walking down the street in some areas it was difficult to believe that this beehive was still Paris. What a wonderful leavening! The Boat People, those who didn't drown or who hadn't been intercepted by Thai pirates, had meanwhile arrived in France. The thirteenth *arrondissement* was transformed into a Chinatown which, for you, meant good eating as your studio was on the edge of that sector. The eighteenth *arrondissement*, la Goutte d'Or (the Golden Drop) and bordering neighbourhoods, had become little Africa. In summer months you suddenly realized how many Black people now lived in Paris, perhaps because they were too poor to leave town for holidays the way Whites did and they stood out more as the white sea drained away to beaches and mountain resorts.

Older generations of clochards had gone the way of the flesh. It is perhaps in the nature of clochards to die young bearing very ancient traces on their bodies. In vain did you search for One-Eyed Paul, or the Man with the Mattress, or the Red Emperor. (Though you'd swear a successor had inherited his perambulator and the brindled little dog.) Still, there were more than enough candidates to take their place. Unemployment was here to stay. There was a progressive impoverishment visible to the naked eye, mustering the ranks of the homeless and the unemployed, bringing about the solitude of the White.

The Sheikh now lived on a bench in your street. He couldn't talk, it would seem (though you once saw him ordering a coffee in a sleazy *bistrot* around the corner – by sign language, surely – staring morosely into the cup, the headcloth held in place by string) but could unexpectedly emit a bark-like wheeze when you passed by. He had more sores and rashes on his body than a biblical dog, and a way of inspecting and scratching the carcass that could be described only as voluptuous. He could also sleep anywhere with the greatest abandon, be it on pavement or in the middle of the street, arms flung wide, empty bottle by his side, beard pointing Godwards. He was a master of strings: his three layers of coat closed that way too, and the lot was held in place by a rope around the waist.

On the staircase leading to your studio some poor bums regularly came to pass the night, leaving the results of their bowel movements and some mysterious puddles of blood. Once, when going down the steps to the cellar to put away your bicycle, you surprised a couple there. She was fat and poor and her bosomy bazoom was unbosomed, her skirt above the hips, trying to retain an attractive composure. He was thin and poor and pale, cigarette between the lips, shivering uncontrollably. They muttered something about 'the wrong address' and, when the concierge came screaming that 'this is not a hotel',[1] left with their pathetic plastic bags and their tails between their legs.

There was an apprentice hobo, a young Black, in the next street. Some building was going on there, and Saturdays he would turn up with a goodly number of beers and stand there under the protection of the scaffolding, so dark that you hardly noticed him, getting very quietly progressively drunker. The changes could be observed from

[1]*Note* Meaning perhaps 'brothel' . . .

week to week – the grey flannel trousers and the blue blazer becoming shinier and shabbier, the face more puffy and the hair more bushy.

The young by and large preserved their politeness. The punks coming to absorb their drugs on the Sheikh's bench or in the courtyard where you lived wouldn't loll or be noisy. Over lunchtime a group of them (three boys and a girl), well dressed but apathetic, would gather at the foot of the staircase leading up to your flat. The three boys had short crewcuts and one by one they'd be given a blowjob by the beautiful girl with the wide glassy eyes. You'd come down the steps and one of them would have his back turned to you, smoking nonchalantly, a leg planted higher, fly unbuttoned. *B'jour m'sieu* they would all say respectfully, except for the girl who would have her mouth full of meat, glancing at you with vacant eyes over the smoker's thigh. You remember thinking an unrelated thought: in the cupboards bone-rests of mice like cracked-open bracelets.

You went down the street to visit that building where Mr Breytenbach had lived until he died, and you found the same inhabitants, but you also heard a raw sobbing echoing in the stairwell. You were told that Mr M—, the once proud boss of a cinema hall, was entirely broken now, and how he wept uncontrollably every night, turning up the noise of radio or television to cover the wracking sounds of despair. One evening when some sequences of a film were being shot in that picturesque building you went to watch and you found Mr M— high up on the stairs (as if in the angel's gallery) looking down upon Lino Ventura's balding spotlit pate. He had exercised seventeen different professions, he confided to you – 'life is hard, the landscapes bleak' – and build life with his own two hands; he didn't have the silver spoon, was obliged to start working from the age of 12 as errand boy, waiter, actor . . . You never learned what his problems were.

And you became a vagabond, travelling with the lady from city to city, from one country to the next. London, under the reign of the flash Conservatives showed off its impressively restored town houses lining the parks and the malls, but you knew that there too poverty was eating into the suburbs. In Vienna the Baroque you stayed in an old-fashioned hotel, a petrified example of the luxury of the twenties, where polite-lipped waiters sported tailcoats and a pianist played in the dining room to an assembly of ancient munching aristocratic bodies; and under the sugary exterior and beyond the rearing statues you could sense traces of that hard intolerance and the bone-headed prejudices that had made the city a strong point of Nazism.

Pretext

Amsterdam disappointed you. True, the friends were as warm and solid and cheerful and hospitable as ever, with the first frost of past tense on heads and down the cheeks, but the city had deteriorated. It was much dirtier than before and some streets were quite sordid. The shop-soiled whores on display behind their panes, bathed in a glow of bluish neon light, were just sad. In the area behind Dam Square going towards the station you went down streets where human flotsam crouched against walls shooting the horse into their shot veins with trembling hands. What a fine centre of rebellion and solidarity it had been once. You saw that what had been a quest for liberation was now reduced to the melancholy pastime of shitting on pavements. The city, like most of the rest of Europe, was depoliticized. The dreamers were gone. In the name of 'freedom' corporatist pressure groups were now raucous bands intolerantly narrowing down and abusing the scope of freedom. And there was a return to patterns of the Middle Ages: the unquestioned acceptance that misery and poverty are here to stay and should co-exist with blatantly reinforced opulence. (Squatters would symbolically break a few bank windows now and again.) You even saw a huge exhibition of medieval torture instruments, presumably pretending to be a protest against the horror, but in fact just there to satisfy a cruel sensationalism. Dehumanizing in the name of humanism.

Berlin the scarred . . . Rome eternally seductive with its light, its attractive and elegant people (be they poor or just half poor), like entering a bath of warm and perfumed oil . . . The outrageously ugly and fat but well-known actress in the café on Piazza Navona, showing off her ankle-length fur coat, claiming: 'All made of prick hairs'; and then referring to a former lover: 'He always wanted to mount me, I never understood why – I hardly ever felt him . . .' Lausanne by its lake, the splendour of the looming mountains, the good white wine, the tough Swiss ruthlessly exploiting all foreigners . . . Barcelona, alive, exciting, but a city of robbers (within twelve hours your car got broken into twice – once inside a guarded underground parking lot – and every other visitor you know of has had her bag snatched or his pocket picked): you are told that it is because of the high concentration of desperate junkies there, and again the growing unemployment . . . New York, the vibrant capital of the twentieth century, which blew your mind with its brutal beauty and its bombed-out desolation . . . The Costa del Sol, Africa already in climate, with rich Arabs from the Gulf States gliding in sun-windowed limousines to their blindingly white elephant houses, and British criminals in exile pottering around the golf courses . . . Antwerp, surprisingly lovely and homogeneous labyrinth of guilds and merchant streets and cobble-stoned squares, the excellent beer, the friendly people . . . Los Angeles the Sham City ('I've seen the future, it works, and I'm so glad I won't be there to live it') . . . Frankfurt, depressing . . . Copen-hagen, a city and its people on the human scale where you experi-enced the felicitous marriage – in objects, furniture, the proportions of rooms and of urban architecture – between the aesthetically charming and the utilitarian; you were deeply at ease there, but you also remember jogging early in the misty morning down an esplanade facing the open sea and the cars drawn up, each with only one occupant wrapped in grey clothes, motionless, with maybe a smoke-curling cigarette between the fingers, staring grimly at the water: what a hard loneliness . . . Then there were Lusaka, Harare, the whole of Australia, Bangkok, Bombay – but these localities you'd like to return to in later writing, except to remark for now upon how all Indians have moustaches and how their heads wobble on their shoulders when they want to show agreement . . .

Two other trips did stand out in the mind though: the night crossing from Civitavecchia to Golfo Aranci, the lingering light (after the sun, like the red embryo of an egg, had dissolved in the shimmering horizon), a silvery grey, a pale lilac, a dove green, and passing the moon as if an unknown vessel, dolphins cavorting under the bow, to disembark on a dark island proudly displaying a firework of stars and smelling of Africa. The whole of Sardinia was fragrant with herbs and spices. Travelling through the night the houses in the villages were secure behind their Arab walls. Beauti-ful like a dream of death. (A graffito was brought to light by the car's headlamps: *l'independencia per la lithuania*.) You were to encounter daybreak in a small port on the northern tip of the island, near Capo Testa – was it Palau? S. Teresa di Gallura? La Maddalena? – and a group of boozed-up American servicemen arrived after a night's dry drinking, waiting for their ferry to come and take them back to their Polaris base. One very sozzled boy tried stumblingly to make contact, but his paranoid companion, probably taking you for a Soviet operative in the thin half-light, kept warning him off. 'Don't go hanging with that question, boy'/'Watch it now, boy'/'It's not applicable' (meaning – don't answer it). Coming from France you had forgotten the visible evidence, in the presence of foreign military personnel, of the shadow of nuclear death under which Europe lives; that the continent could any day be the battlefield for imperialist powers. (Two years later, one balmy night on the terrace of a restaurant not far from Venice, an old Italian poet would explain to you how the simple introduction of nuclear arms on a country's territory diminished the freedom of that people. 'It is like a poison. It destroys independence. It generates fear. It makes people less sensitive. It blunts their humanity.')

And you returned to Africa. Inevitably. A film-maker wanted to shoot a part of your life for a foreign television channel. It had to be *cinéma vérité*. First they took you to a prison in Corbeil and it was like walking back into the instinctive mind. You felt at home. The harsh reverberating sounds, unclear down the steel-barred corridors, the mixed odours of fetid humanity and antiseptics and soup, the prison-coloured walls, the feel of authoritarianism and sullen obedience – these were so familiar. In the cell where you were interviewed your conditioned reflexes took over: immediately you checked the means of communicating with adjacent cells through the window, you tried to establish the field of vision of a screw leering through the peephole, your eyes evaluated the cell's potential hiding places – cracks around doorjamb and windowsill, ledges, nooks or crannies behind toilet bowl . . . It was raining outside. A warder had to lock and unlock grilles as the crew moved from one section to the next. A young actor had been hired to play the role of your personal keeper and he was adamant that the credits should show he's not truly a guardian . . . You had long and contradictory discussions with the director about the nature of cinematographic reality. Could life be staged? Why should the viewer be lured into the illusion of 'this is what it's *really* like', or even, 'you are present now at the unfolding of reality'? To make him/her an accomplice, a participant? You objected to the (Germanic?) conception that 'there is a darkness beyond the light which must be explored, and because it is non-rational it will be more authentic'. You felt that fooling the viewer/reader, fucking around with his mind, of necessity manipulating him, was proof of contempt. To which the director replied that all reality was staged; that from the moment you introduced the lens you modified the behaviour of the person (object?) observed/ filmed. (You felt that the man was a voyeur.) Later you reflected that he ought to have used the argument of the one-eyed Turkish writer, Kemal, who shouted at you, in an explosion of fraternal affection during a meeting in Paris, that reality could be apprehended only by the imagination. Reality can only be imagined! Just imagine that! (And coming from a communist author too!)

In any event, you were re-enacting your life for the camera. Playing it. And so, since you couldn't return to the Heaven of Albinos, you and the lady were taken to Botswana, to film Africa. In you flew to Harare, landing early in the morning, day dawning over endless landscape. Crisp air. Change of planes. Small 15-seater (Fokker) from there to Francistown and on to Gaborone. Slow timeless glide over the semi-desert expanses. Gully and rift below as soft wrinkles on immemorial face. You realized: the mystery of Africa is in its light; metaphysics is a matter of horizon, clarity, sand, bush . . . Francistown, two-roomed blue-painted airport building. The pilot got on top of the plane to fix something there. Gaborone. In the evening you would stroll with the director around the swimming pool of the hotel, his Davidoff cigar, his flowing silk scarf, his *Schnurrbart* (turned-up moustache and goatee), while he reminisced with great nostalgia about his youth in Vienna, the flight via France to America (interned before the war in Northern France where, when hostilities broke out, the guards trained their guns on the inmates and not on the aggressors), the films he'd wanted to make. By day you would drive out of town to go and look for Africa (the reality had to be married to the cliché, you see; always give people what they expect!). The way people could be come across walking through the bush miles from any visible habitation – apparently in a hurry on their way to nowhere. The nonchalant way people dressed, putting anything on their heads, wearing a jacket back to front, displaying baubles made of electric flex, clothes pegs, spools, tobacco tins. The cars, each carrying ten passengers at least, in gut-busting stages of dilapidation. The stars at night; majestic buildings of cloud by day. The breakfasts consisting of fruit and cereals and steak and eggs and kidneys and sausages and toast and bacon and jam and tea. The way the wine glass would be filled to the overflowing rim. Generosity. In the middle of the night people would be sweeping corridors in the hotel. The sweet smell of smoke from cooking fires hanging low over the town when evening comes. The police marching, singińg. The slender limbs, high cheekbones, yellowish skin of some of the people (where did all the Khoisan go?). Two friends from Jo'burg, Schwartz and Rot, crossed over. You waited for them just this side of the border. Ah, what joy! The hours flew, you got drunk together, you watched – incredulous! – Afrikaans television from South Africa; a nightsticked watchman came to tock against the window, offering (in Afrikaans) the services of any one of the nubile young prostitutes hanging hip-a-swivel around the entrance of the hotel. (White man, he seemed to imply, could come to Black country for one purpose only.) Night paled into day. You have a photo of you and your two friends against the African sky, squinting into the camera. So serious. Way back. Another of you with some Black kids with their toy cars made from baling wire. You were home!

Pretext

Past tense all. And the need to get it all behind you. You have identified with the agony for too long. The stage is bare. Rot and Schwartz are gone. The eye opens. The inner space, a hall or a book, is vast and desolate. Death comes easy, easy. As to Ethiopia. (Or in a blossoming of blood and smoke as in Azania.)

[ix]

The world is becoming greyer, smoother, less textured. By world you mean environment and customs, both visual and auditory and olfactory. The patterns have set. There are of course the obvious examples: the digitalization, the ordinormalization, the computerization of the human and her word. The getting accustomed to living by balance of terror. The acceptance that survival can be assured only by fabricating and selling death-doing instruments. Existing with the necessity of torture and wipe-outs. Wiping the mouth and voting. Having the WC fixed, buying polyester shirts. Drip-dry minds.

The world is becoming uniform. All over Europe from north to south, in the States and Asia and Australia too, you can stay in identical rooms in the same air-conditioned hotels looking through the same smoked unopenable windows eating the standard 'continental' breakfast consisting of exactly one-size little wrapped slabs of butter/beurre/boter/mantequilla/burro and plastic dollops of apricot and raspberry jam. Not a glimmer of difference between ad and assassination on the concave screen: all image. Processed through Number One Airport guided along by the dulcet imprecations of the Mother Hostess of them all embarking no sweat to eat disembodied (how you love that plastic food!) at referenceless hours of the daynight while having the same canned music flood the droning mind through stereo-reality earphones and be spilled from the belly of the silver bird into the same fume-filled cities. No sweat.

You have to go to the Third World to the other dimension to meet stench and crying and colour and the laughter of people laughing in the pre-air-conditioned-period way. With bodyshakes. To experience the deadlines and the death of your adaptation. The deafness of your glib skin. Also the vague unease, the raspy breath and the guilty gut.

There never will be full employment again; there never has been – except under Mister A. Hitler's reign. 'Full employment' is a lark-

29

luring mirror, a barbaric object of painted wood and glass shards twirled to entice the singer to its death. Progress is producing classes and categories of unemployed, work-seekers, recycled and re-formed labour units, pre-pensioners. They are the fodder turned over by politicians with white cuffs and satin ties; they form the heavy and expansive matter of statistics.

So, to satisfy the mind hooked on not-facing-the-mind – to keep up the grey buzz filling up all emptiness which otherwise may have provoked confrontation – to deodorize the processes of decay – to create the illusions of viability and usefulness: there must be the nothingness-makers. They will establish and keep up the dimension of soothe.

The extras. The orchestras of Muzak and the thousands employed in piping same to lobbies and arcades and lifts and departure halls. The hotel-lounge pianists. Those filling up waiting lines or using vehicles to produce traffic jams. The artists making colour-scheme works to blend with walled vision. The background noise-makers. The canned programme applauders and the sitcom laughers. The wrigglers in blue movies. The brochure writers. International civil servants. The conference organizers. The intellectual circuit and the international jet set. Those who have to wear caps with slogans to have a claim on 'identity'. The camera-carriers. The buyers of detergents. T-shirt fabricants. The communicators and other experts in publicity and prattle. The opinion pollsters. The happeners. Taiwan. The political class. The American dreamers. Journalists.

[x]

Paris, July 1985

Dear Don E.,

Yes, I've been looking for you and I did hear you, whatever you may think. I turned around and I saw you – you who are known as the Old One to the people – I saw you lift a smoky finger to ask: may I? (A laughable thread of smoke climbing to heaven, to show that we humans may burn!) Of course you may. We cannot avoid it. You think I've been beating about the bush for too long? Your questions have been churning in my mind though. I shall try and answer them to the best of my knowledge. It is time, anyway, for me to explain how and why all this came about. *If wishes were horses, beggars might ride . . .*

Pretext

The how part of it is quite simple. The texts you find here in the first section – essays, extracts from a diary – were written during the years of preparation for prison; those in the second section are among the articles, reflections and *etceteras* I wrote, on request or for myself, since returning from No Man's Land. I have now arranged them in chronological order and I added a batch of notes, hoping that they will help you situate the papers more precisely. Of course there are retakes, cutbacks, repeats: it is difficult to step back from a hard-won insight, or to move away from poor sight, and the things were thrashed out blow by blow you may say. *Nothing is quite as wonderful as the tree – all the colours of green.*

I didn't tamper with any of the texts, not because of an imagined concern with historical veracity or vanity (history can be only the version of the dominators, or an interpretation, it is false like the looking-glass), but because that too was an element of the *how*. I hoped there might be a fugitive or furtive or fugal light glancing off the waves of actuality and I saw horsemen breaking through the foam, shaking their empty bowls at me.

Part of the *how* was using the I as prism, inevitably so, unavoidably also as some sort of prototype of South African sensibility. A prison. Perhaps not just any old I, but, at various moments, the ever-changing 'historical' *bonhomme*. Also to get him out of the way. (So that I may get on with the life at hand.) To do that one must remain on the run – the I, the sense of self, the Whiteness, keeps catching up with one, like shadow. Now using the I as prism makes you cross-eyed. To quote Don Octavio: 'Du point de vue de la réalité vraie (la vacuité), l'ego n'est pas seulement une infirmité, c'est aussi une erreur d'optique.' But what other observation point did I have? How else was the unit to strain the brew with the hope of isolating some fragmented experiences?

I hear you going *ka-ka-ka-ka-ka!* You say I'm producing shit, cack, shite, dung, turds, droppings (like a Parisian dog); *whitish* excretal thoughts; that it is a high-blown, fly-brown, bloated exercise in the pastime and past tense of *cacavecdoigt* . . . Maybe so, but that too is intrinsical to the *how*. And in any event I know there will always be, when least expected, an eruption of the irrational, the poetic . . . Strange comparisons grow out of the writing! We all have inside us a subterranean and bottomless pit of ink which wells up, making its way to the surface through immense limitations, strained through the brain, eventually emerging in weak squirts called words – and when enough of these pale and dried reflections of the 'inland sea' fall into line on the page or the ear an environment, an interaction called 'thought' or 'feeling' may take shape. We can't just vomit.

Why? Many reasons. Frivolously – to get to the real writing: the Other Silence . . . To counteract the slackening of the cheeks . . . To unearth the skeleton of the mouse . . . To move beyond, to shake off the constraints of 'the situation' . . . To trace the dotted line, or the zigzag course . . . To sharpen the tongue, make it more penetrating. (How come, you'll ask, the tongue is not yet digested – given the juiciness of the mouth? Or – there's butter, ghee, oil, smoke: and nothing has changed?)

To get through with it. To break through to clarity. Also to continue the struggle. I know power structures are practically immutable and when broken down they're more likely than not to be replaced by others which are as exclusive and manipulative; I know that the individual's grip and grasp of reality is illusory; that politics is a matter of magic, and therefore ritual, and not of rationality. But I must keep hold of Ariadne's thin inky thread, even with the tongue-taste of defeat in the mouth, because every little effort may just contribute towards destroying the old labyrinth. I must hang in there, hoping to help set off some alarms somewhere, and at least to add to the quality of the reflection, to keep some options open by keeping the cells alive. I know, don't I, that I need not believe or trust in the possibility of attaining the objective in order to keep moving. *That* would be falling into the progressist trap. Besides, continued commitment may just succeed in being perceived as a form of solidarity and support – by those in their transit areas and their prisons who need to feel *some* human concern in order to survive. And, also, it is a means of continuing the work on the self, chipping away at the crust of indifference, squirting light into the dying eyes, diluting the pessimism flowing from non-involvement, learning to live with the monkey in the mirror . . . I can situate myself with reference to 'the situation' . . .

What? Moral rectitude? There are areas of vulnerability that need to be investigated. I sense the need for lucidity, but also for dialogue – even if that dialogue has to be forced. To my mind it is important to point at some of the shapes 'modern' colonialism and imperialism have taken, to point out the role of culture, to linger over the act of writing, to know that being is a process just as structure is a process.

You ask me what the real questions are that need to be dialogued about? It is like asking me whom I'm writing for. For the larks, I suppose – using the twirl with its light-reflecting tongues to bring down the birds, to blind them and to burn them. For my African compatriots surely, you may object. True, and if you forget the high-flying phrases, which hide the real issues, hiding like devils in the light, we are down to kitchen gossip. Can it interest outsiders? It ought to, you know. Apartheid is an export product; the plague of racism – of domination and exploitation – has spread over the world; the canker of White violence has infected Africa's fibres. Bloke Modisane wrote a book called *Blame Me on History*. We, the horrible South Africans, could say: blame us on the White-and-Black world.

What the truly vulnerable areas are? I know, you have pointed out before the insidious mixture of private and public. You have accused me of avoiding the sensitive issues by pre-empting them, by going, whistling in the dark like a courageous freedom fighter, to scout for them over the hill . . . You say I have succumbed to the temptations of the minor prophet, belabouring the obvious and counter-attacking viciously when results don't square with my predictions, my wall-eyed schemes; that I'm so imbued with my own 'insights' that I cannot hear or see or translate 'reality' on the other side of the hill . . . Worse, that so much of my criticism is just thinly disguised anti-Communism. Or that it is motivated by jealousy of the authentic freedom fighters, that I try to camouflage the dissipating frustration of not 'belonging', that there is no way in which I can backtrack to Paradise, that I show the typical feeble-mindedness of the self-taught technician of morals, that I can't stand not being Black . . . Guilt complex? You say that my idealism, like all idealism, is more posturing than practice. I plead for a cultural embargo, you say (spluttering from the sidelines), and I don't wish to admit that it is a form of censorship. I lend myself to propaganda. You say I imagine that I know the Blacks (note, that they can *be* known as a group, a race), and why won't the Blacks drive the Whites into the sea? Why do I support a movement, you ask, knowing that if it succeeds it will try and install a Stalinist control over the country? Then to throw my hands up in aggrieved *naïveté*? Where are my African friends, you ask. How gratifying to prance on the world stage! You say that people like me are the true bastards – adroitly courting acceptance by claiming to be 'bastards' – because we do not really think things through. We are the real demagogues. Finally we wash our hands of the responsibility for violence and dislocation and death: aren't we just the 'writers' and not predicators of the climate that will make violence inevitable? (*Writers*, you scoff: 'tortured' and leash-led producers of shit, cack, shite, dung, turds, droppings . . .)

You would take it amiss if I said I agree with you! But allow me at least (at leasht!) to illustrate, or comment upon, your reference to violence: in Boston, I believe, there was a certain Cardinal Cushing who was a great one for brandishing the Word. One day, so the story goes, he happened to be passing by just as an Irish mason came screaming and tumbling off his scaffolding. The labourer lay splashed on the sidewalk dying, gasping for a take-away blessing, and God's mouthpiece leaned over him, held up the cross and asked: 'Do you believe in Gawd? Do you believe in Jesus Christ His only begotten Son? Do you b'lieve in da Holy Spirit?' The worker looked at his mates and rattled: 'Here I'm on my way and dis man comes to me wid metaphysical questions!'

Ah, dear Espejuelo, you make me fancy my contradictions. I suppose the true confession would be that my 'adaptation', there and since, inside and outside, blind and burnt, has been a charade . . . that I'm dying away even from being a Whitish Afrikaans-speaking South African African . . . that I desperately attempt to hide the shame of not having had the courage of my convictions in prison . . . that no amount of 'sensitive self-analysis' can obscure the fact that I cannot forgive myself, or accept that others have forgiven me . . . that I allow myself to be drawn into valorizing actions, trying to fill the bottomless pit of deprecation and disgust . . . trying to spew out the mountain of silence in the mouth, the inertia . . . that all this and all the rest have been a headlong forward flight . . .

True, all so true, as you so correctly said – and even more so at given moments. But it behooves us to talk more gently, for we speak of the Dead. They articulate through us. Let us go then.

With comradely greetings,

BREYTENBACH

Paris, June 1986

Blind Bird

I delight that man is nothing, all things nothing,
a thousand worlds complete in my one cage.
Blame forgotten, mind demolished, a three-Zen joy –
who says Devadatta is in hell?

Sesson Yubai

Boland
(to D.S.)

You say that Helderberg lies shiny with snow
– isn't that how it got its name? –
that it's cold, and wine only
can give the blood the essential throb,
but that one may perceive as ever above Gordon's Bay
the white gnaw and gnarl of Sir Lowry's Pass against the grey:
thus then winter, and you don't say
but already I know: the vineyards are blackened,
Table Mountain's raincape is blown out of wind's way
and waves as toppling as galleons slip through the spray,
I hear a fisherman wailing 'fish!' from his dune
so that man and child lope yelping into the froth
to rake in the splash of sardines
and, why not, the odd whale and hippopotamus too . . .

when I last saw them – how long since? –
the very mountains were aflame: the sea fell quiet
in awe at this pageant: a mirror where embers glowed
and orange fires fired the depths; how was one ever to know
where hell has its limits and the peaks begin to grow?
it was dark then, and summer, the flames an unbridled joy,
and quiet all, one had to be still, the night was white
with smoke, we aboard a foreign vessel
with spyglasses tilted high on toes perchance
to put an eye on God's table; and someone
                            whispered/choked/sobbed?
'the Southern Cross has run aground against yon peak over there'
as also 'the fish scouts must be eating devil's meat tonight'
(the taste not really unlike that of angel's spareribs)

Blind Bird

you know, we're not getting any younger; tonight I envied you,
or rather, your voice pierced the cuirass of my longing,
that hankering of mine which is a mountain fastness –
I craved to slash a pass through the grey of festered years Europe's
grey pus-cities,
to go pluck stars outside in your company,
with snow-silvered shoulders and smoke in the eyes wipe
away the hoar-frost and together quaff the wine
so that the ache of our words may flicker down to soot
and we now know: summer always overtakes the winter,
and then our scars will be invisible!

for that coast – those mountains where the south's gallows
stands flashing like a pharos, those dunes with people
as brown as the wine – that sealine traces the contours
of my caring, the love of mine which is an occupation:
there I wandered before shoes
could know my feet, its coral behind my teeth, its sand
under my nails, its rain whorling my hovels,
its moon had spikes for me to hang my dreams on,
its sun made me lie at night shivering among the reeds:
I am forever addicted to that prehistoric terror
when I was as nothing as all this

therefore: in exchange for your voice I'll mail you these two eyes
wrapped in the very paper – look after them well –
put them outside in the thinnest breeze of all –
that the sun may bruise them pulpy enough
to complete tomorrow the only trip, close the lip,
and grow fat, wait on the doves,
that they may spy on all this beauty
through binoculars of tears

and hunched I'll squat on the roof-ridge here
watching out for news, whether hippos bellow still,
if there be hope for being human, one day, after all, there,
whether winds still free-wheel down the cliffs
and the sand always be salty, the tears be sweet,
the weeping of fisher-folk and tramp workers?

Boland

as for you, my friend: here's a glass lifted to us:
and I do wish: that we may grow calmer than seasons,
and Helderberg stay so light that on its highest crest
we catch the fish to be simmered in wine
over coals of snow
at the foot of the Cross
in the hearth of the house of stars:
then how we shall laugh winter to fire and to flame!

The Fettered Spirit

I want to express by means of the plague the suffocation from which
we all suffered, and the atmosphere of menace and exile in which we
all lived.

Albert Camus

There are certain concepts and principles that, in the Republic of
South Africa, must be stated and restated until one is blue in the
face. This is necessary because of the constant modification, erosion
and exploitation these concepts undergo in the country at the
present time. To the extent that leaders and members of the White
community justify their laws and actions and aspirations in terms of
the universally accepted *meanings* of these concepts and principles,
the pretence must be shown up. One must apply this constant
debunking to nearly every form of organized human activity:
education, legality and the laws, politics, the racial concept, the
right to work, trade unions, private and public business, travel,
marriage and the free association of individuals, etc. And, of course,
culture. And here we touch not only upon the organized manifestation of culture, but also the right and freedom of the individual
to create, to entertain or be entertained, to think, to express himself,
to laugh or to cry.

Culture, to me, is the uttering of a nation's dreams, hopes, fears,
fantasies and desires. It is national in so far as the individual or
group of individuals formulating and expressing these belong to a
nation sharing a common heritage, living in the same country,
exploring a mutual present and moulding a brighter future. Culture
is the way in which the members of a nation find themselves and
their countrymen. It should never be a privilege – the free expression of culture through the visual and performing arts and literature,
and politically free access to cultural manifestations should be a
right never even questioned. This is patently not the case in South
Africa.

Tribal White man has imposed a way of life on the nation that has
reduced culture to folklore, or rather, has denied the progression

from folklore to culture. Apartheid, which puts the accent on – and favours – that which distinguishes one group from another, inevitably means the glorification of the banal and the local as opposed to the original and the universal (or even merely national): handicrafts and postcards as opposed to sculpture and painting, the beating of the tom-toms as opposed to the discovery and enjoyment of richer musical forms, inferior journalism as opposed to creative writing.

Freedom is inseparable. There can be no rich cultural life when man can hardly aspire to the possibility of attaining political and economic freedom.

In which way does Apartheid then destroy culture? It seems senseless to point to recent laws, which, for example, prohibit racially mixed audiences or create a board of censorship so obviously politically motivated. Complaining about these is what I would term 'giving battle', a token resistance to what is considered excessive – whereas the whole ideology underlying Apartheid must be abolished before we can think in terms of culture, and therefore in terms of human dignity. Advocating the liberalization of a situation is another way of condoning the status quo. It is like treating the patient for bilharzia without purifying the water.

It is the basic ideology of the White people in power (and those they represent) as embodied in all the Apartheid laws, which denies culture and human dignity – to *all* the people of South Africa, including themselves.

And this ideology is one of Christian Nationalism or Calvinist Tribalism by which one tribe is trying to perpetuate itself (according to the image it has of itself) by monopolizing all power and dictating to the other tribes their supposed lines and forms of cultural, political and economic development. The development must always exist in relation to the White man's central perpetuation of exclusive power. This tribe dictates to its own members in that it refuses any opposition to or questioning of its ideology of supremacy which may undermine the monolithic power structure.

Apartheid stifles the cultural contributions of the Black, Brown and Yellow man – but in its denial of morality, humanism and dignity, it is probably well on its way towards killing the contribution of the White man.

Other contributors will be able to show in greater detail how the Apartheid laws prevent the growth of culture or affect the existing cultures. My intention is more general – to try and define this death for myself. Apartheid is the big effort to curb the forming of a South African nation – politically, economically, culturally and therefore also racially – which should be one of the most normal things on

41

earth given our interdependence and mutually hybrid origins. And culture and cultural exponents would have been the links. Now it has become futile to hope that one ethnic group may fertilize another, and the brittle contact established previously among writers, artists and musicians of the different groups is being dismantled progressively. It seems to be part of a general movement of contraction and falling apart – a cultural and national death wish.

At this stage of the contraction and the spasm we have influential cultural leaders of the Afrikaans community asking the Government to stop the flow of immigrants from non-Germanic countries (as they fear the extinction of Afrikaans culture) while launching a campaign to replace English by Afrikaans among the 'Bantu'.

We are going to have a new law – to be tabled during the present parliamentary session – which is to seek the prohibition of one race 'interfering' in the political affairs of another: the Prohibition of Improper Interference Bill. For political affairs read anything from social gatherings to plays or jam sessions or writers' discussions.

One would hardly have thought it necessary to pass new restrictive laws. It is estimated that 1,800 people were punished without trial for their political beliefs in recent years. At the moment, there are about 70 people under house arrest; 600 more are banned or restricted; another 40 are living in banishment in remote areas and over 2,000 people are in prison as 90- and 180-day detainees.

Every Government Gazette adds to the list of people whose creative works are no longer allowed in South Africa. The *Classic*, a literary quarterly has this to say in a recent issue: '*Classic* regrets . . . present rules that writers of the calibre of Ezekiel Mphahlele, Lewis Nkosi, Can Themba, Todd Matshakiza, Bloke Modisane, can no longer be read in the magazine or country.' There are many more.

It is not surprising. In the atmosphere engendered by these laws one can see how simple human acts or the description thereof can be given quite fantastic values, interpretations and implications. For a Black man to kiss a White woman is revolutionary. If this act were to be described (enthusiastically) by a writer in a book or on stage, or even shown by a painter, the life of the work would be endangered. And in this environment unfortunately a 'literary' or 'artistic' importance would be ascribed to this work far beyond the import of the simple description. The daring young man on the flying words.

And to the extent that culture is also the expression of social ideas and values, the writer, the artist and the musician must use it as such, and use it to fight for political freedom, for dignity and for justice. Man lives only in other men; he expresses his dreams only in *human* terms, his only real fear is of other men. It should be up to the individual to decide how much 'message' or propaganda his work can carry, and in which form.

Already the final decay has set in South Africa's cultural world. If the Coloured people of Cape Town can no longer attend concerts in the now all-White City Hall, then music must eventually suffer. If our painters are relegated to painting esoteric pastoral scenes and 'Bantu' motifs, then our paintings will be just decorations on the wall. If plays with a mixed cast can no longer be staged, then the spirit of the theatre must become atrophied. The non-White writer may, if he is lucky, leave the country for a bitter exile. If the White writer, to be able to continue writing, must compromise his humanism (his love) – for Apartheid is practised also in his name – then the illness has touched and discoloured the very blood of his being, and his writing will be an aberration of European culture. Perhaps the fact that no Afrikaans writer has been banned yet is a measure of this.

> And that is where the catch lies. Most White South Africans have simply never opened their eyes to the reality of there being other humans besides the Whites in this country. They do not 'do unto others', but unto an unidentified mass of Natives.
>
> *Nat Nakasa*

As long as we have Apartheid – and the mutual fear, distrust and hate this inspires – it will be impossible for South Africa, or any of its ethnic groups, to develop a living culture.

Paris, March 1967

Cultural Interaction

Questioning is questing.

No man is uncultured. Article 1 of the Declaration of the Principles of International Cultural Co-operation (Unesco) states: 'Each culture has a dignity and value which must be respected and preserved.' Here, we can substitute the word 'individual' for that of 'culture'.

What is culture? For the individual it is certainly a quest for knowledge, an effort at understanding the unknown, a way of situating himself and probably a way of passing on knowledge (concepts, memories), or just passing on the questioning and the need thereof. It embodies the hopes, the fears, the pride, the joy and the misery of a family or group or community. Seen as a conscious structure it can be (and is) used to expand the power of the community over members of that community or other communities; as a structure it sometimes serves as a nostalgic refuge for the economically weak and the politically disinherited. There can be no criteria to measure and compare various cultures without those criteria being defined by the relative political and economic strength of those cultures.

What is cultural interaction? In the working paper prepared for this meeting by the Secretariat we read: ' . . . culture is the essence of being human.' Being human – to be – is to exist in relation to others, to communicate, react, influence and be influenced – in short: to interact. Interaction is the essence of being human. Therefore, culture is interaction – on an individual, communal, ethnic, national and international level. Interaction is what cultures do. Interaction is the practice of culture.

I shall therefore look at cultures not as structures (or edifices) but as vehicles of thought and action; not at cultures as they are, but cultures as they do and as they are becoming.

To do the above, and in order to show up the lack, the presence or the necessity of 'rights' in cultures, I shall discuss briefly (a) the right to interact of the individual artist/protagonist/teacher; (b) cultural interaction on the national level, i.e., within the boundaries

44

of one state (and here I shall have to use South Africa as my example, it being the country I know best and also because we are in the presence there of starkly opposed cultures); and (c) cultural interaction on the international level – where we may talk of 'active' and 'passive' cultures and where, as far as the Third World is concerned, it has been rather more of a penetration than an interaction.

(a) There can be no doubt that the most strenuous efforts must be made to protect the cultural rights (the absolute freedom of expression) of the individual, who is the basic cultural unit. The artist, the writer, of our epoch is often living under conditions of intense stress and with a growing sense of alienation and personal frustration (because of a rapidly expanding and industrializing and dehumanizing society). In order to adapt, he is bound to question and contest the structures (cultural and other) of his society, the assumptions and the dogmas upon which these structures are based, the individuals, instances, groups and interests, that benefit from those structures when other groups suffer through them.

This need for protection – and often the absence of any protection – is shown up the moment the individual actively starts to contest and criticize customs, structures, institutions, mores, accepted ideas, etc. It is essential that the individual, the cultural unit, be protected so as to interact freely – and therefore ultimately constructively. This should not be a privilege extended by a permissive society, but a universally accepted and practised right. Cultural interaction on the personal level is the constant re-evaluation of existing frameworks.

(b) In the present world – and this is particularly true of South Africa – all culture, literature and art emanate from particular classes and convey specific political ideas. Art for art's sake, art separated from the class from which it grows (or the ethnic group or community), art independent from politics or parallel to it, does not in reality exist. Proletarian culture, for example, is part of the whole proletarian revolution; it is, as Lenin put it, 'the nuts and bolts' of the machinery of a revolution as a whole.

Arthur Bryant wrote (in the *Illustrated London News*, 9 July 1964):

And since man lives in communities, the test of a community's virtue is the capacity of its institutions and traditions to evoke the spiritual greatness of its members. A community which fails to do this is failing as a community and will in the long run

45

perish, because it will come to consist of men and women who never become what they were intended to be: it will consist, in other words, of human failures.

This is the case in South Africa where we presently have little or no cultural interaction. There is nearly none precisely because there is a complete denial of the human rights of the non-White majority, let alone their cultural rights. The White minority in power pretend to 'preserve the separate cultures' – which, in practice, means preserving the folkloric – by eliminating and suppressing all contestation, which, through culture, may threaten the existing established order.

It is impossible to evaluate the extent of recent cultural interaction, brought about by the cohabitation of various ethnic groups over three centuries, because not only is all such interaction now forbidden but a conscious effort is made by the White community to destroy that which did take place. This acculturation (and mutation towards a greater, more comprehensive culture) can only temporarily be checked though – it can never be stopped entirely. Already we know that the cultures alive in South Africa are themselves products of earlier interaction: Afrikaner culture is essentially the offshoot of a shotgun marriage between European, Malay and Khoi–Khoiin elements; the African South African culture has been profoundly influenced by this resultant White African as well as by European cultures. Here, remnants of a 'Western' culture will survive only in its positive (i.e., valuable and assimilable) aspects to the extent that it can be used by the people to further the cause of freedom and on condition that it is not used as an excuse or a means by those now in power to justify their domination.

For culture to flow freely in South Africa, the present political hierarchies will have to be abolished. To have any meaning at all, cultural activity in South Africa will have to be revolutionary and Socialist in the real sense of these concepts so often warped and misused.

(c) Let's face it – we seldom react to the abstract merit or beauty of a culture or of its exponents but to the ideas transported by it. Culture (when consciously expounded by a group) is not a matter of kind but of degree and the uses and abuses of it.

It seems to me that we have internationally (at least as concerns the First and Second Worlds, on the one hand, and the Third World, on the other) the same situation we have on a national level in South Africa.

Cultural Interaction

I think the problem lies in the fact that we have basically two different kinds of societies: that which is expansionist, which needs to 'penetrate' and occupy other cultures and areas, which needs to impose its views of society on others, for which it is necessary economically – or at least according to its own estimation of its economic needs and wants – to exploit foreign markets and peoples; and that 'other', humanist and 'passive' society, which seems to content itself with what it finds within itself and at home.

In Africa, for example, culture nearly always stresses the family or the group and cultural means are used to maintain the human and humanist elements.

In the 'White' world it would seem that individual achievement is emphasized and wittingly exploited, either to impose the European view and way of life or to maintain the status quo where the settler, or his élitist representative, plays a dominant political and economical role. In this way their culture became a tool of penetration and not interaction – though one may ask whether it is possible to penetrate without interacting. Thus do the 'members' justify their dominant positions.

Nowadays we see examples of international financing used by rich powers to propagate their cultures, their views of 'freedom' and 'unfreedom'. At least since the late 1950s and the early 1960s these efforts have been well camouflaged – in the use of gullible individuals, the ample but discreet flow of money to finance publishing for example, in the manoeuvring of national and international agencies – all geared to the massive effort of trying to contain real contestation. Whereas before we could talk of colonialism as the rape of the Third World, we can now qualify neo-colonialism as the prostitution of the same for the benefit of rich customers.

Internationally the most influential powers have for a long time reacted as a bloc highly aware of its vested interests, highly skilled at preserving these and using all necessary concepts and organs to promote them. We should be very careful lest international organs reflect only the supposedly 'liberal' ideas of these members.

The Third World, whose only vested interest for so long has been physical survival and whose vested interest for the present and the future must be the freedom of real independence and the freedom to forge revolutionary cultures from old fertilizer and new seed, must take its rightful place on the world scene.

Here, too, we shall have to abolish the existing hierarchies if

47

any free interaction of cultures is to take shape. But it will be of no use to ask for this or even benevolently to legislate internationally to bring it about. There will be a free flow only when the hierarchies of power are abolished or when these hierarchies do not feel their power threatened by free interaction (which is inconceivable).

Human rights in culture – the right and thus the possibility to interact – must, in the international agencies and councils, be reflected in the proportional presence with the proportional influence and power of the Third World. This is internationally a *sine qua non* for cultural interaction, i.e., the mutual dissemination and receiving (sharing) of education.

Finally, the proof of the value of a culture will not lie in the extent to which it 'coloured' other cultures, but in the extent to which, if it was a 'strong' culture, it allowed other cultures to coexist and fully to share that knowledge (technological and other) upon which its strength was based, or, if a 'weaker' culture (i.e., exploited culture) the way in which it was used to subvert and break the grip of stronger cultures. You will have noticed that in addition to pointing to some of the things cultures have been doing, I have also tried to say what – to my mind – they ought to be doing.

I have written this as a writer and painter and as an activist interested not only in the function of culture as a vehicle for thoughts, but also as a vehicle for social and political change.

Paris, 1968

Beda Breyten

Beda Breyten,

I want to write to you about the happenings of the past several days. I wish to write to you in the manner which you would have used if you were to write to yourself – and thus the two of us may well together reach a new low point of make-believe, or is it hypocrisy?

The two themes which I want to touch upon are *covering* or cover-up, and *curiosity*.

Covering, like snow. Because the snow has come, was loosened from somewhere and came to cover everything, the lowest slopes just as the high ones, those of distress and those of joy. Death, this whiting, can certainly not be painted any better than the way it is done by the hands of snow. Snow makes death. There is neither life nor electricity nor sugar in snow. But snow is already decay: the decomposition of the cold. Then, if it gets even colder, a layer of ice may come to preserve everything for a little while, but finally it will rot with the finality of all rotting to life-giving water.

You are an open book for me. I only need to write you. (But I often doubt whether it is worth the trouble – and I do not even need to tell you again that a book 'at its very best' is only an elegant façade, a more effective way of covering.) I know for instance that you always associate snow with Japanese landscapes or townscapes. The gutters and the rooftops or the outlines of hills stand out black and stark against the white rest. A sparrow or a raven or even a motorcar on its way somewhere against such a background becomes quite a dramatic notation. There is to top it off the ephemeral effect of faint feathers of smoke emerging from the chimneys, in contrast with the terrible heaviness of the white world all about.

Snow is above all else a cosmetic. There the trees stand powdered from tip to root – like old and lethargic whores. In exactly the same way death is a face-paint, a disguise, something which glitters and is attractive only under artificial light. There is something fake about snow, and yet death is not false. Decomposition exists, is perhaps the one and only unchanging factor. And snowballs sit in the forks of the tree in the courtyard like tits of water.

Snow is exactly the perishable made visible. Snow is nothing; it is the very core itself of transience. Snow is that nothing, the void which you can eat.

Last evening you were in the house of a Mauritanian – a Bedouin. Among the other guests there were, apart from the desert Arabs, also Egyptians and Algerians. With them you lay down next to the communal platter to eat the couscous and chicken with oily fingers. In the entire flat there was not a single chair. One by one you all drank camel's milk from the same wooden bowl, and mint tea after the meal. The host, his wife and his friends, were all clothed in loose-flowing djellabahs, and with the soft sibilant sounds and glottal occlusions of Arabic in your ears, with the arabesque letters against the walls, you could quite easily imagine yourself in a nomad's tent somewhere in the Sahara. But everywhere outside, just beyond the walls, Paris waited: harsh, snowed under, careless, embittered. And the conversation touched upon the court-martial in Burgos, on the Fascist repression in butcher Franco's Spain. (Why do I tell you this?)

When you go to bed the snow does not cease existing. In the middle of the night you may get up to see the white stench glinting outside the windows. And the flakes keep on falling against the windowpanes: an unwelcome visitor continuously and soundlessly knocking, knowing that you will eventually have to let him in.

Mr Breytenbach is dead. Since two days and two nights already his corpse is laid out in the building down the street from where you live. You have started wondering whether the carcass may not begin to smell and you stayed on the look-out for a convention of flies – which would have been most beautiful to see against the backdrop of snow.

He was not very aged – probably 40 if that – and a friendly person; one of the few neighbours who did not greet you from on high but always with an attractive if slightly frayed smile. The cause of his demise was a drying up of the lungs. They say that his death was a true relief, like snow coming after the excessive grip of cold.

Today they arrived to put him in his coffin. Your *curiosity* became too strong. You did not go to work but just like the fat and hairy concierge shivering in the cold, you tried to stay close to that house as unobtrusively as possible until your feet in their shoes were soaked and frozen.

The undertakers are dressed in black uniforms with on their caps small insignia showing the image of a minute coffin. They look a lot like traffic wardens and you half expected to see the bump of pistols on their hips, as with the park attendants. One of them carried a small blue toolbox, just like that of a plumber. This was, as could be expected, rich fertilizer for your feverish imagination. You expected that the corpse – in the process of embalming – would be emptied of all its innards. You would even have liked to see the intestines chucked from the window on the fourth floor out in the snow, so that the sickly doves might come pecking at it, so that the errant cat with all its hair standing on end might come to enjoy some of it. And you expected that the pale carcass would then be packed in snow in its box.

You are obsessed by death. Your whole life is a preparation for that one pure note. You are addicted to the idea of dying and your only fear is that you may miss that appointment.

Then you went to wait at the foot of the wooden staircase while they carried the coffin down, slipping and sliding on the icy steps. Secretly you maybe even wanted them to drop the coffin, for it to come plunging head over heels down the stairwell, so that it might spring open and eject the carcass on to the snow. Like an observer you stayed there staring at the red and bloated (and how endlessly vulnerable) face of the widow. It reminded you of the faces of women who had been deeply wounded on purpose, and the look they then carry afterwards, exhausted by crying, as if at a loss, and incredulous.

You disgust me.

The coffin was shoved into the car of the deceased to be transported to the South. There the last resting place will, the day after tomorrow (with New Year), be chopped in the ice and the snow of a frozen earth. And with your imagination you accompany them on their voyage – voyeur! . . . in this vehicle of sadness. The *autoroute* is closed for all traffic because of snowbanks and black ice. But the concierge assured you that a car carrying such a burden might at its own risk use the road, by exceptional permission. You wonder whether one would need complicated permits for the entirely private transportation of dead leftovers. You ask yourself whether a dull and heavy-minded policeman, importantly on guard at the entrance to the freeway, might not insist that the box be unscrewed so that the declared contents be presented for inspection.

And when it was over you came back home, to sit here next to the hearth so that I, your better instincts, may put it all to paper for you. Because you are ashamed of your own morbid interests, of your obscene imagination with its cogs sometimes slipping and not

Blind Bird

getting a hold on reality? Or was it only to double the pleasure and make it last longer? Of course you tried to imprint upon your mind the mind-fracturing ceremonies of your own death. (Was that perhaps the reason why I had to write this?) You would have liked to stroke the coffin with your palm, to throw a fistful of snow over it, or even to be allowed to touch the cold head with your fingers. The most important, when there has to be dying, is that there should be a friend at hand to take you into his eyes and perhaps touch you surreptitiously and shyly; that you should not disappear without tracks or a change of address; that something of you may be taken back, behind the eyepeels, enfolded in the memory or even the imagination of the onlooker, to the old country, to where distance commences.

I pity you. You cry over nothing. Over spilt milk. Just like that. Over the snow which has already obliterated the markings in the courtyard, very softly, but pitilessly.

That we may be cured of life.

The snow on the streets has become ice. High through the night, reasoned out above this desolate earth, the wild aeroplanes growl: on the way to a warmer, therefore more humane South.

Vulture Culture

The Alienation of White South Africa

It is my contention that the culture of the White people in South Africa is an organic development of 'Western civilization'. It may be a perversion thereof, it may crystallize only certain elements of that civilization and omit others, which, at a pinch, might have softened the features – but surely this crudeness is due to their being cultural settlers. White South Africa is Western and Christian just as French Algeria and British Kenya were, just as Alabama and the Vietnam War are; it is as Western and as Christian as large sectors of the Western world's population would want them to remain or to become.

Looking into South Africa is like looking into the mirror at midnight when one has pulled a face and a train blew its whistle and one's image stayed there, fixed for all eternity. A horrible face, but one's own.

Apartheid is the state and the condition of being apart. It is the no man's land between peoples. But this gap is not a neutral space. It is the artificially created distance necessary to attenuate, for the practitioners, the very raw reality of racial, economic, social and cultural discrimination and exploitation. It is the space of the White man's being. It is the distance needed to convince himself of his denial of the other's humanity. It ends up denying all humanity of any kind both to the other and to himself.

Apartheid is the White man's night, the darkness which blurs his consciousness and his conscience. What one doesn't see doesn't exist. Also, at night one doesn't balk at the skindeep peculiarities of the girl you sleep with. They are all pink on the inside.

But that which may be a psychic purge for the White (his binoculars to see the end of his nose with), is a physical straining for the Black; the confines and the confinement of his condition, the maiming of his possibilities. White is the Black man's burden and what he wishes for most, probably, is for the man to get off his bloody back and stand on his own two feet.

Blind Bird

Apartheid is at the same time the implement of exploitation and the implementation thereof. It is the lion-tamer's whip and stool. The lion sees stool, whip and man as one.

Obviously, this instrument of repression is also used, structurally, on White society itself. In the name of the state – the state is the daughter of Apartheid – all dissidence is suppressed. White workers too are told to sacrifice their legitimate claims on behalf of Apartheid.

It is Fascist. ('Fascism: the principles and organization of the patriotic and anti-Communist movement . . . of the *Concise Oxford Dictionary*.)

It is totalitarian. ('Totalitarian: relating to a policy that permits no rival loyalties or parties.')

Apartheid is alienation – estrangement leading towards insanity.

It is schizophrenic – a mental disease marked by disconnection between thoughts, feelings and actions.

It is paranoic – mental derangement, especially when marked by delusions of grandeur, persecution, etc.

For the White man, Apartheid is a distance of mind, a state of being, the state of apartness. From the assumption of apartness – from the necessity to stress this apartness, to justify and rationalize it, to obscure that which may strip him naked – White culture in South Africa is born.

Apartheid is White culture.

What is culture?

In a Unesco publication, *Cultural Rights as Human Rights*, it says: 'Culture is a process of communication between men; it is the essence of being human.' It states further that this communication can take place effectively only when the poor throughout the world are liberated from poverty, disease and illiteracy.

And in the same publication Francis Jeanson puts it this way:

> Culture is the perpetual creation of values which are born only to be superseded . . . A cultural act is, in the last resort, a solemn and even risky decision implying a total engagement of the individual conscience concerned . . . I would add that this amounts to a venture, in the best sense of the word, aimed at arousing in people a profound political consciousness . . . [It] is a venture which is based on a refusal: the refusal to accept a certain exclusion, a certain alienation. This by no means implies any attempt to camouflage the economic causes of such an exclusion; but these must be fought with political weapons.

'The community must be returned to itself' – George Lamming.

Vulture Culture

The culture of the Whites in Saint Albino – this state of White-ness, the prison of laws and taboos – negates all political consciousness. Apartheid justifies itself in the name of Western civilization, in the name of the Afrikaans culture. The tendency is there sometimes to think that Apartheid is an unpopular dogmatism devised by a few bureaucrats and some perverted theoreticians and imposed (also) on the majority of Afrikaners. One must point out that the Afrikaners are responsible for Apartheid, collectively and individually. Without them it would not exist. It is their way of life. If the Whites as individuals, if all those who practise culture (the intellectuals, the academics, the artists, the authors, etc.) were to withdraw their direct or implied support of Apartheid – not only of a particular government, but of the ethics of Albinohood itself – it could not last.

In their thrust for power the Afrikaners defined themselves as a cultural entity. They still propagate this defensive definition of themselves with vehemence and passion. Given their origins one can understand the passion.

They are descendants of emigrants who were forced out of Europe or were ill adapted to it – sailors, mercenaries, downgraded civil servants and difficult minorities such as the Huguenots whom the Dutch authorities farmed out to their African colony. (Europe has always shown the tendency to solve its ethnic, religious and social problems by offloading the unassimilables on to the Third World.) Locally non-European blood was mixed in; the blood of slaves, the blood of the conquered ones. Neglected, unsupported and unprotected by the motherlands – until diamonds and gold were found – they soon imposed, in the first place upon themselves, their view of what they thought themselves forced to be: a new 'people', still White; an extension of European culture – which meant Calvinist puritanism – into hostile but covetable surroundings. Thus we have from the very outset insecurity and a correspondingly passionate affirmation of the nature and principles of the tribe. Doubt will be suppressed, purity must be preserved, descendence is to be whitewashed and there results a pathetic clinging to 'European' culture. (It is the story of the pale virgin with the dark-skinned brood.) One pretends to be what you are told you ought to be – with the outward and fossilized signs of European ways.

Consequently we find a literature that does not issue from personal experience, but is grafted on to another, European literature; art grows out of art; culture is a parody of Europe's cultures; aesthetics are unrelated to any conceivable facet of reality. Culturally Saint-Albino Whites live from overseas offal. (Spiced, it is true, with

55

what can be taken from indigenous cultures – as in the field of popular music for instance.)

Thus we can see that in the beginning there was uncertainty, ignorance and greed. Therefore fear and the need to define. The definition was based simplistically on the aspects that most obviously marked the settlers as different from those around them. This definition (White, European, Protestant) allowed for greed to be rationalized as survival at first; later as independence and guidance and civilization and justice. And culture. The tribe became a power. If you say power you also say Party or Church, and the Party must have priests to protect its Whiteness. But this purity is based on a lie. Yet, the purity must not be questioned. Only, truth is awareness which needs to extend its grasp to survive. Therefore: dichotomy. The tribe's power is to the advantage – in the first place – of the bourgeoisie: they prefer the norm to the truth and they see to it that the priests affirm and reaffirm this norm.

The tribe becomes a closed fist. Now there is ossification of attitudes, ultimately even contraction cramping the fingers and cutting off all the blood flow. There is withdrawal into the unpolluted air inside the clenched fist. In the last stage gangrene sets in. And in any case – uncertainty, ignorance and greed. Therefore fear and the need to define.

The tribal ethos of the Afrikaners consists of negation, suppression, withdrawal and reaction.

What, more precisely, are the effects of Apartheid on White South African culture?

The first thing to point out is that Apartheid works. It may not function administratively; its justifications and claims are absurd and it certainly has not succeeded in dehumanizing – entirely – the Africans, the Coloureds or the Indians. But it has effectively managed to isolate the White man. He is becoming conditioned by his lack of contact with the people of the country, his lack of contact with the South African inside himself. Even though he has become a mental Special Branch, a BOSS of darkness, he doesn't know what's going on – since he can relate only to the syndrome of his isolation. His windows are painted white to keep the night in.

For the White author or artist it results in less contact with reality. He cannot dare look into himself. He doesn't wish to be bothered with his responsibilities as a member of the 'chosen' and dominating group. He withdraws and longs for the tranquillity of a little intellectual house on the plain by a transparent river. He will consider himself a new 'realist', an 'anti-idealist'. 'This is the way it is,' he says. 'It has always been a horrible world to live in. This is the way

I am. I just want to be an ordinary human being, free to write or paint or film as I wish. I don't want to have anything to do with dirty politics.' He cannot identify with anyone but his colleagues, any other class but his own White well-to-do one, and with this he probably identifies by default. His culture is used to shield him from an experience, or even an approximation, of the reality of injustices.

A prominent young Sestiger (a Sestiger is a youngish Afrikaner who kicked up his heels a bit during the sixties) when asked what he thought about the many books banned in the country, wrote: 'Once we've learned to think independently and responsibly, many of my English colleagues will no longer write books that have to be banned.'

How can the White man feel angry about his injustice which doesn't affect him – that is, whose effects he refuses to recognize?

But even so he feels the need, natural to the intellectual, to contest and criticize. Since the 'fight for survival' of the tribe was made in the name of its culture – its language and religion – the Poet-Thinker has always played a very important role. The tribe expects the Poet to be an exponent of its tribal values, not a dissenter. These values are power values only, and at times the Poet knows this. He knows that whatever is published is on sufferance of the Publications Board. The Establishment will spare no effort to prevent the publication of a work that may play into the hands of the 'enemy' – the enemy being the people of South Africa. But this suppression if it concerns work by an Afrikaner – the offensive work in English is simply banned – will be subtle, or at least discreet and out of public sight, for the sake of the façade of tribal unity. Invariably it will take place before publication.

How? Through the classical carrot-and-stick approach. The carrot is the possibility of having the book prescribed for schools or bought in bulk by provincial libraries; of being commissioned to write or translate for one of the provincial theatre councils; the carrot is any of a number of literary prizes; of being taken to the bosom of the tribe by being put on a pedestal – of becoming the Poet.

The stick can be the spelling out (beforehand) of any of a whole series of laws: the law on blasphemy, the law protecting any section of the population against verbal injury, the law on the suppression of Communism, even the law against terrorism. (I need not remind you that these are some of the walls of Apartheid.) Or senior intellectuals when consulted in their capacity as guardians of the Culture will advise against unnecessary and disruptive controversy: 'high instances' will pick up the phone to enquire, to threaten or even to bargain; a member of the Publications Board (who may also be a respected *literatus* doctor or a writer) will intervene (before-hand) to confirm in private.

If all else fails the printers will simply refuse to print the objection-able work.

The Poet is scolded and cajoled; he hears of the considered opinions of publishers' lawyers; he learns that the publishers simply cannot afford the financial strain of being sued by the state, etc. So the Poet sets about changing words; he cuts lines and deletes poems; he cleanses titles and forgets about certain books. The next time around he will cut before sending the work off. And presum-ably he won't bother to write unacceptable things after that. For the Poet cringes. He cringes before the possibility of being kicked out of the tribe, of thus losing his 'identity' and his 'relevance'. He attempts to reduce the area of possible friction between him and the tribe and – with eyes closed – he invariably starts writing right. And now he is cringing before the Word, or – to be less dramatic – before his conscience. In this way our Poet becomes the tongue of the tribe – but not by telling them what they refuse to listen to.

Note that there is no legal precedent that can give weight to the considerations used to pressurize the author; he is convinced solely by the lawyers' interpretations of the law in question. No Afrikaans book has yet been prosecuted. What other evidence can indicate more eloquently the rot to which the Afrikaner intellectuals (and their publishers and teachers) have succumbed?

And to soothe his ego he will, as an enlightened one, push forward and attack certain taboos, as taboos. Thus, for example, the fight against the restrictions on the presentation of sensuality. Thus, too, forms of racial discrimination are attacked as a taboo would be – to shock and excite the attention of a tribe. It is not the reality of discrimination that is attacked, nor its implications, since that would lead into uncontrollable darkness. If you were to start unravelling all that thread you'd soon find yourself with no clothes at all; you'd have to envisage the destruction of the tribe of the Afrikaner as Afrikaners, for discrimination is embedded in the tribe, is the *sine qua non* of its existence.

And these attacks are so much grist for the mill of Apartheid.

Stinging denunciations, the exposing of distressing conditions and passions which find their outlet in expression are in fact assimilated by the occupying power in a cathartic process. To aid such processes is in a certain sense to avoid their dramatization and to clear the atmosphere.

Fanon

Vulture Culture

I have tried to show how the culture of the Whites in South Africa is at present a framework of lies and compromise – and that it therefore leads to dishonesty, corruption, degradation, shame and decay. The tone, the climate of the creative artist's environment, is the system of institutionalized violence. Although this violence is seldom directed against him he still has to live in the system – in fact, he is part of that system. The White artist no longer denounces this violence – the hangings, the shootings, the beatings, the torture in prisons, the horror of 'transit camps', the 'clearing up of black spots', or the slower and more insidious violence of poverty and undernourishment and disease and infant mortality and the pass system and the daily harassment . . . Apartheid allows him to be blind to this and if you tell him he will not believe you; he will accuse you of exaggeration for subversive political purposes. He is part of the bulwark against the dark forces of chaos, anarchy, Communism. In the developing revolutionary struggle in the country the people will be even more polarized. During the time before complete liberation can be won the White man's isolation will deepen. We must expect White cultural spokesmen to become even less sensitive to atrocities perpetrated by their government; yet, paradoxically, their hypersensitivity and touchiness will increase with the growing challenge to their comfortable and comforting assumptions.

The White man has become brutalized. He can permit himself to reason away brutality. And in due course his sensitivity becomes blunted. Man lives through and in man. The writer, the artist who closes his eyes to everyday injustice and inhumanity will without fail see less with his writing or painting eyes too. His work will become barren. When one prefers not to see certain things, when one chooses not to hear certain voices, when one's tongue is used only to justify this choice – then the things one turned away from do not cease to exist, the voices do not stop shouting, but one's eyes become walled, one's ears less sensitive, therefore deaf, one's tongue will make some decadent clacking noises and one's hands will only be groping over oneself.

Although the White artist may pretend to be unassailable behind the arrogant walls of his isolation – 'Why should I go to visit Black writers', a young Afrikaner intellectual told me, 'when they don't take the trouble of visiting me?' – his work will be bedevilled by insecurity and a complex of inferiority. Outside the walls of his prison he will sense the disapproval and the ostracism.

These corrosive effects are clear in the works themselves. One finds that manifestations of culture – from, for and by the Whites –

in South Africa are hidebound by traditionalism, a sentimentalized traditionalism. When you believe what you want to believe, you are a sentimentalist. In this genre one will come across the glorification of simple values, of earthy and patriotic atmospheres. This work, it is felt, gives some mental stability because it speaks of eternal truths. One is reminded by nothing as much as of the works written and painted during Hitler's rule – though the technical ability may perhaps not be of the same order.

The alternative to the above is a frenzied experimentalism with the forms of the arts; it is a wallowing in the cerebral and the abstract and avoiding any content that might commit one to a view of human relationships. It is the all-out effort to keep the hands clean. Whatever the form cultural expression finds, it tends to simplify and alienate the subjects treated. White South African culture is describing, not participatory.

When you are not equipped with the faculties that will allow you to integrate and participate – for to integrate you must be able to move – then the 'knowledge' of yourself and others and phenomena and objects around you become very important. 'Understanding' is in that sense a limitation that you impose on all these unknowns. What is more, you have to impose these limitations quickly; you have to tie them down with definitions, before they flaunt their dark natures at you in some disgusting – because unknown and untyped – way. To do this, you yourself and all around you must be reasonably static. How else are you going to be orientated? And so you simplify and cut right down to the image of the outer garments. The protection of one's purity implies the straining of one's surroundings through a simplifying eye.

We must not make the mistake of assuming that serious differences exist between the Establishment and its cultural exponents. The Establishment could not exist without its élite and vice versa. They are in the continuous process of creating one another. They are in fact the same people: the power structure.

The totalitarian regime existing in a hostile environment must draw the noose within which it protects itself from contamination ever tighter; it must continue to create new and more abominable laws, it must constantly redefine purity or its cultural values – closely identified with its politics – are strangled.

If you write or paint or film as an Afrikaner you have to compromise the only raw material you have, yourself, your own integrity. You become alienated from yourself, which is worse than being cut off from the tribe. You become a hack. The fine intelligence you may have possessed becomes a raw wound; you deaden your insides with money or with editing – and then you are immured into the façade you may once have thought of cracking. You are now stinking while still on your feet. And in turn you become fodder for the tribe; you become part of the pressure that will be brought to bear upon fools more audacious than you permit yourself to be. Because your corruption must be seen as having a necessary and pragmatic adaptation to the reality of South Africa.

The South African authorities have nothing to fear from their intelligentsia. The boys are good and they will improve as they outgrow this infantile need to rebel.

But the reality of South Africa is not theirs; the future of the country is in the hands of all its people. There is no other fight for culture that can develop apart from the popular struggle. The cultural death wish of the 'representatives of Western culture' will make them the strings on Nero's fiddle.

1971

The Writer and his Public or
Colonialism and its Masks

The very notion implied in the title of the subject I'm asked to write about – that is, the notion of dichotomy, of distance between writer and public – is to my mind a Western concept reflecting a specific view of society and of the individual's role and place in that society. This is a view peculiar to societies based on 'Western' culture and not necessarily indigenous to other areas. Underlying this dichotomy, we find the notions of specialization, separatism, compartmental-ization, free enterprise and the glorification of individual accomplish-ment; above all, the idea that 'reality' can be grasped and understood must indeed be known. This basic expression of loss and insecurity leads to exploration and conquest, but also to the need to prove and to convince – to dogmatism, puritanism and its corollary: repression of dissent. In its application this is a culture built on interest and thus on exploitation. When we thus discuss the problems of the creative artist and his milieu in Third World countries, we are tracing the extent of cultural colonialism.

In the limited space at my disposal I have restricted myself to generalities pertaining to Africa, for I am from Africa. I hope that my black thoughts will not be taken only as belittlement or con-demnation of Africa's real cultural achievements (but I have not come to praise any Caesar). In recent times no other continent has been so horribly gutted by colonialism: its kingdoms and insti-tutions destroyed and new arbitrary borders imposed at the con-venience of the occupier; its cultures crushed, its languages scattered, its people sold and bought and exported like cattle. No other continent is still so completely under the heel of the imperialist, the colonialist and the racist.

Colonialism is a system operated by identifiable groups and administrations for the benefit of men with faces and purses belong-ing to certain classes. When colonialist powers withdrew from Africa, it was also to protect their investments better. Those left behind to safeguard the interests of the exploiter could be trusted since they shared, and still do, the same values.

The Writer and his Public

All over Africa small men are hanging on to the outside mani-festations of power: a high hat, trinkets to pin on tunics, long motorcars, French friends and the power to take life. These forms of power know no colour or culture. Blinded and awed by the power of the colonizer, we situate ourselves in reference to him. We adopt his trappings, try to understand and imitate him. We have not yet rejected his creed, the basis of his power. We may have denounced the White mask, but the spirit behind that mask is still active. It can be argued that the most insidious form of colonization has been that of Africa's mind. The conditioning of the élite is calculated to fulfil the functions previously carried out by missionaries, expeditionary forces and cumbersome colonial administrators. In sum – to use the language of business – a more 'liberal' and 'rational' utilization of assets through 'participation'.

The *only* language colonialism listens to is that of strength. One doesn't have to be rich to be strong. One needs to find that which is strong in oneself and with that strength fight the oppressor. The power comes from the people. Colonialism doesn't just go away. It has to be cut off, exterminated, thrown out. Freedom is not granted; it is won. Until colonialism is beaten it will always return in other, more practical disguises. One such disguise is the medium of the intellectual or the creative artist, strutting about, fattened on the slogans of 'brotherhood' and 'tolerance'.

For it is time to speak about the writer. What kind of culture will he be part of? What precise tasks must he put to himself in today's Africa?

I think it of little use to re-create artificially a traditional or even a purely national culture as a counterweight to colonialist culture. This too can be a way of hampering progress. Too many cultural exponents parade behind the masks of 'Blackness'. I rather suspect that those who bask in it – as an alternative – are reacting against the shame they once experienced at their own impotence. They are violently reaffirming something which they had denied themselves.

People must take themselves in hand. They must create their destiny, not just submit to it. When the people sweep away the parasites and the caretakers, when the people take possession of power – and so of themselves – then they attack the system of exploitation. The struggle against exploitation is international because exploitation and discrimination know no frontiers. This thirst for change and fulfilment, this is the culture of a people.

A writer in Africa can do one of two things: he can express the culture of the people, precede it and clarify it; or he can be the masked clown who stayed behind when the king left town, now writing letters of longing and indignation to his departed 'brothers', hesitating between insult and self-pity.

As a South African freedom-fighter once remarked: *'Culture is a gun.'* This is clearly illustrated in South Africa. The majority of South Africans are held down in the name of Afrikaner culture and European civilization. The White writers themselves are the Establishment. Likewise, the writing of the oppressed can only become more radical, must correspond more and more to the legitimate claims of the people.

Writing should be a broadening of consciousness: in other words a politicization. An awareness of the conditions under which people live, an analysis of the functioning of the systems that impose these conditions, must assist the taking of power by the people. (I am, of course, talking about real power, not just a manipulated and limited say as funnelled through 'representatives' and filtered through 'parties', but the power of direction and control, individually and collectively at all levels and in all fields of human activity. This is the prerequisite for democracy.)

The writer is responsible first to his own society – and in Africa this means a society that has been deformed by colonialism. It is only when his work is true to the aspirations of his own people that it will contribute to universally shared human knowledge and understanding without which no tolerance is possible.

Faced as we are by the 'natural' collaboration between those who sell and buy slaves, we must demand of our writers – if they pretend to speak for the people (and all writers long to be spokesmen) – to articulate and *shape* resistance to the collaborators.

Unfortunately, it seems to me that the kind of recognition most of our writers from Africa aim for can be extended only by those whom they imitate – since they themselves are part of the uprooted élite. Their claim to speak for and from the people is as flimsy as that of the politicians created and sustained by foreign interests. They have become translators, speaking out to reassure and interpret to a Western public.

The perceptive intellectual feels that he is the product of a cultural bastardization. He is full of the pain of alienation, frustration, humiliation. He is a man without buttocks to sit on. And he rises and shakes his pen like a spear: a measure of his impotence.

What we hear are tortured cries of the torn-apart souls of imperfectly integrated native intellectuals. Even the violence encountered in their work seems to come from disenchantment; the writers have realized that they were only *pipelines, contacts,* and tokens – and now they shout (and that too has been foreseen and will in due time be reinvested) because they wish to purify themselves from the White food they have partaken of. One is what one has eaten. Their violence is self-destructive.

One must not blame them. One must learn and go further. No writer can exist outside his people. Writing is not just a voice, not just a language. It is communication and an opening up. For too many of us, writing is still a Cultural Value. Value is a power symbol. Wanting to be a 'writer' in Western terms is subscribing to a particular kind of power structure. Cultural values are Colonialist Investments.

We can set out on the road to real freedom and independence only once we've stopped seeing ourselves through the eyes of those whom we've tried to emulate. Redefining ourselves is obviously not just a cultural matter. The redefinitions – as expressed by the creative and interpretive artists – will come naturally once these definitions reflect economic and political realities.

But we must realize that cultural activity – as stimulated from the outside – was used precisely to prevent or retard those changes. The very least we expect from our writers is that they desist from being the tools of a continuing colonialism.

Paris, 1971

Notes from a
Political Discussion Paper
Contributing Some Elements
Towards a Strategy for
Revolution in South Africa

One spark can put fire to the whole valley

Introduction

Political realism demands that you understand clearly the role you can play; that you recognize your position and what you can do within specific contexts, and that you do not overestimate your importance; i.e., that you do not take your desires for reality.

It is not for a small group, however revolutionary they may consider themselves to be, to propose a strategy for revolution to the South African people. One cannot be 'revolutionary' by yourself, or in the abstract. Any effective strategy for revolution must be based upon the experiences and the desire for change of the masses. Once this is understood and practised we can contribute towards the struggle for change, we can have some incidence on the South African reality, we may hope to prod 'the joints of history'.

I move from the premiss that our ultimate objective is a Socialist South Africa and that that society, when one can envisage a 'new man' who can come into being only once his social environment has been transformed by Socialist economic structures, that society which will abolish exploitation and discrimination, can be constructed only after a taking of power by those who genuinely represent the workers and the peasants. The taking of power itself is only one instant in the march towards that society. (I do not wish to hold up the goal of 'that society' as some paradise, some shining country in the future; a Socialist society is also one of struggle and change; the advent of a classless society is certainly not for any foreseeable future.)

What is specific to South Africa

Our situation is a particularly complex one. The complexity of it should however be no excuse for not attempting to understand it as a whole and in detail. I propose to present here a summary list of features and statements, some of which may be contradictory: all of which need to be clarified, discussed and ultimately forged into concepts which can be used as tools in our struggle.

(1) Broadly speaking, half of our population is urbanized and the other half lives and works in rural areas. It is unlikely that this will change much, even in the event of more developed and diversified industrialization. (This is one of the factors that defines our choice of an example when we look at the history of revolutions – Russian, Chinese, Cuban or Vietnamese. This is also one of the factors defining any political organization which can best lead the people.)

(2) The strategy of the racists in power is to divide and rule. The Bantustan policy must be seen in those terms. The semblance of territorial independence will be given, but in the absence of economic viability it will be empty. Economic control will remain in the hands of the White minority and/or in the hands of foreign capitalism. The ethnic diversity too of our people is exploited by those presently in power. The National Liberation Movement must reflect the views and demands of the totality of our people.

(3) The Whites cannot be considered as 'foreigners' in exactly the same way as the South African Indians are not foreigners to South Africa. In that sense South Africa's problem is not that of classical colonialism.

(4) White South Africa (and the potential danger exists that the independent Bantustans will do the same) does reflect the interests of the traditional colonialist powers – Britain, France, Germany, Holland, Belgium, etc.

(5) White South Africa is itself a colonizing power. Vorster foresees the creation of a 'power bloc' consisting of White South Africa, the Bantustans, and including neighbouring satellite states (Botswana, Swaziland, Lesotho, 'Rhodesia', parts at least of the present Portuguese colonies and perhaps Malawi and Namibia). The White state will of course monopolize the economic power. Beyond this grouping the

penetration of Black Africa to the North must be seen as the creation of client states. There is colonialism not only to the inside, but also, based upon the producing and exploiting power which the large and cheap proletariat generate, to the outside.

(6) The colonialist grid fits over that of class conflict. The Whites constitute the ruling class. Among the Whites, though, a subdivision of classes can be perceived, which, under certain circumstances, can lead to important internal contradictions.

(7) The class struggle in South Africa gets its own specific nature from the fact that it is overlapped by the race conflict. Black Consciousness is thus a necessary rehabilitatory answer to cultural colonialism, to humiliation and to the alienation from one's own culture.

(8) South Africa is also a strong point of imperialism. There is a concordance of interests between – and similar regional roles ascribed to – South Africa, Brazil in Latin America, and Iran in the Near East. They share the same virulent anti-Communism and consider themselves to be bulwarks against the spreading of 'red' ideology. Their economies constitute, on the one hand, havens for multinational concerns and, on the other, are largely state-run capitalist. They are the *gendarmes* of their regions. Their laws are repressive and often Fascist. They control vast labour resources and sources of raw material and energy.

(9) South Africa is destined to become an exporting power, not only to underdeveloped countries, but also to re-export manufactured goods to Europe. South Africa, like Brazil and Iran, will become a producing area for Europe. They are sub-imperialist powers.

(10) With colonialist and imperialist help, South Africa will try to subvert African unity and, more concretely, neighbouring African states such as Zambia.

What to do?

What has marked our country over the last year is (a) the awareness among the people of a pending armed struggle and the acceptance by the oppressors that this may be the beginning of a protracted people's war; (b) the wave of strikes, continuing economic unrest and labour demands, and a growing consciousness among the workers of their power; and (c) the beginning of a break among the ruling classes (the Whites) themselves, the loss of hegemony as the pressure upon them from within and without increases.

In trying to define what to do, we must also identify all the various forces that can be counted upon in this strategy for transformation. The taking of power by representatives of the people is a prerequisite for a redistribution of economic and political power, but in a sense this taking has already started in those areas of economic, political, cultural, and social activities, where people are aware of the implications of their struggle. To the examples elsewhere of 'liberated zones' must be added the notion of 'liberated concepts'.

The first and most important task is to regroup the progressive elements, even those outside the liberation movement, into a revolutionary avant-garde, which will be closely, organically linked to the masses, work within the mass movements, learn from the people, help the mass organizations and the Liberation Movement in particular to evolve a clear strategy for revolution.

There is the need to build out the Liberation Movement, so that it becomes a true 'common front' against the common enemy.

There is the need to re-evaluate the experiences of the people and the Liberation Movement up to now, to criticize the errors in a spirit of unity and strengthening, to valorize the arms that have been forged, to accumulate and transmit the positive experiences.

We must learn from the examples of working-class movements elsewhere. We must know, analyse, and understand the ideology of the enemy and his allies.

We must redefine, if necessary, the programme of the Liberation Movement. The people lay claim to the whole country and to all its riches, not just to the barren 13 per cent it may be granted.

We must understand and explain the continental and international role of South Africa. Progressive forces everywhere should be alerted to the implications for them and for us of our struggle. For instance: to counteract foreign investment in South Africa and the immigration of skilled White labour.

Armed struggle must be linked to other forms of struggle; armed struggle must be seen as a support for mass struggle, as the arm of a long people's war, as the expression of legitimate revolutionary violence against the violence of oppressors and racists. Armed struggle by itself and alone is self-defeating. The people must recognize themselves in the armed struggle, which is one of the forms our struggle will take on.

WE MUST REGROUP OUR FORCES. WE FIGHT FOR FREEDOM FOR ALL OF SOUTH AFRICA AND FOR ALL THE SOUTH AFRICANS.

The Liberation Movement must head the working alliance of Black Workers, of exponents of Black Consciousness, the Church leaders and the White Radicals, and reflect the struggle at any level at which it expresses itself.

Paris, 1972

Random Remarks
on Freedom and Exile

1.0 Much of what I have to say here will sound contradictory – but that is inevitable given the contradictory nature of the writer's condition and perhaps also my own lack of clarity on the subject. I do believe that there are very basic contradictions which mark the writer, and the first one is that between the private origins of his work and the public impact of his role as a writer and/or an intellectual. It is the contradiction between the sound, which is born somewhere inside, deeper than the ear, and the word, which comes out of the mouth and which is both a utensil and a convention. My intention here is not to try and resolve any paradoxes but only to attempt a description of the experience of exile, to indicate some of the negative and positive aspects of it.

1.1 I have not tried to order my thoughts in the shape of an essay but rather as a series of statements or aphorisms. And of course the totality of what I have to say, of what I do, of what I think and how I say it, is inevitably the image of my state as an exile. In other words, given my condition and conditioning it is difficult if not impossible for me to indicate and describe the state of non-exile, of belonging, of integration.

1.2 Also, since writing is to my mind a form of combat, you will find in my paper the traces of *positions*. There is no such thing as objectivity. One can perhaps be impartial, one can attempt to see both sides of any question – that still doesn't guarantee any objectivity. You are always part of the struggle whether you want to or not, whether you *know* it or not.

1.3 Indeed I believe that only the conscious participation in the struggle can supersede the paradoxes from which I suffer. But the struggle is a way *forward* – *not* an escape.

2.0 In the Third World wherever people are still dominated – be it politically, economically or culturally – the role of culture is a very important one, and the role of writing particularly so.

Colonialism, imperialism, manifests itself in many ways but it is its cultural form, the colonized mind, that is salient in our discussion. The colonization of the minds of a people (or of a privileged sect of that people) making second-class citizens out of them – since they will now have to relate to the culture of the oppressor – is as destructive as its political and economic counterparts and perhaps more insidious. When you alter a person's sense of his own value you are in fact poisoning his ability to resist and reject the other forms of domination. Political and economic colonialism is oppressive; cultural and intellectual colonialism is subversive.

2.1 Writing is about the way people see and experience themselves. Most of the countries that we refer to as the 'Third World' have been partially destroyed and continue being exploited by colonialism – for the most part coming from the West. The process of reconstruction where liberation has been obtained, the struggle for freedom where it has not – are slow. It often includes the need to cleanse the mind. These tasks are complicated by the existence of 'élites' – i.e., people who had been formed or co-opted by the colonial master. In some instances the élite may be drawn from the traditional or pre-colonial hierarchy, but generally these are people created (or secreted) in the area between oppressors and oppressed: middlemen, entrepreneurs, overseers, *assimilados*, puppets.

2.2 The writer in the Third World, in those societies of conflict, is practically without exception a member of that so-called élite. This explains, I think, his ambivalent position and the fact that he is often an outsider to his own people.

2.3 In a situation where cultural awareness can be a weapon for liberation or a tool for reconstruction, the writer is not only either 'proletarian' or 'bourgeois', but quite literally either for liberation or not. As Fanon said – we still have to write our own history; we cannot afford to exist only in terms of the history of the rulers.

3.0 I have briefly indicated, I think, the way in which the line of writing is part of the political drawing. The exile is someone who is artificially removed from the heart of this debate. He can continue to participate in some way – he can attempt to eat from a distance – but he is now no longer part of the mainstream of the development of his people.

4.0 I now come more specifically to the subject I've been invited to

72

talk about: 'Freedom and Exile' – or how the exile experiences freedom and the absence of freedom.

4.1 What is freedom? I cannot conceive of freedom as an absolute, like 'wine' or 'bread'. Freedom is not an object, it is the means to something else. For me it always triggers off another series of questions – freedom from what? For whom? To do what? In which way? Perhaps the only absolute freedom is death because it seems not to be subject to modification.

4.2 Freedom is linked to power. For instance, if we say 'freedom from oppression and repression', it denotes a certain power – it would in fact mean that the people have power.

4.3 But even more, the idea of freedom is linked to class. For the bourgeoisie certainly it means the right to private property, the right to exploit labour, etc. – and all of these 'rights' (obtained and retained by power) and their justifications add up to a class definition of 'freedom'. This allows for freedom of expression (within limits). Freedom of expression in bourgeois societies, where the writer is at best considered to be an entertainer, is a hollow concept because it concerns only the élite – and *this* élite has no control of real power, not even really the power of forming opinion, which is done by other more popular means – and those other means will reflect the vested interests of the class in power.

4.4 I hope it is clear though that I am not pleading for any form of restriction on writers. 'The intelligentsia', to quote Osip, Mandelstam's widow, 'has a certain degree of education, the ability to think critically and the sense of concern that goes with it, freedom of thought, conscience, humanism . . .' and all of the above must be developed and preserved and made functional. But I could never justify the granting of any privileges to writers that are denied to others.

5.0 There are many kinds of writers: some travel into the night and bring back strange and disturbing observations – they speak with their ears and their eyes; some travel in the day and hold their words up to us like mirrors; some don't travel at all but still relate to us the exotic places they've been to – for them the tongue is a road; some tell us where we *ought* to go, how we *ought* to get there. The writer can be the single exploring voice, or he can be the attempt to give tongue to the silent, to a period, to a class, to a struggle. We should not be afraid of debate and confrontation among all these various points of view – debate and confrontation are needed for progress, they are essential if we are not to become stagnant.

5.1 The writer is a product of his society and his times – however camouflaged it may be. But the writer also helps to shape, in an obscure way, his society and his times. He produces – that is his basic satisfaction. That object which he produces is in itself useless. The freedom of the writer lies in what is done with his product, on how it is spread and used; his freedom lies in the relationship between him and the people of whom, and for whom, he writes.

5.2 The greatest freedom for the writer is to be in a position to serve, to communicate, to contribute.

6.0 The lack of that freedom is the first, the most obvious 'unfreedom' from which the exiled writer suffers.

6.1 When we look more closely at the position of the exiled writer we see that exile contains a certain number of advantages and disadvantages. First we must ask ourselves – exile from what, from whom?

6.2 The exile of South African writers is provoked by political repression first of all. People don't leave because they don't like the climate. They don't even leave because they think that they can make a pile of money abroad. They leave because it often quite simply is a choice between prison or exile. They exchange one form of living death for another.

6.3 To be exiled means, in effect, to be exiled from your own people. This cuts at the umbilical cord essential to any artist – the close and continuous contact with your people, the possibility of staying alert and alive on the feedback, the possibility of diversifying and deepening your literary activities – through readings, lectures, etc. The real *language* of the writer consists of two components: the sounds that disturb him from within, that push from inside – and the *people* who speak his language. Language is *people*. When you are deprived of one of these it is as if you have only one leg, which keeps on getting weaker because you use it too much.

6.4 Of course, one might say, you *do* take your language with you wherever you go – but it is rather like carrying the bones of your ancestors with you in a bag: they are white with silence, they do not talk back.

6.5 In exile the writer becomes a borderline case – he tries to recapture from outside that which he possessed from the inside – which he possessed so completely that he didn't even *know* about it. He becomes alienated and detribalized – his intelligence becomes that of the 'clever' immigrant who belongs by adaptation and not by instinct. He never quite fits in anywhere else. It is as if he carries the *absence* within himself as an unspeakable disease – and this disease keeps him separate from others.

6.6 This *absence* and *distance* eventually kill the inner sound – particularly for novelists whose work grew directly out of local social conditions.

6.7 With whom does he identify? Being in another country may broaden his horizon. He may identify with other intellectuals and, as it were, hit the international circuit. Or he may – through his exile and because of his politics – identify with a cause as represented by the oppressed classes. But that is likely to be a one-way identification. It is rather like a dog loving the moon.

7.0 What are the advantages attached to his condition? For South African exiles it is obviously in the first place a freedom from fear – if he is Black he no longer has to carry a pass; he may sleep at night without fear. We must never underestimate the freedom to be away from Apartheid.

7.1 For some writers *exile* can be a country to explore.

7.2 Then, also, you become much more intimately aware of your language; it can become a new exploration – but that may ultimately turn in upon itself, turn into a well-turned shell.

7.3 One is, of course, also far more exposed to new ideas which may prevail in the *métropoles*. You may be stimulated by new and foreign social and political conditions. Your thinking may be broadened by internationalism, you may be better equipped to situate yourself and the struggle in your own country in an internationalist and anti-imperialist context.

8.0 What are the obligations of the exile? I believe they are several. I think he should consider himself as an interpreter abroad who can constantly try to focus the attention of the people with whom he comes in contact on the nature of reality back home. He should consider himself to be an envoy even if he has no mandate.

8.1 He must force himself to maintain a dialogue with the inside. He can be a conduit through which ideas that may be upsetting for the self-satisfied Establishment on the inside can be filtered back. He must bark all along the borders.

8.2 He may have to try and maintain and save that which is menaced by extinction on the inside. It can be called 'the hiding away of books' – but more concretely it can mean trying to solicit help abroad for work that cannot be published inside the country.

8.3 And, of course, he must try to 'survive'.

9.0 Ultimately, the exile is marginal. The struggle lies *inside* and it will be decided *inside*. But it is his privilege to use the freedom of exile to the utmost of his capabilities in terms of that struggle inside.

Paris, 1972

Conflict and Literature
in South Africa

Originally the intention was that I should write a paper on the situation and the difficulties of the South African writer in exile. For it is obviously only one form of exile when you are far away from the society that gave birth to your work and for which it is destined.

Nearly all South African writing reflects varying stages of exile and alienation. That is what our literature is all about. One could nearly postulate that *South Africa is the homeland of exile*. There are many kinds of banishment: the physical one to which I just referred, but also a spiritual or cultural one when people have to use the language of the colonizer; then there is the exile of Afrikaner writers in South Africa itself, those who have no true insight into the South African reality because of the restricting laws or an induced tribe-bound blindness; and the political exile of those whose works are quite simply forbidden in the country. And if we were to generalize some more – could it not be said that all literature as we know it today, wherever its origin, flows in fact from exile? Isn't it true that one writes (or paints) to expel Time? (And that one deforms the latter in the process of creating it?)

Ex Africa Semper Aliquid Novi

I must however not dramatize needlessly. (As if writing were all-suffering, or all-important.) That which writers live through as the many mansions of exile translates in fact the inequality, racial discrimination and oppression prevalent in the country. These conditions have been fought, are still being fought. The struggle of the majority of South Africans is a long one.

It is at present certainly entering the most difficult and the most decisive phase. Even at the time of writing some of the structures of White colonialism are crumbling – at least in the buffer states around the citadel – and soon it will have to start happening in the heart of darkness itself. Our land, my land, is filled with bitterness and wretchedness and hate and anguish. But at last the discovery is dawning that it has become urgent to dream a new future – a dream as old as the exile of the people. The conflict, which is now so clearly visible, has been there ever since the advent of European occupation; the profound causes for the conflict have scored our lives. And now Southern Africa is on the move and already we may claim: 'Tomorrow, next week, very soon the portals will open and we shall walk on the green earth and see how richly fertile it is, and we shall see that the mountains are blue with birds and that the heaving oceans are alive with fish.' Agreed, it is certainly true that it is too early to discern a timetable, but the ultimate outcome of the conflict is clear for all to see. In my country it is often said: 'Freedom in our lifetime.' A Black African singer once formulated it thus: 'All of us have to die one day, but there are some deaths which will not have been in vain: deaths do not all convey the same meaning.'

We cannot write ourselves out of exile, we can only hope to comprehend its roots and its working through our writing. Only the redistribution of political and economic power – whether it comes about abruptly (and bloodily) or slowly – will bring an end to exile.

I am no specialist in the field of South African literature, perhaps because I'm not interested enough in literature for its own sake. I shall nevertheless assume that you know even less about it than I do. You will realize soon enough that I am quite unashamedly a patriot. I am indeed of the opinion that our dismembered country has produced the most interesting written work coming from Africa south of the Sahara. How did it come about? Is it because we are so rich, or so poor? Is it because we are so different from one another, or because we have so much in common? Can it be ascribed to the walls that we have erected between the different groups or is it the result of our cultural mixing? The Word, spoken at first and then written, has always been important in South Africa. Maybe the reason for this can be found in the relative poorness of other cultural expressions (but then our music too is as strong as the thudding of the heart . . .). Or can it be due to having so many living languages coexisting in the same territory? With us the word can be a caress, or it can be cruel. Not without reason is it said of us that we are pegged to the Law the way a goat is tied to the stake. Does it sometimes rain a little too much? We shall have to have a word with God; we shall do away with excess by passing a Law. Do we at times harbour a touch of doubt about our identity? Then we shall break forth in Protest, we shall Protect our narrow-mindedness by Law. We shall employ the Word to create and invoke pain, and others will use words to gloss over the unbearable.

Conflict and Literature in South Africa

Let me now attempt dividing South African literature in different categories. First of all it must be said that *a South African literature* in fact doesn't exist – or if it does then it is simply defined by the South African *situation*. What we writers share is the specific South African situation but we experience its influence in different ways depending on whether we belong to the exploiters or the victims. (Some will of course try the pretence of being neither fowl nor chicken, of being above and beyond all this, and for them the Word would have been conceived without stain, from eternity to eternity, not polluted by blood or water.) We all write: around, because of, by means of, or despite the same situation; we write about a display of facets of one shared reality which can be clearly isolated and studied. Nearly always it will be a literature of non-acceptance: to some refusing any responsibility for themselves or for the powerful, to others the non-acceptance of defeat or the denial of degradation and dehumanization. In varying ways we are all branded by the same shame.

A first way in which South African literature could be grouped would be (1) Black literature in indigenous languages; (2) Black English-language literature (and some in Afrikaans also); (3) English-language literature written by Whites; (4) Afrikaans literature written by Whites.

You will notice that I'm obliged to generalize in a clumsy way; I leave out of consideration the many exceptions to these categories: in reality they can perhaps be discerned less starkly. (When you have to handle definitions you often discover that you are busy fixing the boundaries of ignorance, and formulating or restricting something can sometimes be a way of eliminating all other potentialities.)

When I look a little closer at my grid as described above, I establish the following:

(1) I know next to nothing of the literature written in 'Black' languages. People who do know and who can read Zulu, Xhosa or Sotho, claim that much of it is of excellent quality. Oral poetry has always had an essential function among Africans. In the case of the Zulus, for example, the poets were also the guardians of the history of a clan or a regiment; the consciousness the Zulus have of themselves as a people is formed by their poets having traditionally assimilated their history by heart and passed it on from one generation to the next. From quite early on a written literature in the indigenous languages took shape in South Africa, in all probability helped along by European missionaries. A few of the classics have been rendered into

English. Vilikazi, the Zulu poet who lived until the first half of
this century, is known not only for his epics but also for his
'contemporary' political and social consciousness. When he
exposes the misery of the mineworkers' lives, for instance, he
consciously expresses political sentiments shared by his people.

Present-day writers in the African languages are perhaps
overshadowed by their colleagues writing in English, better
suited to interpret the uprooted culture of the urban proletariat.
We must furthermore consider the fact that the industrialization
of the country and the concomitant phenomenon of migrant
labour contribute towards the continual development of a
national consciousness, which can best be expressed in a lingua
franca such as English. Besides, some writers will shy away from
writing in an indigenous language exactly because the
government tries to promote that in terms of their 'Bantu'
Education Policy. If the so-called 'Bantustans' were ever to
become political reality we could perhaps observe the
establishment of a new breed of writers choosing to use one or
the other African language.

Because of the promotion of indigenous-language literature
by the government – through broadcasting and publications –
those willing to be enrolled are nowadays often seen as
collaborators. One noteworthy exception is the young Zulu
poet, Mazisi Kunene, who is also a militant combatant in the
Liberation Movement. But his work is banned inside South
Africa.

I must, however, point out that the African languages are used
insistently and popularly in song to give voice to resistance and
political aspirations. These songs are indeed popular in the true
sense of that word since they are composed by the people.

(2) Black literature in English has a long, difficult and proud history
in South Africa. I imagine that much of it is already known to
you – from Sol T. Plaatje, via Noni Jabavu to present times. The
fifties and the sixties were defined by a generation of writers
introducing the rush and the rhythms of city life into their
works. I'm referring to the likes of Ezekiel Mphahlele, Can
Themba, Nat Nakasa, Bloke Modisane, Lewis Nkosi, Dugmore
Boetie, and many more. They are sometimes described as the
'Drum' generation, or the 'Classic' writers, after the publication
for which they worked or the literary journal which served as
their platform. Their writings, permeated by a sweet bitterness,
were often based on exposé journalism, and they consciously

employed their art to show up and denounce the horrible conditions in the locations situated on the peripheries of White-ruled cities or the even worse plight of the people confined to prison farms. Through repressive legislation, 'banning orders', exile and suicide they were forced into oblivion. The government intended destroying maybe the best and the most creative group of writers in Africa.

Now, after a decade of silence following upon the destruction of the above-mentioned generation, we witness a new flowering of Black authors expressing themselves through English. Like a trail of blood the humiliations of the Apartheid system have soaked into the work of the Black writers. At times the writing mirrors true experiences, as in the poems of Dennis Brutus culled (or should I say 'squeezed'?) from his 'life' in prison on Robben Island; very often it is an expression of solidarity with others going through the same hell; now and then the writer withdraws into himself, or he explores the nostalgia of exile, he describes how people are forced to become refugees always on the move.

In this new work we also find present the pride of being Black; a new combativeness is surfacing and it is as if the writers want to announce to the whole world that the end of suffering is in sight. It is significant that these new strains are expressed in poetry and not short stories as was predominantly the case during the fifties.

Pascal Gwala, Wally Mongane Serote, Steven Smith, Benjamin Takavarasha, Oswald Mtshali – these and others represent the voice of power shaping up in the country. As Ilva Mackay says in her poem 'To All Black People':

> the truth will be heard
> we will be their tongues.
>
> Arise from your comfortable shanty
> from your cold cosy room
> and shout
> I AM! LET ME BE!

The above poem appears in a volume published by BLAC Publishing House – an indication that writers are searching for their own way of publishing and distribution. It is of great importance for the first step towards cultural liberation must surely lie in controlling the *means* of spreading one's own culture. Too much Black literature is still born with the help of a liberal White midwife, unfortunately an effective if treacherous way of cutting the authors off from their own public.

(3) Our South African literature can seldom brag of its wealth of ideas or themes; it is rather impressionist, sometimes a literature of sentiments becoming ever more expressionist. It is a stylized literature, though quite often somewhat slovenly so. Perhaps the clearest illustration is given by the White English-language writers. On the whole their work gives the impression of being descriptive of, rather than participating in, the despair of a South African existence.

While no one can possibly mistake the origins of Black literature, the literature of English-language Whites comes across as if it constituted an integral part of another world. By this I mean that their works don't seem to be rooted in a local reality. An Africa is suggested to us that is completely hostile and inhospitable, where the narcissi do not flower, where you cannot dreamily meditate under rustling trees and pastel-tinted clouds – mostly because the flies will damn well eat you alive, etc. Local reality is painted as strange and artificial. So much for *couleur locale*. Thus we often stumble over words intended to lend authenticity to the writing, because of their supposed autochthonous origin – 'veldschoen', 'kopje', 'sjambok', 'laager' and so on. One must point out that these are obsolete Dutch versions of Afrikaans terms. English books written by South African Whites all too often imply a rejection of Africa and its roughness. To be fair – the local English aren't really accepted by any of the other groups either. Perhaps it can be ascribed to their ambivalent position – they have the lion's share of economic power without exercising the accompanying clear political privileges (the latter power being still, provisionally at least, in the hands of the tougher Boers). Politically, they stand for a *laissez-faire* liberalism which is in contradiction with traditional British economic imperialism.

To this I must of course immediately add that South Africans can justifiably be proud of many of their English-language compatriots of the past and the present. No one has better staged certain aspects of South African life than Athol Fugard.

(4) Afrikaans literature, as all the others, has passed through several stages. When people started using Afrikaans consciously, at first, it was also to explore and to glorify the continent that saw the birth of the language. Eugene Marais and Louis Leipoldt

were certainly 'African' poets. This initial period – of discovering the new wings of the language – was followed by a more 'proletarian' one during which the writers incorporated the conditions experienced by the poor Whites – those then pauperized by the war against the British and uprooted by their migration to the mining cities and the first factories. The farmers, once so self-reliant, were now broken displaced persons. Literary works of the time often show a homesickness for lost innocence, for open spaces. The following period coincides with the Afrikaner tribe's struggle for political predominance – and ultimate monopoly. The works produced then reflect a strong nationalist bias, with a lot of loose talk about remaining 'true to the blood' (which was pure, or so one tried to pretend), and often show definitely Nazi traits.

This exclusive political power was wrested from others, and subsequently consolidated to the detriment of all decency and justice. But we hardly took any notice of the rot mildewing our souls. When we finally came face to face with it we took refuge in the unattainable but convulsive search for purity and justification. The generation of *Sestig* (the sixties) represented the final effort of identification with Europe. If we can't communicate, so we reasoned, we can at least be intellectually decadent (and analyse the pitfalls of communication).

Another and more interesting reading, cutting across the ethnic and linguistic dividing lines as indicated above, would perhaps be as follows:

Conservatism or Conformism – those chattering with mouths closed shut by fear; Collaboration – the corrupt ones, and certain manifestations of opposition are of course ways of collaborating (*saampraat*, mouthing along – that's how I describe it); and the literature of Resistance, or – in some instances – Revolution.

What is the clarifying factor provoking these new groupings? To my mind it comes from the growing force of Black Power and its allies. We are at the present moment living through the pre-revolutionary period. The converging and sharpening conflict is smoking all of us out from behind the protective hedges of our words and our illusions.

The approaching eruptions will be a source of joy for some and the cause of pain for others. But the inevitable redistribution of power will snap the chains of exile; then at last we shall be free to contribute constructively to a South African literature.

Paris, December 1974

Burnt Bird

Wonderful, this three-foot sword of the Great Yüan,
sparkling with cold frost over ten thousand miles.
Though the skull go dry, these eyes will see again.
My white gem worth a string of cities has never had a flaw.

Sesson Yubai

Pierre Mesnard's Story

My name is Pierre Mesnard. I am to write a story about Jorge Luis Borges. In other words. He would have written it himself had he not been so old and weak. Now I am the swaggerer. Actually this is the central fillet of a story; the beginning and the end have already been gravestoned in time.

Wednesday, 13 January. Paris weather is, as Oma always claimed, running dogs. Sidestepping the turdy drops you scurry from *métro* to *bistrot*. You are drinking to the stained trickling of the world. Invited to go to the Ministry of Culture, out of the blue, a reception for Jorge Luis Borges it would seem. And one's first reaction is: is this living myth still alive then!

He lives. In a wing of the Palais-Royal there is this hall with high stuccoed ceiling, the light-tinkling chandeliers; there he sits hunched over his walking stick, photographers and cameramen in a dangerously close half-circle around him and Cultural Minister Jack Lang. Spasmodic flickering and the artificial sun are continually and blindingly reflected from the gold-framed mirrors. Strange flamboyants. Reality is a multiplying image.

One of the nits slowly approaches his lens to within centimetres of the mummy's mask.

In prison, I am reminded all of a sudden – because memory is a prison – I made use of this head in an illicit drawing: a healthy dier lies on the ground; blind Borges holds up a mirror in which the blind sun is centred. It is called: *bringing the image to the dying*.

Jack Lang delivers a neat and squarely wrapped-up little speech. The old one is in France to receive, this coming week, the *Légion d'honneur* from the white hand of François Mitterrand.

They bring microphones to Borges's mouth. He is hoarse. He thanks his multitudinous invisible (and sometimes visible) friends; he says that he is happy to be in France, that it is easy to be happy in France.

Then there is white wine, whisky, dainties and other goodies. Borges drinks a spastic orange juice. One by one the literary mandarins come to bow over his hand. The news-suckers do not fall back even one inch. What are they photographing? His blindness?

You get the chance to speak to him. From close up he is fragile, ancient, archival – you could say stained green with age. In my grip his hand is a glove loosely filled with slender bones. And yet there is still about him, faintly, nearly like the aftercling of an echo, the air of a dandy. He is somebody who can afford smoking canaster and sporting diamonds.

'South African?' he tilts an astonished head and immediately starts uttering a veiled French murmuring about Roy Campbell, 'the great poet. I know his works by heart,' he says.

His brittle knuckles in my hand grow warm. I must tell him about the curious coincidence that my gaol life practically started and ended with him. At home I have a list, in the scarlet ink of a security policeman, of the possessions with which I was arrested at the time. There it is written, amongst others: *one book, A Universal History of Infamy*. A fond recapitulation of the careers of some great criminals. That book was not allowed to stay with me for very long. But a month or so before my release I managed to get hold of another Borges volume: *Labyrinths* . . . I inform him about Sheila Cusson's translation. He enquires after Afrikaans, already knows something about the origins thereof. He is a language archaeologist.

Suddenly he starts reciting the Our Father in English. 'Our Father *which* art in Heaven. It is much more terrible than *who*. It is a thing, not so?' And then repeats the complete prayer in the long since deceased Old English.

What it may sound like in Afrikaans? I am bent low over his ear. Remember the first few verses. 'More! More! Say something else in Afrikaans.'

I say: 'You are the greatest living writer,' and translate it for his benefit.

'No,' he contends. 'I am an old man who has lived too long, blind.'

I: 'For us you will always remain young, and present . . .'

The novas in the mirrors lose their glow. The novena is finished. I hand back to him his little pillowcase of phalanxes.

Later I return by underground train to the Left Bank. Life is a greedy little journey. In the subway an old beggar with two squinting blind orbs is posted – he turns the head in my direction when I come by. In the train itself I am pushed up against a middle-aged Spanish-speaking gentleman engrossed in his homework. The language guide he totes is in Spanish and French. The chapter heading above the day's lesson reads: *Quién es usted? Qui êtes-vous?* He smiles over my expression of interest. I commiserate: 'At the outset it will be difficult, but that also passes.'

Pierre Mesnard's Story

At Saint-Michel station I emerge on the street again. Above ground at the *métro*'s mouth, a bus is parked. All the *clochards* of the neighbourhood are shooed together and carted off. Those doing the collecting are called *les bleus*, they wear blue overalls, and they are of the same age as these stupefied human specimens without work. Why are there so many *agents*? Are jobs created this way to prevent them from becoming bums also?

From the Place Saint-Michel it is uphill to the Collège de France, hardly a cock's crow away, where Borges will be giving a lecture on 'Poetic Creation'.

Here the neck-craners trample upon one another – Latin Americans, scholars, aged grey-haired bodies. Breast against breast we fill up the auditorium. Foucault's shiny pate sits in the first row.

Borges is led in, fumbles for a seat – the butterfly hunter, entirely clear and sharp of mind – in a circle of flickering camera flashes. A wrinkling of applause. He starts his recital. Hoarse. Sometimes he stutters a bit when encountering a bony word. The crowd stare at him as if studying something inside themselves, as if staring down in the core of that which never passes and which will never escape from the maze.

A youngster climbs on a chair, the better to see. His eyes fill up with tears. 'How much longer will it go on?' he asks.

'Perhaps for a quarter of an hour,' I say.

'But that is too short, too soon!' he whines . . .

And when there is time for questions the inevitable shrill militant just has to ask something about the Falklands (*Les Malouines*). To my astonishment Borges falls into the trap. Someone else wishes to know what his relationship to suicide may be. He says that he cannot now remember ever having committed suicide.

I tried penning (pinning?) down some of his thoughts. He says that he is 83 years old with a long past and probably a limited future, but that he would continue writing, not baroque works as in the past, but simple ones. The difficult things are simple. He speaks of an interior literature.

'Luckily memory is not unlimited: one may forget in order to create anew, to imagine again.' And: 'Each language is a way of experiencing reality.' And: 'The gods do something horrible to people so that later generations may have something to sing about.'

He quotes Valéry: 'Tout aboutit à un livre.' Literature grows from literature. Why publish? 'We publish because we do not want to spend our lives correcting old manuscripts.'

'What would Pierre Mesnard have written now?' a voice from the audience enquires. The contorted old grey-headed man, with the light emanating from him, does not answer. Later he does say: 'I know the beginning and the finish (of a tale); it is what happens between those two that one has to invent.'

12 January 1983

Freedom

I have a small series of paradoxes for you:

'Freedom' has a manifoldness of forms and shapes, it has many meanings, like death: perhaps that is why there are so many similitudes between the two.

(1) Thus one gets what I would call 'freedom which is no freedom'. It is a kind of loosening of the very concept 'freedom' – exactly a liberation from the conceptual. It means simply that you have found an equilibrium, the Middle Way of absolute experience-through-living which is at the same time entirely relative.

   This way of cancelling freedom can be encountered anywhere, even – and particularly – in prison. I am free.

(2) One cherishes freedom as an ideal, you live with it as a reference point. For instance – freedom of thought, of expression, of association, of development, *one* freedom: in short, the freedom of the individual in a modern state.

   Sure, it is stupidly utopian, because this freedom is never realized: but it remains above all important as an aspiration, nearly as an all-consuming obsession. I am not free.

(3) There is freedom as exact measurement: to be free *from* exploitation, free *from* oppression, free *from* discrimination. As long as society is typified and conditioned by exploitation and oppression nobody in that society can be free. The oppressed is not free from poverty, hunger, squatter's conditions, illness, bitterness, humiliation, corruption, collaboration even; the oppressor cannot be liberated from his fear, his greed, his ignorance, his prejudices and his illusory constructions, his degrading way of life, his political and economic and cultural corruption.

   South Africa is of course *the* concretization and expression of a lack of freedom. The South African is not free. I am not free.

(4) One gets a freedom of perception, the breath-losing of a

91

growing awareness. For me, since I've come out of gaol, it is an
intoxication.

A few examples: this morning we left Paris very early – it was
dark still with against the firmament a sprinkle-spray of stars.
And at once I was back in Pollsmoor.

Winters, very early, when cold still walks around outside with
a painful nose, and it is night in the lee of the mountain, we had
to go into the courtyard to be sorted out in work teams. And then
one unexpectedly came, nearly as a voyeur, upon a rich but aloof
and *free* world of dying stars, of morning smells, of mountain
shade, of first light. The most intimate bedding of night is aired.

And that fleeting moment of intense experience was a
suspension of imprisonment.

Or, later today in the train, we suddenly entered a powdered
landscape with a rising sun the spitting image of a red-painted
moon, and then the punctuation marks of black birds in the
snow. There were no impediments. I could *see*. It was real –
neither dream nor fantasy.

(5) You know, there is the inestimable freedom of the trivial. In
prison every inmate may, once a year at Christmas, receive
twelve cards. It has happened that the censor withheld one of
my cards, sent from Holland, because it had been signed by
several friends: for the authorities that constituted more than
one card, exceeding my allowed quota.

Now I may be receiving twelve postcards a day, each signed
by ten or twenty people. Is that not freedom?

But this freedom is conditional. While I sit here writing this
the shadowed world of police cells and prisons continues
existing. Truly an impressive *gulag*!

The average daily number of prisoners in South Africa is
110,000 out of a total population of about 25 million people. To
compare – in France, of a population of 55 million, there are not
yet 70,000 prisoners (and the French consider that they have too
many people locked up).

The human beings there, gaolbirds, have names and tongues
and faces. Mandela is rotting there, Sisulu is there, Goldberg
and Kitson are there – and all the others, to you the nameless
ones, for me the maimed people of flesh and of blood. They are
dreaming my freedom – stars and birds in the snow, an
unlimited amount of postcards, a stroll through the streets, a cup
of coffee in a restaurant, stretching out a hand so as to touch *the
other*. I am free. I am not free.

Freedom

Does all of this sound a bit sombre? Listen then, there exist two further forms of transformation and thus of freedom. I'd like to touch upon them briefly . . .

(6) The most definite *taste* of freedom is when you are struggling for it. That mobilization – despite the weaknesses and the breakdowns – of the freedom-loving and generous and comradely qualities of man, expressed through the political *act* in the economic or cultural or moral dimensions of the freedom struggle – that mobilization is an exceptionally precious *approach* to freedom. Better still: the struggle for freedom *is* already the embodiment thereof.

(7) And finally: the poem too is an expressive structure and an instrument of freedom. I know that the poem has a multiplicity of faces – simultaneously puzzle and labyrinth, illusion and reality. For me the contradiction action/dream no longer exists. Word *is* act. (And act, in its actualness, is also word.)

One must walk on. It's important. Only yesterday I read in a French translation of the writer Luxun's work (called *Le Journal d'un fou*): 'L'écrivain est celui qui lance quelques cris d'appel pour encourager le combattant qui galope dans la solitude afin qu'il ne faiblisse pas.' Somewhere the fighter moves in solitude. We must strengthen him.

To you I wish to convey and entrust the knowledge of that other, unfree, twisted world of bars – which is nevertheless so totally human.

Paris, February 1983

Paris

A little while back I received a letter from an esteemed young Afrikaans-language South African writer – this description, expression of the maniacal cutting and chopping that Apartheid entails, and we stumble and slip among the signposts, is a little laborious because I do not know whether he considers himself an 'Afrikaner' or not: it is after all a controversial conception: I, for instance, am not an Afrikaner although I have from time to time a whitish skin and even though my heart-language is Afrikaans, the same one he uses now – I'm talking of my colleague – to hit me over the knuckles with.

'Whyn'tya write something decent for a change,' he says. 'What are you doing over there in Paris? It is no longer cool to be in Paris in 1982, there is immorality at home now too . . .' (And a little further along in his letter a nice image is offered. 'Imprisonment is like paying off on a hi-fi set which has already been stolen.')

You miserable little bugger, I thought: you really think people flee to Paris just to be in fashion? Also: do you have any idea how exciting this old city can still be?

This run-up, my patient reader, I chewed over in my mind on the weekend of 12 February 1983. The occasion was a jamboree in the Sorbonne of about 400 'intellectuals' invited there by François Mitterrand and the Ministry of Culture; the theme of the get-together was 'Creation and Development' (or actually 'Culture in Times of Crisis'); the undisclosed contents (and intention?) was a glorious eating and drinking, eyedropping and manoeuvring to be seen (one of the *boopboere* always exhorted us, the *bandiete*: 'Look sharp, that's the thing! Don't try to be wise; just notch!'), and especially for those whose heads of hair have been thinned by the dizziness of cloudliving, to make new acquaintances and to plot together with old ones. What a joy to be running again into old friends like Edoardo Sanguineti.

More than that could not really be hoped for. The participants constituted a veritable Babel of tongues. Writers, painters, film directors, actors, excusers; also philosophers of fame and economists of name and sociologists of same; and some wheels from industry; a politicologist or two and – believe me if you will – even a culturologist. People, one and all, who go hurriedly bent double with the runny word. It would have been unwise to expect resolutions or even guidelines to emerge from these circumstances. Although many of the communications did show insight, were pithy and peppery, aphoristic, or funny.

Listen, Kenneth Galbraith was there (he says that he had been invited many times to go to South Africa but that he hesitates whether to accept or not, and my advice was: rather hang on), Francis Ford Coppola was there (cheerily apocalyptic) and Francesco Rosi (he knows his pictures are being shown in South Africa), William Styron, Amos Oz, Sean McBride (as strict as a mummy), Norman Mailer, Graham Greene (he remembers his trip through the country and is hugely surprised that his works are not banned there), Leopold Senghor ('Yes, I follow developments in South Africa very closely. Pieter Botha has been to see me.' And when we speak about bastardization, Africanization, he points out that some of his ancestors were of Portuguese origin – that's where his name originated), Peter Ustinov sits spread over three seats, Melina Mercouri is dolled up in pastels, Susan Sontag is there, Joris Ivens, Mary McCarthy (crotchety but terribly brittle), Sidney Lumet, Volker Schlöndorff, Ettore Scola, Vassilikos . . . And all the French: Régis Debray . . . Annie Girardot . . . Milan Kundera . . . Artur London (what an impressive man!) . . . Claude Simon . . . Françoise Sagan . . . Bubi . . . The fashionable people?

You don't want to be letting any cats out of the bag but, yes, it is true, Sophia Loren remains an attractive dame, uncomplicated and hospitable, and we had many reciprocal gaol experiences to exchange.

Scola also goes with a heavy ticker: he has a small watch-like counter attached to his belt to control whether he does the requisite distance every day, to keep the pump a-pittering, although, he explains with an ashen grey face, one can cheat by swinging the thing around for a while.

Ugo Tognazzi, resourceful cook, knocks together a very passable spaghetti ('carbonara') from nothing plus nothing at la Loren's hideout. I give him a scarf as a present to protect his neck from what he describes as the 'bestial cold'.

Such a tumult – a filching of thoughts, a thinking aloud, a pummelling of paps – evidently cannot be summed up. Except for, as if thrown off nonchalantly, phrases or echoes which one picks up here and there: the small seeds for poems. The Sorbonne is a veritable treasure cove. The scars of May 1968 have been effaced. At that time the popular graffito was: 'L'imagination au pouvoir'; now one hopes for slightly more power to imagination.

From his niche in the big amphitheatre, with Puvis de Chavannes's mural of the swapping of females as backdrop, Descartes sits peering down at the audience, with a red stain in the side – the mark of some student prank? Or must he also during major events start bleeding like Saint Gennaio of Naples?

'The economists admit that they have made a schmuckup of everything,' Schlöndorff says, 'and now they want us artists to clear up the mess. And to think that fifteen years ago in this very same Sorbonne we chucked culture out the window!'

Ernesto Cardenal, now Nicaragua's Minister of Culture, reads us a statement in his essy-ish Spanish. Parts of it could be straight from a poem. 'The blind must see/The cripples must walk again/The fish must be multiplied/We have 50,000 dead/We must learn to dream in another way.'

What is it that we long for? We are searching for more justice, true human dignity, the privilege to be allowed to participate in the edification of our lives, a more profound responsibility, and – why not? – a more concrete freedom.

And in passing you hear other references. 'Struggles', for example. Or 'Socialism'. What matters, (my young colleague, my patient reader), is that the authorities here give a certain importance to this type of thinking together, that they attempt to create a space for the generation and expression of opinion. And isn't that already a whole blooming lot?

On top of it the intellectuals are willing to explore the problems arising around artistic activity in a production-orientated society. 'The artist', Ka'afir contends, 'is the go-between between the actual world and the future.' It means, at a minimum, that we are facing forward.

Naturally the deeply seated obscurities remain, the dichotomy between technology and nostalgia. Must it necessarily paralyse us? Artistic expression is also the fight to rhyme and reconcile the extremes, the irreconcilables. And there has always been a creative dialectic between content and form. That is after all our task: to give to these new techno-miraculous forms of expression a human content. Look, culture really exists only there where we attempt to master the possibilities of communication and to use them; when we try to make ourselves understood – first to ourselves, and then to others. Look deeper, through the liberation struggle in South Africa, painfully, a *South African* culture is forged.

True, it is so that our bleating about cultural repression camouflages a political impotence. But the camouflage is not in the culture. For to be able to wrestle politically you must first of all know who you are. And thus culture is also an attempt at identification, personally and collectively.

Yes, I hear you, my china. I know of Benjamin who said: 'Every cultural document is at one and the same time a document of barbarity.'

We were tongue-tired of talking. But something I still have on the heart: that development, on the cultural terrain too, must move in a Socialist direction. Man's future will be Socialist or else we have no future to envisage.

Mitterrand closed the proceedings (the Sunday streets were cold to the soles but a little later we would right smartly go and break the fast in the Elysée Palace) with a quotation from René Char. Some line to the effect that we should now, 'turn the face to the rising sun'.

13 March 1983

The Writer and Responsibility

I am particularly grateful for the chance to address the Dutch PEN Centre. You are probably aware of the fact that one of the purposes of imprisonment in South Africa is to isolate the prisoner from the outside world. (This, by the way, is largely true for all prisoners and detainees, including the so-called 'common criminals'.) In the case of a political prisoner everything is done to destabilize him, to keep him off balance: for instance, not only is any expression of outside support kept from him, but the authorities try hard to create the impression that he is forgotten, rejected even, by his friends, colleagues or comrades.

But prison is never a watertight world; it cannot be so. Even behind those walls life manifests itself, sometimes taking on strange shapes. And rumours of 'real' life in the 'real', 'outside' world do penetrate. Thus I learned at various times, in bits and snippets at least, of actions undertaken on my behalf by the PEN Club of several countries. I know that PEN International sent a delegate to South Africa in an attempt to intervene with the authorities.

Such manifestations of solidarity are indeed terrific morale boosters for the incarcerated people. It is a confirmation of other realities, other values, other commitments existing beyond the frontiers of the penal universe. Life does continue!

For what you did and what you attempted to do I wish to thank you. And for your ongoing concern for authors in difficulty, in whatever country they may be, I'd like to congratulate you. Permit me to remark that it is with this type of intervention, concerning specific people and within the framework of our communal craft and concerns as writers, that you have the most effect and obtain the best results.

I'd like to say a few words on the theme, a very extensive one of course, of 'The Writer, and Responsibility'; and then more specifically on the writer's responsibility within a given social and cultural context, and perhaps a little also on the writer's stance when it comes to international issues such as, for instance, censorship and the oppression of free thought, economic and cultural imperialism, genocide even, and Apartheid particularly. Obviously the writer's basic commitment is to the integrity of his own work; he acts first of all through his work – it is his means of exploring himself, the network of his relationships, the objective world. I'm not ignoring this initial dimension; in fact, I think the writer's public actions form an extension of his private honesty or lack thereof.

You must forgive me if what I have to say at times sounds inevitably like a confession of faith. At this stage I'm not particularly interested in the cerebral debating of arguments. What's more, I cannot pretend to speak for anyone, I don't represent any group or school of thinking. I'm sure a few writers in South Africa, or even among you here, agree with some of my statements while fiercely disagreeing with others. And that is as it should be. All I'd like to do is to sketch my own position at this place and time.

A first conclusion obviously imposes itself: moral or political evaluations can never be used as literary criteria. We all know that 'good' writing can come out of profound dishonesty, decadence, treachery.

A second conclusion: a writer, any writer, to my mind has at least two tasks, sometimes overlapping; he is the questioner and the implacable critic of the mores and attitudes and myths of his society, but he is also the exponent of the aspirations of his people.

In the poor and colonized countries the writer plays a more visible role: faced with acute social and economic iniquities he is called upon to articulate the dreams and the demands of his people. From these contradictory responsibilities come the dichotomies of the writer's existence giving rise to so much tension and ambiguity. And from this flows the impossibility of the writer ever fitting in completely with any orthodoxy. Sooner or later he is going to be in disaccord with the politicians. He can be at times the expression of politics, even directly so, but the demands of his freedom and integrity may isolate him at other moments, may make him marginal. Call it the impotence and the glory of the writer if you wish!

And this holds true also for those societies and cultures where the writer is considered a 'cultural worker'. The highest and most difficult state of the writer is to be totally aware and self-questioning while contributing to the endless struggle for greater justice and more liberty. Yevgeny Zamyatin already claimed that writers should be heretics. 'Heretics', he wrote, 'are the only (bitter) remedy against the entropy of human thought . . . The world is kept alive only by heretics: the heretic Christ, the heretic Copernicus, the heretic Tolstoy . . .'

Burnt Bird

Yes, I too would want to wish with a Jan Campert 'that I could erect barricades between myself and the world' but I know that it is impossible.

There is in fact no Truth. We are too fragile and volatile for that; we work with too many uncertainties. There is rather the continual shaping of something resembling, poorly, provisionally, 'truth'.

I must try to situate myself more clearly. You are aware of the context within which any South African writer works, be he in the country or in exile. I am referring of course to Apartheid. But what does it mean to me personally?

Sometimes one is more impatient with one's friends than with one's enemies. We all agree that Apartheid is Evil. We often take the short cut. We oversimplify, we condemn out of hand. And perhaps sometimes we do it more out of consideration for the good of our own souls and not necessarily because we reject in a reasoned way the socio-political and economic (and cultural) exploitation, discrimination and humiliation of the history and the system that, inadequately, we call Apartheid. It is not so easy to wriggle out from under our responsibilities. Absolutism doesn't always imply absolution. In our simplicity we expose ourselves to the White masters – and to some Black lackeys too. Also, in our generalization we make it possible for some so-called 'allies' to oppose Apartheid while strengthening the foundations of the system. It is, as Mao might have said, like waving the red flag to combat the revolution.

Let me explain. You will find in the very cabinet of South African ministers people who claim to oppose Apartheid. And correctly so. In their prime objective to retain power they will abolish racial segregation. All they ask for is some 'understanding', the time to effect the necessary changes in an orderly fashion. Which foreign capitalist investor would disagree with them?

Many false impressions are created along the way of trying to improve their image and thus their respectability and thus their defendability. What we witness taking shape down there is in reality a controlled experiment in co-opting a number of non-Black politicians to bolster the present power structures against the Black majority. The real scenario is a militarist one; the strategy – against the so-called Total Onslaught (of Communism) – worked out by non-elected security 'experts'; the real power already in the hands of the military and of the political police. Meanwhile we shall hear more about South Africa being an outpost of Western culture, a bulwark against subversion, the strategic treasure house of the democratic powers, the economic turbine of the subcontinent. As the misery and the unrest elsewhere in the impoverished world deepen, more and more 'realists' will lend out their ears to this hogwash. Already American investment in South Africa had risen by 13.3 per cent in 1981 to 2.63 billion dollars and it is estimated that it had risen to 2.8 billion dollars in 1982. (These figures come from the US Department of Commerce.)

We should nevertheless have no illusions. Some of the structural changes being effected down there, such as the creation of the Bantustans, have already altered the landscape to the extent that any future solution of South Africa's problems will have to accommodate the changed and contaminated situation.

Yes, Apartheid remains a barbarity. But what I personally am more interested in is a feel of the grittiness, of the texture of everyday life. Here are a few recent examples.

It was revealed in the South African Parliament on 29 March this year that 722 'Coloureds' had been reclassified as 'Whites' between July 1981 and July 1982. That means, if they are employed by the state, that their salaries and pensions will now increase by 20 to 30 per cent. Seven Chinese were similarly 'upgraded'. They may now live in White zones, drink in any bar, send their children to the best schools. Fifteen 'Whites' were declared 'Indian' and three 'Coloured' – losing all the above privileges of course. Thirty-nine 'Coloureds' were changed to 'Indians'. One hundred and nine 'Blacks' were 'promoted' to 'Coloured', now no longer needing passbooks. Last year 135 people were caught and sentenced for 'immorality', that is mixed-race sex.

In the Transvaal the little village of Driefontein has been declared a 'black' spot; in terms of the government's resettlement policy all 5,000 inhabitants are to be displaced to a distant 'homeland'. (The village had been bought legally by a group of Africans in 1912.) On Saturday, 2 April, the village leader, Saul Mkhize, tried through his bullhorn to exhort a meeting of his people to remain calm, telling them that non-violence was the only solution. Two policemen arrested him for holding an 'illegal meeting'. In the ensuing confusion they shot and killed the old man.

It was announced in Parliament that 1,259 people have been killed by the police since 1976. These figures do not include people who died during the riots, nor those executed by the state. On an average 1,500 people per year are wounded by the officers of law and order during shooting incidents.

I cite these few examples to give you an indication of the tenor of everyday life in that bastion of democracy.

It is seen against this background that I, as a writer, growing through my own experiences, must take personal responsibility for my actions, all the while pursuing my journey on the two legs of theory and practice.

I subscribe to the cause of liberation and of majority rule in South Africa. At this juncture I believe I can best support that cause through my writing – and in not attempting to pull the wool over anyone's eyes. This is not an abstract idea I pursue (although I am committed ideologically to the transformation of the South African society) but the total sense of my life. I should like to see, through the pain and the hopes and the mistakes even of our struggle, the tempering of a truly *South African* culture, drawing its richness from the diversity of its origins – and I think it *is* gradually happening. The common roots are there: they need to be valorized. Even the common denominator, Apartheid, is there.

But I dispute the right of any orthodoxy or pressure group to tell me what and how I must write. My loyalty can be true only in my freedom to remain an agnostic.

I write mostly in Afrikaans. Now that I am relatively free to make my own choices I shall attempt to see to it that my work is handled by publishers who are not dominated by or in the pay of the Afrikaner Establishment. I cannot compromise on censorship in any way. If I cannot publish legally in South Africa, I shall try to explore other means of doing so.

I do not consider myself an Afrikaner; the definition, whichever way you turn it, has a political content with which I cannot identify. Even culturally I can't claim to be an Afrikaner. (I'm not particularly concerned about being a South African either; in fact I'm just a *bandiet!*). The Afrikaans language doesn't belong to the Afrikaners. I have no anguished feelings either way about its survival or its disappearance or its mutation. I recognize that it is fatally tainted and classified as the voice of the Master; I also know that it is a means of awareness and expression of astonishing beauty. But people will sing in whatever language they happen to dip their tongues into.

If I have any contribution to make to the changing of that tormented society it will have to be as a non-Black exile. My effectiveness inside South Africa, however tenuous, can be only within the White community. But I am isolated there. Although many White writers are against Apartheid, or rather the effects thereof, in varying degrees of disgust and anxiety, I do not know of any identifying with the Liberation Movement. (Admittedly, it would be suicidal to do so inside the country and it is completely unfair of us to expect them to be martyrs.)

The gulf created by Apartheid exists. The problems, although springing from one and the same source, are translated differently by the various population groups. If I were to deny this reality it would be a crass denial of class analysis.

The White writer is either a traitor or a hostage or a sell-out. In the deeply polarized South African environment he will be out of touch with some sector of the population wherever he may stand. In trying to heal yourself, in trying to recuperate some human dignity by spewing out Apartheid, you will find that it is a lonely business. But ultimately it is the only way to self-integration and possible brotherhood. Life is shitty enough as it is.

You, here in Holland, have been called upon to support the Cultural Boycott against South Africa. I should like to raise a few questions pertaining to that subject.

What can a Dutch writer do? What can PEN do? What exactly is the aim of a boycott? Who benefits from it? Who is touched by it? What is its effectiveness?

Let me say immediately that I support entirely the cancelling of all cultural links and exchanges between Holland and any official or officious or South African government-tolerated bodies. This is not something you can go back on, however much paper may be used by South African cultural organizations trying to cover the cracks in the ugly face of racist reality. You will have to be vigilant though. When they find it convenient the South African agents will break your ranks with the corrupting lure of money (big money too, as they have shown themselves capable of when buying sportsmen or journalists) or the equally tempting illusion of importance accorded to mediocre writers.

But the Dutch Cultural Boycott doesn't really make the headlines in South Africa. W. F. Hermans going there, for example, is locally perhaps a hotly disputed event – which may be what he intended to achieve – but nobody outside the restrained Afrikaner academic community cared or even knew about it. I doubt whether the authorities there saw his visit as an endorsement of their policies. Nevertheless, the man going there, fully aware of the implications of his visit as seen from this end, and Hermans is certainly not stupid, must be interpreted at the least as tolerating the set-up.

And apart from literature and some art collectors and museums down there acquiring the works of Dutch artists, what cultural exchanges have there really been?

I take it for granted that as concerned and informed Dutch writers you would want to express, through your positions and actions, abhorrence of racial discrimination. You would also want to show some form of support and solidarity with the oppressed majority, perhaps even an identification with the hunt for freedom led by the liberation organizations. Some of you may want, in the process of supporting action against the South African power élite, also to come to a clearer delineation of your own role and responsibilities as writers, not only with reference to South Africa, but in your own environment.

One must be clear about your motives and your means. In this equation cultural or collective guilt feelings have no place. I believe any support for the liberating of the South African people – in all the multiple devolutions and expressions it must have – implies the responsibility of at least knowing exactly what one is about.

Responsibility implies the freedom to be critical. Few positions are as demeaning as that of the 'fellow-traveller'. Too often the intellectual is a sheep, one of the bourgeoisie who, as Lenin pointed out, will make the revolution for us. All too often also the intellectual, ill at ease because of the contradictions of his condition, is hood-winked by the promise of 'playing an important role'.

The cause is a good one, the issues at stake and the implications (worldwide even) are momentous, encompassing our emotions as well as our reasoning and our interests; but we are dealing with political organizations employing political means for political goals. I repeat – the cause is noble: be entirely aware in your support however of both the ends and the means employed to attain those ends. Not so that you may be paternalistic in any way, but as responsible writers knowing the scope and the limitations of your actions.

I must insist that I find it totally unacceptable that any organiz-ation, however representative it may be, should decide what writing is to be allowed and diffused and what not. If you agree to that you must also accept potentially at least the tragedy of a Mandelstam or a Pasternak or a Solzhenitsyn. What do you do about Céline or a latterday Hemingway? What about a poet with the stature of Roy Campbell who ended up supporting Franco? And, closer to home, what about Mazisi Kunene who, as far as I know, is not at present in favour with the ANC?

The difficult balance to achieve is clarity of principle and purpose while refusing any oversimplification of the options. To insist on a blanket boycott of all literary work produced inside South Africa is politically stupid. It denotes a blindness to the reality of the situation there with all its cracks and interstices of freedom; it is furthermore a running away from your own responsibilities, taking the easy way out. You are denying to yourself the means of political action and of moral manoeuvre.

The Writer and Responsibility

Athol Fugard's *Master Harold and the Boys* is at present being staged in Johannesburg. In a review, published internationally, I read:

> When the lights dimmed on the powerful last scene, in which the two Black waiters affirm their self-respect in the embrace of a slow, heart-rending foxtrot, roughly half the audience rose to give the play's three actors a standing ovation. The rest had yet to emerge from the private world of grief and loss into which the play appeared to have plunged them. Many, Blacks and Whites, were crying.

So what are the alternatives? It seems as if we are all waiting for the Apocalypse down there. I too am frustrated by the monolithic nature of the South African set-up, the fact that nothing seems to have any effect on the smooth surface of repression – at least not anything one may be able to do from here. But although you may not always realize it, some things have happened here. It may take years for an idea to come to fruition. I remember that we discussed, years ago already, with some Dutch friends present here, the need to get South African authors and artists, both in exile and inside the country, to meet and get to know one another. Well, we weren't the only ones thinking along those lines – I still have some correspondence pertaining to the matter – and eventually the meeting did take place. I also remember how particular attention was paid in Rotterdam, years ago too, to Zulu poetry. Over the years quite a few poets have participated there – Kunene, Pieterse, Kgotsitsile, Brutus, Serote. I remember discussing with Dutch students of Afrikaans the need to dissociate Dutch from Afrikaans, to see Afrikaans as just one African language among others – Swahili too was shaped by a non-African language, Arabic – and to shift the accent to *South African* literary studies. This concept, I believe, is no longer as foreign as it may have sounded then.

In South Africa I know of at least one university where a similar healthy development has taken place: Dutch is taught there as a totally separate foreign tongue, not only as the prehistory of Afrikaans.

I believe, in the question of a Cultural Boycott, that alternative links should be forged strengthening and amplifying the real voices of resistance in the country – always keeping in mind that these are the people being smothered either by censorship or other ways of harassment and suffocation.

I am not suggesting a dialogue with any official body, neither am I advocating the idea of keeping communication lines open in the hope of influencing the minds and hearts of the racists.

Burnt Bird

Of course, as far as selling books through official channels or exchanging lecturers, etc., are concerned – that should be totally out. But always remember that there are some brave people there who need your support, a few Dutch expatriates even; I'm thinking of one, for instance, who is instrumental in having most of the Black poetry inside published. They must be helped to survive.

Why not try to be more adventurous? Why not, for example, try to get good quality Dutch works to prisoners in South Africa? You may not succeed but at least you would have made a point. Protest actions, standpoints decided upon here, should be brought to the individual attention of the South African authors themselves. The crux of the matter is that as far as the Whites are concerned you can really influence only those writers and academics who look nostalgically to Holland for approval – rather in the way the Calvinists there are sensitive to the authority and the influence of the Calvinists here. Why not attempt to have books against Apartheid published there? You should in any event try to assure that critical works printed there, and most likely banned, are translated and made available outside. It is also a form of protection for the dissident writers.

It is even more important to help create the possibilities of printing here in the original languages publications banned there, and to find ways of getting these back into South Africa.

You see, there is no easy solution to the dilemma South Africa poses, neither for me as a non-Black exile, nor for you as sympathetic Dutch writers.

'Brakke Grond', Amsterdam, 9 April 1983

Keep Clear of the Mad

Life is not entirely correct or tender in its treatment of the human being. Put another way: characteristic of the human condition is that you are a broken rhythm, that time catches up with you, that you quite simply develop too tardily to be able to digest effectively the dollops of 'liberated' wisdom you may have managed to imbibe through a tight gullet.

Everywhere around you, like tiny unscripted fables, you become aware of the paradoxes and the ironies of the matter . . . In the big gardens near your rooftop house (now a sea of pale green leaves asway with birds like twittering baby dolphins in the branches) every morning you come across an old grey-haired lady in her electric wheelchair. The miserable little bundle of humanity, practically diminished to glasses and coat and shoes, wheels with a humming sound from one garden dignitary in stone to the next, to spread again and again little clawfuls of crumbs for the flutterfolk, doves and sparrows and the odd blackbird. She half hides behind the granite figures, each embodying some woman, probably a muse, still young but already lascivious and mature.

And Petitloup tells you about the accident that befell Blanche, the butterfly-friendly friend of yours. Blanche, fluent in Chinese, works in a bookshop with the name of 'Phoenix'. One day, while leafing through the ashes of some ancient oriental text, a fire flitted up and translated both her hands and a strip of her face in smoke and burnt-out flesh.

That is the way in which life makes its way, you would be led to believe: it is a sadness that via a Sunday newspaper will duly be transformed into circulation figures and therefore into hard money. It goes without saying. But as if your objective condition isn't cruel enough you furthermore find instances – people, institutions – which seem to obtain endless gloating satisfaction from the destruction of others. A whole career, with pension pending at the end of it, is apparently not sufficiently long to slake their dirty desires.

Recently I met an activist who was bent to go round the bend while in the hands of these selfsame officials. Thin he was now, shivering, with damp hands, a haunted and unbalanced glint in the eye – his spirit endlessly twisted. Detention, isolation, interrogation, psychological manipulation – all of these with a sham of 'security' considerations, but in the final analysis it was sadism only. Anguish, in fact, more than anything else: as if we could penetrate to the nitty-gritty of the reason for our existence by taking each other apart and squashing the parts, as if loneliness could be exorcized in this fashion.

Such a person, such a released but contaminated one, must become 'God's clown', always on the edge of explosion or breakdown: a cocked arm for assassination or self-destruction.

You see, thus your greyed haslet secretes a first conclusion (sometimes, when you are already limping): that the ground is broken but that the only way through is to walk on, to continue the hobblededay. But then, if you don't want to boob into any of the traps, only in so far as you are *without interests, without expectations, without belongings,* without the abscess isolated as 'I'. It is only through meshing entirely with life that you can prevent it from getting a grip on you. That is, I'm sure, what Randy Newman implies, in one of his songs, with: 'Looking at the river without thinking of the sea.'

Where the hogs are many the wash is poor. This is why I am so grateful to prison, which relieved me of so much – trust in the fellow human animal, idealism, self-respect . . . so that I may survive as some burnt-out extra.

Naturally you will want to continue creating your environment from nought to nothing. Because writing is a reality transcription just as it is the furnishing of a reality. *That* you cannot do without. (It is an ancient gnaw . . .) The writing is a dead snake slithering sneakily from inside you, and you the skin that will be replaced. Writing is the recognition and the realization of your alienation, it is the living death with all its coils and foils. No echo – neither does it have any echo – with only language as the interpretative, if piecemeal, structure.

Translating oversimplifies terribly. (The first limits of our thinking are the expressive possibilities of language itself.) Language has its own frightening beauty. At times it is a convention worn smooth, with a taste of pebbles, and at other moments it may become a lip-frothing dictator. I know, even while writing this, that much of what is sincere and warm and irrecuperable will fall away in the cracks between words. The real is in the interstices. And *that* is replaced by the living image, the illusion – this premiss which we de-scribe as 'language': shattered and propped up by silences.

Perhaps I am so fidgetily aware of this crumbled reality image, of the dialectic of communication, of the necessity to identify the interstices (not by way of runaway but as punctual actions to bring the rhythms in harmonious transport) because it ties in with similar preoccupations in society.

Last week, in Holland, I could, enlightened by many exchanges of views, get some inkling of the spirit that is prevalent there now. (I was there to explain why I support the boycott of official cultural links to South Africa, but also why I refuse to be squeezed or boxed in by whatever orthodoxy or combination and concoction of activists.) All of a sudden it is as if many people no longer care about the contradictions and the paradigms of the Establishment. And not so much because the dominant value systems are questioned and combated; they have quite simply lost their relevance. The postulate 'hierarchy' is itself ludicrous so that every periphery may now become the focal point or the central. You no longer have to buy face.

As illustration of the situation I was told of the huge communal concern about nuclear armament as expressed in a march upon Rotterdam. Apparently there were close on half-a-million protestors, all very calm, without any aggressiveness. That same evening the Minister-President of the previous Dutch government put in an appearance on the television altar to try and capture the massive landslide with the aggrieved ceremonial countenance and the make-believe wittiness of the typically hypocritical politician.

'I comprehend the fears of the people,' he asserted, but he was handling the question by the wrong end, because that was not the case at all, people are not apprehensive of the Big Bang, they are just not interested any more in all that tommyrot. People simply want to live.

One encounters widespread 'dissidence' (if you still insist upon arguing from the point of view of archaic tenets) which appears to be due to depoliticization. People have lost all confidence, even in the labour movements. It is unequivocally accepted that all governments lie and that all politicians (representatives and other senaphors) are crooked. Besides, that the language has been poisoned.

We have nothing, that is why we are not afraid – that seems to be the common denominator. To concretize this realization you must, even without having to go into opposition, pull the plug from the ruling classes' bath full of holy water. Once you submit to the thought restrictions of the power managers, enter their game with their options, cultural and other – they have already won the day.

Our first victory is the breakthrough of knowing, exactly, that we *may* reflect, conceptualize, chip away at the taboos; that we are *not* afraid. Thus after all do we create space, even if the latter serves just to demarcate the conflicts more clearly.

What a glorious day it will be when all secret services, occult organizations and masturbating fraternities sink away in their own unimportance, or rather, are left soppily floundered in their empty beds!

But our interstices must be suffused by tolerance. 'We are an army of the ragged and the impecunious,' one of my friends says while we stand looking at the rain in his garden. Not all of us are strong labourers. *The dumb and the halt and the lame and the drunk must also be included in our cortège.* (These words are believed to have cost the late L. P. Boon his position as editor of a Communist publication.)

> how sad your face is
> like an empty white page
>
> the winter was not quite stiff enough
> for the canals to grow their ice,
> winterbirds didn't come to search
> for cake-crumbs in the gardens of the city
>
> and it is said that the aged pigeons
> while still alive
> are finished off by the younger ones
> coo-coo beaking open the hoary heads
> to gulp down the brains
> (so much for the peace symbol)
>
> the magnolia tree has bated blossoms:
> when it starts flowering
> the grey wall behind it will go purple
>
> in the newssheets reproductions
> the size of palomas
> of dead humans
>
> shore up your face with the crawl of words:
> fleetfooted you must be
> to keep clear of the mad

24 April 1983

Berlin

The two poles remain freedom and restriction. And, like other pairs of opposites, the one exists only in terms of the other. Even quite recently Claude Lévi-Strauss asserted that we cannot express ourselves unless there are limitations. It was a reference to Gide's well-known: 'Art lives on restrictions (or obstacles) and dies from freedom.'

I should like to express the same in trying a somewhat different tack. Namely that freedom can be uttered only through structure. Even: that structure is the embodiment of freedom. But that is a working truth, an organic or even an organizational law. Metamorphosis, after all, 'manifests' or accomplishes itself from form to and into form. It has no truck at all with repression. (The structures I have now in mind concern rhythm and pattern and repetition and reason and space, edges of the silence, rims around silences, signs of and towards meaning, the play between matrix and fuck-all, which is what text is all about, and jutting from those all the relationships . . .)

Could one conceivably claim that censorship is a structure or the structuring of expression? Certainly not! Censorship is an act of shame. Censorship is a motion of no confidence in your fellow and in yourself. It has to do with manipulation, with power, with the repression of freedom seekers out there and the phantasmagoria or even the bare bones of enjoyment within. That is one of the hallmarks of a totalitarian state. 'We recognize that the enemy of the individual, of freedom, may use any mask, but that he will always have the face of the state.'

Structures of language, of thinking, of action on the one hand, manifestations of repression and hooding on the other, and also patterns of survival and forms of resistance – these are the things that you inevitably cut into when you find yourself in Berlin. Especially when you are there within the context of the fiftieth-anniversary commemoration of the *auto-da-fé*, the burning of the books. On the evening of 10 May 1933, thousands of books were destroyed on the Opernplatz in Berlin – by students accompanied

111

by their lecturers, professors, rectors: the intellectual rectum of Nazism!

In the name of the national community and an idealist attitude to life, of a moralist family life, of loyalty to the people and to the state, of nobility of the soul, of respect for the past, of responsible participation in the process of nation building and national edification, of respecting the national patrimony (and combating the disparagement of the language), of honour and esteem for the undying national spirit . . . works of Marx and Kautsky and Mann and Glaeser and Kästner and Förster and Freud and Hegemann and Wolff and Remarque and Kerr, etc., etc., were thrown into the flames.

Now, you may very well say, yes, but these authors survived the incineration whereas Hitler and his riff-raff are relegated to the rubbish dump of History (except for hither and yon . . .). Partially true, I grant you. But only partially. Because there were also other writers whose works were unavailable for long enough in Germany for them essentially to cease existing. A book is after all both product and expression of its time, has a vital interaction with its readers within a specific time span, and may then, and perhaps then only, contribute towards the development of society. To read the works now, in our present set-up, of Casey Motsisi, Nat Nakasa, Can Themba, the assassinated Rick Turner, the gagged Beyers Naudé . . . is of only historical interest still. Like eating dead bread. And then: the spirit of totalitarianism is not dead, it keeps on poking out its beastly head (with helmet); it flourishes still in, for instance, 'democratic' Chile and South Africa, just as it does in some so-called Communist countries.

Yes, we cannot hide behind the supposedly 'unique nature' of South Africa's problems; in spirit the country is but a banana republic. Fifty years ago a 'freedom library' was started abroad to conserve the forbidden German works. I hope that with us today too there is at the very least a literary faculty somewhere trying to index the history, methods and results of censorship, and seeing to it that the works are saved.

The cold burning. That is, appropriately, how a German newspaper characterizes the present spiritual persecution in totalitarian countries. It was to talk around this reality that I had been invited to Berlin by the *Autorenbuchhandlung*, together with Jorge Semprun, Milan Kundera, Lev Kopelev and György Konrad. Kundera had to be off to America and was replaced by a young Czech who writes in German, Libuse Monikova.

By the way, the *Autorenbuchhandlung* embodies a concept worth imitating. It is a Berlin bookshop (in other German cities there are similar ones) which belongs entirely to a group of writers; an association of people employing specialists to run the business professionally. The general assembly meets annually to discuss the report of past activities and to consider new ideas. One principle is that even the rarest German book in print will be available. Those books of which only a few remain will be bought up, and the last copies will go to the adjacent archives belonging to the bookstore. The shop has naturally become a watering hole where local and visiting pen-sufferers gather to exchange their whimpers. Three or four evenings a week the long-suffering and slow-to-anger authors will read there from their works in preparation: a book may sometimes be modified for its own good after such a confrontation with a critical reading public.

We who were there for only a few days also had to read. (I am becoming a polyglot: during the past months I have had to mumble my way through French – on France's national poetry day; through Dutch, not long ago, during the national liberation celebrations in the Eusebiuskerk of Arnhem, and that in the presence of Beatrix, quite fetching in her blue boater; through German and through English; and in between, bless my soul, through Afrikaans as well, (But, oh dear, despite the blurring of foreign languages the verses remain 'obsolete nonsense', as Brink would have it.)

After the readings there are discussions, and the public joins in. The guest writers are, each in his own miserable way, at odds with their countries of origin, and the declarations and questions all pivot on this central perception. There are exiles in the audience, certainly an ample number of spies to boot, because someone like Konrad intends eventually to return to his native land.

'We ourselves constitute censorship,' he says. 'State man represents the norm, autonomous man is the deviant.' And then recounts with much tenderness how he respects the 'field work' of the secret researchers. At least an ear somewhere captures his sighs. He only hopes that they labour with their listening devices and their voyeur eyes, down on all fours in the dust or hidden up in lofts or patiently spying from their state vehicles – at the behest of the philologists of the future. State power drives the author out into the open. Strips him. You look and listen to yourself from outside. How then can you not identify with that person in you who has been prohibited?

Later he also says that the only relief from censorship is simply to ignore it. He refers to the undermining effects of repression, of how it takes root inside you as a kind of interiorized paternalism. And a question then: should you resist through your writing the platitudes that have become 'statified'? You yourself are the platitude too. 'All true literature is an everlasting inner struggle against clichés.'

Lev Kopelev recites with a sonorous voice, with dramatic gestures. His white beard is all a-tremble. A veritable Tolstoy figure. And whenever he stumbles over a whatsisname or the infinitesimal matter of a date, his wife helps him over the hurdle out loud from her seat in the front row.

(Mornings, in the hotel where we stay, the breakfast table may as well be in little mother Russia: the paterfamilias bickers with his wife and smoothes her feathers down, devours five simultaneous conversations with intense co-expatriates armed with bloated brief-cases, sniffs his way through ten newspapers and passes on to me an article with a photo of Blacks in Pretoria crowded around the pedestal of 'Ohm Kruger', tells anecdotes of his life in prison – he is the 'Rubin' character in Solzhenitsyn's *The First Circle* – praises the merits of Peter Abrahams and German jams, and all the while the pots of coffee disappear.)

But to listen to him is to have a knife painfully in the stomach. He entered the camp a convinced Communist and when finally discharged he was still as much of a believer as before. We must suffer for the good of the cause. Only then though – because one must attempt distilling some sense out of one's life – he started questioning the impeccable wisdom of Stalin. The crumbling of his idol, so it is written in the confession which he reads us, cracked the very foundations of all his other beliefs. Now he is completely disenchanted and no longer attached to any ideology or church or group. His only guideline? *Tolerance.*

A young Black compatriot of mine gets to his feet. He wants to know from me whether it is true that there are differences of opinion among White Afrikaans writers. And didn't the Sestigers in the end direct themselves to Europe? And what legacy will the White writer leave his offspring? What are they doing to make their own children aware of Africa? What do they contribute towards the destruction of that racism which defiles people? In what way do they help make our common future liveable?

Come now, dear reader, what would you have said in my place? He's right. We are entering the bloodbath with blinkers on. And the renewal that we, feebly, called *Sestig*? (This 'Sestiger' label is the doing of lazy historians looking at all costs for a little peg to hang History on, and with noses in the dust they keep on thinking in terms of decades and races for writers.) It is true that our worlds of reference, and finally our public, are European-orientated, however

114

hard we may try to break through the topsoil of African reality with the borrowed tools of existentialism and structuralism. We live off the fat of suffering, particularly since 'courage' (according to Nadine Gordimer) has become a *literary* attribute. Worse still: our 'bravery' obfuscates the existence of the Black writers in the country. And aren't we, we who are courting liberty, making Afrikaans acceptable to the outside – and in the end taming Apartheid in this way? I mean: by exhibiting the queasy feelings we may have about Apartheid we, the White writers, the Masters' voices, are making the monsters human and banalizing the horror.

Other prickly pears thrown about for discussion were, *inter alia*, the question (as pointed out by feminists) of the visual pollution and the verbal exploitation of the female body, and whether it should be censored; the statement also that interdiction may scramble literary values – a work may well be considered good just because it has been forbidden by bureaucruds.

Konrad tells us about a nice elementary form of *samizdat*. In Hungary forbidden work is printed specially to be distributed among Party bosses only – as a kind of perk? Or because they should be familiar with evil? Thanks to the brats of Party leaders opponents obtain these books and 'liberate' them by illegal proliferation.

Berlin? So much to say about it. The wall. The wall jumpers. The wall in the mind. The Turkish quarter. The huge pink letters on a wall spelling simply ROSA. The enormous feast–protest against nuclear weapons. The city as the petrifaction of human folly. The grass-covered chancelleries. The night life. The S-Bahn, East-owned, with its Western employees. But there is not enough space . . . One should in actual fact quote Jorge Semprun: 'The barricades obstructed the routes and opened up a new perspective.'

29 May 1983

9 June 1983

I have something on the heart
it is hot again in Paris today nearly an African heat
trains rumbled through tunnels underground
and pigeons took off with a rustle of wings
to look for security in the plane trees
the way words revert to a mouth
to be concealed by the green rustling

I have something on the heart
this day doesn't want to pass away
interminably the evening star stood burning over the city
like a lighthouse having to entice the night
to a feast of joy above some Bethlehem
and news from the realm of death flickered on screens
I must weep I cannot weep

this morning in Pretoria three black fighters
were dropped down a well
for high treason against the whites' white state of terror:
I know that place of iniquity
have heard the grey sounds of chained people
climbing the steps to paradise

hamba kahle!
Marcus Motaung age 27
hamba kahle!
Jerry Motsololi age 25
hamba kahle!
Simon Mogoerane 23 years young
    . . . hamba kahle . . .

Transvaal winters can be so cold and dry
early day-labourers have hands chapped and still with the cold

9 June 1983

the people are awake the time is at hand there
Ukwezi still swings from night's crossbeam where
daylight hesitates to venture
waiting for the sun till the sun advances masked
through smoke blanketing township and enclosure

far however far across this arid earth
of covenants reverberating trapdoors open in the people's listening

behind the walls of Maximum Security
the lifesongs are rhythmed like breathtaking
the revolving of night to gladness
behind the ramparts of the state's supposed safety
the raw singing will open too with the day
on to the larger chant of silence:

everyone will have an ear close to his cell door:
the heart a soft pigeon in the throat:
there will be a physician in the procession
and a spiritual cripple who has to try
blanching the legal murder
with an illusion of christian clemency:
the head of the prison too (will he
press the shackled black hands in leavetaking?)
and warders who have to pair life to rope

I am 43 years old
I must weep I cannot weep
it is hot in Paris with a kind of African heat
this Thursday tomorrow will be Friday Saturday
Sunday the butcher-birds will be in church
with flowery ties recalling slightly stained necklets
I must weep I cannot weep
I have something on the heart

Simon Mogoerane
blood on the ropes
Jerry Motsololi
blood at the neck
Marcus Motaung
three corpses dangling down death's slope

Burnt Bird

like words in the mouth
and in this anonymous grey earth
three offers will be burning as a wound
bleeds resistance, and freedom fires

A Festival of Poetry in Rotterdam

(1) When you enter the city of Rotterdam by train you first pass over the Rhine, here as wide as a hand above the eyes, and then across other bridges over a latticework of waterways. Along the outer perimeter of the city, against the wall of a watchtower standing guard over one of the bridges, you will see painted in big red letters: DROOM UW DROOM. DREAM THY DREAM. Towards the end of the week we, shepherded tourists, sail through parts of the port. Mr He Xianglin, of China, dutifully jots down all the information broadcast in four languages over the squawk-boxes. Ships from Panama, Korea, Norway. Bobbing. From on high over the boat railings sailors with faces like wrinkled brown fists peer down at us. Grey light. Tang of rope, tar, salt. You suddenly realize that that child, which hesitantly wanted to cross the threshold of the limitless dream, is still alive inside you. A harbour will always remain the antechamber of the unknown. Rimbaud: 'Oh que ma quille éclate, oh que j'aille à la mer!'

(2) Must we slavishly take for granted the pollution of neon advertisements? Why not harness the shallowing medium for other purposes? Against the skyline on top of one of the buildings there glows, traced in tube lights, a line from Remco Campert. *Poetry is an act!* (The word-feast then continues: *of affirmation*, to finish at last with: *death is an emotion*.) My proposal that there should be a grave for the unknown poet somewhere in the city will most probably be realized also. Perhaps even in the shadow of the gigantic old tree standing surrounded by water above its own reflection in the Westersingel. We call it 'the tree of poetry'. It resembles the grafting of an oak on a baobab.

(3) Poetry International 1983 runs from 12 to 18 June. Impressions, fragmented musings, whispering mirrors, light nights, interpoet sympathy with the sickness of being a poet, not too much bragging, confrontations, frustration at the inadequacy

of the Word, warm fraternity – I don't think I could distil it to something coherent.

(4) Why is the poet (like) a whore? Because he has to go and sell himself. The intimate is exposed, exhibited, and thus loses its exclusive power and validity. We are all poseurs, even those among us who do it reluctantly. Communication is corruption. Professional declaimers like Rafael Alberti and Kazuko Shiraishi make a proper performance of their readings – multivoiced, with music. But giving away the private also transforms it into something else, powerful communal property. You must accept that you are a public convenience. Yehuda Amichai: 'Poetry is the last truly human activity on a human scale; the single human voice speaks to the other human being about things and emotions of man. And you can do everything with that.'

(5) The diet is however too rich. Too much verse-dreaming verses you in the perversions of poetry. Like a parrot. A kind of swooning or some frenetic *frémissement* of emotion leads you to believe that your most banal on-the-spur-of-the-moment inspiration, or ingenuousness, must have poetic value. You become a practitioner of the beheaded poetry. Puns will cover the floor, snarled like mares' nests. But if you were to look more sharply you will also notice the cracks of pain. The monsters cannot help themselves. Inevitably all of us will be fondling the frontiers to knead and knit the *poesia* in us, always engaged upon the testing of words and concepts and ways of telling an anecdote. One just has to escape. I give the translation project a wide berth (we are to translate Remco) with the excuse that my Afferkaans is too close to Dutch for comfort and that I shall make my contribution by helping Yehuda with his Hebrew (nobody can check up on us); then we go and hide for hours on end in some eating place. Bert Schierbeek proposes that we should, for the sake of our souls' health, go and do something concrete. Like watching a football match, for instance. (I thought that I could already master enough psychic energy to face all kinds of music-makers during the week, but halfway I realized how weak I still am. You need psychiatric help to survive prison, and whilst you have been turned properly into a prisoner you as much need psychiatric advice to come alive outside again with your dead strips.)

(6) Yehuda recounts a previous get-together of poem-makers in London. Both Montale and Ungaretti had been invited, but

there is not much love lost between the two of them. So Ungaretti had to be fêted specially, all by himself, two weeks later than his countryman – when the Italian ambassador duly presented the guest as: 'The best poet in Europe and one of the best in Italy.'

(7) I am pestered by journalists. Each of them wants some core substance to devour. There is a cannibalistic search for the 'nice story'. Why is it that the Dutch seem to be more interested in the doings of a whitish South African than in that of a blackish one? Eurocentrism? I come upon myself mouthing senseless sentences, such as – that love poetry may also have political implications! One young lady comes to interview me for *Die Waarheid*, the mouth-organ of the Dutch Communist Party (NCP). Her questions however are statements several yards long, to which I can only answer with a muffled 'yes' or 'no'. An illustration certainly of how the question can sternly manipulate any answer. As Ford said: 'You may buy any colour car you wish as long as it is black.'

(8) The NCP, I hear, has been taken over from within by feminists. Probably the only 'current' that could succeed in prying the party loose from Moscow's apron strings. On one wall I read a grafitto (no obvious link to my previous sentence): *Big sister is watching you!*

(9) 'Open' conversation with three compatriots in the presence of a Dutch journalist and a tape recorder (which pulls everything out of kelter). Superficial and false. Hackneyed propaganda strewn like dice over the table, with closing fists and many imprecations. The conversation points to questions like nationalism and patriotism, exile, the Taal, culture (for whom do we write and what is the purpose of our writing), Eurocentrism, censorship, the position regarding the ANC. When we go to that little place where you pass–ss water (for the conversation is continually irrigated by beer), then there is much fraternization. But back by the tape recorder there is a wailing and a belly-beating about exile and further half-cooked recriminations. A double-facedness. Profound South African disease. My accomplices-in-conversation speak as Blacks although all three of them are Brown. I am the Whitey although I don't consider myself an Afrikaner, am not particularly sure whether I'm a South African, and never again want to founder in the miserabilism of being a refugee. (If ever nostalgia catches up with me again, I shall doctor it to death with

memories of Pretoria.) How can you justify your writing in
Rapport, a government mouthpiece? The question makes
sense. My defence: I take the gap where I can, on condition that
I retain control over the contents. But is the spoon really long
enough? It is held against me that I am not Nelson Mandela.
Yet, the only difference between the two of us is precisely that I
am not Nelson Mandela. Did I not prove irrevocably that I am a
political stumbler? And anyhow, I say, I was not going to tie a
rope around my neck only to gratify the expectations of those
of you sitting out here on your big fat arses. How dare you
allow the Dutch to carry you on their hands the way they do?
Look, I must say, if you think I am standing in your way it is
your task to sweep me aside. Influence, power, can never be
granted; it must be grasped . . . Nevertheless, the positive
aspect is that we *can* at least have this conversation. But such
conversations should be taking place down there in Babylonia,
and at all levels, with no holds barred.

(10) People who attacked me and spat upon me while I was
lying in the belly of the beast now come to kiss me on both
cheeks. The feeling seems to be: the Breytenbach bandwaggon
is on the roll again, or, let us look and see how we may use him.
But people make errors.

(11) There are Fascist structures of thought and means of expression
that are not recognized as such because they live under the
tongues of people who consider themselves to be 'Left'. When
you tilt your head a little more intently to listen to the rhythms,
you will hear the machismo, the intolerance, the references to
'blood' and 'fire'.

(12) Everywhere South Africans pop up. Old exiles, fresh
expatriates, chaps who are there just like that without any
rhyme or reason. One or two of them hang about, beer glass at
hand, self-conscious amongst all this poetry. There's a poison-
head from Durbs, musician – no man, it's sweet, but could I
perhaps see him right with a possy for the night, I say? There's
a laitie who has pushed two years first in Big House and then
in Crown Town. (Whatever became of so-and-so?) One berk
wants to head me off at the pass, has urgent needs, wants to
unbosom himself at all costs, wants to tell me the soggy story of
his life. Behind him his wife – her heart too is heavy with life.
Behind her, two more pals, *idem*. A whole commune. Sadness,
sadness.

(13) Everything that Mr He Xianglin hears and sees, data and addresses, scrupulously enters his notebook via the drip of his pen. He teaches English, has a long string of titles, and to top it off he is a member of the Central Committee. We all buy him books because it would seem that one book alone is priced at half his monthly salary. Somebody says that his Humphrey Bogart-like suit of clothes (it looks like that of an old ape being discharged from boop) was issued to him by the home authorities so that he does not have to walk about in his Mao uniform, but that it has to be handed in again upon his return to the country. Somebody else remarks – now if the Dutch were to give him an extra suit he would probably defect to the West. But he also has a blinding blue satin tie, embroidered with a silver dragon, around the neck. What would he be thinking of the discos and the decadence? He is an old fox. Has to be. How else could one survive Maoism, the Cultural Revolution, the Gang of Four?

(14) Kazuko Shiraishi's volume of poems is called *Sacred Lust*. Exceptional poetry. She is 52 years old, but just watch now how sexily she presents that long epistle to a penis, with music thumping the background. Offstage she is a worried little mother. She looks me deep in the eye, shows me a few shiatsu pressures which should stimulate the blood circulation, and strongly recommends that I eat 'blown lice' (brown rice).

(15) Together with Denise Levertov in the bus during the 'school trip', the excursion taking place on our last day there. She was born in England – of a Welsh mother and a Jewish Russian father – grew up there and then went to America. Where does she feel really at home? She reflects for a long moment. Then decides: probably only in the language. In the end only language can be my home.

(16) The Westerner's wanting to know, wanting to understand, is in reality already an attempt at appropriating the alien culture. So-called 'scientific' observations modify in actual fact that which is being studied. Anthropology, ethnology – these are cultural–imperialist disciplines implying a hierarchy of civilization values.

(17) The walls are often filthy. I read: *porno and justice – two hands on one belly*. Above a supermarket is written, confusingly, as some form of advertising: *change is valuable so that the oppressed can be tyrants*. In a shop window a dusty collection of obstetric

instruments, fancy condoms, manuals about the various positions. Also a mysterious little tin as if for chewing tobacco, with the reproduction of palm trees and a text on the lid: *Impotent? Zumba helps!* Bert says: as soon as Holland started getting earth gas there was immediately no more petroleum available.

(18) You can tune in to at least eleven television channels, in German, in English, in Dutch and in French. And late at night there would be a blue movie. A terribly polite demonstration of holds and folds and falls and grips imagined and illustrated by bored and black-fingernailed old bed athletes. I never knew that pornography could be so pernickety about etiquette.

(19) I propose that worldwide – quarter by quarter, city by city, country by country – a survival organization should be formed, flowing from the population itself, intended to unmask and to combat all security services, information or intelligence groups, secret organizations, political police. Those of your own state, and all the others as well. That would be an effective way of becoming an outlaw and a hunted prey. But it very definitely has everything to do with poetry also.

(20) The last poem read by me on the last evening is 'Letter to the Butcher'. The list of names at the end of the poem, of those whom the masters have suicided in detention, has grown considerably since 1973. Now *there* is one piece of writing of which I should love to be able to say: it is done!

28 July 1983

My Dear Unlikely Reader

The temptation is tempting – now that it is summer, and warm (up to 46 °C the day we arrived in Sardegna) – to let go, to relax on this terrace in Rome where you sit with a view over the fishbones of television antennae, to be bewitched anew by Mozart, to enjoy the succulence of fruit, to hide from the midday fires in cool hollows behind slatted blinds, to perish in mattress music. There are three knacks, once acquired, that to your astonishment you never unknack again; there is cycling and swimming. There is the recuperation of the subtle body when swimming in emerald-green waters and at night, when the moon is but a ship passing offshore, when breathing in the accumulated sweet-smelling heat of the fig tree. Under the crust of the old the new forms other structures.

But not yet, not yet. You see double. And words still tear the soft-bellied spaces to pieces. Too many matters have been left untouched, too many things unsaid. Here above the city and its sun, which is like a roaring lion, you respectfully take off your well-worn cap. To rid yourself of sense and nonsense with a bare head.

The problem remains how to clothe the odd thought 'in such a fashion that it does not offend'. Not that you can be bothered about giving offence (see to it however that the hair without cap does not grow too long in order not to confuse the masters), but you do wish to speak also to the reader who'd rather have gossip stories, snot and tears, and the praising of sundown. With from time time, the tickling of a taboo.

You want to believe that spaces may be recovered or remembered or invented so that the *chi*, the essential breath, may circulate freely. To fit in effortlessly and without proper interests with the rhythm and the structure, which are not subject to opposites.

But your probable off-White Afrikaans reader lives in his/her Afrikanerhood which is a shell of anaesthesia and brutalization. In the land of Apartheid, which by definition means self-lopping. In the land of ideological arteriosclerosis. In the land of the Great Silence. In the land where shame is not a current concept. In the land of state murder and murder and exploitation and maiming.

Murder in the name of survival and murder in the name of the right to exist. In the land where torturers get promotion and the men of God pray down hate from the pulpit. In the land – let us say it – which, like Israel still, and like the Iran and the Argentine and the Chile of yore, is supposed to be a solid citadel for Western imperialism. In the land where Calvinism and nationalism mouth, through the same trumpet, on racism only. In fact in the military camp.

The simplest way to combat totalitarianism (and the computerization of humanity) is *to disturb the silence*. Therefore it is also the land of banning, censorship, prisons. Where, when you are Black and wish to survive, it must be impossible not to fall outside the law in some way or another.

But those are serious head problems, to be fitted into other spaces. Let me rather sing the tune that nobody can take away from me again. At least I know what gaol is about.

Prison life, that dark dimension which by and large is ignored in the country – and the dark doings are blocked out by walls – is a world of its own. How many White Pretoria citizens will pause, say, once a week or once every fortnight, in the early morning with the thought: now they are hanging again in the Hills? And who really worries on his picnic rug next to the highway, about people slivered like sardines in the big tin trucks ('mobile units' they are called, but we knew them as 'batch lorries') which speed by now and then? Who will send up a little grey thought as he comes breasting the neck of the Old Cape Way in his motorcar on his way down to the beaches of Muizenberg, when he sees the labyrinth of Pollsmoor prisons spread out at his feet? If he were to pass by there on a winter's morning before daybreak he might notice the searchlights and hear the snarling dogs; he would not get close enough to see the men waiting crouched down, hip against hip, behind the wires in a circle of light and dogs' barks, waiting to be counted and sent out in spans on the tasks of the day.

Disorderly impressions. Generalizations certainly. I speak only of that which my eyes have seen.

In that 'other world' the decisive factor, the idol, the master of the farm, is the state. Never mind it being the White man's state, grounded in White prejudices and priorities, entrenched behind White man's laws, deeply affecting the lives of the Black majority. Of course, there is a relationship. What inkling of responsibility can the Black man have about the White man's laws and courts? And how can a Black man from Soweto, with a minimal sense of enterprise and self-respect, succeed in not becoming a gaolbird?

But, so you are told when you are inside, nobody can be held to task – it is exactly the bureaucrat's heaven. There is always a higher authority, an edict, a main office; and behind it all the state, which says this or demands thus. A Boer will make a law.

It will not be of much use to try and make your potential uncoloured reader aware of the barbarity and the final obscenity of capital punishment (yes, certainly, with as many sweets and visits – non-contact – as the condemns may wish during the last weeks), because your likely reader assumes that he is a Christian and finds his convictions on the principle of an eye for an eye (it is after all not that covenant that Christ came to do away with): he would also believe that the rope is an effective deterrent – human lives must be secured, just like the belongings of the bourgeois, and especially, oh especially, the state must be protected. And even if the 'civilized' world (England) were to show that these considerations are only confabulations from the Middle Ages – well, the world has always been wrong (or undermined), sick with liberalism, and it does not know our South African reality; besides (as Professor Barnard would show), 'it is much worse in Russia'.

But perhaps your reader can emit a little sigh at the thought of what it must be like to go about with death for those who have to do the actual killings. Keep in mind that more than 95 per cent of your uncoloured warders are reasonably naïve Afrikaner boys. Think about it that even for them (after a time, sometimes) the people whom they have to put down become humans. Make a slight little space for the consideration that such a profession may be morally corrupting.

One would demand that the firebrands shouting outside the walls for revenge come in and do the dirty work themselves. One would want also that, in the first instance, it be the politicians and the people's leaders and the senior officers and other rejects and dummies who should go to the border to attempt there to buy time against the inevitable. Just as one would have liked, when it comes to what is euphemistically described as 'death in detention', that there should be one minister at least who feels: 'Up to here and no further. Before God and man I cannot justify it.' Not because of an acceptable image or some such political skulduggery. Only just. And that that one minister should have the courage of his convictions to say it also – not in the closet but on the podium. Or lacking such a little flame of conscience in the Cabinet, why not a senior civil servant? A general? A colonel? A captain? Isn't there even a miserable sergeant feeling the tug of nausea somewhere? One would be hoping for the impossible.

For one asks oneself what is worse: the gallows or living death behind walls – conforming to international requirements, thank you? I do not know how many people Nelson Mandela killed, how many women Dennis Goldberg raped and how many banks he robbed – I only know that they have been languishing in the cooler since 1963.

And repression does not even work. It only makes your opponents more determined, cleverer; and it creates more grounds for uprising. Repression of your opponents, so it seems to me, is in fact more with the intention of mobilizing your own supporters. Trying to scare them with a big darkness. And even that can have only a temporary effect – ultimately it will brutalize and depoliticize your own people utterly. You allow your own power base to crumble irrevocably.

All right then – these are known names, old arguments. One would have to be childlike to wish to believe that with the so-called *realpolitik* of the ruling class another system or another state of affairs could come about. With tears you will not break down any steel portal, even if you lament also the tragically maimed souls buggering off into damnation – dragging the rest of the country along with them. But what about the 'coats'? I remember the empty-eyed old apes – men who had been inside for seven years and more for stealing, for instance, a bottle of milk or a few packets of cigarettes – because taken all together they already had more than five years on their records.

One such old gentleman whom I am acquainted with – he has a wife and grandchildren – had committed crimes, over a period of forty years, which caused about 70 rands' worth of damage. For which by and by he has already spent ten years in the Alcatraz. His date of release he still hasn't got. And when he comes out? Where would the graft be? In prison they would have told him when queueing up for food and talking with the mate in line behind him: 'Look in front of you – the welfare will look after you.' How long will his parole be? How easily he will be hit with another 'coat', or have to start his indeterminate sentence all over again because of some minor parole infringement?

But then probably 75 per cent of the off-White inmates in boop are Afrikaners. Nearly without exception they will attempt speaking English amongst themselves. And, in contrast to the Brown prisoners whose visitors over the weekend will cover the ground outside the walls like people coming to a carnival, many Whites are thrown aside by their families. Certainly some interesting deductions ought to be made by the protectors of our laws, and by the ubiquitous shrinks.

Or perhaps even worse: what about the 'juveniles'? Will you believe me, reader, if I were to tell you that I saw boys in prison whom I could pick up in my arms with the greatest of ease? Do you want to know how they get their first chops? How their virginity ('nice water') is broken? How they are made into little females? And the Whites – how many of them one sees returning! What can prison do for you except make of you a prisoner?

Or take the 'awaiting trials'. Did you know that they may sometimes be lying there for a year or more awaiting trial, only in the end to go free on the charge, or, as the men would say, to end up with three months? Can you imagine what it must be like sometimes to be living three in a single cell – one on the bunk cemented into the wall, one below it, and one on the floor next to it? Don't you want to go and see how your sons or your brothers are doing, reader? Or your servants? In any event – for what it may be worth – I wish to submit to that reader who may be entrusted by the Publications Board with reading material that the legal system is White, protecting the sacred interests and investments of the bourgeoisie, that it is the embodiment of institutionalized inequity, that it tries to sweep insoluble social problems under the carpet, that it makes prisoners out of human beings, that it is ultimately ineffective.

Night is dawning over the tiled roofs of Rome. And perhaps in No Man's Land also. Sleep safely, my dear potential reader. You live in a fool's paradise. So blunted, so white that you will not even hear the bullet come keening through your church.

21 August 1983

Palermo

sleep is the tump
and waking-up the snouted harvester
consuming the darkness flash by flash
with a glutinous tongue

but the earth-pig also has his lair
this globe thrashing through space
an other-earth hole by spathe
to widening flow into another space

awareness, tiny signal in a school of signs
between learning about structure, and digestion

Even before the sun drapes a first glittering petticoat over the
mountaintop (the stars shining through) to cover it later with a blue
robe its seams stretching from hem to haw, Bangai can be seen
trotting up the streets of dawn around the Piazza G. Verdi with its
baroque lamp-posts dimly evoking Lampedusa's world of luxury
and putrefaction. Palermo is a city of nearly indescribable opulence:
godhouses and palaces as if trickled from the hand of some Gaudi,
mysterious courtyards, luxuriant botanical gardens with alleyed
palms and ficus trees dripping their aerial roots, rank sub-tropical
plants tendrilling over baldachins – you smell the frangipani – little
altars with the effigy of Santa Rosalia, the patron saint who expiated
mankind's sins by sojourning in a cave along the mountain slope, or
that of Jesus – *Gésu ti amo* the scribblings say – nooked into a wall
every hundred yards, framed by candles or coloured bulbs behind
panes and always crocks filled with carnations and fresh roses,
arabesques and mottoes and family crests carved in the stucco of
façades (a delicate mixture of chalk, gypsum and marble dust),
canopies, elegant cast-iron railings, statues on the roofs, houses of
devotion down every turning, churches which started out as
mosques – up to three hundred at the time when the city, called
Panormo by Phoenicians and Carthaginians, becomes Balarm, with

public baths and walled-in squares and tinkling fountains, truly 'the pearl of the Mediterranean' – Paul de Musset says one should describe the city as a lady of pleasure fit to seduce even the haughtiest conqueror and to make him sit at her feet; churches transformed into dwellings with high up in the air a single bell awry like a mouth stilled around the final uttering: for everywhere there is crumbling and decay: one may well get the impression that the present-day Palermitans are barbarians investing a civilization beyond their grasp – but it would be unfair, because the city is *alive* with old and new death, existing in its very heart, staggering and nodding a hoary head, life and death side by side in one unbridled frenzy of procreation – from the Capucin catacombs where about 8,000 embalmed mummies (in diverse stages of going-to-dust) of generals and merchants and monks and married couples and writers and babies tricked out in their very best gold-embroidered coats and three-pointed hats and shawls and evening gowns (a moth's paradise!) sit gaping their grins, through alleyways to the Virgin's Square where one goes knocking on the door of a cloister to buy in a whispered voice from a nun, behind lattice in a dark inner court, sweetmeats made on the premises, or from the adjacent abbey little cakes baked by the brothers, called 'virgins' breasts', to the markets – which are in reality only *sukhs* and sometimes still sport the Arabic names in time-slippery distortions, even as the residential areas do: Cassaro, which used to be Al-Qasr, Kalsa, Lattarini, Zisa, Pellegrino, Cuba, Mazzara, Albergaria, Kemonia, Garrafo – all that's left of three centuries of sickle-moon rule except for the rapture of the tiles to be glimpsed everywhere with blue and white and brown and green motifs leaving the thumbprints of an ancient sense for decoration, and the typically Arab consonants and guttural sounds interwoven with the dialect as also with the Sicilian songs which unexpectedly rise coiling from beyond a wall, the fluttering notes a continuation of the deep breath – or the intertwined maze underneath the old city, hiding place for fraud artists and bandits: when you enquire after its entrances and exits you are apt to be referred to so-and-so who as it happens just moved house – but where was Bangai – ah yes, still loping down the Via Roma (past a graffito saying VIVA LUMUMBA!) and back in a wide arc, he re-enters his ward by a narrow street, passing Amato's *laboratorio di dolci* (not for nothing is the city famous for its traditional sweets, from tiny palm branches and dolls in finely spun sugar to the perfect almond imitations of fruits and nuts) and further past the historical puppet theatre always depicting anew the epic adventures of Orlando and other northern crusaders – and overlords! – when they sally forth

with helmet and sword to smite the Saracen heathen, and in the
next street the last remaining workshop where oxcarts can be
embellished in the old way; sounds captivate him and lead him by
the ear: bells chop logic rumbling and trembling for long minutes
on end unable to decide who is to have a monopoly on the exact
time, and smothered in inner rooms the bone-beaks doodle-do
contemptuously, and randy young dogs sniffnose open the plastic
rubbish bags, and silverfish is the light over the huge paving
stones, and the nextdoor ladies are long since stooled on the
thoroughfare without sidewalks, fans in the hands and piffletosh in
the mouths – mothers and other initiates and the whorled grannies
who have healed finally facing the traffic, young damsels face to the
wall, 7 o'clock's horse conveyance with its load of fresh tomatoes
comes clippety-clop spark-at-hoof down the road, the barber's first
client is lounging, with frothy chops, on his coccyx in the chair: the
day is sliced open in a municipality of noises – a jesting back and
forth (the street is so narrow that you only need to stretch an arm to
steal the neighbour's washing from her line, and every living being
can be seen on these balconies, which, if there are young lasses still
at home, are primly cordoned off below with cloth, as protection
against those astronomers scouting for stars at noon with a naked
eye), a yelling when from the upper storeys baskets are lowered on
ropes to howzit and hoist up the groceries, scooters and decibel
bikes and cars forever burping like soldiers having ingurgitated too
many bloat-beans for breakfast, lottery-ticket sellers and other
beggars; up the stairs (he heads) and into the living room with its
tiled floor and its green shutters, quickly under the shower (you
have running water only from 6 in the morning till noon) and down
into the *casbah* again to buy bread for breakfast (of the delicious
hand-length kind, with sesame seeds in the crust), while a chopper
scurries overhead, leafing the blue book on its way to the daybreak
raid of a *mafiosi* stronghold, in vain of course, but the baker greets
you with his white flour-hand and refuses your soldi 'because it's
yesterday's bread' – man! bread and honey with the freshly ground
coffee, and fruit fruit fruit, the way it will be fruit with cheese and
strong white wine for the midday meal and fruit with the supper's
pasta and wine, with just a few nibbles of fruit in between in the
course of the day to counter the stomach's rumbling; but Bangai has
to get down to his writing before the 'Cinesa' drags him off to
market – to the profusion and the plenitude! of meat (unskinned
cows' heads dangle from hooks, the eyes bursting with light and
with flies), silver-blue swordfish and octopuses, bunches of herbs,
pumpkin runners (offered as a vegetable with the pasta), tomatoes

and grapes and peaches and plums and figs (a fig is a *fico*, please, never a *fica*!) and green almonds and olives and corncobs and prickly pears and watermelons and sandwiches with an ice-cream filling and meat-and-rice-and-cheese balls and sandwiches with slabs of maize-bread between the bread slices; because it is time to prepare for the beach, to leave for Mondello in the crumpled Fiat 500 put at their disposal by Michele, the car which stitches a blue ribbon/ asphalt road while pedalling along like an old-fashioned sewing machine, and to swim way into the sea (till the heart in you flounders with joy), right out of sight to where the yachts nibble at their neckties and to float on your back there, looking at the land, the rounded grey mountain-heads and cloud grazing through the blue with its shadows lively like a flock of sheep down the slopes – there you notice the smokiness of arsonists in the hills (after all, this is also an archipelago of volcanoes) and nearer at hand the shabby German fire-eaters under the pine trees on the beach not far from the covered terraces where oysters and mussels and *polipo* may be had (the 'Cinesa' is anxious for Bangai not to divulge the identity of the locality fearing the arrival of South African locusts) – and then to come and stretch your heavy puffing on its belly in the sand and thoroughly to study the indigenous birdlife, the topless thrusts and tits: look at the gherkins and the *Cucumii africani*, the wee limmins, the googooseberries, the kiss-apples, the peachies – and back to town, the heavens a blue blowtorch (driving through areas run entirely by the Mafia – the state has a precarious foothold – to a city that has become synonymous with the most intricate and delicate conspiracies, how else when one has had to live for so long already, reluctantly or with a measure of enthusiasm, under the heel, successively, of the Phoenician and the Carthaginian and the Greek and the Roman and the Arab and the Norseman and the Swede and the Austrian and the Aragonese and the Spaniard and the Inquisitor and the German and the man from Anjou and the Bourbon and the Neapolitan and the Carbonari and the Garibaldian and the Savoyan and the Fascist – kings and regents and presidents and dictators and army commanders? – the city is dotted with memorials and wreaths where judges and prosecutors and police chiefs have been shot down or blown up, the city from which you cannot escape: Tomassino was to catch a train for Rome, got into a coach in the station, departure time as always somewhat flexible, opened up his food parcel and unconcernedly ate all his provisions to the last crumb, seeing as one has to wait before being on one's way one might as well do what is at hand, and when sundown came and he realized that he'd all the time been sitting in the wrong train left on a side line, he meekly returned home), so as to get back to the work which will justify a siesta, so that this day too may perish, and perish the thought – such a long day finally, like a convoluted phrase, a tongue in many orifices, turned in upon itself, like that worm which is the noose tying life to death, binding to decomposition, and gradually it is getting quieter, a coolness traverses the house, the gecko behind the tub emerges with its throb-belly in the lamplight – you may meditate, sir, you may lay down your thoughts, you may climb on to your bed to risk a ride through the passes to heaven on your donkey, legs apart. Beyond. Over hill and valley. Over and out.

18 September 1983

from Notes of Bird

[i]

We attended a performance of the Wuppertal Tanztheater directed by Pina Bausch. It had something of the Punch and Judy show about it, or was it a specifically Germanic type of cruelty? The Parisian audience became fidgety, perhaps because what we saw shadowed on the stage did not involve the intellect; it was also neither witty nor spiritual nor sentimental. Every night people outside begged for tickets to get into the sold-out auditorium; halfway through the act many would leave the hall, snorting their indignation with red faces.

What was striking (of the production we saw) was that the performers were formed and informed by a discipline, *dancing*, which they then did not make use of. It was the invisible matrix. It showed – or shone through – in an absolute control of small movements.

The total effect created was that of a play being displaced or played to the inside. Because of the intentional questioning of communication there arose a stillness, an interiorization. So you became more aware of the surface too. You looked harder. It left the spectator paradoxically in a total space. That must be why the cumulative result was one of obliging the looker to confront himself analytically. (This 'wall-looking' can be seen as an analogy of meditation.) In such fashion was the alienating effect brought about. And that forced participation. Which is why the theatregoer became hostile. (We go to be entertained, not to create.)

These are some of the techniques by which the results were obtained: the apparently senseless repetition and thus the making of patterns and thus a re-evaluation of 'normal' rhythms and meaning; the decomposition of the context – it became a dialectic between what you saw and what you expected to see-feel-experience; conventions were invoked only to be discarded, to be mocked, to play with, to employ in a contradictory way. You realized the extent to which *comprehension is recognition*, a shorthand, a code. You expected

135

a suite to the most banal actions and you didn't get it, or if you did it was in a totally different set-up. You were confused. It was a straight twisting. And even the most ordinary gestures – the placing of a chair for instance, or the eating of a carrot, or the gouging of an eye – were isolated in time and space, imbued with other implications. A clear obscurity.

Increased awareness. (Awareness staged.) Breaking of pattern. The more patterns you make, the more you destroy pattern. It becomes, fatally, a play on language itself. Language is therefore by definition doomed to extinction, I mean to becoming invisible; it disappears to re-surface organically in rhythm and pattern, in inexplicable tensions and seizures and ruptures and relapses. Language as de-finition. Brought about by immobility, by doing the nothing, being nothing. Stretched to extremes. Until the audience is embarrassed and provoked into reaction because the way of conditioned expectations has become one of pitfalls.

The poor text too was cut down to size, smoothed to mumbling. One participant declaimed: 'Le coeur de Chopin repose dans une cathédrale à Varsovie,' and immediately afterwards read from his wrist, in the same tone and intensity of voice, the correct time. Time read as at the time of reading. It was now exactly . . . What seemed like disdain for the onlookers was ultimately a measure of real respect. Our collaboration was solicited; we were treated as adult and reacting (if non-consenting) partners. Never does one listen as creatively as when one doesn't understand the other.

The foregoing intentions and results are also encountered/ experienced in the theatre of the absurd, through the skein of some 'modern' music, via techniques of filming, in the stylized plays of an Eastern world. Are we extending our illusions to areas of new myths, of new rituals? Contemporary sensibility moves into spaces unknown to the ancestors. It is now more and more a *looped* consciousness, dizzying, stripped of the skin of referential security that may be identified as 'priorities', 'systems', 'judgements', 'ideologies', etc. This consciousness doesn't even want to be funny – except incidentally so, in an offhand, white-clown, unconcerned and disconnected way: a man (he may as well be a painted effigy, or a bus conductor) will draw on his cigarette, turn to face the audience, and let a nonchalant plume of smoke escape from his fly.

Perhaps we are advancing into greater density. Perhaps we should be computers, programmed with no questions, unencumbered by bombast and pomposity.

from Notes of Bird

I conclude – that perception is a point of departure
         that space is essentially paradoxical
         or that the essence of paradox is space
         which is why we fix (on) the surface
         to exorcize space by the rituals of movement
         that perfect pattern is the no-line
         and meaning is (a) light

(Also that one shouldn't look at paintings: one risks losing part of oneself there.)

[ii]

Gradually the workspace is taking on shape. Returning to Paris was like entering an unknown past. You know you knew it, and yet all is new all over. A knew where you had forgotten the k. You have with you a conditional space – the area within which you move, the pattern of your displacements, the limits along which you display your presence. The contours of the space are imposed on you: sometimes they are arbitrary, sometimes the result of agreement and convention – the rubbing together of my space and yours. When your area is arbitrarily delineated it could be because you are handicapped, but in fact it is because you find yourself locked in a power relationship implying hierarchies, restrictions, rituals, tithes and tits for tats, thines, times, mines, thisses and thats. (In nospace all thats are grey.) This is the nature of the prison-space you carry with you. By constant foraging – remaining alive, waiting for the slightest weakness or camouflaged fault, sniffing along the lines demarcating night and day, exploring every ridge and knoll and whorled brushstroke and masjid and pistil and pistol and monticule and pessary and mask – you try to extend your means and your frontiers. You transport your consciousness and like the dog having to define itself you squirt a measure of it against this barred door or over that blind wall. Mobility is important. To vibrate in absence of any integration with a landscape. A cardinal precept in prison is: to *move* with the thing. Home, home on the range.

You have learned that space is not a matter of size. You create it – extend it – by structuring it, by having hides for the eye to seek out, and strokefields. You have also apprehended the dawning realization that the I is just a thing. The point of it all is – the paint – that it is a transportable mobility (if you see what I mean) – a shiverishness. You must take it out to have it shriven by the light.

137

Burnt Bird

Space, this implosion – like a word with its walls giving way. To silence. Take space, or the illusion of it; plant the I there as your point of reference or of measurement; and you have the space of illusion. Now move!

Over this last year (1983) you moved many times. You remembered how important it is for the painter to have his lair, somewhere to depose the odours of his materials and his hands. You found again how difficult it is to find a studio in Paris. It is all very well to say with Leonardo da Vinci: *la pittura è cosa mentale* – but it is exactly one mental activity that needs to become tactile to exist. It must die into definition and shape. And for that you need room. A place or a space to do your *apocalypso*. To exercise your *métier* as echographist. During your absence, during that space of deathlife when the echo went looking for its ego, another painter occupied that *atelier* with the yellow mellowish imprint of wood. The understanding was that you'd be reinvesting it upon your return. The return did take place. Someone came back. (Such is the obnoxious nature of miracles.) And sure, you had forgotten what selfish bastards painters can be. He whined and kicked his feet. He had made his your space.

So you went from pillar to post. Pillar and Post and all the other holes (as you moved five times) were minute, and either with direct light or no light at all, or bone-achingly damp. And like a crow in the throat the knowledge that you could stay there only for a week or for a month. You had meanwhile gathered most of your old works, which had been stored hither and thither. These you now started destroying, excising the images, as it became senseless to drag them from one temporary refuge to another. A salutory experience. I recommend it. It is important to keep on burying the past.

You were very tired. It is exhausting to come alive. Sometimes you had to lie down on the floor, limp and gone, staring at the ceiling, so as to find a reason for surviving. You said: *la vie est un métier à apprendre; actuellement je suis au chômage.* You knew what it was like to be on your knees in the night before the toilet bowl, bawling. Tired, so tired. Broken, torn, but clean! The Great Begin-Again.

Until you found these 35 square metres, perched high, from where you can watch the cloud silently avoiding any collision or definition. And the space is gradually taking on its rhythm, it is starting to move. From the ceiling is suspended the plastercast that used to encase the broken knee; and the skull – because it is vital to have the mind exteriorized and visualized and localized. Part of the skull has been cut away to allow for new ideas to circulate. The walls have been painted white. On one shelf is the trunk, with head and two disconnected arms, of a display model who, when young and varnished, must have lived in a shop window somewhere. She is better off here – although the legs-and-buttocks is standing separately on the floor; at least you don't insult her virginity by draping clothes over her. No tits. The head has a hole in it, large as a fist, its edges eaten away by the grey rotting of papier mâché. Inside that there's a dark nothing. Big as the fist opened. She has two stiff blue eyes (one is peeling) like those of a Saxon maiden.

Her name is Joyce O'Foyles. In the corner Horse sits with patient knees, waiting for his tot of brandywine. You have the work table (3m × 1m) which you and Loufiot went to fetch in some dead master's stilled, dust-stifled studio. (It was too long to enter the workroom in one piece; you took it apart on the pavement outside and brought it upstairs to be reassembled; it fell on your foot and broke the skin; you have the obsession of playing Christ.) Now it is loaded with material, with possibilities. You have another, smaller table, painted red. On this you write the lines for a monograph. You have Bonhomme looking at you with his hat of blackness hiding the black hat of his blank thoughts which are thinking the thoughts of all hats. You have the stuffed head of the green parrot, born far away in Africa, decapitated and emptied of all imitations and echoes and illusions, far away all the visions of Africa's green hills too, and put up for sale among old men's teeth and boots and coughs and mirrors and other knick-knacks on some fleamarket. You have had it for many years now. It was always dead but never as dead as now. You unearthed it again in Loufiot's cellar in a battered suitcase (the traveller's desire) with paint-tubes that had gone dense-eyed and hard, and photos of Mao and Che, and posters in many tongues clamouring for FREEDOM FOR NOMANSLAND NOW. The imitation of an eye has fallen out. The green feathers are moth-eaten. The orange beak no longer glistens. It is blobbed and ungainly like a brain. It cannot stand on its own either. You have brushes and rolls of canvas and rags and music (Mozart, Dollar Brand, Bach, Chris Blignault, Lemmy Caution, Chopin) and a book in which the words of Master Eckhart are written: *Only the hand that effaces can write the true thing.* It is also written: *L'oeil était dans l'anus et regardait Cocteau. C'est caca de le dire.* You don't have any idea. You don't have time. You do have the cracks and the ruptures and the knee.

This echo-space must now secrete the paintings that will end-lessly and futilely attempt to occupy the space, to put a term to the void. Outside the window, entirely in the day, birds are going to the emptiness of trees. Clouds are sifting the light, shifting the eye.

[iii]

Painting – any manner of making (even the performing arts, although the guidelines will be different there) is always a *process* of never-ending decisions. Every step represents and then respects a choice. At every step you are faced by a number of alternatives. (Why must the white which you are painting stop here?) 'Completing' a work is simply a matter, step by step, of reducing the choices. Or increasing the bid. The final form, if successful, is arrived at by eliminating the has-beens and the progeny; it ought then to be unquestionable, perfectly 'natural', preferably without trace of the murdered what-ifs that have fallen by the wayside (by way of expression). Without history even.

Every action, step forward or into recollection, chases up a multitude of faces. Pray don't pay too much attention to them. It is like in meditation: let them come and go of their own free wills while you continue along the way of searching for the original face. (I don't know what it is but I'll recognize it when I see it.) Easier said than done. The saying is always easier than the doing. Here it comes. That's why I talk so much. Talking instead of walking. Taking its place. So many sounds on the road I can't see the tree for the forests. Painting is cutting out the tongue. The silent art. Sliding through the gap between the real and the imaginary. (Bumping trees?) I paint Bonhomme with a jacket on – but it is a coat of paint, and no bones underneath. (When you look at people on the street you don't normally see the bone cage under a coating of flesh either.) How nice it must be to wear a coat of colour. Bit sticky perhaps. Madman's garb. So, manipulating signals, signs, systems of reference (never discover: always recognize) – to slip in *other* shapes and discordancies. Pretending to be speaking the same language. The art of silences. Shouting with a closed mouth.

Sometimes you paint (you choose) in accordance with a structure or a colour or a tone or a 'feeling' which will become invisible (non-existent?) as you abandon the work. Suppose you have a ground colour of blue. As you open up and fill in your painting you will be taken in hand by the blue. The end result may have no blue in it. (But all of it there.) Originally there must have been an uncomplicated communication with the natural forces. Rather – that 'originally' and that 'eventually' are continuously present. It's just a matter of making room. Shut up and open up.

Many of the decisions you make may be entirely arbitrary. Don't wait and don't question. Self-doubt slew the dragon. If you are walking the tightrope and you wish to step off it, well, step off it and walk on; if you were to stop and start worrying about whether your socks are smelly or not you will be plunging down fifty storeys of faces dischortled by laughter. When you have moved from point A to point B you must now be at point B and not in the moving or the thinking it out. Thinking is anyway a bad painting medium. It distorts the colours and makes them crack prematurely.

Similarly many of the decisions you move through (informed by instinct, training, mood, the extent to which you are in touch with your environment, the mirage-image you are mirroring, the work already done, the narrowing road, bad eyesight, tax problems, sexual urges, identity fantasies) may be destructive. Good for you! Go for it me ole hansom! It is essential that you should risk (and lose) everything on the knife-edge chance of getting *there*.

Sometimes you have to keep a civil tongue in your head and a straight posture. You may have produced your best at an early stage of the work (the way you painted an eye perhaps) – now you just have to keep it up, continue working at your best. Your own best is a hard taskmaster, a slave driver. You will mostly fail. Since death invaded the land life is no longer a certainty.

In fact you paint very often what you 'know' and not what you 'see'. Don't we in any event just see what we know? We are programmed and we are lazy. We have either/or minds. It is exhausting really to peel the eyes. Better put them on the ceiling. But here I mean that to be pictorially realistic you paint that which you *know* exists (in the gloom around the corner, hey-hey, in the closed box, beyond the horizon) although it has no visual justification from the observation point of the time-situated I. Anyway, 'lifelikeness' is an affair of choice, of dosing the work, of introducing a whiff of illusion (limited by communal history-confined consciousness), of 'creating' a jab of 'reality'.

What the 'reality' is is something else again. I am sure that we produce it all the time. We can't help it. We have to, since we are ever running out of it. (With reference to the preceding paragraph: contradiction is my privilege.) Obviously we don't really have standards. Standards were invented when we proclaimed ourselves damned and lost and furthermore decided that we needed standards and guidelines and disciplines to unlose ourselves, to pull up our smelly socks by. You have an idea. Idea is so beautiful and so logical that it must be true. Thus we descend from the apes. In this way we created the universe with the Big Bang (BOOOM! We are still deafened by the echoes.) So we measure by means of the Great Shift. We think up a universe and a history tainted by the fallacy of an ego ensconced in mortal meat. Or the phallacy. Evictims of starvision. Foul fools.

But if you have nothing to say it is still no reason for shutting your mouth. If I may quote God.

Fumbling Reflections on
the Freedom of the Word and
the Responsibility of the Author

The theme is a vast one, and it may well intersect with some of the preoccupations of our time. I'm not going to tackle it philosophically by attempting a closer definition of the concept 'freedom' or 'freedom of expression'. Neither do I wish to present a historical exposé by tracing the evolution of this notion, or situating it in the present time. I can't even put the question in its ideological context.

Why would the artist – whether expressing himself in literature or in art – have a special responsibility? Can it be because he embodies the universal need, one could say the genetic desire, of the human being to define his life-spaces by expressing them? Is it because he permits man to place himself, and thus to be recognized? Is it because he works away at the structuring of the unknown, or that which is sensed obscurely, and thus brings it to the surface? Is it because he manufactures illusions? It is true that illusions are as many veils, masking or transforming a reality that is too harsh; but the artist's craft lies also in the awareness and the application of illusions by way of disguising the real: a mirror game, if I may say so.

We need to *feel* ourselves alive. We are imbued with the sense of impermanence, of mutilation, of not-knowing. And we are haunted by the need to know, to understand, to be integrated. Quite paradoxically we should like to be sure, once and for all, of our fate and our place in the void, the better to be able to disappear into forgetting and non-definition. Must the artist be the agent and the definition of this research and this flight? In a recent interview, published in *Lire*, Milan Kundera says: 'People have become blind to their own lives. They live by day, at night they forget. We live ever more in the forgetfulness of being. Rendering this sensibility to life, this concern about coincidences, that too is the novel's intention.'

It seems to be a thought worth retaining: the artist as nightfall visitor. More: that life is a sensitizing trip. Or: life made conscious is an awakening method. But there's another way to conceive of the artist – not necessarily contradicting the aforementioned. Aren't we perhaps intrigued by his position because he is the precursor of alternatives? Is it because we are blocked off and need to be shaken loose, that our preconceptions must be questioned? Guido Ceronetti, in his *Le Silence du Corps*, proposes that 'the author is a supporter of the fuck-up hiding behind the façade of an erudite fellow'.

I think it important to raise these questions – not because the artist is of greater value than the cobbler or the bank teller, not out of some umbilical self-absorption either – but only because, via these questions, we touch upon the necessity ceaselessly to refashion the relationships, the convergences and the contradictions, linking the individual and the collectivity. Just as, in the words of a Russian dissident, the pig must continually be beaten over the snout so as to become human, we must go on asking these questions about the writer to refine his usefulness as a conductor of the finer feelings. Communal space has form only if we keep on redefining it anew. You must become alive to yourself also. And you must remain sensitive to the implications of your conduct and your points of view.

So, if I may be permitted a first conclusion: one, it is absolutely essential to continue suggesting questions in order not to be blasted by a final answer; two, it is all-important to walk on, especially when you have given up on the mirages of *goal* and *destination*: that's when walking becomes a discovery; three, the artist is a tool with which awareness and conscience can be made real. (Well, as 'real' as 'real' ever can be.)

It flows from my conception of the writer that his thinking and his wordthinking be formulated as questions or hypotheses. Art is ambivalent. If it were otherwise, we'd be spouting propaganda. And propaganda – precisely this effort at formulating certainties – kills the alternatives, that is, scepticism and irony and doubt and questions. Propaganda more often than not is the enunciation of hierarchical power. No, I think it is more *true* of the artist to be taking part in the creation, by recognition, of a mutual space concerning us all, ever re-formed, than to be wanting to lay his visions or his principles upon us, however noble and high-falutin these may be.

Let me go back a space or two. I've had the opportunity elsewhere to say that I could not conceive of 'freedom' existing as an absolute. But we have to go on living *towards freedom*, we have *to extend our liberties*. I've also said that the sense of freedom exists only when one is hustling for it. To live freedom is therefore to be implicated in the struggle.

Burnt Bird

How does one define totalitarianism? Some aspects jump off the page: for instance, that it consists of structures feeding on 'informing' and betrayal, or else that in such a state you are made to renounce or hide your inner convictions. There are also, it seems to me, other characteristics more germane to our discussion here. A totalitarian state is marked by the blocking out of any idea that may jeopardize structures of authoritarian power; such a state imposes an arbitrary and rigid space upon its citizens. The mind is shown its blanks. It leads to immobility. It is death. And then, totalitarianism, by its very nature, unavoidably spawns corruption – if only because all artistic activity must express itself by cheating, by delusion, by telling lies to the self, by collaboration. Believe me, South Africa is a fine example of how Apartheid (which is the rotting of morals) has corrupted masters and oppressed ones equally.

The danger of censorship, as pointed out by György Konrad, is that one integrates it. You become your own castrator, the *Staatmensch*, product and expression of the state. Ultimately this condition is illustrated by the acceptation of the wielding of the commonplace. Nowhere are sunsets as pretty as in a language that has had its eyes poked out. The word becomes wall – no longer, as it ought to be, instrument and means of seeing. So you have to spike the self incessantly, you have to probe and to prod the numbness, you must pickle the heart, you have to resist, you have to fight the levelling or the burying and the forgetting brought about by commonplaces.

And corruption? On the one hand it is generated by the fact that even a mediocre work may be made important by proscribing it. Totalitarian censorship often evokes simplistic reactions. Democratic societies too often put the dissident author on a pedestal, even making a hero out of him, only because his voice is choked off in a totalitarian environment. In this way censorship itself is accorded artistic value judgement. You are corrupted, on the other hand, because to survive you must compose with the powers that be. You live the lie. You also live the dangerous delusion that structures of oppression can be made more flexible from within, that totalitarianism could possibly be liberalized through evolutionary progress! What blindness! And that through art, by means of which we were supposed to see clearly! Any opposition from within to totalitarian structures, which does not have as a prerequisite the dismantling of these structures, can only serve to strengthen them.

The artist's responsibility must be: to resist by all means the foisting on society of clichés and lies; to struggle for the refinement of the means of expression, to preserve the preciseness and the integrity of the word; to be technician of the conscience – not in a moralist way, but to the extent that the only 'sin' is that of ignorance. I am convinced that freedom must be concretized along these lines. And if a moral dimension were to be required of artistic activity, it would be in the formulation and the expression of the ethics and the aesthetics of resistance.

Do I need to add that it doesn't mean that it will be forbidden or even dangerous for the author to take part in, and of, power? Recently I came across the following declaration by Philippe Sollers:

> The intellectuals are in opposition. By definition. Out of principle. From physical necessity. As a game. They are opposed to all majorities as also to all oppositions hoping in turn to become the majority. They write, they move in the invention of language, and with it. It is referred to as creating a culture. A live one. Critical. Original. Aggressive. With its memory and its diversity . . .

Well, I find this statement a poor one. Pathetic even. Why must the intellectual remain in his ghetto? It shows, I think, an inability to distinguish between different types of political regimes. Besides, it is arrogant. It is unfortunately true that the artist (or the writer) is the first to be blinded by the neatness of his formulations, corrupted by his activities as communicator, led astray by the word . . .

I imagine that, from afar, I have pointed at some food for thought related to the problem of freedom of expression. Much remains to be said, undoubtedly. I should have liked to advance a claim – had I known how to go about integrating it structurally with my paper! – for the artist to be allowed, in Cioran's words, to be as useless as God. I wanted to say – a commonplace? – that exploring communication (with the I or the Odder) inevitably makes you more deeply alert to the true nature of the means of expression; that understanding is structured (or layered), that language is a hodgepodge of conventions, that you are tied down by your own visualization of limitations, that you understand for only as far as you can express yourself, as far as you can see down the road, that you therefore have to proceed – to advance, if advance you must – by breaks; that comprehension is released by the crack-ups. I should have said that you ought to push the self over the lip into the void, if you bank on finding gaps of survival and freedom, that is. I furthermore wanted to linger on the idea that painting (like writing) goes through two simultaneous but contradictory shifts: making clear the process of clarification or that which you feel called upon to express, and creating the incomprehensible. But precisely this contradictory movement constitutes one of the joints of communication. See, that is why it is so important at one and the same time *to understand* and *to not try and understand.*

We are here to attempt formulating the interstices of freedom where our vital spaces and our essential silences may coincide. After all, artistic say so is neither affirmative nor politic, perhaps not even direct. Art could be the conquest – or the creation – by allusion. I say that art is the coming to grips with a feel of reality by way of illusion. That's it: creating nothingnesses, appearances, ersatzes, make-beliefs – in an attempt that more than likely is desperate and springing from the despair of ever crystallizing the concrete – or at the least that which had been experienced. As there is also the perennial surface-content dialectic. One is barking up the wrong tree, to my mind, if one expects to be able to grasp the core, the *ne plus ultra*, the ineffable, the unique, the nitty-gritty of the artist. One has to know how to be satisfied with the exterior, with inculcation by example and not by explanation; one has to know how to put oneself in the correct position for being available and receptive. It is not a matter of reticence, but of clearness. And to accept that you're never going to 'get to the truth' by digging for it. Digging, wanting to circumscribe, trying to provoke a psychological tearing of the veils – what cannibalism!

So I finish with three sentences:

One, Art is the matter of survival.

Two, Cioran who says: 'To be born then seems to be a calamity which, had I not known it, would have made me inconsolable.'

Three, it is bad manners to talk with your mouth full of words.

Amsterdam, March 1984

Upon Hearing about
the Hertzog Prize

I have just now learned that the Hertzog Literary Award for this year has been given to Henriëtte Grové and myself. I should like to express my gratitude to the jury members who, so it would seem, weighed up my work – and I want to insist that I accept their decision as having been arrived at through personal literary penchants.

Whether ('*Yk*') is any 'better' than my earlier attempts or 'better' than that of other candidates, naturally remains a point of debate. I myself am ever more convinced that the largesse of a literary award, or any literary value judgement based on the comparing of that which cannot be compared, because every *oeuvre* is by nature unique, turns into a miserable mess. Except where you can wield explicit literary-scientific or ideological criteria. The pen-pusher ought to be *encouraged* or, when already lying bodkin with old Devil Death, *appreciated* – so that he may enter the refrigerator at the top of his self-esteem – but we must refuse to see books – like exegetists with their mouths stuffed with wooden expertise or like some of the unconcerned taste (de)formers unsuspicious like mirrors of wood do – as mouth-frothing ponies in a race. And we should be able to break away from the kindergarten attitude of rating a work as 'the best yet in Afrikaans'.

It is urgent that young South African authors particularly be enabled financially to continue with their work, in whatever language. And that can happen only in a structured way, under the auspices of a fully-fledged *South African* ministry of culture, doing the necessary in conjunction with other interest groups such as consciousness organizations, educational departments and public libraries.

It is only natural that I should be aware of some of the implications flowing from giving this award, in part, to Breytenbach. I know of the fluid situation and of the pressure building up for internal realignment, maybe even for change; I know, up to a point, of the fermentation in Afrikaner ranks. I should not wish, by my conduct, to block off even the tiniest rift through which a wee wind of change may yet whistle.

Burnt Bird

For some judges it must be hard to square this award with their treasured convictions. Many old bones are mouldering in the history of Afrikaans, and to unearth them now will serve no sense. I must assume however that a man like Professor Cloete is obliged to make a clear distinction between what he writes for the security police or the Broederbond, and his literary tastes. I therefore do not question the *bona fide* of my peers. I am especially at pains not just to slap away the hand of acceptance and cordiality which I make bold to glimpse emerging from Stellenbosch. I take it that the jury wanted me to have this prize knowing full well that I would turn it down – for which I thank them and assure them of my esteem.

For I cannot but turn it down. Not because I've become petrified in the image cleaved to by some – that of 'agitator', 'trouble stirrer', '*provocateur*', or 'outsider'. So I'm not doing this to please my mates. Neither to provide copy for journalists sniffing for sensationalism nor, worse, for those, the English-language ones, who back in an opportunistic way any so-called 'Afrikaner' deviationist (or deviant) in the hope of thus getting a lick in at the Afrikaners as group. Not even (and I think I'm reasonably honest by the mouth now), not even because of old injuries, a twisted personal *parcours*, mean-spiritedness, or because it is, alas, 'too late'.

But for the simple reason that the South African Academy for Arts and Sciences remains as ever *the* bulwark of the Afrikaner Establishment. And for the majority of my compatriots the country *remains* a land of terror and alienation and sadness, a political and economic and cultural set-up propped up by the pale citizens. Were I to accept this garland I could not, in my own minor mumble-bumble, contribute towards real transformation – no, I should then be helping to grant an illusion of flexibility to the structures of a system that is still exclusive: minority, discriminating, and therefore oppressive.

No indeed. If I could harmonize with what a Brown church recently put as question to a White one, and adapt it to my preoccupations, then I should wish to call upon the Academy to give us a review (possibly leading to the taking up of a stance) of cultural phenomena such as the Pass Laws, the Immorality Act, the Group Areas Act, the death in detention of Biko and Aggett.

What remains? Each must accept responsibility for his acts. Clarity doesn't dawn in the span of a day. And you schlepp your life with you like a little shit-bucket, in order – when you want to relieve nature of death's bowel-twisting need coming upon you like a thief in the night – to have something at least to kick. And know that chatting (chattering) about literature is really only making a bee-line for boop. And then I ask myself – as it is totally germane to culture – if someone could give me *one* decent justification for Nelson Mandela and Walter Sisulu and Dennis Goldberg still being in gaol?

Paris, 27 April 1984

Dead Locust Rumours
and Language as
the Random Thoughts of Camels

Vin de Chiraz et les *poèmes*,
c'est aujourd'hui ton seul recours
Il n'est plus d'autre compagnie,
durs sont les temps, durs les coeurs.

Hâfiz

(1) A few weeks ago I came upon myself walking down the rue de
la Tête Qui Marche, minding my own business as always. At
the end of the street one may turn right to go clip-clop-clop
down some steps leading to the boulevard des Petits Pas. At
the bottom of the steps a young man accosted me. He had the
frail physique and the haunted look of a poet. Under his arm he
carried a thin but well-thumbed folder.

Of course he wanted to communicate one of his creations. I
saw his meek eyes behind dirty eye-glasses. Time came by in a
rush. It always does. Right sharply I handed him 10 francs,
hoping to short-circuit the process. I was in a hurry to go
nowhere in particular. It can be embarrassing to stand by while
a soul is being fondled. (Even a shop-soiled one.) No no, he
held me back by the sleeve and said thanks and all, but he
nevertheless wanted to share one short poem with me.
Anyway. For the love of it.

The verse wasn't all that bad. I remember it as being about
the descent to earth of a fairy, of how she died and decayed to
ink, and of the poet now tracing her life (a post-mortem as it
were) in her own words. It had the virtues of not being very
long, of rhyming, and of conveying simple ideas.

The man then insisted that he wanted to tell me how he'd
written the work. It had taken him ten days and eleven nights
of uninterrupted labour, he said. He survived on aspirins and
black coffee. 'Poets suffer,' was the solemn conclusion that he
breathed into my face.

He had bad teeth. A breath like the soiled flag of a revolution
now degenerated into a dog-eat-dog power game.

I came away with some insights: the poet has a keen sense of guilt that needs to be exercised; he works hard at the effort of making poetry sound like work; he continues struggling even after he has been paid; poetry can pay; it never pays very much.

(2) Poets of the world unite:
You have nothing to lose
But the words you write . . .

There should have been a fourth line to round off the quatrain, ending with *booze*, or, *use* or *noose*, or *fight* (*flight*?) – but I can't seem to find the connecting knot just now.

(3) The category 'poet' doesn't exist. Poetry is neither trade nor craft. The writer writes more or less well, the doctor doctors or dithers and describes death, the politician manipulates, the security agent secures by exterminating the enemies of the state (or the people), the man of God keeps on kneading God – but to the poet the fact or happy hazard of having written one poem is no guarantee for writing another ever again. Committing poetry is a process of stumbling from breakthrough to breakdown. In fact, every poem sounds to him suspiciously like the last rattle in the throat. Was Rimbaud really a poet? or just a kinky adolescent? (I'm told he turned out to be a better than average trader.)

That which is so intensely personal and unique – midwiving a poem by marrying the non-verbal to that vice-ridden old bridegroom Verb – is in fact done by all of us at one point or another, and in the same way. We all have written at least one poem. (Some of us are still trying: witness the books of published fragments!) That which is essentially formless (otherwise it wouldn't interest us) is construed in forms (allowing us to type the shapes as 'poetry') which are ancient, limited and restricting.

The *poet* doesn't exist, or at best he is an ephemera, having been freed from the yoke of 'normal sense' for the fraction of an eternity. We have all had our blebs. Those who continue beating their heads against the wordwall are obsessed with the mechanics of consciousness, the nuts and the bolts and the buts and the nots. They use life as a technique for enlightenment. Or a survival practice.

(4) Language is a blindness. Form is a limitation, a construction of our basic condition of laziness. It is tradition made concrete –

151

or is it at the consecration thereof? The tongue looks for the
familiar, for the taste of wood. Normally we don't *see*; we
recognize. Seeing should be rupture. The eye, to survive intact,
must break. To peer ahead resolutely but in such a way as to
notice from the corner of the eye, fugaciously, the congealing
moments where worlds move and the chair shades into mad
meaning. To be alive to the interstices, to the entry into
imagination. To the old people living in the trees of the
Luxembourg Gardens.

And yet, our limitations are our tools for apprehending
reality. Such is our condition. Our becoming is reality.
Structure is an ongoing shifting of understanding.

(5) Yehuda Amichai once said that poetry is the last purely human
activity – using the individual human voice with all its
inflexions and associations and history – to say something
personal to one other human being. Thus, I assume, without
having to pass through the 'screens' of computers, usefulness,
exploitability, commitment, sense, or even communication.

'The communication of poetry' – isn't that a tautology?
Poetry itself is communication: a complex transmission of
meanings, of which 'meaning' is only one element. We must be
careful when we translate poetry (and printing or public
readings are only different manifestations of translating) that
we do not shave the dog to make it conform to the idea of what
we assume a dog or its idea is supposed to look like. If you
understand what I mean.

I believe that *posture, structure* and *texture* are important
helpmeets when conveying poetry. Individually it is the
posture of receptiveness (I'd even say 'availability') that makes
it possible to discern the structure partially defined by the
texture of images and sounds and rhythms and silences.

Poetry editors and organizers could, I'm sure, use the same
guidelines – adapted to their disciplines of course.

(6) With whom or with what do we communicate? Reading (out of
physical and cultural and historical context) the haikus of Issa
and Basho, I sometimes feel that they were conversing with
Nature only. Or were they also just talking to the Word? But
then I know too that the poem, to exist, needs a listener, a
reader, a participant. Otherwise it is a dead letter. All the poet
really does is to trigger the reaction in the receiver that will
provoke that impossible *feeling* or *process* that we describe as
poem.

It is, as someone pointed out, like debt: the more you make use of it the bigger it becomes.

(7) What we try to distil is, I suppose, the limitless wonder of the word. (It is first of all a musical love affair between tone-deaf and untrue lovers.) And then the derisive attempts at making believe that life is worth living. It is like admonishing ourselves to 'walk tall!' when we know we're going nowhere. (One should write a volume entitled *Slow Walk to Nowhere*.)

What do we communicate? Often the sadness or just the bloody-mindedness or peevishness of living. The harsh struggle for death. The painful efforts at honesty. The breath worn thin. Perhaps also the 'positive' statement (or existential conditioning?) that there is a purpose to communicating. Certainly not *Truth*. Truth sank with the *Titanic*. Though some people are still trying to salvage it.

But poetry is also history, and more truthfully so than the work of historians. Poetry can be ideas, it can be ritual, it can be dreams, it can be opinionated and prejudiced, it can convey moral strictures and ethical precepts and even slogans. I don't think all the odes to Stalin were necessarily bad or poor. Poetry can transmit or be used by power. It *is* a force. Above all it is a destroyer of barriers, perhaps because of its intensely private character.

When I think of Turkey I hear Nazim Hikmet. When you mention modern Greece to me I understand you through the prism of Yannis Ritsos. I know – I *am* – the Palestinian through the keening songs of Mahmud Darwich.

(8) Who does the communicating? Most often – in the West at least – it is the individual torn from his 'natural background', perhaps even from his cultural environment. (Think of Joyce, Cortazar, Genet, Gombrowicz . . .) In a way exile is a blessing in disguise. Exile becomes a confrontation with the I, leads to a mating with the phantom ego. The destruction of the ego-perception, that *deus ex machina*, opens the way to the kaleidoscope of creation. We have the (desperate) communications of the disintegrating seer coming to grips with his broken vision of an incomplete reality in and through a language going to pieces.

Please don't read this as a glorification of the outsider. True, the poet – seeing the humbleness of his means and the fragility of his conceits, and seldom being a power junkie – could be considered as marginal to the value system of his society, even his literary one. But he retains a function within that background – one that may be hard to define and could perhaps be reduced to that of the subvert. The *poète maudit* is a self-seeking cultural cliché.

(9) Better to talk about the precise ways in which the poet fits, as misfit, in his social environment. Better still to point out the concrete ways in which the work can be transmitted.

Poetry is mainstream.

Yes, there has internationally been an increasing awareness of poetry: of its slow but sure power to break down separations (because I can identify essentially with a poet from some far-off land writing in a language unknown to me); of its curious ability to span time (because I can recognize as being relevant now a poem written centuries ago); of its universal nature and still of its richness in cultural variety (because I can participate in the religion of the Aztecs and the politics of the Brazilians through their word-pictures). One thing we know: that the nature and the quality of poetry have nothing to do with cultural or social 'development' as evaluated by Western standards.

And this greater awareness must be ascribed to the generosity of the 'transmission relays' – the translators, the poetry editors, the festival organizers.

(10) I think it is important to rationalize and to extend the means of communication – particularly through the publication of original and translated work, and through poetry gatherings.

1.0 In some ways – even in France today – poetry is seen as some borderline activity: obscure, unrelated to the country's life, for all intents and purposes a secret movement . . . It is necessary to make concerted efforts, nationally and internationally, to valorize poetry, to remove its effete mask and to move it out of its intellectual ghetto.

2.0 Why not imagine a worldwide organization grouping the poets? *Poets International*? I don't think the interests of poets always coincide with those of other pen-pushers. Who can be better positioned than the poets to address themselves to the specific problems poets are faced by? Who can better identify the options or the development possibilities?

Most translators of poetry are also poets. Those few who aren't could certainly be affiliated to such an international association of solidarity among poets.

3.0 Why not imagine a *Poetry International*: a small and not too formal body of experts grouping poetry organizers, editors and/or publishers, plus somebody representing Unesco, who could, in conjunction with poets representing their association, better articulate and co-ordinate poetry festivals and intercultural exchanges?

3.1 Working together in this way an index on poetry festivals and similar manifestations could be established.

3.2 They could promote the creation of a video bank: films on or by poets, films on poetry and poetry festivals, to be used for educational purposes also.

3.3 They could search for and suggest more coherent ways of subsidizing the publication and the translation of poetry.

4.0 All of this can come about, it goes without saying, only if we rigorously avoid the attitudes of élitism and hierarchy in our appreciation of poets and poetry. There must be no cultural charity ever. No more Eurocentrism.

(11) It is difficult to believe that people are actually born in the trees of the Luxembourg Gardens. We never see the young. Since they have to sit very quiet so as not to be discovered, they tend to assume a great age and excessive thinness even when still young. Those who really are too weak to continue clinging to the branches can sometimes be found on early smoky mornings, close to the trees from which they have fallen, hunched in rags and tatters. They are then mistaken for *clochards*. (That is why the dream of every *clochard* is to return to Heaven 'up there'. And that too is why they drink so much: to deaden the pain of having to live the low life.)

Not very long ago the tree people were faced with a crisis. A rumour blew through the perches, agitating the leaves, that swarms of locusts driven North by the drought were about to invade the park. They would devour all the greenery and thus decamouflage and expose to ridicule the native population: the bourgeoisie, alerted, will call in the *flics* to dislodge the squatters.

The only remedy, they knew, was to get hold of a camel. Locusts don't like camels – there is an ancient desert enmity between them. They are frightened off by the remorseless munching of the camel's mind. But a camel, being the symbol of hospitality, costs money.

And so a young fellow was sent down to the outside to go and raise the funds, if necessary by selling the story of the upper world. His only defence against the avid foreign myth-gobblers was to be his fetid breath.

But he stumbled. He couldn't bear the thought. He just could not communicate – and there was no Poets International to help him. So he took his words and changed them into a fairy . . .

Muiden, August 1984

155

Poetry Is

*In memory of a Round Table session
Muiden, 25 August 1984*

The coimportance of mutually exclusive inclusive contradictions.

Michel Déguy

Poetry is an odd passtime

Poetry is a way of maintaining that which cannot be maintained
Poetry is a do-it-yourself survival method
Poetry is a do-it-yourself survival mechanism
Poetry is an improvisation upon pessimism
Poetry is consciousness running away through the words
Poetry is a trickle of consciousness
Poetry is a gift from the ancestors
Poetry is our curse because of the sins of the ancestors
Poetry is a verbally transmitted passion of words resulting in silence

Poetry is politics, or the appearance of politics
Or the appearance of the appearances of politics
Or the politics of appearances
Poetry is language taking a risk
Poetry is language coming apart at the seams
Poetry is existential communication
Poetry is crippled prose
Poetry is a reconstruction of the already existent
Poetry is a tautology of silence

Poetry is translating into a non-language
Poetry is a raping of the poem
Poetry is narrow-casting on a broad base
Poetry is a sacrifice with words the victims
Poetry is a pollution of silence

Poetry Is

Poetry is that which can be learned by heart or by head, or by word
Poetry is a way the poem has to reveal itself to itself
Poetry is a useless commodity
Poetry is the celebration of an aristocratic act
Poetry is poetry talking to itself through the poem, using poetry
Poetry is constitutionally incapable of convincing anyone

Poetry is memory
Poetry is souvenir
Poetry is the art of forgetting
Poetry is the form of memory, or the formula for forgetting it
Poetry is the shape of memory shaping poetry
Poetry is the tracing of forgetting
Poetry is the husks of forgetting
Poetry is a form of training to be different from others

Poetry is the elemental grammar of culture
Poetry is the Fifth World
Poetry is the Fourth Tense
Poetry is the consecration of useless definitions used uselessly
It is cheaper to keep a poet alive than to programme a computer for
poetry

the rabbit hunt,
September 1984

there is the child – what does he do?
look, he skips barefoot over the veld
cold the wind and gaunt
in his ragged tatters; who comes too?
the squatters of the world
chirruping kids hopping like Cape kangaroos
Jack and Jill and Humpty Dumpty's second wife's
unlawful offspring black-breeding in the Sebokengs
and Sharpevilles of this land where they are not
supposed to be: what are they up to?
big and small will clenchfist and sing
protests against the higher rates
and by the way look for a whiff of life also
put fire to rotten tyres and other junk
to signal smoke just like real Redskins
and jive and pose for vulture photographers
perhaps use knife and stick over heads
of pimp and sell-out profit-cropper:
the stone is a secret weapon

there arrive the boere with their musket-bearers
to do what?
they come dressed as heroes in camouflage brown
to blend like tigers with this earth
that must be tamed
and trundle armed and cigaretted in their huge
steel-plated trucks
through billowing smoke and puerile barricades
to go safeguard God and God's own children
from the Devil Communist

the rabbit hunt

look, there are the beer-bellied border warriors
now they'll unveil the Face of the Law;
many hand-raised henchmen are fed fat and black
with shoes and some even wearing socks
to let it be seen it's not always foredoomed
to be Bantu; look, what are they preparing
for now? go one-kneed kneel as if
to pray to shoot tear gas and plastic
bullets and other bullets too
and up to flay with batons over heads and kidneys;
just like in the movies, mate
except that the stones are mighty cold;
look what happens now: *ecce homo*:
boer lifts his gat with elegant concern
to blow away the bastard: *click* shouting
Africa shouting the odour of justice
and blood
without a pass *click* the funny fall-guy fixed
mid-air in wonderful whirligig Olympic jump
just like the jumping-hare look
the chap is chopped
bulls-eyed and on the map
(also to hell)

the minister sits in his office – what lies ahead?
the minister announces – what edicts and announcements
do the minister enunciate?
the minister lays his seriously concerned hands all
prepared on the authoritative executive desk and says
violencewillnotbetolerated, and says
agitatorsweshallsooneliminate, and says
cowardsletkidsdodirtywork (and ands)

over here at a safe distance the poet –
what's he doing there what's he doing here?
look, look, with little hops and skips of words
he gives writing write to a perambulating poem

Letter to a Figure
in Manet's *Olympia*

Dear Ka-Ma,

You don't know me – it doesn't matter. I'm writing to you on behalf of Ka'afir. I'm lending my pen to others, to track the pulsing of their hearts, in the same way that the painter always substitutes himself for the observer. The painter paints what he *thinks* the viewer will see.

(But don't ever ask the painter what he thought he was doing. The risk is that he may tell you. He will prance, purse his lips, and start wagging a pretentious wooden tongue. Poor soul. What is it that really interests him? Perhaps only the attempt to translate into colourshape the *feeling* of a dark hole. Or the voluptuousness of a knee. And most artists end up doing paintings inspired by other paintings. It is after all very hard to leave an odour of the self on the canvas. Or to depict someone from inner space.)

Ka'afir, I am sure, you will remember. He is the young man who was standing to your right and just behind Victorine's left shoulder in that painting where she is lying naked – like a white cat with a black ribbon around the neck. (The kind of animal one sees in advertisements for cat food.) He says you will recall how the two of you made fun of the White slave with the dwarf-like dimensions, and of the silly dress the painter asked you to put on. How hot you were, and how cold Victorine!

True, he was then later effaced from the work. It is of course the prerogative of the painter to erase the essential, to alter reality by changing his mind. Ka'afir says that he asked Eddy about it afterwards and that he was told: 'Taking you out of the painting, now *that* is Beauty!'

I often see Ka'afir. We spend hours reminiscing about Africa. It is like talking about the dream and its image. When I told him that I'd been approached to write about a work of art, he laughed and said: 'I have something far more interesting for you to do.'

Letter to a Figure in Manet's *Olympia*

Before leaving he wanted me to give you the following message:

Tell Ka-Ma that we are linked forever. Look, she is still glancing at where I stood. It is said that one can make a cat disappear completely, except for its smile. In the same way one may wipe out a person and even the story of their love, but the way they looked at one another will always remain. For I loved her. I close my eyes and I see her slender legs behind the uncomfortable couch. Even now I still know her smell: the freshness of linseed oil and something of cloves. I had a letter in my hand. I was too shy to give it to her then. Please send the *non-dit* to her.

This then is the result of his request.

He also said that he doesn't know where that black cat to your left came from. It is not a good omen.

Like him, I permit myself to embrace you tenderly.

Breytenbach

Angel

Yesterday I go with Y to have lunch at Angel's place right on the other side of town, beyond the dog cemetery where streets start twisting uphill. Going there water pour from the heavens, stream down the streets, gurgle in the gutters, cocoon us in the car with the steamed-up windows. A cloudburst.

The building in which he lives has a very ancient lift. Slowly we ascend to the last floor. From the third floor upwards we start hearing the music: the watery flow of some sonata comes drifting down. We enter his apartment. In a largish room he sits before a grand piano, running fingers over the keys, like laughter. A young girl with lank dark-blonde hair leans on the piano, her face mirrored, chin cupped in palm, lost. She wears heavy legwarmers over her tights. 'Tight' must be derived from thigh. The windows are opened wide, giving on to shiny wet roofs and curling sky. And immediately the day, which had been slippery and closed in and sad with fog, is transformed into a translucent and silvery presence. We embrace.

Then the other guests arrive. A lady doctor from a far-off town, expert in treating marginals – those who've had their balls desecrated by torture, ex-inmates, raped women. Dressed all in brown (the doctor). Short hair, nearly no make-up, strong odour. Accompanied by a man from another country with a raincoat of anonymity, a discreetly fashioned moustache, small granny glasses.

He is an expert too, a *responsable* with an organization enquiring into the lot of detainees and prisoners with the objective of having minimum conditions of decency honoured. They embrace Angel. (Angel embraces everyone.) We are introduced by hand and by smile.

The people living in Angel's house gather round. M, his secretary, with the severe hairdo and the shining face of a disciple. His son (*il est beau comme un dieu, mon fils* – and the boy shrugs his shoulders angrily) with curls and dark eyes. The young girl is a dancer. She bobs, and walks off into the wings with toes pointing outward.

Drinks. (During all the time that we are there I remain aware of the dark piano's silently thrumming presence behind me, but the

162

outside day stops fluttering.) Down we go on the floor, the other two guests perched slightly higher on their chairs. Not good: as if we are in the posture of people about to be interrogated.

And the interrogation starts. Very friendly, very concerned, it must be said. But the other guests had come obviously with the purpose of hearing something, of hearing it again. It must be said. What a terrible punishment to have to be plunged back in prison. Will we never be released, Angel?

The lady analyses, sharp as a knife. The problem is that you cannot really use the knife for writing or for making music. Why do people imagine that they have *the right to know*? Why do people think that *everything can be known*? Why do people expect that there is *something hidden behind or below the façade* (the *truth*, because covered)? Why do people believe that *knowing* (understanding, teaching) can be a cure for all our sins and our despair at living, *le mal-être*?

The lady has read my book and she serves up lashings of it. She remarks upon the recurrence of themes, of images. The same pictures are dredged up in all the confessions or decodings or the jumble-mumble of her patients. The flying, for one. The visitors from outside. All over the world maimed people are taming the feathered ones. Or the evocation of water. It must be time. It must be, since you are narrowed down to living by ear, the flow and the no-taste of nothingness all around you taking on the ripples and the undulations and the swish-swash of water. There is the constancy of silence.

The lady expounds, probes, sums up. The gentleman intervenes with precise questions and then he fishes a tiny notebook from an inner pocket and with a slim pencil he starts scribbling. Notes? Observations? A game of noughts and crosses? I learn that the delegates of his organization are briefed on how to address themselves to the humans they visit, what clothes to wear, the duration of the contact, balanced – using a knife metaphor here would be a slip – between giving the prisoner enough time to relax and let go, and not too much, lest the come-down of withdrawal be too traumatic. The gentleman pauses, peers around his eye-glasses, purses his moustache. He also relates how Master Basie, a senior South African prison official, came to inspect the gaols in his country, and of how he remarked that, 'You guys have a bleeding cheek to put the eye on *us* when one contrasts ours with the shitty conditions here!'

It has started raining again. (I must think: the tongue is a bird.)

Food arrives. Angel says that he also helped preparing it. Meatballs and rice. Too salty. Salad. Too salty. The wine is a Château Quelconque '84 with the blue taste of added chemicals. Ice-cream. Coffee. No one tastes the food. We are in the company of militants today.

The lady is confirming her theories. She says that she understood raped women only once they started talking to her. Of how talking – like having to reconstruct the crime for the police, or testifying before court – is a tearing apart process. Yes. A violation. (I think: yes, but talking is also lying; doctoring reality with the balm of the lie.) But the young women don't talk much, she says. They seal their lips. They have broken mouths. It is the old ones who seem to have less qualms about explaining how they were forced. (I think irreverent and piglike thoughts: that the old women had less to lose, that the old women were furnishing their lives.) She understands when people open up, she says. And though they be locals or from Latin America or the Orient, the wavelength remains in essence the same. The only hitch is with the Africans. We do not speak the same culture. Perhaps there is speak-culture and other-culture. When you ask them, she says, to tell you exactly where they were tortured by electricity – in the office or the corridor or the cell? – their tongues take the grey road of vagueness. Do they have a black reality? (I think: ah, but in Africa electricity is still a miracle, madame. See the snake come flashing down. And I think: *bliksem*! I think: when everything else has faded, all the textures of the tongue, I shall be left with a few curses. Like *bliksem*. And, perhaps, *lief*.) We are isolated in our misery.

Angel is illustrating certain ideas by anecdote. His face has become tense, his profile shows the knotting of muscles. I know that he must be having brackish spittle in the throat. He clasps his hands. His eyes have the Christian look. He speaks too good a French. The sad thing though is that I have heard him tell exactly these same stories before, in similar images. He becomes obdurate; his forehead and cheekbones pale. Love is the message. (I think: brother, you and I will never forgive them for what they showed us about ourselves. Also: how easily we talk! The sense of privacy has been destroyed forever. It is enough to enquire, and immediately all the beans are spelled out. There is no distance, no filter, between you and what is asked of you. You cannot help yourself. The throat thickens. You are back, bitterly, in the situation of humiliating exposure. Nothing can stop you now. You must run your line to the point of choking.)

But Angel comes up with a new twist which I hadn't heard before. In the place where they kept him, Libertad it was called, he was punished (a hundred times, he says) for smiling. Don't laugh! Open your mouth and take that smile off'n your face! He turns to me and shows me the blue opacity of his orbs and the long teeth between parted lips. The light is fish-like. The teeth are not his own any more, and they are not all of the same colour. I imagine a story of a human being tortured to death until only his smile is left glittering on the floor. How do you wipe out a smile when there is no more face framing it? Will that smile be discharged? Suppose one has no more teeth, does the smile remain the same? Time passes.

The lady broaches the oh-so-delicate subject of sex. Like the breaking of the water. Angel adds a laugh to his smile, and I too must snort. People aren't really *cured* until they are willing to come clean about their sex lives, single or complicit, the lady doctor remarks. But so few do. Ah. Maybe they suffer from fears of withering. Maybe they have to prove that they still can. Again and again. 'Tis not easy to put the hand in own bazoom. Silence. Birds in the rain. Angel says that he knew of only one (!) incident of homosexuality in his time, and that was the one and only time the word 'love' was used. Cellmates were discreet, he recounts, leaving you be with your handkerchief for half-an-hour to pray and/or to play with the private member of the family. (How far do you have to go if it takes half-an-hour to get there?) I laugh and claim that the question never arose in my instance: was I not always alone in my cells? And then I repair to the toilet and feel the fool when I shake the droplets from my tool. Should I tell them about that vomiting dream I had of screwing a warder?

Don't talk. Better to cry. The sublimations can become too laborious, too involved.

The time has come to go. Angel doesn't want us to leave. We are all on our feet. He puts his arm around my shoulders. I feel the tenseness, the shocks coursing along his body, choking the flow of his limbs. Music he will give us, he says. We must have music before we go. He plays. First a water piece. Then, he says, something for or about the birds. I think it must be Mozart. Birds scatter their wingbeats in the rain outside the open window. Droplets on the sill. We lean our elbows on the piano. I can feel the vibration communicated by the coffin of the instrument. Angel's face is closed. It is also asymmetrical – a crooked line of concentration cutting it vertically, like a scar. He doesn't play very well. His fingers fumble. The lady is seated behind him. She is watching his hands intently and avidly. All her body is slumping relaxed, her face now gone soft and wistful, gone, going, gone. Then she notices me watching her and the mask promptly returns. Taking the form of smile.

And so Angel plays a popular air from his country, and his big heart sinks (sings) into the piano. All the expressiveness is there – the proud affirmation alternating with the bombast and the tenderness. 'Mon pays,' he says.

On the piano there is a framed photo of Julio Cortazar, taken a few months before his departure for the Great Big Prison in the Sky. It shows him standing upright amidst a sitting crowd, a brooding crowd, applauding with hands as big and as white as birds. Light glances off his bearded moonface, off the whirring of his hands. The silence of it.

A Reading of the Present Situation in South Africa, Autumn 1984

For an observer looking from a distance at the South African scene the recent picture must be quite confusing. (It is not necessarily less so for those living in the country.) One had become accustomed to a brutally simple black and white situation where racist oppression could be traced along the lines of *mega Apartheid* or *big Apartheid* with divide and rule and the inferiority of the *non-Whites* as the guiding principles for the cutting up of the country into Bantustans, the permanent exclusion of Blacks from any power sharing, the inviolability of indigenous and foreign White economic profits thanks to unlimited natural resources and abundant cheap labour, for the fundamental laws governing race classification, education, living areas, political expression, work, etc. A country where repression could be read in the crude daily sorties of the police or minor civil servants, in institutionalized state violence, in the banning and exile of political opponents, in the humiliating pinpricks of *petty Apartheid*: separate and inferior facilities with the absurd consequences known to all, arrests for pass offences, torture . . .

Now all of a sudden things seem to be in a condition of flux. Did the ideological ground of *Apartheid* shift? Has there been transformation, change even? The observer gets conflicting information, made more difficult by partisan interpretations – a complication compounded by the fact that disinformation, a carefully cultivated smokescreen, is part of the rulers' campaign to bolster their position. They have understood the impact of language, and how to present that which the outside world needs to hear to calm the twinges of conscience. But reality is sometimes resistant to the palliative of language.

Take some recent happenings, at random:

- Inhabitants of the black townships around Johannesburg protest, ostensibly against increased rates and rents. The protests burst into flames and some Black officials of local councils, considered traitors, are killed by the crowds. The police and paramilitary units (many of whom are Black) trundle up in their armed vehicles and open fire. More than sixty demonstrators will die, some very young still, and many hundreds more are wounded. Hospitals are forbidden to provide casualty figures. The township dwellers are organized by a group called the Free Mandela Campaign.

– Freshly elected Coloured and Indian parliamentarians take their places in the institutions provided for under the newly enacted constitutional dispensation. Two of them, the Reverend Alan Hendrickse and Mr Amichand Rajbansi, are drafted into the Council of Ministers.

– Black and Coloured students on several campuses and in many schools boycott all classes. Some radical White students support them. Riot police intervene repeatedly, firing tear gas and rubber bullets. (People die from rubber bullets. The mourners bury their dead with revolutionary songs.)

– The National Union of Mineworkers – a Black union – using channels provided for by labour legislation, officially announce a 24-hour strike in support for claims for higher wages and a demand to have the 'normal' working hours of 96 per 2-week period reduced to 94. The strike is legal and perhaps 70,000 miners participate. Police disperse the strikers. Seven are killed initially; more later. The Chamber of Mines refuses to give in to the demands. During subsequent, illegal, strikes more miners die.

– Louis Le Grange, Ministers of Law and Order, decrees unlawful any meeting of two or more people – taking place in a private house anywhere in the industrial heartland of the Transvaal, described as the Pretoria-Witbank-Vereeniging triangle – 'where the Government or the Government's actions are commented upon or criticized'.

– Eleven thousand soldiers of the South African Defence Force engage spectacularly and expensively in war exercises at Lohatla in the barren Northern Cape. The Minister of Defence, Magnus Malan, claims that no 'enemy' can prevent his troops from reaching Cairo should they wish to sweep through Africa.

– Increasingly bombs, often limpet mines, explode in or near power plants and government offices and installations identified with Apartheid practices. These incidents, ascribed to ANC 'terrorists', occur particularly frequently in Natal and the Eastern Cape.

A Reading of the Present Situation

- The Coloured Labour Party announces that it now admits also Black, Indian and White members – in defiance of the Improper Interference Act specifically forbidding this.

- Without any explanation all restrictions are lifted on the Reverend Beyers Naudé, an outspoken White opponent to government policies who had been banned for two successive five-year periods.

- The Government decides that the Western Cape will no longer be considered as out of bounds to Black labour. Previous laws obliged employers to hire Coloured labourers on a preferential basis. The change seems to imply at least a tacit acceptance of the permanent presence of migrant workers and squatters.

Confusion, as always is partly also in the eye of the beholder. There is a lack of clear vision, made more misty by overlapping ideological views and blind prejudices. But if we look correctly the underlying pattern will emerge for all to see.

The pressure for change is on. Apparently contradictory movements are at work. Historical and conjunctural conditions are sharpened in the process. The level of political consciousness – some would say the despair – among the Black majority remains high. The fighting spirit is undaunted.

The Background

This imperfect inventory of recent events must be seen, if we want to make sense, against the backcloth of major occurrences and permanent features of the South African society.

A basic – one could say endemic – source of unrest is the dire economic situation. The country's economy has moved into a period of recession considered to be the worst since the thirties, marked by a stagnant market, a weakening rand (due mostly to the consistently low gold price and the correspondingly high dollar), mounting inflation and foreign debts. Nobody knows how many people are out of work but in a set-up of non-existent or minimal social security for Blacks, and certainly no dole money, of no alternative economic activity permitted due to the impermanent and often illegal nature of their presence in economically viable 'White' South Africa, their present plight must be horrendous indeed.

The economy is suffering also from the results of the drought (crumbling Africa elsewhere as well) starving the rural Blacks and affecting the traditional backbone of Afrikaner nationalism – the farmers. The Government must pander to the farming community, for electoral reasons, but also because in terms of border and internal security it needs to keep White settlers on the land. Another traditional support sector, which must be kept satisfied (milking state resources), is that of the civil servants – and the ranks of the bureaucrats will be swelled considerably by the multiplication of structures called for under the new system.

At present though the first priority of the state is not to relaunch or revitalize industry or agriculture, but to keep going the war economy, which is draining off an ever larger portion of the national budget. Those in power are caught furthermore in the cleft stick of ideological paralysis on the one hand, and the need to survive on the other. To continue at the approximate level of accustomed privileges the Whites have to develop the indigenous market and thus favour the establishment of a Black bourgeoisie – a necessity recognized by the private sector and accounting for some of the 'liberal' White opposition to the regime. But developing more sophisticated Black consumerism and promoting productive incentive would play havoc with the master plan which presupposes that Blacks are transients or foreigners in the land of honey and milk.

Poverty and misery are unevenly distributed – explaining in part the recent and continuous unrest. According to an AMPS (All Media and Products Study) report issued in September this year the average monthly income of a White household is now R1834, of an Asian household R1072, Coloured R624, and Black R273. The total income of all South African households – of which there are 6.1 million – now exceeds 4,235 million rand per month. The calculated 1.5 million White householders earn 2,714 million rand per month, or 64 per cent of South Africa's monthly buying power. The 138,000 Asian households earn 148 million rand, totalling 4 per cent. The Coloureds with their 428,000 households earn 267 million rand or 6 per cent. The Blacks with more than 4 million households earn only 1,106 million rand monthly, accounting for 26 per cent of the national earnings. (Another interesting aspect shown by the AMPS report is the declining wealth of the Whites and, paradoxically, the rising average age of White wage earners. Only 22 per cent of Whites are now between the ages of 16 and 24; in 1983 they still formed 24 per cent of the group.)

Whites are now curbing their spending or their foreign travels complaining that South Africa is becoming 'like Argentina or Brazil';

Blacks are dying from hunger, stunted by malnutrition, chucking the stones they cannot eat.

A second feature helping to understand the flare-up of resistance among Blacks is the new Constitution, which took effect from this September. Seen in its simplest shape the new dispensation embodies the strategic and structural changes necessary to ensure the White minority's power monopoly. By doing away with some of the overt manifestations of Apartheid the power élite hope to expand its base and thus be in a better position for the inevitable confrontation with the dissatisfied majority. In a way similar to the placing of local lords in the homelands, the Whites have offered extended privileges to the Coloured and Indian minorities. Their fond hope is that the parties representing those two minorities who have now entered the game will henceforth realize that they too have vested interests in the system.

The new system has, to my mind, several distinctive characteristics. Parliament consists of three separate chambers – one each for the Whites, the Coloureds, and the Indians (whatever happened to the Chinese?) – plus a Presidential Council where nominees, on a quota basis, from the majority and official opposition parties of each house and including some further presidential appointees, will sit. By entrenched law the Indian and Coloured representatives are to remain in the minority, even if they were to combine forces. Each house concerns itself with what is known as 'own affairs' – agriculture, local government, housing and public works, finances, education and culture.

The electoral college – consisting exclusively of each house's majority-party representatives – elect the Executive President (P.W.Botha) who now enjoys vastly increased power. It can be seen that in this way the president must inevitably be the candidate of the White National Party. The president in turn, after having appointed the ministers' councils of the three chambers, forms the national cabinet of ministers responsible for 'common or national affairs'. Thus the country now has five departments of education – three relating to 'separate cultures', one supra-separate to co-ordinate separateness nationally, and one separately national for the Blacks; four departments of agriculture and waterworks; but one ministry only of Law and Order, one other of Justice, etc.

The president appoints his ministers, if he wishes to, from different parties and any of the houses (or even from outside these), thus theoretically promoting 'consensus politics', but also effectively doing away with party-political control. He also names the Chairmen and members of the many special and permanent intra-cameral committees, where, behind closed doors, real policies will in fact be formulated under the guidance of non-elected experts.

The system is said to present a break with the Westminster model. South Africa of course never did have a democratic representative parliamentary structure: the Westminster model existed only within very strict limitations for the White minority. The new dispensation is sometimes referred to as 'vertical or pillar democracy'.

The real thrust and the overall effects are however evident. There is no entry for Blacks, no majority participation is foreseen. There is no devolution of power, and the local administrative structures meant to contain Black political aspirations are rejected by the people. Indian and Coloured political participation has been co-opted to form a loose coalition grouping minority interests and to create the appearance of moving away from power monopoly. The Whites – and specifically the National Party – have secured and entrenched their exclusive political and executive power by refining the structures of discrimination, extending their room for manipulation, and effectively freezing any possibility for the peaceful replacement of the party in power. Coloureds and Indians, lured from a position of limbo into the system of the masters, will be sharing the blame for government without sharing any of the real power. (Their leaders do get fat salaries though.) The decisions and directives that matter will emerge from committees staffed by the president's appointed experts – and these mainly military and security advisers. There, behind the screens of the president's secretariat, you see the hands pulling the strings that matter. The question is: who are the puppets and who the puppeteers?

It is interesting to note that Whites were called upon to pronounce themselves by referendum on the new system concocted by Whites only – and 60 per cent duly voted in favour of it – whereas Coloureds and Indians were given no chance either to accept or to reject the principles proposed: they had to proceed directly with the election of representatives for the new chambers. In the event 30 per cent of the potential Coloured voters (that is, those who bothered to register as voters) and slightly more than 10 per cent of the Indians participated. Government spokesmen nevertheless blithely insist that the results constitute a mandate and that they consider the tail-waggers elected by the minorities as the only spokesmen for their people.

A country-wide campaign was started by organizations active in the Indian and Coloured communities – supported by Black and some White groups – to oppose the new dispensation and to boycott the elections. These organizations, over 400 of them, ranging from rate payers' associations to churches to sport organizations to trade unions, are grouped in an alliance called the UDF (United Democratic Front). The registration and voter percentages show the effectiveness of the UDF campaign. The Government, nursing its newly respected international image and not wanting to poison the carrot, could not repress the UDF immediately. Several of their leaders were however arrested on the eve of elections. Six of those later released and on the point of being rearrested (the Government had issued detention orders) have since taken refuge in the British Consulate in Durban, forcing Mrs Thatcher's embarrassed Foreign Office officials to quarrel publicly with the South African Government.

A third component of the picture, which may go some way towards explaining the recurrent uprisings, is the atmosphere of violence permanently impregnating the South African scene. The country is a police state. (There is a dialectic involved here: the police and the soldiers formed and strengthened and mandated to protect the state come more and more to control that state and nudge it into a direction that would justify their increased power. The state is their hostage.) The physical presence of police or army units in camouflage outfits and armed to the teeth, patrolling the townships in their armoured vehicles (the real borders that need to be protected are within), or using dogs and whips to terrorize people – these have become everyday sights hardly commented upon.

An average of 110,000 people are in prison at any given moment, many for pass offences. Detentions without trial continue. More than 100 people are executed every year by hanging from the neck – by far the highest number of any country pretending to subscribe to Western values. Between 150 and 200 people are annually killed by the police in shooting incidents – not counting those dying in riots. Over the last two decades the authorities have forcibly moved 3 million people, to 'clean up black spots', or to resettle them in terms of the Group Areas Act; 4 million more are earmarked for uprooting.

The Government seems to manoeuvre cynically within the parameters of 'acceptable' violence, always raising the threshold though – and the outside world, particularly the West, stuffed to a dazed apathy by the media, appears to have become inured to the horror and to tolerate a certain level of degradation. Soweto deaths are merely morning news items.

Finally the background needs to be completed by a cursory glance at South Africa's recent foreign-policy initiatives. The nonaggression pacts signed under duress by Mozambique and Angola and Swaziland and the enclaved Lesotho, and soon Botswana too – the continuing strategy to destabilize Zimbabwe through a combination of using the economic noose and military support to rebels (even furtive incursions by South Africans themselves) – the control of Malawi, the interference in the internal affairs of some African states and the enslaving support extended to others, in fact the economic and security penetration of a large part of the continent – the establishment of close ties with Latin American military dictatorships, with Taiwan and with Israel – the *de facto* integration of South Africa's military capacities with that of NATO – the effective maintenance and servicing of South Africa's arsenal despite a supposedly total arms boycott – the successful establishment of South Africa as an arms exporter (viz. South-African-originated equipment captured by Polisario from the Moroccan forces) – the entry, not admitted but hardly contested, of South Africa to the nuclear club – the failure of Western powers to impose their (admittedly tepid) peace-making efforts on South Africa regarding Namibia – the unequivocal involvement and support of South African incentives in the subcontinent by the USA – the visit of P.W.Botha to Europe as visual confirmation of his regime breaking out of isolation – all of these are the achievements of a structured long-term strategy, probably worked out in collaboration with some Western agencies.

A few salient facts must be pointed out. South Africa's foreign policy during the sixties and the early seventies – that of *détente* and dialogue – came undone with the fiasco of the first Angolan war, the accession to independence of the Portuguese colonies and the so-called Information Scandal. South Africa's buffer zones melted away and even its attempts to bolster the Muzorewa alternative for Zimbabwe/Rhodesia were doomed to fail. These setbacks certainly contributed to the fall from power of John Vorster.

With the feeling that they were all of a sudden at the barrel end of a gun (and a Black gun at that!), the ruling caste evolved a more aggressive or interventionist foreign policy; one where subtlety and subterfuge would play a larger role too. The main concern was still the need to buy time: time to refashion physically and politically the internal landscape and situation, to enlarge and to consolidate their power, to defuse the revolutionary potential of the majority, to prevent a non-White coalition by completing the cutting off of slices of land to shove Blacks into and by evolving a process by which Coloureds and Indians could be co-opted, especially also to prevent a possible joining up of outside and inside opposition forces.

A Reading of the Present Situation

To achieve these goals the so-named radical states had to be isolated and unmanned (South Africa supports and pilots Unita in Angola and Renamo in Mozambique) and the OAU had to be prevented from effectively aiding and channelling resistance. In the process South Africa's subcontinental foreign policy became essentially, in the first phase, a military one, with the concomitant rise to a position of decisive influence of the Defence Force and of security advisers. The complementary stage will be a larger economic penetration of neighbouring states, condoned by Western interests and favouring these. South Africa, posturing now also as a peace-maker – and still using as levers the rebel formations that it services or creates where necessary – is starting fully to play its role as regional *gendarme* and dominant economic power. (By creating colonies internally and client states elsewhere, South Africa must be one of the rare examples where we see what we thought of as the thrust of history being inverted. More soberingly: we are witnessing a 'modern' colonizing process, a hundred years after the scramble for Africa, which is rapidly becoming a *fait accompli* and which will in due time be justified as corresponding to a 'sphere of influence'.)

These policies clearly coincide with what the major Western powers consider to be their essential and strategic concerns in Africa. The White regime's 'total response' to what it describes as a 'total onslaught' dovetails very well, for instance, with the United States's policy of 'constructive engagement'. The stakes are high. In 1982 the USA had invested directly no less than 2,300 million dollars in Southern Africa and it had a two-way trade with the region amounting to 7,200 million dollars.

The USA's ambassador to South Africa, Hermon W. Nickel, in 1983 described 'constructive engagement' as:

a regional policy, directed not at South Africa alone, but at all of Southern Africa. Progress towards a more representative government in South Africa and economic progress throughout the rest of Southern Africa are inseparably linked to region-wide stability. That is why we have been working towards a set of interrelated goals. These include:

(1) An internationally recognized independence for Namibia;
(2) a negotiated withdrawal of Cuban troops from Angola;
(3) some form of *détente* between South Africa and the other states in the region; and, since internal conditions in South Africa also contribute to regional conflicts:
(4) the peaceful evolutionary change in South Africa towards a constitutional order to be defined by South Africans themselves, but

175

one firmly rooted in the principle of government by consent of the governed;
(5) recognition of the need for internationally supported programmes for the economic development of the region.[1]

Already in 1978 however Nathan Shamyurira, now a cabinet minister in Zimbabwe, analysed the policy enunciated above:

> The imperialist US strategy for Southern Africa encouraged explicit recognition of and support for South Africa . . . The US also accepted South African hegemony over the Bantustans and the neighbouring states of Botswana, Lesotho, Swaziland, Namibia and Zimbabwe, even if the last two states fall under controlled Black rule. Finally, the US supported strengthening the neocolonial ties among the frontline states so as to weaken the rearbase for liberation movements . . .[2]

It has often been stated (by South African government propagandists) that the purpose of the Nkomati accords was to bring security to South Africa by depriving ANC 'terrorists' of their sanctuaries in Mozambique. This purported desire to 'weaken the rearbase for liberation movements' has been, I think, very much a red herring to camouflage their true strategy of subjugating the neighbouring states so as to impose a hegemony translated, economically and constitutionally, eventually in the structure of a 'constellation' of Southern African states.

The Opposition Forces

It would be a mistake to read South Africa's foreign policy as divorced from the internal turmoil. The White minority's exclusive exercise of power, expressed through racist discrimination, economic exploitation and cultural deprivation, has defined conditions all over the subcontinent. It is clear, if only because of the infrastructural links and the uneven levels of development attained, that the frontline states cannot ever be completely free until South Africa is liberated. The 'liberation' of South Africa simply means the coming to power of an equitable majority government. The explosions of violence we see from time to time in South Africa are manifestations of a festering, low-level civil war – in which the adjoining states are involved too, whether they wish this or not.

[1] 'Quoted in *Azania Worker* vol. 1, no. 2/3, Summer 1984, p.4.
[2] *Ibid*, p.5

A Reading of the Present Situation

Resistance in South Africa is furthermore not only a blind reaction to the prevailing circumstances. Increasing the rents or trying to enforce the teaching of Afrikaans in Black schools may serve as catalysts for the eruption of discontent – but linking all these incidents there is a political awareness and a tradition of organized struggle for freedom.

Despite the fact that all effective organized political opposition has been banned for more than a generation now in the country, there still prevails the willingness to mobilize and articulate alternative ideas on a national scale. The authorities have not succeeded either in stamping out ideological questioning, the fermentation of idea systems and even – to a limited extent – the dialogue and the testing of strategems among different opposition formations.

There is a certain amount of opposition to the National Party coming from the Whites themselves. Leftist opposition is diffuse and ineffective, emanating from some intellectuals, students, and in an organized fashion from the PFP (the Progressive Federalist Party, the official White parliamentary opposition). These opponents suffer from not being able to identify with the ultimate aims or forms of struggle of the oppressed majority, and from not being accepted by that majority. Their demands are for human rights, dignity, humane decency, Christian tolerance and a liberal economy. To the extent that they are tolerated by the authorities and that they fail to sever their links with the White Establishment, they risk strengthening the dominant ideology from within. Their situation in a context of radical polarization is as ambiguous dissident members of the Establishment (culturally so at least, if not politically – but political discrimination is rationalized in terms of cultural identity); they stand accused of 'softening' the perception of Apartheid.

The rightist opposition to the National Party is by implication much more of a threat to them. The contest is for the soul of the Afrikaner – reviving primitive fears and crude prejudices, exploiting the decadence and corruption of a National Party (originally with an anti-capitalist, Poor White and proletarian base) after 35 years of power, and the social inequities evident in White society. Apart from a few extremist pro-Nazi and semi-clandestine formations, the two most important rightist parties are the HNP (Refounded National Party) and the Conservative Party – both led by disaffected National Party leaders.

There is a shading of opposition coming from trade unions (excluding those affiliated to TUCSA, the grouping of White unions – some of them rightists) and some churches such as the ethnically integrated Catholics, Anglicans and Methodists.

177

But the hard opposition forces, representing the Black majority, are expressed by two tendencies: the so-called 'Charterists' and the exponents of Black Consciousness. The Charterists, in other words those who identify with the ideals expressed by the 1956 Freedom Charter, are led, outside the country at least, by the ANC. Inside the country this stream of attachment to explicit non-racism and by implication to the Socialist transformation of society is reflected by the UDF.

Broadly speaking the Black Consciousness alternative flows from a break with the traditionally non-racist opposition parties, a break provoked partially by the apparent ineffectiveness of the ANC and to some extent by the revival of a mixture of dormant Black nationalism and the cultural re-evaluation or roots revalorization of a people who had been subjected to, and tainted by, a foreign culture. Outside the country this radical nationalist tendency is represented by the second internationally recognized liberatory organization, the PAC (Pan Africanist Congress); inside, the leading body at the moment, after several mutations, is AZAPO.

Both tendencies are involved also in trade-union organization, and taking part in the present discussion on the function and the role of unions. (In the absence of permitted political parties there is the temptation to see unions as conduits for Black political aspirations; the unions are at the moment in the process of evolving a definition of their function, independent of ideological overlords.)

The cleavage between the two streams of struggling is a real one and can sometimes be bitter (AZAPO is blaming the Free Mandela Campaign for the deaths during recent demonstrations), but it is not necessarily along Marxist/anti-Marxist lines as is sometimes averred. The ANC is certainly, at least as far as the directing core goes, an orthodox Marxist organization – and in that light the UDF can be considered a national front englobing, for tactical purposes, bourgeois elements too.

It is important to realize that the struggle is a process that will continue way beyond liberation.

What Does the Future Hold?

Has there been real change in South Africa, either structurally or in the attitudes of people? Or has there been only a pragmatic adaptation to a situation that is subject to changes provoked by the world outside? And if there was change, what motivated it? A sense of guilt because of the obvious injustices? Did it come about under concerted foreign pressure?

I do not believe that there has been real change – although we witness a lot of manoeuvring and some obfuscation. I think we are assisting at the unfolding of a major strategy for the preservation of privileges and power, which indeed includes some social engineering and a big effort at creating the impression of change. There may be some modifications brought about by interacting interests (foreign powers who are involved in Southern Africa may conceive of their basic interests in ways not necessarily compatible with those of the South African regime), but the end goals – in terms of the type of economic, social and structural environment they wish to establish – remain clear.

I believe there is little chance of the present constitutional and attitudinal modifications generating an uncontrollable momentum for change: we are seeing a very controlled development and the machinery does not allow for alternative growth. I believe at the same time that the interests of the minority (perhaps one can already say the minorities) as conceived by them, and the aspirations, goals and interests of the majority, are incompatible. Conflict is inevitable. It may vary in intensity, it may also express itself in unexpected ways, old forms of struggle may again become applicable and be revived (non-violent resistance for instance) – but the majority will carry on the struggle.

It is my contention that it is not the intention of the rulers to obviate confrontation – but to contain it, exploit it if possible, and to let it peak at times of their choosing when, for example, they are better situated numerically and straddling more defendable borders – at moments too when they can count on more active international support.

Ultimately of course they are confronted by a build-up of demographic pressure, and economic imperatives. The first short-term crisis may well be provoked by having to share and make funds available corresponding to the rising expectations and needs of the co-opted minorities.

It can be expected that South Africa will move rapidly on the external front to consolidate its dominant position. This position or breakthrough will conceivably be consecrated by an impressive visit by P.W. Botha to several African countries in the near future. It is not yet clear what they intend to do about Namibia – or rather when they intend to do it. They will use the conflict there to the hilt to secure concessions and international condonation. But ultimately the takeover by SWAPO does not constitute a threat to their own security. Namibia will remain a satellite state and, as the humiliation and taming of Samora Machel is showing, they can obtain and retain control even via Marxist leaders. It is not entirely clear either whether they want eventually to depose Machel, and Mugabe in Zimbabwe. Machel, having been thoroughly discredited, may well have become a lame duck by now. If he remains in power it can be only as a figurehead.

Internally we can expect a further series of moves going towards the creation of an impression of thaw. In the process some sacrosanct symbols of Apartheid may well be disposed of. In truth, I believe that Apartheid, the way we think we know it (as the abscess adroitly used by those in power to divert attention from other developments), could be done away with without in any way modifying the bedrock of control and exploitation.

The Group Areas Act will probably be modified, at least to provide for the development of the Coloured and Indian middle class – allowing them to do business in the White cities for instance – and establishing so-called 'grey zones' where ethnic mixing will be tolerated. The Immorality Act and the Mixed Marriages Act will accordingly be scrapped also.

Urban Blacks will obtain a measure of security and permanence in 'White' South Africa. Structures will be provided through which they will be supposed to express themselves politically, having enough autonomy to justify being grouped as representative entities in a larger constitutional set-up of a confederal nature. The cutting loose of the Bantustans will at the same time be accelerated – to come rapidly under the same umbrella structure. Some form of supra-ethnic or supra-'national' Southern African nationality or citizenship will be devised.

Mandela will be released at the opportune moment – that is, when they can use that card with optimal effect. Popular and/or organized violence will increase but not get out of hand. Death, already banal, will become even easier.

The ANC, suffering from blocked or cut-off pipelines into the country, and very likely going through an intense period of internal upheaval caused by their diplomatic setbacks, may well be amenable to talks.

All of the above will reinforce the power of those now ruling South Africa, and it will be self-indulgent blindness – or scarcely masked collaboration – to pretend otherwise.

Desmond Mpilo Tutu

Throughout the long years that the South African people have continued striving for freedom, for equality and dignity and justice, there were always women and men who became emblematical of the struggle. During the early years of this century there was Mohandas Gandhi, and later on Albert Luthuli. Now, in prison for already more than twenty years, we have Nelson Mandela, and his wife Winnie, banned to no-where in the Free State. Others also have shone as symbols, appeared fleetingly, were silenced: Bram Fischer, Robert Sobukwe, Helen Joseph, Steve Biko . . . The patriots. The best.

Foremost among those keeping the flame alive, giving a renewed sense and adding a depth to the liberation process, is Desmond Mpilo Tuto.

Is the Bishop any different from the leaders mentioned here? How does he resemble them? He would probably define himself first as a Black Christian. A *liberator* he is in the truest meaning – not just relentlessly exposing and denouncing the oppression suffered by Black South Africans, but imbuing the most wretched with pride by the quality of his concerns and the tenor of his actions. His role, in the absence of freely elected Black leaders, is indeed eminently political, yet he is not a politician and unlike Zimbabwe's Bishop Muzorewa he certainly nurtures no personal political ambitions.

His contribution has been rather to help formulate Black Theology – a consciousness that has given a new thrust to the concept of Christianity and made it relevant to African politics. He is above all a passionate warrior for peace, where peace *must* come to mean: no more blatant racism, an end to institutionalized state terror, the abolition of the pass laws, stopping the forcible removal of millions, the dismantling of Bantu Education and its replacement by one educational system for all, the right of residence and the right to property for all, urgently organizing a national convention grouping the authentic spokesmen of the people. Modest, minimal, realizable demands. What would pass anywhere else for basic human rights . . .

Burnt Bird

For, as he wrote:

> We consider that the freeing through Christ concerns not only internal
> enslavement, but external slavery as well . . . Through vigorous action
> the Black people must be delivered from their slave mentality, their
> inferiority complexes, their lack of self-confidence and the perpetual
> dependence on others leading to self-hate.

The Bishop, responsible for the Anglican Diocese of Johannesburg
since November 1984, is a product of South Africa's urban slum
culture – sharp, streetwise, witty, cool, tenacious, with the gift of the
gab, courageous, outrageous when he has to be. Born on 7 October
1931 in a 'location' near Klerksdorp, to parents who could be
categorized as being of the Black petty bourgeoisie, Desmond Mpilo
Tutu must have known from the outset what it was like to be Black
and looked down upon in the country of his birth where all power
was usurped by the Whites.

His mission in life was affirmed quite early – to teach first and
then, his formative years having been marked by Trevor Huddleston
(he who 'laughs nearly like an African, with his entire body') and
Ambrose Reeves, to enter the Church. The faith and the practice
though were not to become means for knuckling down to humiliation,
no:

> 'Following our Lord's example we are beckoned to work for the
> prisoners, the poor, the oppressed, those who have been deprived of
> their country, the despised ones.'

He rose in the hierarchy, travelled abroad, continued studying.
Appointed Dean of St Mary's in Jo'burg he preferred to stay on in
Soweto and to renounce the mansion in White Houghton going
with the job. The vision remained clear. Purple wouldn't blind him:

> 'Those who rule this country have embarked upon a road of conflict
> with history.'

In 1976 he was, briefly, Bishop of Lesotho, and then invited to
become Secretary-General of the South African Council of Churches.
He would continue 'obeying God's commands only'; he would, as
before, combat the cancer of racism expressed by a government
described by him as:

> 'One of the most perverse regimes . . . the most vicious system
> invented since Nazism.'

He compared the deportation of millions of Blacks to Hitler's 'final solution'. His stance became more resolutely anti-capitalist; he pointed out the importance, internationally, of the South African Problem; he stated pleading for disinvestment – let foreign capital be withdrawn from the arena of exploitation.

And inevitably he came in for his share of harassment from the White authorities. His passport was withheld on several occasions. They tried to smear him, appointing a commission to investigate the finances of the SACC. They wagged warning fingers and tongues, they threatened him, they tried to link him to terrorism, they even now accuse him of fostering tension.

> 'Those people called terrorists by the Whites, they are our sons, our brothers, our fathers . . .'

On 16 October 1984 the Nobel Peace Prize was awarded to Desmond Tutu. Luthuli had been similarly honoured many years previously. And the country was now more blood-smeared than ever before. 1984. A few old and ailing political prisoners released (after having done more than twenty years!). Beyers Naudé unbanned. But also armoured vehicles trundling through the streets of Sebokeng and Sharpeville. The army occupying the people. Hundreds dying in the name of White order. No yellow stars needed – a black skin will do.

Desmond Tutu, carried on the shoulders of the anonymous ones. He must be a thorn in the side of the rulers. (And yet -

> 'Why be afraid of me? I can't even vote in the country of my birth.')

How much longer will they tolerate him? Will he have an 'accident' the way Chief Luthuli had? Will he be 'murdered mysteriously by person(s) unknown' the way Rick Turner was? Will he die of 'natural causes' like Steve Biko and Neil Aggett and all the others? Or will he receive a parcel through the mail the way Ruth First and Jeannette Schoon did?

He has said to the Whites:

> 'Time is short. It's a miracle that the Blacks are still willing to talk to the Whites.' And: 'Whether you like it or not, you are our brothers and sisters.'

Whatever happens, Desmond Tutu will be present in the heart of the struggle and in so doing honour and inspire us all.

He has also said that which we must never forget:

> 'Victory is certain!'

Paris, December 1984

On the Ethics of Resistance
as a Writer
in a Totalitarian State

Power, which translates as an unquestioned sense of superiority supposed to justify manipulation and exploitation, *power* is equated with historical and conceptual and moral *right*. I include the moral dimension because the powerful never seem to doubt that they have the mission and the ability and thus the right to decide what is best for the deprived ones. In this way the North – to cut for a moment along the North–South power line – considers itself the locus where history (being progress, justice, knowledge, etc.) is generated.

But do we really care about 'the others'?

An ice-cap of indifference has started moving over Public World Consciousness, crunching to glass the resistance of the outsiders, paralysing all activism, engulfing the Human Mind in waves of silence. We are saturated by information, gorged on *news*. The salients of our perception are evened out: distractedly, we assist at the slight puff of exploding hearts and the glorification of a new shape of underwear – presented to us in the same format. *These are equally important*. Nothing is of any importance. We witness the fact of males and females, be they infant or adult, dying like flies, leaving a slightly black messiness on the flickering blue screens. The image is wiped out. Or rather – the images exist as predigested matter. Death is a statistic, like sales figures. We live it. It leaves us cold. We bury it. We feed the digits of our consented and registered identities into the Central Data Bank and are given to read our needs for the day, the headlines, the third-division scores, the latest discount on slightly used brains. We are the process of emptying by saturation. We are the means of survival for voracious microbes. We imbibe our chemicals and we stumble off to oblivion, perhaps to embark on the ancient vehicle of dreams ... Awareness tumbles in upon itself, implodes, a balloon wrinkling to nothingness. Consciousness, that border between nourishment and decay, has become the flat line of the encephalogram.

Far away – in the Third World or the Fourth World or the Fifth

World – where humans grow up stunted by physical and mental and moral malnutrition, by cultural colonialism, growing poorer all the time – far away, something stirs. True, the best minds may be spiked, and many lives are destroyed by the convulsive efforts at breaking through to freedom (or an approximation of it). But there is movement. It may be the look from eyes shaded by a hat brim, or a sudden white baring of teeth in the night, or a bowl of food put out by the hedge under a tree, for the essential rebel. *It is the slow stirring of survival consciousness*. It may want to take the shape of revolution, of transformation and metamorphosis even. Some may mistake it for big-R Revolution. There is a red glow embedded in the ice. The heart recoils at the thought of thaw. And yet it must thaw to survive at all.

Indifference, revolution; revolution, indifference. The one spawns the other.

A writer, as we all know, is someone who uses the written word, in its textual and intra-textual and infra-textual contexts – to fashion and/or to reflect a reality. In a larger sense, ideally at least, the writer is someone who expands consciousness by means of the written word – that is, by structure, texture, and association.

The above constitutes, to my mind, a possible minimal definition of his craft and an indication of his function. I am well aware of the fact that it doesn't say anything about his social insertion. To be a witness, to be a revolutionary or a subversive or a heretic or a sceptic, to be a spokesman or a dreamer or an interpreter: any or several of these roles may be incumbent upon the writer – essential at a given moment, marginal or optional at another, depending of course on the history and the conditions of the society he is part of. At all times, however, the writer is a communicator; he always interacts with society.

A totalitarian system – to try and circumscribe a further component of my theme – is found where a single party, expressed in a power structure usually operating on behalf of some homogeneous ideology, rules a state to the exclusion or, more likely, the repression of any really valid alternative. Here one must take into account, of course, the practices and their effects and not the lip services of the dominant Establishment, which may well range from 'centralized democracy' to a seemingly democratic multi-party set-up. Dissent may be allowed in certain instances, 'opposition' may be tolerated – but only to maintain the appearance of tolerance or to the extent that resistance can be incorporated to make the oppressive system stronger by rendering it more flexible.

Since a totalitarian system is nearly always run by a minority of the people to benefit their perceived interests, military and police methods have to be used to impose the system on the majority. Repression with its concomitant violence and corruption will inevitably be justified in the name of 'state security'. Arbitrary administrative measures take precedence over representational politics. The army and the police – particularly the security police and the intelligence advisers – become the mainstays of the regime. The power élite more likely than not will be organized as an occult 'brotherhood', 'lodge', or 'league'.

Totalitarianism promotes a police state. Not necessarily because the streets will be crawling with policemen, but because treachery and informing will be the name of the game, and often seem a survival technique. Also, because people living in such a state will have to camouflage their true beliefs and pretend to opinions of convenience. Nationalist sentiments and class or cultural or ethnic differences will be exacerbated and manipulated for ruling-power purposes.

The remarks I wish to make – obliquely, I'm afraid – will be about the role of the writer in a totalitarian set-up, his attitude when in the presence of resistance to that set-up, and the ethics that will inform his behaviour. I shall be referring to the South African situation, partly because it is the one I know best (to the extent in which a White living away from that country with its 'hidden' majority can pretend to know its problems), but mostly because South Africa is at one and the same time a unique case *and* a microcosm displaying so many of the symptoms and the problems bedevilling colonialist societies, or imperialist outposts, or multi-cultural nations, or simply developing countries. Plus – if I may be so imperialist – because the solution to 'the South African problem', the White problem, will be exemplary to the world, will set Africa on the road to freedom.

Let me put some questions to myself.

What is the true nature of the South African state? I propose two series of answers.

Talking of South Africa as a reality (and keeping in mind that 'reality' is not ideological by nature), one could say: that it is a fairly developed industrial state, the economic giant of the region (using, for instance, 60 per cent of all electricity generated on the continent); that it is self-sufficient and endowed with excessive natural riches, with space enough for all and room for expansion; that it is the granary of the subcontinent; that it is a land laid waste by recurrent droughts and erosion and mismanagement, its arable surfaces diminishing yearly; that it is a Third World country showing all the archaic features of a feudal society, with the vast majority of its citizens living – or dying – under the bread line; that it is a country made up of a rich patchwork of cultures but already – due to acculturation and centuries of mixing and a long exposure to American clichés – exhibiting a distinctly recognizable *South African* culture, making it different from Zimbabwe and Mozambique . . .; that it is a country where 'differences' are enforced and exploited and rewarded by the privileges of discrimination; that it is a country cut off from the world, with thinking and political activity smothered; that it is a depoliticized waste land where the mind is stultified by imported dogmas ill-equipped to provide solutions to local discrepancies – neo-Nazism, Stalinism, to name but two; that it is a country rich in theoretical innovation, with minds stretching to provide sense-making interpretations of its pecular social realities, finding novel forms of political expression, inventive structures; that it is the country of the Devil, of alcoholism, of despair, of heart ailments, of hereditary high blood pressure, of obesity, of hard-heartedness, of wasted bones, of apathy, of crusted-over insensitivity, of daily violence and nightly murder; that it is the country of tenderness and hope and generosity and hospitality where the believers are truly involved in the burning issues scorching the communities; that it is the place where you find Africa's foremost military force consisting of White professionals and conscripts, and Black volunteers, capable of both orthodox and irregular forms of warfare, ready to strike fast and far beyond its borders; the land where the army, made up of jittery young Whites – brainwashed, taking to drugs – and brutal Black flunkeys, is employed at squashing internal uprisings, an occupation force; land of rain and wind and dust, of storms and desolation; land criss-crossed by borders; land of death and regeneration – of death mentality, suicide mentality, border paranoia, revolutionary *élan*.

My second group of answers would be touching upon the world of madness, of calculated madness, of sublimated madness – the world of difference between pretensions and reality. Those in power in Pretoria claim that they, as arbiters of peace and progress, are carrying the illuminating force of Western civilization into the heathen darkness, that they are God's lonely soldiers battling against Communism and barbarism. Many of them believe it. (Some power-ful instances abroad do too, or pretend to.) They further insist that they are the only ones who can ensure Western capitalist invest-ments in the subcontinent. In the process of so pretending, they are, *inter alia*, corrupting the powermongers of the West, often, alas, so easily corruptible. They are also raping Africa, but that would seem to be by the way, the West would seem to be closing a complacent eye, leering tolerantly at those goings on as just healthy sexual romping . . . They say they are uplifting the Natives, near and far. They can even be heard to boast that they *know* and *understand* Africa and the Africans . . .

The truth? Communism has found, objectively, a recruiting agent in the South African regime embodying (boldly) the basest manifestations of capitalist colonialism. They are destabilizing and ruining the region, and mortally humiliating the entire continent. They are destroying the credibility and the viability of Western values. They are endangering, in the long run, whatever strategic and financial interests the West may have in the area. They cannot know the Africans. Not even themselves. How can the master ever understand the slave? Control and repression are not tools of perception.

The veritable nature of the South African state is that it is totalitarian – in the classical definition of that concept, including the identifying characteristic of the state itself (and especially its supposed or so-called security) becoming the highest good and ideal. The state is God's carcass inhabited by the pure and the just.

South African totalitarianism's claim to fame lies in its constitutional, institutionalized, structural and codified racism colouring (excuse the pun!) all forms of human intercourse and enterprise – politics, economics, religion, social life, culture, sport, sex . . . It is unique in constituting a living alternative solution to the problems of cultural and economic coexistence, problems of an increasing urgency for all of us living on this planet: the alternative of camps, homelands, border industries, mass removals, classification, repression and crisis control. It is unique in its shaping of new forms of colonialism – when we thought that history was at last pointing the other way. It is unique in its introduction of massive state violence against its own citizens, in *the controlled enlarging of limits of acceptable violence subtly implicating and rotting the Western nations by their tacit approval of it*. It is unique in its conscious banalization of inhumanity. It is the cutting edge of a new *Realpolitik* expressed in the callousness to hunger and poverty and death.

What does this state aim for? To perpetuate itself, to increase the good fortune of those loyal to it, whose interests it promotes. Since it is totalitarian and expansionist – but also encircled from within and without by growing numbers of agitators, antagonists, barbarians and others, it must extend its hegemony – particularly if it wishes to preserve its privileges. And so, despite breakdowns, fuck-ups and temporary setbacks, it moves along the wounded lines of Big Apartheid: farming out the indigenous majority to manageable homelands, depriving them of their nationality as South Africans, ultimately aiming to regroup them, together with the neighbouring client states and/or colonies, in a 'constellation' of Southern African states – with White South Africa, sitting as the spider at the black hole-heart of the universe.

Did this state evolve? Is it amenable to pressure? No, it has shown no evolution – except for an adjustment to changing circumstances, a refinement of the theoretical matrix underpinning the praxis, the introduction of some flexibility to make it more resilient – *all that in terms of overall goals and basic assumptions that have not undergone even an iota of change.*

Nobody can tell how it would react if it were put under real pressure. No effective pressure, apart from low-level internal resistance (flaring up sporadically), has ever been brought to bear upon it. Ideally, as things move now, there could be a point where they become enmeshed in their pretence at effecting structural and conceptual changes – where they unleash more momentum than they can handle. After all, there is a dialectic interrelationship between form and fiction and function – or appearance and reality. (I have always maintained that it is not important to expect the racist to undergo a change of heart, but that he should be forced by circumstances to pretend he's non-racist: the contents will eventually supplement the posture. It sounds nicer in Afrikaans: *Die houding sal uiteindelik die inhoud aansuiwer*, meaning that the pose will in due time purify the portent.)

But I'm not optimistic. First of all, because they have enough blanket control and strategies ranging far enough to guide events and direct them. Secondly, because Afrikaner consciousness is grounded in a profound willingness to self-destruct. This armours their fanaticism. The Afrikaner, with the rigid sense of insecurity of the halfbreed, is culturally incapable of absorbing or translating or accommodating transformation. Let alone of provoking it.

What are the real problems, the true obstacles threatening the present South African state as finicked and run by the White élite? One: demographic pressure. They cannot breed fast enough (and the tribal survival instinct may well be blemished), neither can they incorporate sufficient numbers of foreign Whites fast enough without submerging their identity. And even if they were to succeed in making real allies of the two co-opted minorities, Indian and Coloured, the dike will not withstand the flood. (And they have run out of minorities.) Two: economic pressure. They can only safeguard their own privileges by allowing the economic growth, and ultimately the integration, of the Blacks. Which doctrine forbids!

And there's not enough money to go round. A certain Dr Frank
Shostak, economic researcher, foresees that we shall see during 1985
the price of gold slithering between $270 and $300 the ounce; that
the prime interest rates will be 35 per cent; that the South African
rand will not be worth much more than 25 cents, and that it may
well plunge to 10 cents; that there will be zero economic growth
probably until 1988. (To compare: when I was in prison, the gold
price was reaching for $500 the ounce and the rand used to be
pegged to the dollar on a one-to-one basis. Perhaps I should have
stayed inside!)

The fat of the land is turning rancid. Economic and financial
hardship will accentuate the rifts in their own ranks. The Far Right
will become more militant, more influential. And then, resistance . . .
No way – there is just no way in which they can, once and for all,
eradicate Black political consciousness hardening into a resistance
evolving specifically South African forms of struggle against South
African totalitarianism. Time, you may say, is Black.

Who is the opposition? Ultimately they are confronting the South
African people. (I'm not for one moment attempting to deny the
South Africanness, the *Africanité* of those now ruling; I am, however,
saying that opposition is patriotic, coming from within, in the name
of the healing of the South African nation.) More precisely: effective
opposition more and more clearly situates itself in relation to the
aims and the practices of the historical avant-garde *and* mass
organizations (and foremost amongst them the African National
Congress). In a land of crude extremes, the liberal alternative is a
non-starter, a non-adaptable transplant from more clement climes,
ill-equipped to do battle with nationalism and extremism. In the
final analysis, 'liberalism' (the old-fashioned kind, not the present
one where 'liberal' equals New Right) can but fit a more humane
mask over the embittered features of the clowns running the show.

The battle lines are thus drawn: on the one hand, the White
minority (with some Coloured and Indian and minimal Black
support), using a fearsome repressive machinery, having a power
monopoly, strong in their favoured position as caretakers for Western
interests; on the other, the Black majority (with some Coloured and
Indian and White support), led by the ANC or by organizations
hewing the line.

What does this opposition propose? The opposition programmes,
vague as they are, need not be discussed here. Their salient aspects
form the very heart of the struggle exactly because they reaffirm the
total commitment opposing the Government's goals and strategies;
they are the zero demands which cannot be negotiated. One unitary

state. Unconditional citizenship for all. Majority government. These are the essentials, and can perhaps even be reduced to: *one people, one nation.* Beyond that, obviously, there are many concerns – freedom of movement, land ownership, the same opportunities, decent and free education, one justice for all, etc. But what matters now is the quality and the lucidity of the opposition struggle – the extent to which, by their principles and their choices, the resistance organizations show the way to moral acuity and nation building. Oppression sharpens the mind, resistance cleans it.

What are the possible scenarios? There is no cause for optimism. Blood and suffering, treachery and bestiality. Those in power will stretch their claws to the Congo. Where among the nations of the world can the political will be found to thwart them? And who, in Africa, or what combination of forces can mobilize the necessary economic and military power to prevent the implementation of their schemes? This is the first, most gruesome alternative. But they will be building on sand. For how long could they maintain the state of drawn-out war, sapped by internal unrest, needed to impose their *pax africana*?

The second possibility hinges on a rapid deterioration, a cave-in of the national economy and widescale Black uprisings becoming better co-ordinated. I don't think this likely. But the ferocious commitment to the struggle of those at present fighting with bare hands, and their willingness not only to endure suffering – general unemployment, no electricity or water in the townships – but actually to sacrifice themselves, could become a decisive factor. The Government has shown a willingness to use troops for internal security purposes, and now it cannot undo the escalation: it has been manoeuvred into the classical trap of being an occupation force.

A third possibility I have already alluded to: that the powers that be lose control over their attempts at reform and adaptation. If the politicians fail, will the army take over? Why not? Or need it be pointed out that the Defence Forces are already, surreptitiously – and then sometimes quite openly – in command? Wasn't the takeover by Botha from Vorster also the army taking precedence over the other special forces, even over the politicos? Witness the fact that we have now, in the best banana tradition, a professional soldier as Minister of Defence. And look at Namibia. Isn't it really only a military province? Surely the negotiations can be described as essentially a military process? Look at the way foreign policy – towards Angola, Zimbabwe, Mozambique – is conceived of and put into application as acts of war.

Burnt Bird

It is perhaps useless to speculate, or to project a 'Jericho solution' – you know, the all-encompassing and purifying revolution inexplicably bringing down the fortified walls. What can be foreseen is that the official White opposition – the Progressives – will focus on three areas of dispute: urbanization, influx control, the nationality question. The Browns – in Parliament – will want to do away with the Group Areas Act, the Immorality Act, the Mixed Marriages Act, the Improper Interferences Act. (They are puppets who must show that they can dance without strings!) The Blacks will harden and diversify their total rejection and opposition. Economic or trade-union action will become more important. The psychological freeing from dependency through a revalorized consciousness will again become relevant. But they will suffer from the split between 'Black Consciousness' and 'Charterists' (meaning essentially the ANC/UDF). The ANC will go into crisis. Deprived effectively of bases, the External Mission finds its primacy, as architect of a developing armed struggle, threatened. Paradoxically, the 'inside ANC' is growing in strength and popularity. Does this mean that the 'outside' leadership apparatus may lose its grip on events inside? Is that perhaps one of the reasons why the ANC has for the first time agreed to official talks with the South African rulers?

I think that, on the one hand, the struggle will be more diversified, become more complex; and on the other side there will be repeated offensives by the Whites to shore up their recently confirmed position of regional dominance: Botha will swing through Africa, there will be regional alliances and development aid from abroad funnelled through the White government; there will be the occasional military incursion alternating with the economic throttle to weaken Zimbabwe and Zambia; they will play footsie-footsie with Zaïre; they will ignore Tanzania and have no reason to be reminded of the existence of Malawi (except as a feeding trough for Renamo); they will pray that the Cubans do not leave Angola too soon so that they may continue extrapolating their internal contradictions into an East–West conflict. They will also continue being the midwife to the extending American influence in the subcontinent.

Having said all this – having dwelt far too long upon these matters – you may well ask: Well, what about the writers, then?

I think the answers have been pointed at, at least implicitly so. The situation is extraordinarily complex, but the writer, if he really wants to write, if he wants to hone his craft, must face the splitting of the mind, the supping with the Devil, the writing in dribbles from the corner of the mouth – but also the exhilarating challenge of rising to the need.

On the Ethics of Resistance

How? We don't even speak the same meanings. If you say *man* (quite innocently) in Afrikaans, you are of necessity referring to a White. The language has other, derogatory terms for indicating 'the other'. Similarly, *peace* in the White mouth demands maintaining a strict order by law, protecting the status quo – with everybody 'knowing his place'. No adaptation without peace which is upheld by order! For the Black, this peace spells poverty, oppression, indignity, humiliation, and being driven to the despair of violence in the bitter quest for recognition of his essential being.

Justice is White. For the Black, it is alienation. Imagine a Black raping a White not being sentenced to the rope; imagine a White condemned to death for raping a Black! Imagine what it is like to be – naturally, by birth – an alien in your country, needing a pass to move through it and a permit allowing you to settle there temporarily, on sufferance. Imagine, if you can, how many Black males attain adulthood without a sojourn in prison.

I can go on in this way. Do you think *beauty* says the same, then, to Black and White? Or *politics*? Or *resistance*? Or *commitment*? Or *literary quality*?

And yet we all speak the same world seen through different prisms of ache. This is not the place to give you an overview of the history and the actuality of South African writing. Suffice it to say that the best Black writing comes from the profound shared, popular aspiration towards freedom – but that this identification does not obviate the conundrum of not having an audience, not really, and neither does it of necessity confer a quality on the work. As for the Whites, despite the fact that some of them (us?) are passionate observers, and sometimes diligent escapees into the exquisitely vibrating space of No Man's Land – we are alienated, marginalized, irrelevant, depoliticized. The heart is shrinking.

And yet (I repeat) the tasks remain the same. To keep the word alive. Or uncontaminated. Or at least to allow it to have a meaning. To be a conduit of awareness.

To remember that writing imposes an obligation of dignity, even if idiotically so (in the Dostoevskian sense . . .). To try to see that one shouldn't confuse writing with politics, given the fact that *writing is politics*.

To keep up the noise level. To create confusion at least. To be an underminer campaigning for *alternatives*; that is, for *thinking* (even if it has to be through word thinking), that is, against the laming of the palate.

To keep an uncivil tongue in the head. To write against that fate worse than death: the wooden tongue clacking away in the wooden orifice in order to produce the wooden sing-song praises to the big bang-bang and the fluttering flag!

Not to knuckle down to oversimplification. (Which need not imply that one drowns every sausage of words with globs of Joyce either!)

To keep tending to freedom. Which means possibility. Which means means. Which means responsibility.

To write like a bat out of hell always screeching for the line of truth. Writing as the expression of revolt, not the sublimation of it.

You see, I believe that ethics is a craft. A tool. And beyond that? Sure, the compromises to survive. Publishing by hook or by crook or by *samizdat*. Beating the breast and gnashing the teeth if you're that way inclined. What else? Propagating violence? Condoning mayhem? Penning praise poems to some home-grown Stalin? No, I think you will agree that the above precludes that.

To accept, though, with humility and compassion, that we have areas of rottenness within us, that which was stilled and killed by the censor, or weakened by fear. And to realize that ethical considerations, in this instance, do not mean subjecting yourself to a communal moral restraint, but rather sharpening your perception of the quality of your work as a writer, of its import too.

For the White writer, it also means avoiding the twin paternalist pitfalls of either trying to speak in the place of the oppressed Blacks, or indulging in special pleading when it comes to their work. It means, at all costs, avoiding having his work or himself be tainted by 'martyrdom' or 'courageous actions'.

Above all, it means to project the *feel* of feeling, the feel of thinking, the feel of what it is like, the horror and the joy, to be balancing on the twin legs of birth and death. That is, to my mind what revolution, which is resistance, is about. In terms of writing.

New York, February 1985

I Write

simply because by now I no longer have a choice; to survive; to
seduce; to please my publishers;

to be – and the writing is a sense-organ, a possible decoding of the
environment, a symbiosis with what is other, a coming to terms
with matter; it is as much the way of being on the run

as it is a way into the labyrinth, the labyrinth itself, the de-scription
of same and thus the thread which negates the maze;

I write in order to invent an I which can be the means of survival
and multiplication of the word; to fashion a truth, to erect
sandcastles against the onrushing silence of the sea; to find the
spiralling sea-shell of amnesia;

ink-pregnant (like the sea) I write because mind-hand-heartmoving
is a primitive and futile game,

but also because it is the conduit of awareness structuring
conscience, a metamorphosis, a communion of the endless struggle
for justice;

finally to know that life is death deconstructed and death is
semiotically alive; and to merit then that silence secreted word
by word.

Paris, March 1985

Can Reform
Still Obviate Revolution?

Why is South Africa (for 'South Africa' read 'Apartheid', 'settler colonialism', 'East–West confrontation' . . .) such a major cause of concern? Part of the answer is probably suggested by the synonyms used here. We know that the complex of interests symbolized by the concept 'South Africa' is a running sore on the body politic of the world community; we all vaguely sense the urgency of the issues and the importance of the solutions. But the occultation of the real strategies, the duplicity of the world powers criticizing the South African regime in public whilst strengthening it discreetly – these make it difficult for the non-initiate observer to get a clear picture.

During this century successive generations of 'informed opinion' have had to face the phenomenon of what I'd call national or ideological rabies. The Turks killing the Armenians was a case in point. The Germans exterminating the Jews another. The never-ending wars in Vietnam . . . The squashing of the surge for freedom in Budapest and in Prague . . . The Cambodian genocide . . . The Iran–Iraq madness fuelled by hand-wringing nations pouring in arms . . . In none of these instances could international outrage bring the horrors to an end.

Is it because moral persuasion has no political force? Must the perpetrators of these 'injustices' – to put it rhetorically but mildly – be considered renegades, mavericks, mad dogs? Or is it dangerously naive to expect some decency in the practice of politics? Are inter-group relations defined only by the short-sighted perceptions of national interests?

In the case of South Africa the hanky-pankying of the Western powers, the discrepancies between words and deeds, can probably be ascribed to the sense of shame resulting from the collusion. Or maybe the protagonists just don't give a damn about world conscience. Are they not hard-headed pragmatists after all? Who is going to force them to make their play public?

As the last White colony of any consequence, South Africa is a historical oddity. Although its history cannot be interpreted exclusively, or even essentially, in colonialist terms, its system does reflect the insensitivities and the arrogance flowing from conquest and occupation. It would seem as if history passed by the Afrikaners, the ultimate settlers from a previous and picaresque epoch. In the folds of darker and more pristine ages they live an archaic contradiction: they are a people with a mission, put there by God with a purpose; they cling to the belief of predestination – which accounts for their obstinacy and their fatalism – and yet reject utterly the notion of historical determinism. They are a *White* African tribe tragically defending a superannuated vision of Western civilization, thereby dooming themselves and their values to extinction. But the odds building up against them, demographical, or of blood debts if nothing else, do not faze them. There is no link between cause and effect. There is no limit to their cruelty. They are not responsible for their own fate. God has created, hierarchically. God decides. He is terrible and wrathful, spitting fire these days from armoured vehicles called 'hippos'. He may provide, but if we do not follow his precepts, He will turn His face away from us . . . In any event, securely outlined against the background of a weak and hungry and corrupt Africa, the economic recession of large tracts of the world, a resurgent anti-Communism, the bolder reassertion of Western interests in the continent, they know they can count on their allies. Even if they have to bribe or blackmail them . . . The rest is but atheistic plotting and propaganda.

(I'm concentrating on the White Afrikaners here; the Anglo-African Whites by and large squat flabbily behind the ramparts of Afrikanerdom – carping, but profiting hugely.)

It is true that White South Africa – as the regional superpower flexing its strength, putting into operation its 'forward policy' (which is the step following upon destabilization), and as a virulent force of oppression denying basic citizens' rights to the majority of the land – is experienced by Africa as a perennial humiliation, an intrusion on the continent, a foreign evil. (The relative apathy and silence of Africa must reflect their impotence and their dependence on Western economies.) In its unique role as the only state wielding racism, however attenuated, as official dogma, South Africa is furthermore a challenge to world precepts of morals and civilization.

What I have said thus far is that White South Africa is a historical anomaly, probably regressing disastrously; that it is a political generator of unrest and dissolution in the subcontinent and, by extension, a menace to the developing North–South dialogue; that it acts in defiance of what we fondly take to be international criteria of civilized conduct. These observations are, of course, interrelated.

The pat explanation is to blame it all on Apartheid. If that were so the equation for redress would be simple. In Desmond Tutu's words: 'Apartheid cannot be reformed, it must be dismantled.' But what is Apartheid intrinsically? In the starkest terms: White minority power monopoly. This is the kernel condition deemed essential by the Whites for their survival. On this they will brook no negotiation and I cannot see the perception evolving. Apartheid as an edifice of racial discrimination is only the means of maintaining this desired end. The pragmatists, or 'new realists', would be willing to jettison the appearances of Apartheid in order to retain essential power.

It is equally clear that the Black majority cannot eventually settle for anything less than full participation in the political, economic and social processes of their country, on equal terms, with the same privileges and the same responsibilities. We tend to forget that the organized expression of unitary national conscience has been muzzled since the early sixties. Despite the best efforts of the White minority – bannings, Bantustans, gaoling, mass removals, depriving Blacks of their citizenship, killing – this conscience, resolutely anti-racist, is more alive today than ever before.

Given these two irreconcilable positions, what are the chances for an agreement that would embody the minimum conditions acceptable to both sides for some form of ceasefire if not coexistence? Recently, in Washington, Elliott Abrams – the Assistant Secretary of State for Human Rights – opposed my excessively sombre reading of the South African situation. He argues that many changes had indeed been effected since P. W. Botha came to power. The proof of Botha's moving out and away from entrenched domination would be the hiving off, to the Right, of part of the Afrikaner tribe.

Mr Abrams had a worry-bone there. I'd agree that, from the Afrikaner's point of view, at least two significant shifts did occur. The first was the break-up of Afrikaner tribal orthodoxy, the split between Far Right and Pragmatic Right. This break, caused by the realization of the pragmatic Nationalists that they'd have to co-opt the Asian and 'Coloured' minorities to extend their power base against the inevitable onslaught of the Black majority, could not but blur the outlines of Apartheid. The cosmetic blurring proved too much for the keepers of the tribe's cultural and ideological purity. This shift to a base that is no longer exclusively White is probably permanent: the Government's declared intention to abrogate the laws pertaining to 'mixed' marriages make a healing of the split impossible.

The second shift is illustrated by the increased militarization of the country, and the growing political influence of the military Establishment. South Africa has moved from an old-fashioned colonialist set-up, with Westminster political structures assuring vestigial democracy for the minority, to a Third World autocracy typified by pervasive state control, a rampant bureaucracy, antiquated economic structures, endemic and structural weaknesses, which cannot be overcome because of ideological blocks, progressive impoverishment, and a transfer of power from the politicians to the security experts.

There has been much effervescence but no progress. Reform, in the present context, consists of the piecemeal deployment of methods of adaptation. The underlying pattern, however, remains one of military containment. We capt conflicting signals emanating from South Africa only because the game is veiled. I am convinced that the strategy is a military one – apparently incoherent and sensitive to pressure – but in fact with clear goals and a timetable.

The strategy takes account, I am sure, of the way the scenario may be influenced by, say, the cultural factor, or foreign-policy developments. The goals and the methods remain constant: sectioning the country according to a military grid that would assure control and allow for a containable level of upheaval and resistance: liberalizing some abhorrent and obsolete Apartheid fixtures to procure 'Coloured' and Asian support and to assuage foreign faint-heartedness; creating alternative representative structures for Blacks to divert their demands, strengthening the homelands, driving a wedge between rural and urban Blacks, ultimately regrouping this mare's nest of institutions and bodies (at diverse levels of representation, based geographically or ethnically or both) in the semblance of a participatory confederation that would leave White-run political and economic power intact.

These internal readjustments are accompanied by an aggressive foreign policy, which is expressed, *inter alia*, by creating or supporting rebel factions in neighbouring states as means of intervention in their affairs (Unita in Angola, Renamo in Mozambique) by direct incursions when they see fit (as in Lesotho, Angola, etc.); by establishing a military presence of sorts elsewhere in Africa, or weaving a tissue of complicity by selling them arms (Somalia, the Comore Islands, Malawi, probably Zaïre too); by putting the world community before a *fait accompli* in Namibia.

In all of this they serve the interests of the United States, which has no quarrel with South Africa's military stance and considers the present political Establishment as privileged partners (or conduits) for funnelling aid and influence to sub-Saharan Africa. To do so the policy-makers in Washington must consciously misread and mislead their own concerned public.

How else can the world live with the raw terror emanating from South Africa? Officially more than 250 people have been killed (including one White) since September last year when the new constitution came into operation. Recently 14,000 miners were sacked for striking, and forcibly sent back to their 'homelands'. New treason trials are going forward, setting up the United Democratic Front for liquidation by linking it to the ANC and thus to the Communist Party. We know from the inquest into the Uitenhage massacre that the police have orders to shoot to kill. And they do. Women and kids. From the back.

Despite the continuing insult of neo-Apartheid to humanity, and although majority spokesmen have repeatedly asked for a total isolation of the country, a consortium of twelve European banks (the Kommerzbank of Frankfurt, the Union de Banque Suisse . . .) a few days ago granted a loan of $75 million to Pretoria.

Among the contradictions that those people nominally in power may have to solve will be a certain overextension of their military capacities, the economic palsy that makes it impossible to follow through after breaking a neighbour (with what are they going to rebuild Mozambique?), and losing policy control over their own armed forces.

But I would suggest that the true changes – if I may thus risk an updated reading of present-day South Africa, and taking into account that any interpretation, limited by language and confined in space, must be a blunting instrument – are the following. There has been an all but total collapse of the 'middle ground', where, with mutual goodwill, the future could have been talked into shape. (It is true that borderline contacts with the ANC have been established, but these are as yet too timid to start a *process* of discussion that would pull the parties into an interdependence and provoke a *need* to continue talks, which in turn could *create* grounds for negotiation.) The Black man no longer pleads for participation. In fact, the White state, as authority and promoter of change, is massively rejected.

The strategy of reform, although modifying some elements of the data, has ultimately no grip on the future. And although there is not yet a majority strategy for revolution, there is a depth to the despair and the bitterness and the resolution of the people (and an inner liberation too: a cultural awareness, a political tempering) that expresses itself in the willingness to die for the cause, in the burning of corpses, in the attempts to create autonomous power centres and germinal people's armies. The mourning, the strikes, the marching, the acrid smoke, the breakdown of White-imposed civic structures, the refusal to accept White 'peace' – these flash one clear signal: the point of no return has been reached. The civil war has already started.

Paris, April 1985

Black on White

There seems to be a taboo, or an area of painfulness in present-day South African cultural politics, that few of those concerned are willing to discuss. I'm referring to the convergences and the discrepancies, the posturing and the paternalism, the breast-pummelling and the silences marking the relationship between Black writers and White ones.

There is, to my knowledge, no longer any professional writers' organization grouping representatively both Blacks and Whites. (Apart from the *Skrywersgilde* – essentially an Afrikaans group formed to fight censorship and to promote Afrikaans literature – which does have a token number of Brown members.) The Johannesburg PEN slit open its own belly in January 1981 because it was felt that 'the non-racial character of PEN had proven more of an impediment than an impetus to the cultural struggle which most of its members sought to further'. According to the Executive Board, 'Internal Black resistance in South Africa, led by various Black organizations . . . has placed a taboo on the involvement of Whites at the decision-making level . . . even though the White writers (on PEN's executive) are committed opponents of the Apartheid system.'[1]

It was in fact a public play by Blacks slapping away the White hands, but also a way of saying they can no longer swallow the paternalism, explicit or implicit; that the sitting together cannot quench the fires of rage and humiliation ignited by the Soweto events; that a multi-ethnic (or anti-racist) superstructure such as PEN reflects do-goody idealism – corresponding neither to the reality of polarization nor to the consciousness of the people.

[1] The pamphlet in which I find the above quoted, called *Censorship and Apartheid in South Africa*, a Report by the PEN Freedom to Write Committee, then continues (p.38): 'The decision to disband Johannesburg PEN, a decision initiated by both its Black and White executive members, was a move towards solidarity and not confrontation with the Black resistance, reflecting the complexity of the "cultural struggle" against Apartheid.'

Burnt Bird

It is interesting and perhaps inevitable that Whites, in the true guilt-rotted liberal tradition, should have acquiesced in this demise. White writers often experience a sense of being discriminated against because of their Whiteness (more discriminately because they are constitutionally part of the privileged, and thus weak-sighted, class) whilst, paradoxically, encountering in private real expressions of appreciation and shared concerns. The illuminating fact is that they *know* (be it gut-knowledge or induced realization) when they do appear in Black ranks that they are tolerated there as 'token Whites', as 'Oom Jannies', and yet they will never admit to these mortifications. They prefer biting the pillow in the dark of night.

Black writers in the same way dissemble their frustrations, though the causes for these may be somewhat different. If you could meet on 'neutral ground' (abroad, or out of earshot of an audience, freed thus from the obligatory bloated 'revolutionary' rhetoric) you may learn from the Black writer how worried he is about not having an audience, or at least not an identifiable one. He may well tell you about the contradictions that ensnare him: insisting upon a cultural boycott (that is, recognizing the cultural identity dimension of the liberation struggle, the need for 'decolonization' and self-sufficiency) and yet yearning to be let out of the ghetto. He rejects the imposition of 'bourgeois' values, but his own, unacknowledged, criteria are apt to be Western and orientated towards accepted 'universal' norms of literary quality. He will be a Black nationalist (often a euphemism for being anti-White) and still hold up foreign White revolutionaries as paragons. (Someone said to me recently that most Africans think of Che Guevara as having been Black.) Admittedly, the local variants and devolutions of White are *the* enemy, and you'd be hard put indeed to find a revolutionary among the lot of them . . . Worst of all – he may still be in a position of humiliating dependence on the White for literary breakthrough and survival . . . One could continue. There is, for instance, dislocation between written and spoken languages – for individuals who are by birth and by circumstance 'social realist' writers.

All of the above naturally illustrate the painful passages of mental decolonization (decontamination) and a dawning national consciousness. It is a process of positioning, but also one of objective transformation. But isn't the fact of not talking out just another facet of paternalism, of self-confabulation, of calculated deception? Are we, White and Black pen-splutterers, doomed to be cuckolds and cuckoos? We do no one a favour by masking the prancing and the lying and the pain. At most we promote and aggravate the prevalent ignorance and distrust. (It is healthier to trust a bold-faced 'enemy' than a hood-eyed, hoodwinked, 'brother' or 'ally'.)

The truth is that the literary world – as also the spheres of political, labour, and religious activity – is shot through with often unrecognized rifts. The Afrikaners do not trust the English. The English libs tolerate the Afrikaner libs only in so far as they don't compete for the same commiseration. (There's a sense of 'turf' involved; just watch the widening irk between them.) And Afrikaners, however often they may go down to the springs of remorse and opposition, remain stained by their Afrikanerness. Whites more often than not still reflect the old insensitivities of the 'baas' to the Blacks, or else they attempt to communicate from the dock of the accused in which they sense themselves to be. Blacks look upon Whites with a rage and a distaste so overpowering that they have become inarticulate emotions. Blacks by and large regard the 'Coloureds' – and their strained attempts at identification with *Black* – with scorn. At best with distrust. The Whites consider the 'Coloureds' their poor and untrustworthy cousins. The 'Coloureds' are engaged in an old family feud with the Whites: they are the half-brothers banned from the dining room to the kitchen. They are caught in the cleft stick of pleading and threatening. (I had a communication recently from some Southern Brown writers who are having difficulty having their Afrikaans works published: 'insufficient literary value' is used as excuse by the publishers, meaning essentially that these authors are talking from within about a non-White environment, but the true obstacle lies with the political affirmation of the work. There is still a long way to go to complete cultural disaffiliation, before Afrikaans is taken possession of by those who intrinsically created it.)

Writers' solidarity is only page-deep – a lacquer holding the furniture of cracked inlaid patterns together by dint of demagogic shine. But these symptoms – the 'revolutionary racket' and the 'conceptual double-vision' – are normal in a situation where the old order (the gleet-oozing disorder) is violently rejected and the new one, already largely shaped, has not yet emerged or imposed itself.

Having said all this – how do we function in terms of a wholeness that is desirable but chimerical? What are the alternatives? How do we get out from behind our masks – that is if we can – that is if we deem it useful to do so? Do we want our public institutions, including the writers' organizations, to reflect the *reality* of South Africa? Which reality? The ethnic one? Then we are talking, surely, of majority 'rule'. Do we insist then upon 'minority protection'? (Thus institutionalizing the separate approach, 'separate but equal', which brought us to where we are; thus also reneging on our willingness not to see our society in a fractured way, but whole.) Does a 'middle ground' still exist, where a willingness to prevent the total rending of mutually woven fibres can even yet be negotiated? Or have things fallen apart irrevocably? Has the centre burst asunder? Can a 'middle ground' of shared cultural affinities be created?

Let's try a different tack: what are the levers for change in South Africa? Which are the rifts and the cracks through which a shift in awareness can be promoted, and how could these shifts presage and functionally provoke transformation, and transformation towards what is it that we want, and are we willing to be involved in a process without being able or allowed to foresee and/or control its parameters?

I cannot speak for the Blacks; I cannot help but speak as a White. A political 'middle ground' – not to be mistaken for state occupation, meaning centralized or 'legitimized' control over society's essential digestive functions – could have been established only were there to be, by now, say two to three thousand White political prisoners. (Because that fact would have denoted a significant pro-South African minority among the masters and the foremen.) That did not happen. And it is why the Whites are irrelevant to the revolutionary process – apart from being a component of the problem, the old order, and of being a minority whose position will have to be accommodated beyond takeover. A cultural middle ground, cushioning political excesses, could have been hammered out – had the White writers the foresight to break with their own tribal authorities, forcefully so, along lines of absolute solidarity with their Black colleagues, *even without any recognition from the latter*. This did not happen. We were/are too thoroughly depoliticized. Which is why our writing must oscillate between snivelling and despair; between sloppy romanticism and demagogic junk.

CAN ANY OF US SEE SOUTH AFRICA WHOLE? No, of course not. We are institutionally (historically?) incapacitated. And we have to accept the maiming, the limitation.

The goal – egalitarian, classless justice – we cannot quibble about. (But are we willing to see it through, even to its most blood-curdling implications? Are we ready to realize that 'peace' and 'law and order' serve only to shore up White privileges?) The slip-ups *en route* to understanding often occur in the misapprehension or the faulty appreciation of the points of departure. But we have to remain alert to the dangers of self-deception, to the siren voices of 'special pleading' as much as to those of self-deprecation. For instance: as a wordsmith aware of the political implications of writing ('there can be no dichotomy between writing and politics: *writing is political*') I could argue – well, yes, I must blow them out of the bathtub, see, I'm trying to yeast Afrikaner sensibilities from within and therefore I start with the bread we break together, even if only via the basic complicity of a common mumbo-jumbo, I mean language, I mean *taal*. How else could I have a say so? Ah, but how do I avoid the twisting and the bending, the kneeling and the back-stabbing, the compromises, the ethical corruption, in my attempts to 'hang in there'?

One is obliged to register that the commitments of Black and White writers will spring from different grounds – but the one need not be considered any 'better' or 'purer' than the other. Not even more essential. In fact, we share many of the motivations. We all need to purge, break down, come to clarity, cultivate responsibility, rebuild. We have to realize that we are fuck-ups, with treacherous failings, and we have to show some compassion – even where we don't understand or sympathize. It is possible to come to the acceptance of tactical alliances. It is above all primordial to realize that we are scaffolding convergent strategies.

But the harsh realization is there for all to see: White is *not* deemed essential by Black. (Even though Black will still accept the White hand-out, surreptitiously, late at night before the cock's third screech, at the bottom of the garden.)

No cause for undue despondency there. What we are experiencing is also a cultural revolution in action: a mixture of good intentions and distrust and manipulation and peacocking and politicking; 'more revolutionary than thou' put-downs; anti-'bourgeois' rhetoric; but at the same time a coming to grips with the complexity of the situation, with the shattered vision, with the *unthinkableness* of the options, with the horrors of our history, which, like it or not, we made together murder by murder.

I have to accept that Black is as much responsible for Apartheid as White is – without denigrating the heroic (if partly futile) struggle of Black resistance – while recognizing that the point of no return has been attained, that there is now a significant willingness to drown the pestilential Apartheid in blood . . . I cannot act differently from what I am . . . I cannot abide by my situation, or condition: it must be changed . . . I cannot allow my involvement to be decided by the acceptance or the rejection, the appreciation or the disregard, of my Black compatriots.

As a writer then one must continue pushing for the limits. Or keep testing and extending them. One must remain vulnerable and open to change, to other insights. One has consciously to cultivate a sense of insecurity (and *that* needs no magic, believe you me!) – in the absence of the courage required to commit suicide (to quote Graham Greene badly). One must also keep gathering the positive strands and warp and woof them into one's mantle.

The struggle in South Africa is finally and fundamentally also that of projecting conflicting readings. It is true that we, as Whites, must become conscious of our lack of relevance, and know that such a consciousness leads to pessimism if not negativism. Which, among other reasons, is why the appreciation of the struggle, or the image if you wish, is so important. Yes, if we are impassioned and detached enough a case can be made for a historically justified positive interpretation of present events. And that, surely, is also what we ought to be bending our pen-pecked minds to.

Paris, May 1985

A Letter from Exile, to Don Espejuelo

Dear Don,

You have asked me several times now what it is like to be living in exile. Let us then, as the saying goes, bring light to bear upon the matter. That is, let us be absolutely clear (I am eaten alive by the need to become clear): I am not an exile. I am not even an expatriate. I may be considered, I suppose, an *émigré*.

Why I say that? For several reasons. First because technically and legally I am not. No longer am I a political refugee: since December 1983 I have been a naturalized French citizen. For the first time in my adult life I can now live somewhere without being a 'foreigner' needing a *carte de séjour*: and I can cross most borders without the hassle of obtaining visas or worrying whether my forged documents will pass close scrutiny. I can be poor if I want to; I can go to Africa; I could even vote! No political refugee any more, but should we not look closer at the notion of 'cultural refugee'?

You see, I feel quite at ease in Paris. You mustn't forget that I had been living 'abroad' for well on fourteen years before going on extended leave into South Africa's intestines, and that returning from there on the fifth day of December 1982 was very much like 'coming home'. Remember too that I had been formed – or deformed if you wish – from an impressionable age, by the Parisian way of life, by European culture. Recently I came across a poem by a Latin American cosmopolitan, one of the *métèques* of many nations living in the capital, which said more or less: 'La France aux Français; Paris est à nous!'

Even now I am writing in the language of the hereditary enemy – English. With the consoling knowledge that in so doing I go to sea in a basket like all the other non-Anglos: the Indians and the Nigerians and the many-tongued Americans . . . I also write in French. Primly and properly so. With the requisite 'redundant' demagogic phraseology, stylishly crafted. I have caught on to the tune even if the words still elude me. In fact, a Ghanaian writer reviewing *Confessions* criticized me for using Gallicisms . . . Nevertheless, I remain the only Afrikaans-writing French poet.

Burnt Bird

Is the *émigré* author a parrot? You could say that I ought to be able to give a passable imitation of the European. Exiled? But then, can you imagine a more pleasant place of exile, had that been my fate, than Paris?

The implication, you may wish to remark, seems to be that my sojourn in No Man's Land burned me clean of any attachment to that ancestral earth. Yes and no. It is true that I experience a profound revulsion, shot through with pity, when I think of the Afrikaners, when I even hear Afrikaans! (The pity comes from seeing them foundering apathetically in the mire of their own making – a compassion one senses, for different reasons, for other population groups also. But disgust and pity remain debilitating sentiments.) And yet I feel that my entanglement with the continent has become more complex, my rooting more painful, my involvement deeper, my concern more acute. The hills, the smells, the birdflight, the boom of breakers and the rustle of wind through frost-crystallized grass, the pairing dance of cloud and sky – these and all the other shadings of memory have entered unto me; they are the ground of my being. John Coetzee, in a rather querulous review I came across, remarks upon the Afrikaner's attachment to the land. He implies that the Afrikaner writer's passionate and mystical descriptions of flatland and hillock exclude the non-Afrikaners, and in fact aver: this is our land, you don't belong here. An interesting point (forgetting for the time being that his own books are essentially a communion with the surroundings), and upsetting when you remember the Teutonic obsession with *Blut und Boden*. And it is indeed curious that the White African writer should be so acutely aware of the landscape, as if he needs to reaffirm his puny presence, or exorcize its cruelty or its hostility, or lay claim to it, or tame it by words – whereas the Black African writer quite obviously accepts the land as his natural and unquestioned dimensions.

But more than the land I have a sense of closeness with the people. Not an exclusive sentiment: I feel I can identify from within with all the poor bastards of that ravaged country – the cocky but obtuse White peasant boy, the insufferable captain of industry brimming over with charitable comprehension, the snooty city Jew, the tattooed Brown *skollie* or the prissy Coloured intellectual, the Indian coolie or the silly chap in business, the low-profiled China-man, the Black *tsotsi* or the African migrant labourer. Prison has destroyed the barriers and broken the stays.

More than any of these I feel an association with the human forces battling for betterment, projecting revolution – when that is the transformation of a stultified and fear-frozen society to one of greater social justice. I can identify with the good, with the potential good (the generosity, the solidarity, the tenderness, the will to resist, the respect for the other) to be found in some measure in any South African; knowing at the same time that the percentage of rottenness in that individual, as in me (the corruption, the collaboration, the hate, the despair, the dumbness and the numbness, the apathy, the hypocrisy), will be preponderant. I am the syntax of the people. The tense and the tenseness.

And beyond the borders of terror I feel at one with Africa, with the African peoples, with the resilience and the absurdity and the fragility and the poverty and the decadence and the inadaptability and the garishness of her cultures. With the swaggering dictator twirling his fly-whisk, the strutting murder-man toting his weapon, the gun-on-hip soldier, the poacher, the goatherd, the marabout, the beggar all heel and elbow. Africa humiliated. Africa in exile. Africa with rotten and greedy rulers, and beggar economies.

There are a few obvious remarks that need to be made. The history of exile, of people being displaced or being forced to become refugees, is as old as that of organized communal life, as ancient as the mountains. Or that of property and of power. Yet, despite the legalistic distinction made between 'forced' and 'voluntary' exile, I don't think anyone in his right mind will by choice prefer to live away from the intimate communication with his own people. Abdellatif Lâabi who, more than most, must have been prompted to leave Morocco, says that it is vital to stay 'home' for as long as you have the possibility of operating effectively. Crisp new words, he says, are being coined daily on the streets of Casablanca, and for the wordsmith it is terrible to be deprived of the enrichment. Language, for the writer, is of the essence of the equation; it is to the writer what religion or superstition or traditional cooking must be to others: root-nourishing security. Besides, it is important that there should be present alternative models for the youth particularly to look up to, in opposition to symbols of authority promoted or imposed by the government. Of course, when the choice is either prison or silence, then you move off to fight the silence by other ways, or to go and measure yourself against other shapes of muteness.

There are specific problems relating to 'exile'. Each nation state, conditioned by its history and the level of its moral reflection, has its own attitude to 'the foreigner within the gates'. The situation is complicated when the host nation hearkens back to a long-lost position of colonial ascendancy, which was often rationalized in terms of supposed ethnic superiority. It becomes especially bitter when the exile or the refugee originates from a country that has booted out the colonists. The right to asylum is not yet a universally recognized and practised conquest. The legitimacy and therefore the prerogatives and the privileges of the state (without which totalitarianism ultimately cannot develop) still take precedence over the rights and the protection of the individual. 'New' composite national communities – the Americans, the Canadians – seem to thrive on the influx of new citizens. Older nations, often in decline, are more hidebound, less accommodating to 'the other', despite their own chequered histories made up of different tribes and languages.

France, for instance, is not really a *terre d'accueil*. Maybe its claim to international cockiness is still too much alive to accommodate the foreigner, particularly if he is an ex-subject. Maybe its culture is too centrifugal, too codified, to recognize the extent to which it has sagged on the world market. And instead of admitting to the enrichment of *métèques* writing and painting in French, it is developing a relationship of cultural provincialism *vis-à-vis* America (borrowing from it, without really understanding or sharing the sources, striving for the *look*, trying to be *cool*, and simultaneously reacting against it). There is in France, worst of all, a latent – and less and less latent! – racism, compounded by conditions of economic stress. For instance, a Black person hunting for an apartment in Paris will not find it as difficult as in Pretoria, but every bit as hard as in London. The authorities do not combat the endemic racism vigorously enough. (Its timid policy concerning the immigrant families and its reluctance to do away with blatant White exploitation of New Caledonia, for instance, do not help at all.)

Still, *Dieu merci*, there is the tradition of tolerance of political dissidents exiled in France, of which every Frenchman could rightly be proud. There is also a strong minority awareness of the benefits accruing to France from the contributions of foreign artists and authors – from the East to Middle Europe to Africa to the Americas – having been grafted on to French culture. Less élitist: what a dreary place France would have been to live in were it not for the variety of minority cultures and culinary arts!

When I lay claim to not being an exile or an uprooted drifter (although I am a vagabond), it is also because I abhor the concept of exile, which goes clothed in a myth of romantic lamentation. I have seen too many of them – drenched in self-pity; at odds with themselves and blaming invariably 'the oppressors' or history; petrified in a time warp where the reference points are a rosily remembered past; victims to the corruption of suffering; up to their necks in dog-eat-dog exile politics. And too often have I observed the relations between exile and host: the slightly patronizing attitude of the master of the mansion to his unfortunate guest, suspending the critical faculties when judging his work . . . Only to tear him to pieces once the exotic aura has faded, especially once the intruder starts wanting to be treated on an equal footing . . . And the exile takes refuge in the comforting knowledge that he will 'never be understood'.

But, to return to the subject, what is it really like to be exercising the 'dur métier de l'exil', to be 'climbing up and down other people's staircases', to be 'changing countries more often than changing your shoes, despairing whether the revolt can ever bring injustice to an end'?

It is, when you are a writer, to be living *elsewhere* (*ailleurs*), to be writing *differently* (*autrement*). You live in an acquired linguistic zone like going dressed in the clothes of the husband of your mistress. It may be said that you are caught in a cleft mouth. You live and you write in terms of absence, of absent time (or in terms of a questioned present time). Not an imagined or remembered existence: more an absent presence. A state of instant reminiscence. With your tongue you keep searching for the aftertaste of remembered delicacies, and you may well imbue the tasteless fibres with an unexpected refinement. But the tongue keeps clacking against areas of dead palate. Your relationship with the world around you is that of the foreign observer. Or you turn in upon yourself, turn yourself over, observe the albino insects scurrying away from the light. And you taste a distaste, bloated as the tongue in its orifice of saying.

You risk the rupture of silence: either because the break with your milieu is finally too traumatic (you can't stand being painted into a corner), and the awareness of your declining faculties wears the few existing links down to nothingness; or (which is the same problem seen full face) you lose the sense of inevitability, you stop believing in the magic-making, you break with yourself. Writing, after all, is like breathing. Only more painful.

True, you never really relax. You never completely 'belong'. And yet – your situation is probably a blessing in disguise. Freedom, because that is where you're at, is a nasty taskmaster. You have so much more to learn. You are conscious of the *étrangeté* of life, and your senses are sharpened to needles with which you skewer the grey flesh of dull daily acceptances. Your head too is crammed with clichés and stereotypes, but at least you recognize them for what they are – in several languages! For better or for worse you are an outsider. You may be a mutant, for all you know – like a Jew in Poland or a Palestinian in Egypt or a Black in America! If so you are privileged. And, in a century of Displaced Persons and exiles and those fleeing famine or torture, you are in the position to share in and contribute to a historically important, and vital, human experience. (Not to say experiment.)

Take heart then. Lady Luck has smiled upon you!

With greetings from house to house,

BREYTENBACH
Girona, May 1985

A Letter to Winnie Mandela

Paris, May 1985

Dear Winnie,

When one crosses the mountains separating the Atlantic Ocean from the Indian Ocean, by the Old Cape Road, one arrives at a vantage point above the Silvermine Southern Atlantic Naval Head-quarters (largely sunk into the mountain) from where one can look down upon the maze of Pollsmoor Prison Command: *Maximum Security* – stark and inaccessible, with its watertower where pigeons nest; *Medium* – an agglomeration of bungalows enclosed by two fences of wire netting; *the White Male Prison*; the Women's Prison; the dog compound; the general stores and the workshops; the administrative block; the staff accommodation; the acres of carrots and cabbages and the Boere's playing fields; the watchtowers; the encircling wall . . .

South Africa in a nutshell. With all the demarcations and barriers afflicting that totalitarian society – racial, sexual, the hierarchy of rulers and subjects.

This is where, for the last three years, you have come to visit your husband. 'They' allow you to come regularly, I hope. Although each visit must make your heart go still. (Thus the universe of incarceration functions on petty regulations and a semblance of order.) This is where, for the first time in more than twenty years, they allowed your husband to touch an infant, his own grandchild. Oh, it is certainly a less terrifying place than that other devilish one of death and degradation, Robben Island, where he was imprisoned from 1962.

I find it difficult to comprehend the extent of the evil permitting people, who pride themselves on their Christianity, to keep some-one like Nelson Mandela in prison for so long. If any proof was ever needed to justify the people's cause, it has long since been amply provided by the obduracy and the fear with which the oppressors cling to their victims. Little could they know when they sentenced

213

him to 'life' that they were consecrating a life that would become a living denunciation of their callousness, their immorality, their pathetic efforts at using human beings as dollars and cents to bargain for political acceptance. A life that could now be neither broken nor humiliated.

His cell, as those of his close companions, is on the roof of Maximum. If the walls around the roof were not so high he would have appreciated the beauty of the mountain flanks signalling the changing seasons. Perhaps, during the strictly allotted half-an-hour morning exercise, he looks at the gulls and the clouds overhead being blown down to the nearby coast where waves wash over the rocks. When I left Pollsmoor metal workers (prisoners!) were putting the finishing touches to a rotating machine-gun nest, to be mounted on that roof. He wears rough, prison-made, dark green clothes. Year after year he is given exactly the same bland food. Exactly enough. Never a gram more. The authorities keep him in reasonable health – not out of concern for him, but, half-heartedly, to satisfy the exactions of the international community by exactly applying the minimum Red Cross standards. (And under their breaths they mutter about 'the cheeky kaffir'.)

What does he think about season after season? What does he read? He has continued studying. Through his pre-prison writings, tracing the struggle the way his life has since become a witness to history, we know the quality of his mind. From the comrades who have met him in prison we have learned that he has remained firm.

He has seen prime ministers come to power, prance and shake their bloody fists, and go into obloquy and oblivion: Verwoerd the fanatic, the ideologue plotting the disenfranchisement of millions, the deportation of tens of thousands, the death of thousands; Vorster, cruel as a pig, the executioner, the high priest of repression, giving shape to those mad dreams; only to be pushed from his dungheap by Botha the Party hack and hew, the destroyer of District Six, the invader of Angola, the man who wants to deploy the final nightmare by grandiosely (and with the complicity of the Western democracies) creating a 'constellation of Southern African states' on the broken backs of the South African people and their subjugated neighbours.

Your husband must know about the bitterness and the anger. He saw the gaols flooded with people who dared chant his name. They told him about the sporadic uprisings, about military incursions convulsing the neighbouring territories, about the martyred townships of Soweto, Sharpeville, Sebokeng, Langa . . .

He knows – because such is the reality of the country – of the

A Letter to Winnie Mandela

famine driving people to squatter camps, of the deportation centres, of strikes and boycotts and a breakdown of community life. He will know also that there has begun the terrible internal freeing of the people, a new resolve to drown Apartheid in blood. At what costs? See the numerous corpses littering our history. Some of them children still, shot in the back.

In vain? No, never. They will be remembered. Even if the outside world closes its eyes and its ears to the carnage. We are painfully moving from amnesia to memory.

The hands shooting down the people are the same ones handing him his rations. Could they silence or corrupt him? No, his example throbs in millions of memories, his voice is amplified by a multitude of tongues. His leadership – like that of Biko and all the others tortured to death, like that of Albertina Sisulu languishing in detention, like that of Tambo and all the others dead or alive in exile, like yours and that of other people like you hounded by the authorities, restricted and banned – patriots all – serve to enhance the dignity of mankind.

The inequity does not bear thinking about. And yet we must. We don't have the right to despair. And 'they' can no more destroy Mandela than they can escape from history.

I know you are proud of your husband, the father of your children and the elder brother of all freedom fighters. A meagre compensation perhaps for the anguish, the barren years, the harassment, the deprivations, the sacrifices.

Still, if we, as South Africans, have any chance to emerge from the barbarity of the present minority regime with some decency intact, it will be thanks to people like you and Nelson Mandela.

Please allow me to say how much I respect the quality of your lives, his and yours.

My heart goes out to you.

Africa will be free!

BREYTEN BREYTENBACH

Dear David

Dear David,

A few words. You will remember that I promised to write to you immediately upon our return from the States, while the impressions still had an aroma and a pungency, and because I didn't want to let the chance slip: the first insights are always the most penetrating, and 'America' is an important part of world consciousness, the upper or the sub. Also, suffering from writer's malformation – a drying out of life – I know that an experience doesn't exist unless written down. After which it's a wordworld. Your can't have it both ways.

Alas, it was not to be. To the normal mental paralysis was added the turbulence of Parisian life, the sprinting after deadlines, and I was sucked into committee existence. (We were preparing the Human Rights Conference.)

I tried, believe me, I really did try. I remember vividly how strange it was, back here, to drive my own 2CV. I had of course been spoilt by the car which the UCLA authorities had put at our disposal, the spacious automatic vehicle in which we could glide down Wilshire Blvd to the sea. Travelling in a powerful softly purring car and being isolated from my surroundings reminded me of nothing as much as being taken through the streets of Pretoria by the Special Branch . . . Now I was here forgetting to use the clutch, so that the engine would splutter and jerk to a halt, and Paris looked quite small and frail. (So easily one is corrupted!) And in my mind I wrote to you:

Dear David,

I want to write this down before it gets away from me. It is good to take a certain distance under your wing, to allow the writing to breathe (if I may thus again misquote Greene), but you still better get down to it before the images – nearly an anagram of 'magic' – fade.

216

Dear David

I sometimes regret not having adequately developed mental parts with which to squeeze experiences, transcribe random insights (insides), provoke and forge comprehension. Lack specialist discipline to harness thought and provide recognizable paradigm – but glad to be gadfly, dip into what I take to be philosophy, political science, psychology, structuralism, deconstructuralism, and a few more; makes for hodge-podge, but *naïveté* can be saving grace. Amazing grace . . .

Dear David,

Errant nonsense, naturally. Let me rather save what can still be, and filter it through the memory, whap it into a few paragraphs. To give you a leftover imitation of what I would have tried, succinctly, to give you then. Now just the gobs which survived to become clichés. I talk my best thoughts to death.

When you board an American flight you learn that the notions of space and order are quite different from those you are used to. People don't pay much attention to seats being booked, and vast amounts of 'hand' luggage are tolerated. You are also immediately served a glass of iced water. (This you would find wherever you went, from a traditional Hunan restaurant in Mott Street in Manhattan in the winter to a Mexican eating house in Los Angeles: the first thing you're given is a glass of water with ice, and after the meal you can have as much see-through coffee as you want.)

The women, often, are *quackadiles*. There are peculiar shapes common to all, be they Asian or Chicano or Caucasian or Black: the considerable lower back-parts, the shape or slope of the lips which must be due to pronunciation. You can recognize an American female by her turn of mouth. They practise a walk, or a slouch, which can probably be ascribed to the preference for low heels, but I think it has to do with wanting to project a Puritan-inspired image of unconcern, of innocence, of boredom even: 'We may be nubile but we *know* nothing of sex; we can't be wooed, only raped.' The older ones are often leathery despite fork-lifted appurtenances and areas of sucked-out fat . . . Many a time, during my lectures, I was quite correctly pulled up short for my sexism. But you will notice that as far as male chauvinism is concerned I'm an incorrigible backslider.

The men often have big feet. The pilots favour a Texan drawl. They are supposed to be flying cowboys.

New York. Into town from the airport in a limo. Air-conditioned, wall-to-wall carpeting, television with canned sport, bar, capped chauffeur. Tried not to have noticed how much of a peasant you are.

Burnt Bird

Felt the way a Third World migrant must react upon arriving in Paris. Overwhelmed. The first shock was how familiar it all looked. We, citizens of the world, have all had our inner scapes imprinted by American visuals, overtly or insidiously through fiction, documentary or advertisement. We recognized the steam hisscaping from the manhole covers, the skeleton pattern of fire escapes running down the backs of buildings, the box-like air-conditioners attached to outside walls, single men on the street clutching brown-paper bags from which they drank time and again with bobbing Adam's apples. The skyline of course . . . The second shock was realizing the extent to which one's vision had been restricted by your exported images. There were thousands of *ugly* people (and I had thought that all Americans were *glitzed* by their filmableness): obese ones, dirty ones, gnarled ones, and many who spoke no English at all or else a strange approximation thereof.

New York. To the Gramercy Park Hotel. The manager a French-speaking Belgian. Room, shower, washbasin familiar as a Hopper painting. Ice and slush on the streets. Gutters clogged. Slippery going. Mittened and hooded people jogging with flowering white breaths. Enormous, low, dark cars. Sometimes you see a car parked as if abandoned, but a thread of smoky life at the exhaust pipe. Inside a man would be sleeping, stretched over the front seats, one forearm protecting the eyes. The high wailing of sirens at night. All the lights in the tower blocks: like vertical cities. The immense beauty of some architecture, mirroring and remirroring an icy grandeur. Dead vacant areas immediately adjacent. The exhilarating lift of the heart to wander through the MOOMA or Frick House. The walls of the mind have to move to accommodate.

I remember the bitterly cold winds sweeping down the streets, of a cabby talking of 'taking de turn down toity-turd street', of the uncounted television channels emitting many languages. People spoke to you easily – in lifts, lobbies, on streets, shifting their hats and scuffling their feet. Lifts, in particular, are obligatory talking spaces. It was confusing to go out for a typically Sicilian pizza and to hear the owner and his workers converse in Arabic, being recent Egyptian immigrants. Until we understood that levels of commerce were taken over, from the bottom up, by new waves of arrivals. As the Greeks and Portuguese move up the Koreans will become the greengrocers, the Russian-exile cabbies will progressively be replaced by Haitians. In the process people grow into their 'older brothers" clothes, investing temporarily their national forms of commerce.

We met people. The interviewers can be dispensed with rapidly.

One sly young South African doe with woeful eyes, wallowing in the burns of an exile that was probably comfortably paid for by mummy and daddy, came to talk to me on behalf of the *Village Voice*. An intense, smouldering and unhappy young man, an Afrikaans poet in a brown coat, called De Witte (what an ironic name for a 'Coloured'), interviewed me for a radio station. He was upset at my referring to myself as a 'bastard'. Was I stealing his thunder? 'You may be one, but then a *special kind* of bastard.' Probably meaning a privileged self-proclaimed one. A bastardized bastard, as it were. I liked him. His line was the psychological one – that we have to exteriorize our conflicts. Burn clean! Homesickness! (Odd South Africans popped up at the readings.)

At Tom's discreetly chic place I shook some of the country's fine writing hands – Padilla (maudlin), Ed Doctorow, Bill Styron . . . And Rose, a radiant rose, with a rare depth to her compassion.

The publishers. That was after all what the American trip was all about. I think a real bonding took place. There was Roger, the jovial swashbuckler, sturdy as the best brandied oak, surrounded by a bevy of beautiful and brainy dames . . . And the exuberant blue-eyed young man with the long ears, Ganesh, my editor. He showed us a little of the town. On our last morning he took us for breakfast in Harlem. We had to find a Black taxi-driver; others don't fancy taking fares there. Soul food. Us pretending to be unconcerned, 'normal'. No room for glitsches. Ganesh chuckling up his coat sleeve. A roomy, roaming mind. A mind you can sit down at table with. Harlem desolate, poked-out-eyed blocks, decay, demolished cars under piles of snow . . .

Midway through the New York week I flew to Washington, from holding pattern to holding pattern, accompanied by the firm's Southern belle. A quick lunch at the *New Republic*. (The magazine seems to me to have one full-time obsession: Israel.) A long talk. Back to the airport for a view of its attaché-case-toting commuters.

Then Los Angeles. Balmy after the East Coast's sub-zero temperatures. Met upon arrival by Bob Kirsner, the kind-hearted professor. Whacky as a Californian Woody Allen. Wind in the palms. One-people cars.

I thought LA was one huge oasis. If New York might still have been comprehended by the European-shaped mind – being a 'city' with a 'centre' – Los Angeles was just an enormous mirage criss-crossed by freeways. The airport where we landed was smack in the middle of the agglomeration. LA is a country covered by human habitations, not a town. And Europe no longer exists – neither in the make-up of the people living there, who are mostly of Asian and

Mexican origin, nor in the public awareness. They are perhaps turned a little towards the Pacific, but more hedonistically to the self-perpetuating and self-absorbing image. By sun and by knife, by dye and by wig, by all possible means must time be held back. Death is a process of accelerated ageing. Tall palms dotted the horizon.

On the lawns of the campus clean-limbed, plastic-fresh kids were sunning themselves, imbibing sugar-free acids and eating cancer-free junk. Get your cancer now! Before it's too late! Don't wait! At night police cars patrolled the university city, with loudspeakers on their hoods or roofs through which they could address other vehicles. On television – there was never any transition between ads and news – show, all show – we saw a police tank ram a hole in a house to get at the boarded-up junkies. A man stood up after one of my conferences and said: 'You may be South African but the truth is still the truth!' Kirsner took us, alternately yakking and being his sensitive self, to a Zen centre (which had fallen apart because of the master screwing the disciples). On a wall, as you entered the Mexican quarter was written: *Kill Roaches Dead!* On the beaches gays of all hues were flexing their bloated biceps, rolling their hips and bunching their muscled buttocks. At Little Venice there was all of a sudden all the world's muck available: acres of trinkets and tawdry tourist gewgaws. People with Walkmans and dark glasses went whizzing by on their roller skates.

There were fantastic murals. I talked to an ex-ANC exile who berated me for what he thought were my 'red herring' attacks on the South African Communist Party. He (who had been side-lined because of deviationist nationalism, I suppose) reminded me that the Party had always been loyal in the struggle. 'Why do so many "minority people" belong to the Party? A need for identification, security, a future investment. It doesn't mean they're Communists . . .' I read about two 'Cabbage Patch' dolls getting legally married, in the presence of 200 guests. Maybe they had to . . .

I saw milk cartons with the photos of 'kids gone missing' on them. I heard a speaker pleading for equality for all, 'be they men, women or Hungarians'. A boy held up a dentist with a firearm, forcing him to remove the braces from his teeth. And in a reportage it was shown how all vital information pertaining to a person, reduced to a microdot, could now be implanted on a tooth. Eat up the facts of life! We went to listen to Michel Déguy reading his intricate poems in French, smoke from his cigarette making its way to the ceiling, as if he were back in intellectual Paris. No quarter given. I backed our car into the wrong parking entrance and curved steel spikes whipped up and ripped two tyres to pieces.

Dear David

We had lunch with some senior members of the *LA Times* staff, in a Japanese roof restaurant, exchanging views about the looming catastrophe in Southern Africa. Afterwards the lady and I walked through a part of the 'centre'. On a wall I saw written in an uncertain calligraphy: *The people are lying!/To Ther Self!* and a little lower down: *Keith dose not lie!*

People don't walk the streets in Los Angeles. It is illegal. Except in Watts. Hundreds of youngsters were wandering down the sidewalks there. The houses looked hardly any better or less uniform than those you can see in Soweto. In every yard there was at least one immobilized car with all its springs sprung.

Chief Gatsha Buthelezi was giving a talk in a distant college. We went to listen to him and to embrace him. There was an audience of five. He and his two aides were nattily dressed in the best American-tailored suits, and he carried a short authority stick. He was trying his damnedest, sweating, to undo the impression Bishop Tutu had left on the country, and hinted at commitments Botha had made to him to stop further mass removals. Unfortunately, unbeknownst to him, the boere had killed at least six squatters that very morning in a 'cleaning-up' operation at Crossroads . . . We met more odd South Africans and had supper at Leo and Hilda Kuper's house. A gentle, clear-headed, profoundly humane couple . . . I found California immensely rich in vegetation, but somehow none of it had any smell.

One Sunday we drove down to San Diego with Prince Mazisi and Mathabo, to have a brunch in a palatial hotel overlooking the ocean. We watched the gobbling scarecrows at the other tables. And then we drove back. Soon it will be one built-up area for hundreds of miles from LA to the South. Mazisi explained his views on human rights. It is a Western concept, he assured me – growing out of an urgent need. What is a 'right'? In Africa the accent is on responsibility and duty. There can be a violation of 'rights' only when the code governing the relationship between rulers and those mandating them is disrupted. But people don't *own* land, he said; people don't *own* people. And being human or not was a cultural concept, thus cancelling the ethnic differences . . . In the fireplaces there was the merrily lapping play of flames. I looked and saw that the logs were artificial, made of cement; the ash was probably fireproof wool; the flames were ersatz; the glow was a simulation. Newscasts mentioned buckets of solid human waste being dumped in space by the astronauts. On the small screen I heard an old geezer with a tear in the eye and a red nose speak of his 'infinite absorption in surfaces'. I thought I'd heard the truth at last. It was only much later that I realized he was referring to 'circus'.

Burnt Bird

And we flew to San Francisco for a night and a day. It was a relief to be somewhere again where you could define the beginning and the end of the city, where you could walk the streets. It is probably an arty-farty town. But beautiful. Reminded me very much of the Cape. Same up-and-downness. The harbour. The penitentiary island at large. The pastel-coloured houses. We went to browse in the City Lights bookshop and I was given some books by Lawrence Ferlinghetti. The hotel where we stayed was a monstrous ultra-luxurious palace of marble and copper and jade with gold-braided minions in huge halls. Our suite was on an executive floor. You had to feed the lift a code to get it to go up that high. We were stuck. We hadn't been trained in the art of living in places with music-making arse-warming toilet bowls. We lacked the manuals. A minion had to come and help . . . I took part in a live television show: with the two brown-pasted platinum-smiled spokespeople I sat on a stage that rotated slowly before audience and cameras and offstage a man stood holding up placards to tell people to CLAP! or to OHHH . . .

Time was up. We settled in for the long flight back to winter in Paris. Dear David, don't you think there ought to be a right to remember? We must have flown over the grey Atlantic sometime during the dark hours. And other islands of water. I watched *Country* for the third consecutive time (all Pan Am flights were showing it that month), and thought: I ought to write to David to discharge a debt.

Dont acte.

The very best,

KEITH

Early Morning

Early morning. Step out briskly heading for station early morning train back to Paris. Pavements puddly, rain snicking down tonguing hair and lapels. White headlamps prying into darkness as cars go swishing by. The radio in the hotel room predicted a 'nébulosité abondante' but I'm sure that was one man's cocked-eye view – one wee man locked into the wall. It must be quite something to live in the wall of a neutral space of encountering and passing, darkening dust, absence. See the couples come, slither into bed, copulate, stare glaucously at globe of TV scream, yawn-a-fart, and leave. Red neon signs for JUPITER all over the place. Station area Moroccan, Portuguese and Greek. Flags heavy wet.

Birds migrating. Grey trees winter draped from empty branches: volume in its skeletal dimension. Stretches of water like pewtered table linen. Morons going to work pushing hard with *parapluies* against sky. Skyline gritting clearer, water-logged. Pigeons fighting the damp cottonwool. Space for monks with bristled scalps and black wrists riding mules from one knðll to the next inn-enclosure. Other besotted pilgrims too. Mostly thieves and foreigners. 'Oh, baybee, 'tis a big wide world of forringers.' Psychology of landscape squeezed between words.

Swollen hearts. That's the way I'd describe writers feasting on the remains of others' suffering, dipping pens into the grey clotting blood of deprivation and of hunger, whispering with the torturer. Never wrong. Making big breast of the bleeding feelings. You get the beer-guts-and-balls writers. The bloated kind. Hemingway. Or the brainy soul-strokers. And then the morally outraged and the politically pyure, peddling injustice at the price of ladies' magazines. Swollen hearts.

When I was young I knew a man who went about with words. Vicariously he lived, picking at interstices of private trought, at rubbish mounds and duchesses' thighs. Knew how to keep himself aloof though. Not participating at all. To be exact: all take and no give. I thought: what a selfish bastard! How he usurps, squeezes and sucks without ever getting his mouth wet! But now I know that it was the need of his craft. The fat floating on the water. To be able to practise the giving of writing you have to block off zones of the self – let it lie fallow. Grey impenetrable and unthinking matter. That which absorbs without vibrating or transforming whatsit into ulterior usages. You have to be dead too to survive for the better.

And to plot areas of slowness. What a joy to move into *scheduled* scapes of nought reflection, of paging through *Penthouse* or watching the bird flubbing its flight over wet backs of fields swooping by train window! Neither sentinel nor sentence nor sense nor sententiousness. No other survival, no alternative return to the original inchoate.

And on. And what a privilege to have nothing to say. To sit there, to ass-ist (at) the slow unravelling of thought, the untravelling, and when asked once again to vomit an opinion – be it on the soul-icing of imprisonment or the whimpering of the flogged or the flought of the beard over capes or righting or the state of pootry or the latest nuise from Nomansland or the condition of Marilyn Garble's knees – to lean furrard intensely and to saygh: "Lookit tit hyere: I have nuffink to seigh!"

Brussels, 4 March 1985

Breytenbach by Espejuelo:
The Interview

ESPEJUELO: So you've done it, you fashioned your anthelion after all!

BREYTENBACH: Yes.

ESPEJUELO: I must say I can't quite grasp this book. It is slippery like the proverbial eel – neither fish nor flesh. And not only because of the mixture of genres, though that is upsetting enough and certainly can't please the distributors.

BREYTENBACH: I can only quote Kafka here who said that Truth has, or is, a human face; that is why it changes with time.

ESPEJUELO: You quote too glibly and too often, but you know it. That is not what I meant though. I'm trying to understand the inner reason for its shape. What is its coherence, if any?

BREYTENBACH: Well, it is, as I wrote to you in the *Pretext*, a put-together of papers which had been piling up over the years and I think I wanted to be shot of all of them, to move on to other areas. The cut-off point was quite arbitrary. I mean, before completing the book we had also been back again to Africa and from there we went on to Australia and came back up via the Far East and Italy. Very interesting trip. I wrote about it but I thought I'll save those papers for a second volume.

ESPEJUELO: God forbid!

BREYTENBACH: Eh, yes. Well, anyway, the papers are all more or less polemical, and about South Africa. I want to move out of this monstrous interregnum, to move away from old attachments, from the 'I'. To become the Other, I guess.

ESPEJUELO: Me?

BREYTENBACH: Yeah!

ESPEJUELO: No, I'm not going to prod you about your confused metaphysics. Polemical, you say? Political? I imagine for that you'd have to elucidate the terms you use so easily and, it would seem to me, so incorrectly. 'Struggle', for instance. And 'class' and 'racism' and 'oppression' and all the other catch phrases.

BREYTENBACH: But these words are self-explanatory, or clear within their contexts, surely. Besides, I don't think we should ah – attach too much importance to mere words, I mean, we shouldn't expect them to be original. They're just ah – handles.

ESPEJUELO: And to think that you were the one who claimed from a platform that the duty of the writer is to keep the word untainted, alive!

BREYTENBACH: Maybe I had to use them to get them out of my way, to be rid of them?

ESPEJUELO: That's the very easy way out. The eel's way again. Like just now when, it only struck me now, you had the arrogance to compare your book to Truth with an ageing face! Really! Still, if you used those words it implies that you saw yourself as being of the Left, I suppose. Am I right? And where are you now?

BREYTENBACH: Still on the Left, as ever. You know, as Mayakovsky would have said of words, perhaps even hackneyed ones, such as 'Left': 'Often, neither read nor printed, these words end up in the basket, but they get out again to gallop with the bit between the teeth.'

ESPEJUELO: Even under a Socialist government?

BREYTENBACH: Er–, yes, yes, I think so. In fact I'm sure. It is easy, it comes natural, when you are an 'intellectual' in France –

ESPEJUELO: Isn't 'intellectual' a specific and exclusively French kind of fart?

BREYTENBACH: Of course. What Mao called 'the stinking ninth category'. But I was saying that the intellectual always sees himself in opposition. It's much easier that way. You can blame 'them' for all your vague dissatisfactions. The authorities. It is the oldest temptation there is, to be against the Power. What can the concerned intellectual do? Support those who move in the right direction, even if you don't agree with them entirely. I think the leftist, or the intellectual, ought to look out for three traps. He should try not to become or be used as a precursor, a prophet or a procurator. Because he'll end up being just a procurer.

ESPEJUELO: Neatly said. And what would the right direction be, if I may make so bold as to enquire?

BREYTENBACH: For me, towards greater social justice. And to be resolutely against any and all forms of discrimination. Which must mean the same chances and the same responsibilities and the same laws for everybody. And it must lead to the liberation of people's creative energies, to a devolution of power, to real democracy, which surely must imply decentralization and people's power. I think furthermore that the right direction should establish, ah–, guarantees against oppression or abuses and transgressions of democracy. The army must absolutely be kept down, the police ought to be educated and non-political – particularly in France – and the snooping and spying agencies should disappear. To put it differently: the right direction, as far as I am concerned, would be a mixture of dreams and checks, of means and limitations and limits. But no more of this obsolete 'dictatorship of the proletariat' nonsense. I can't see revolution as an option anywhere in Europe. It's different in the Third World though.

ESPEJUELO: Well, well. As simple-minded as ever. And what makes you think the developed world can just stand by and see world money or market systems go to hell because of upheavals in the banana countries?

BREYTENBACH: Of course they won't just let it happen. They've been interfering all along. The desperate conditions in the Third World are by and large the legacy of Northern domination and manipulation. No, in matters of conflict between North and South I'll always be a Southerner.

ESPEJUELO: Has the Left, by which I mean the present Social-Democrat Government, been satisfying your fierce criteria?

BREYTENBACH: In some areas, yes. In others obviously not. I'd say they haven't even gone half my way. I'd have to ask: do they really *know* what they want? Do they *really* want it badly enough? Have they been realistic? No, they could and should have mobilized the people for their cause. But then the Opposition was very clever in outmanoeuvring them, stymieing them on the real issues and enticing them to give battle on false fronts. In this way a ridiculous climate was created. Remember the row about private schools? Or the colonies? Were the Republican power structures and temptations too strong for them? Were they corrupted? Was there too much of an inbuilt administrative resistance? Anyway, they squandered a historical opportunity by not moving resolutely ahead when they had that vast support and parliamentary majority. And now they seem to be concerned only about saving their skins. Still, I think they have made some excellent progress, some of which cannot be undone by the Right. In culture, for instance, although they won't leave behind much *structural* support for the creative people. And in justice. By doing away with the death penalty. By liberating radio and television. By making some hard but necessary

Burnt Bird

choices in the shift from bankrupt labour-intensive industries
to computer technology – from quantity to class, as it were. In
the field of Human Rights. But their foreign policy was all show
and no substance, their nuclear policy – the weapons, I mean –
an aberration, their labour and education policies disastrous
and cowardly.

ESPEJUELO: Do you think the Right would have done better?

BREYTENBACH: Of course not! Not on your life! I was hoping that
the Left would by now have made the Right as obsolete and
prehistoric as they are in effect! And instead –

ESPEJUELO: Don't you also think liberalism is the wave of the
future? Those smooth-faced and reassuring technocrats.

BREYTENBACH: Don't tease me, please. There is no liberalism. It's
the same sorry old ideas promulgated by the same people – just
a little balder now, or wearing thicker glasses. Surely they still
hold sacred ideals and practices I could never agree to. The law
of the strongest. Elitism. Kow-towing before the idea, the
chauvinistic altar of 'the state'. No, they are only too keen to
exploit ingrained prejudices, which they share. They feed on
the illusion of national or private superiority. They always want
to lead, to think *for* me. They are anti-egalitarian and anti-
worker. Not, you'll say, that the Left has been brilliantly pro-
egalitarian or pro-worker. Not much. But what's weakness on
the Left is constitutional on the Right! No, never!

ESPEJUELO: And South Africa?

BREYTENBACH: Ah, yes – I was going to forget. I think there's a real
danger, were the Right to return to power, that they'd try and
undo Botha's isolation and bring him in from the cold, as it
were, and be the intermediaries also for his renewed
penetration of Africa. Luckily, though, internationally co-
ordinated rejection of the White State should be so strong by
then that even the French Right could not go the opposite way.
That is, if the British and the West Germans could be forced to
swallow their greed.

ESPEJUELO: I see. Just as I thought. If I were to make sense of it all, as
a political profile, I'd say you're an anarchist.

BREYTENBACH: Maybe, yes. An undogmatic leftist anarchist. I'd
pass for 'terrorist' in many countries.

ESPEJUELO: You have the mouth for it. Do you see yourself as
French?

BREYTENBACH: I live in France.

ESPEJUELO: And South Africa? Do you think you'll ever return
there?

228

The Interview

BREYTENBACH: No. I could be rhetorical, smart-arsed, and say: *I am there*. But no.

ESPEJUELO: OK. Don't. That'll be all, thank you.

BREYTENBACH: It's a pleasure. And thank you, sir.

Paris, July 1985

End Notes

Like lightning it flashes through the shadows, severing the spring
wind.
The god of nothingness bleeds crimson, streaming.
Mount Sumeru to my amazement turns upside down.
I will dive, disappear into the stem of the lotus.

Sesson Yubai

On the epigraphs and part-title poems

When the Chinese Zen monk Wu-hsüeh Tsu-yüan (1226–1286) was threatened by invading Mongol (Yüan) troops, he composed a four-line poem to express his indifference. Years later, in 1313, when the Japanese Zen monk Sesson Yubai (1290–1346), who was studying in China, was imprisoned by the Mongols and faced with possible death, he took Tsu-yüan's poem and used each line as the opening verse of a new poem.

I gleaned the poems and the above information from an anthology of Japanese poetry, *From the Country of Eight Islands*, edited and translated by Hiroaki Sato and Burton Watson, an Anchor Press edition of 1981.

Boland *p.37*

Written in Afrikaans upon receiving a phone call from a friend in South Africa. Helderberg (Clear Mountain) is situated just to the east of Cape Town. My wife and I had passed by along that coast one night when the mountain was on fire, it must have been during 1966, on our way back from Mozambique to Lisbon.

The Fettered Spirit *p.40*

This paper was written for the March 1967 issue of the *Unesco Courier*. Most of the ideas repeated elsewhere, or developed later, can already be found here. Note the reference to the attempt at force-feeding Blacks on Afrikaans. This policy – under the aegis of A. P. Treunicht, the ex-minster with the soft white hands washed clean of blood, who has since led his followers out of the governing National Party to found the Conservative Party – would ten years later be the trigger firing the 'Soweto events'. Some of the laws and institutions referred to have been amended during the intervening years, to be made more subtle (e.g. censorship) or more harsh (the notorious 90-day and 180-day clauses in the Security Acts have been dropped, to be replaced by the brutal and unimpeded custom of

indefinite detention; police and army torture is now far more
widespread than it was then). The underpinning matrix of minority
power monopoly maintained by exploitation and oppression has
not changed at all.

A good deal of the banned works of the time, those of the so-
called 'Drum' generation, are now belatedly, reissued by David
Phillip Publishers of Cape Town.

Cultural Interaction *p.44*

My contribution to the 'Cultural Rights as Human Rights' Conference
organized by Unesco, in Paris, 8–13 July 1968. I don't think I have
much to add to the platitudes then uttered. I use the word 'platitudes'
advisedly because, in retrospect, so much of what I said consisted of
pious wishes couched, moreover, in the leftist language so modish
then. On the other hand I do not disavow any of the commitments
expressed. My reading of the situation may have been simplistic
and my reactions to that no more than fiery declarations of intent,
but I still count myself on the side of the less privileged, of those
who had been colonized. I shared many *tiers-mondiste* misconceptions
though, or rather a romantic vision of Africa particularly, and by
implication an overestimation of the role that the concerned outsider could hope to play.

Years later the question would be: Where are we now?[1] The
concern with cultural interaction, between the ex-colonizers and the
ex-colonized at least, or between rich nations and poor ones, can
partially be found in the concept of North–South dialogue. But what
kind of conscience and consciousness are we implying when we say
'North–South dialogue'? Does this dialogue, assuming that it does
exist, translate a true need? What sort of *rapport de forces* is channelled
and fed by it? Are the relationships changing? And to what extent
do the situation and the role of South African impinge on North–
South relations?

[1] Adapted and translated from a paper read at the conference on 'Human
Rights and North–South Relations', organized by the International Federation
of Human Rights in Paris, 17 November 1984. Abridged.

Have cultural expressions been devised for the history, the relationships and the contradictions between North and South? Can cultural conceptions and expressions have the function of transforming values, which, in the end, may promote a political transformation? And how then, within that context, to identify the responsibility of the writer?

One has to learn to live with the taste of ashes in the mouth; to learn also that the roots of inequality are more deeply embedded than one ever thought; that liberation or redressment cannot be brought about by winged words but through changing the power relationships, by an in-depth politicization, through an extended struggle, which ceaselessly renews its forms, and maybe by the patience of many generations.

For some time already we have witnessed a devaluation in the way the Third World is perceived. Against the background of an economic crisis we passively accept the continuation and even the accentuation of inequality and exploitation. (This famous crisis, it must be said, certainly has many causes and manifests itself in multiple ways. In developed countries it is the result of capitalism's internal contradictions, provoking a profound economic mutation ... which in turn brings about the tearing of social fabric and certainly also a modification in its relations with the rest of the world. The crisis means the economic stagnation of Socialist societies, the diminishing of that hope which was the moving force behind the struggle for human values, for a better world. And in the Third World? I'd say the 'post-liberation blues': the folding of survival systems, political chaos with wars and bloody dictatorships succeeding one another, impoverishment, large-scale hunger ...

And yet, despite our disenchantment, we cannot deny the absolute reality: the world is one. If we hope to avoid barbarism or a return to feudalism – or worse, accepting a world order with one super power and the rest of us brought down to caretaker states or to kneeling colonies – and if we expect to live with a minimum of dignity: we must accept that putting into practice the principles of respect for 'the Other', of co-operation and cohabitation, translated as cultural policies also, is not a matter of charity: on the contrary, they are vital necessities. To realize that we are interdependent is but seeing clearly.

We cannot allow this North–South dialogue to become just another metamorphosis of colonialism, a new sharing out of markets and natural or human resources. It must be a true interaction. And within the framework of this unavoidable interaction the plague of racism – humiliating the other and demeaning the self –

threatens to play an ever larger part. Already, here in France, we have a recrudescence and a banalization of racist sentiments; we see a strengthening of corporate reactions, of national egotism.

The reference point for racism and racists, the example you may say, remains South Africa. That racism is the underlying motivation will be camouflaged. But the eventual creation of a 'constellation' or confederation of Southern African states – supported more or less ardently by some Western powers – will indeed be based on the assumption of the superiority of Western cultural values, on racism and exploitation, even if – to achieve their goal – South Africa's masters were to jettison all the appearances of Apartheid. (Over the years the White masters' propaganda has made large inroads into a more than willing Western awareness. It is disingenuous only not to pinpoint the origins. Examples: South Africa is a country of minorities, the Afrikaners being the largest single group, so why shouldn't they rule? Left to their own devices Blacks, because of tribal differences, will exterminate one another. Blacks are better off in South Africa than anywhere else on the continent. South Africa is the only bulwark in Africa against Communism. The Kremlin masters scheme night and day to subvert South Africa, and thus the West; in fact, winning South Africa is a major priority for the Soviets; in fact, South Africa is a foyer of East–West conflict; in fact, there's a co-ordinated worldwide 'total onslaught' against South Africa, which justifies a 'total response'. Apartheid – please call it 'separate development' or 'separate but equal freedoms' – respects the cultural diversities in the land; it protects indigenous cultures and allows them to develop without having to face the more abrasive Western technological superiority. South Africa is strategically important, because of its geographical position and its mineral wealth. South Africa is a peacemaker. If you don't deal with us, the moderate Whites, you will have terrible reactionaries facing you. The way to progress, adaptation, change, goes through the White man. We share the same values, after all. You are being manipulated. Do you really wish *uhuru* for South Africa? Look what Africa has done with it. Look at Uganda, Ethiopia . . . etc., etc . . .)

That, after all, is why we claim that South Africa is a threat to peace in the region.

That is also why the struggle waged for the liberation of the country, for one nation reflecting all its cultural richness, for a democratic majority government guaranteeing the respect for human dignity, for a resolutely anti-racist society – is important way beyond its borders. South Africa is in a sense a melting-pot of history, a socio-political and cultural laboratory.

There is no possibility of the majority accepting, forever, their exclusion from full political participation. Replacing a minority dictatorship and their totalitarian state by majority dictatorship will not be acceptable. South African Whites are African; they are there to stay. The solutions to the above problems will come about within a Black socio-cultural field of references, for the Whites – petrified by ignorance and anguish, encrusted by prejudices – are culturally incapable of conceiving or accommodating transformation.

One way out is the need and the challenge painfully to forge an Azanian identity fed by a variety of cultural sources. And it is through this absolute obligation to find the means of coexisting in a just state, respecting and understanding 'the Odder', that our struggle and our solutions are exemplary. It is this contribution to human experience that will give a cultural sense and content to the North–South dialogue.

Beda Breyten *p.49*

Translated from Afrikaans, excerpted from a notebook, which could tentatively be called *Nightbook/Selfdigestion*; dated 13 October 1970 to 14 June 1972. The book was a kind of collage – impressions, dreams, outcries, trial runs, jotted down conversations, quotations. Such as: 'L'individu, dans son angoisse non pas l'être coupable, mais de passer pour l'être, devient coupable' – from Kierkegaard, used by A. London in his *L'Aveu*. Or: 'When you cease dreaming you are dead. When you stop someone from dreaming you first make him mad and then you kill him. *Quos vult perdere Deus, dementat prius*. It is the technique used by Major Swanepoel and his team of torturers . . .' – a reference to the no-sleep interrogation methods used by South African security policemen. Or again: 'Thou shall not miss thy excretion.' Or also: 'But the White man has a horrible, truly horrible, monkey-like passion for invisible exactitudes.' From D. H. Lawrence's *The Mozo*.

Somewhere in that book there was a description of a meeting with Mb. Mb., who, I should point out, was a gifted writer. I used to see quite a lot of him and then, one day, after I'd lent him a small amount of money, he disappeared from view. I learned many years later that he was too poor to pay me back – he was always down and out, sometimes having to pass the night in public places – and too ill at ease and angry finally to show his face. I have pictures of him in my mind, dating from earlier times: Mb., carrying an outsize alarm clock on a length of twine, in his trousers pocket, to wake him before the janitors open the building to the public; Mb., perched on the toilet off the communal staircase of our building, reading Shakespeare aloud, on his head a crown-like contraption with several candles, 'to save electricity'. Years later, in my cell in Pollsmoor, I was surreptitiously reading a scrap of newspaper smuggled to me by another inmate, when I came upon a photo showing a typical street scene on the Place du Tertre, Montmartre. A folkloric painter with matted beard and bushy Afro was drawing the portrait of a tourist. It was the mug of Mb., converted to painting, no doubt still fighting for survival. Since my release he has called me once on the phone, introducing and describing himself, and addressing me as 'Mister Breytenbach'! I also saw him coming up from the *métro* one day, obviously as poor as ever, a bulky knapsack slung over his shoulder. He explained that he was writing again, that he had nearly finished a book, in fact that he had the entire manuscript right there with him. It won't be long now.

In the notebook I find: He believes that de Gaulle was a god, that he will rise again, appearing on the street among us: 'a Gaullist who will speak with the voice of a man and who will even resemble him physiologically'. Then he clasps his knees, squatting on his rumpled bed, lays his head against the cupboard at the foot of it and says – 'When times are like these then we must stay close to the gods, just like this, just to hear them talking, close to heaven, yea man . . . I thank God that I believe in Him again . . .' And he goes on to explain how he's selling Black Panther leaflets nowadays, that the police sometimes hassle him on the street, but that he could never belong to any organization since he believes too sincerely in 'love', pronouncing it as 'loff', with a respectful mien ('which is modesty, not asking for much, not taking responsibility, just a little love') and because it isn't *in* him to be supporting any political cause. 'I just can't adapt. I don't have it in me. They will have to put it there. But I think I have no holes in which it can be put. I sit here in my room and I watch the world and I realize I am a man without holes . . . I cannot join shit! . . . What is it that I've done? . . . Why can I not make progress?' And he also says: 'There are enough cows in the world for every man to have his steak . . .' I think he must be such a lonesome man that at night, upon returning home to this room, he probably knocks on the door to invite himself in as an eagerly awaited visitor.

Some of the entries are hard to decipher now. I come across the following, for example, written no doubt under the influence of cocaine:

It is within the reach of any human being to become a dwarf. In contrast to popular superstition dwarfs are not *born* that way – one *becomes* a dwarf. Indeed, each of us carries his dwarf within him . . . I know a dwarf. His name is Lasarus. I don't know what he was called prior to that. Perhaps Jan Blom. His clothes stink. And the sea is as pretty as a red motorcar . . .

The terrible part of it is that this Breyten-I in me, this *dédoublement de moi-même*, is an unreasonable monster with the red eyes of a beast. That he – perhaps he thinks the same of me – should neither speak nor understand any language. I am a silent, incomprehensible animal stalking myself, intent on killing.

When I see my self all my hair stand on end from some primordial fear. Caught in the fork of the spirit . . . Words are the parasites living in the wound of experience . . . Experience is the blood welling through the cut . . . A man who speaks is an unclean man . . . But: the abhorrent thought in and about death is: that you *then* lose it. What if you were dead and should realize that it was not a wipe-out, that your awareness atomized with every maggot and digested molecule will go into the world – and then that no further death (wipe-out) will ever be possible! . . . If I could only get myself together again, all the parts of my body, *then* I could die. Self-knowledge, nirvana – which death is – is only being whole . . . For as long as I crawl over the earth – in all directions, an imperialist and an exploiter – I shall be doomed to live, given to the incompleteness and the diaspora – and for just as long my words, the ant spies who are to look for me and drag me back to the anthill of the grave, the ant-chamber, will flow from me. My search is a blind white queen . . . My homeland is a conception. If I could confine myself to one single comprehension, then I'm dead . . . (Don't look at everything your eyes see) . . . If I had to stop lying I should not be able to create any more . . . Written in darkness . . .

Satan – what a mellifluous sound! – was an angel . . . His wings pure flames folded around the shoulders and there was the tang of sulphur. The swallow smells of gunpowder. The swallow chalks its flight against the heavens. Since that time all angels have been wearing swallowtail coats. And as you get ready to exchange the steam-cosy atmosphere of the inn for the street outside where wind sweeps hither and yon like invisible flags of ice – but you have to go, and you are prepared to face the snow and the crystals belling from gutter lips – and your heart softens when you look at the rounded and scorched shoulders of the bald-headed angel waiter so that you try discreetly to slip him a tip, which is declined with a sad little smile while – to help you over the discomfort – he bends to gently try and remove with his napkin a drop of spilt wine from the snowy-white tablecloth, you wonder whether the sparrows too will burst when, frozen like glass shouts, they plunge from the skies on to the pavements below, and whether the beads of blood like rubies will capture the diffused light, to capture and to render. Penetrate more deeply the successive layers of absurdity. Comprehension is Absurd. To go exploring for the lost. Frontiers are points of rest, breathing places. But on purpose! Half-way to heaven he stopped, took off his wings and plucked the thorns from the feathers. And the old people will tell you how red the snow was that day.

Once upon a long time ago . . . Because, taken the other way: the angel is a devil. Sometimes when you run into him on the street you notice the sooty stains on his sleeves. His face is sunken and of a dark red hue about the eyes and the nose. You sense – since you cannot see it – the sombreness and the sadness of his flesh under the garments. He doesn't look you in the eye; in fact, he is never very forward. And if you dare peer into his eye sockets you also will perceive nothing there, or everything as if from afar: you see the universe's blindness as if through the arse end of a telescope: a shrivelled fruit. Then you realize he is so blind that he can see everything, that he is blind because he has seen it all. You take him home with you and draw up a chair for him close to the open fireplace. With his sinewy hands stretched over the leaping licking laughing living fountain of flames he thaws. And out of sheer gratitude he will try and convey an exceptional message to you. Even if it is any old message, even the repetition of scraps and pieces of warped reminiscences, even babblings and gargle-talk – don't deny him. What does it matter to you after all? Brush the dandruff from the lapels of your grey coat and summon Lasarus from the kitchen. Let Lasarus on his odd little legs come to serve you: each a goblet of red-deep wine. And touch his glass with yours, here's to the health of God . . .

Marti has said: 'It is the tree under which the body is buried that will grow the highest.'

The poor man cannot buy a leper's kiss.

Travel pains: We think because we no longer know. (A poet said that.)

Culture is what you have left when you have forgotten everything else.

If a weak baboon is attacked by a stronger baboon it has two means of escape: it can offer up its awful plum-hued rear for passive inter-course or it can mastermind and lead an attack on an even weaker baboon.

I am a translation of myself.

Exile – but I prefer the term 'isolation', because 'exile' is too melo-dramatic, it has the appearance of tragedy – is a method of maiming. It implies that you are turned in upon yourself, that you unremittingly try to fix your place and value in society, without finding a natural outlet in a shared culture or language for your worries and your reflections. There cannot be much intercourse between you and those sharing your concerns: the problems of your country, your language. The little contact you have is easily misunderstood or overestimated. Man is a beast of contact and it is not realistic to expect the incidental contacts over long distances to replace daily communion. Man's obsession with his own shadow is a waste of time. Isolation is arrested growth. I don't know whether I'd have been as aware of the symptoms of decay had I remained in South Africa . . . Does an early dismantling also mean the mummification of a youth? Can my youth thus be preserved? The heart must be pickled. I go looking for death behind the hills, to stay out of its claws . . . I could not decompose to clarity. I shan't be part any more of that wished-for new country – for that I am too full of scars, too impure. But my failure doesn't mean that clarity cannot be obtained along this way. It just shows that the I can only develop as a living part of the us.

Thus far then the plundering of the notebook. The letter included here seems to indicate that snow came early that year to Paris. The Bedouin referred to was Ahmed Baba Miské, at one time the Mauritanian ambassador to the United Nations, then the director of a publication called *Afrique-Asie* to which I contributed upon occasion. The court-martial in Burgos must have been when Puig, an anarchist activist, was condemned to die grotesquely by *garote vil*. I remember writing a poem about the event. There is an error in the letter however. Mr Breytenbach, who died, was then 32 years old, not 40 as stated.

Vulture Culture *p.53*

Published first in *Apartheid*, edited by Alex la Guma, International Publishers, New York; Lawrence and Wishart, London; Seven Seas Books, Berlin; 1971.

End Notes

The Writer and his Public
or Colonialism and its Masks *p.62*

[i]

This contribution was prepared for a Unesco meeting of 'experts' on the theme of 'The Influence of Colonialism on the Artist, his Milieu and his Public, in Developing Countries', which took place in Dar-es-Salaam, 5-10 July 1971. It was an enriching occasion to discover that part of Africa and to make the acquaintance of fellow participants and others then still living in Dar: Samora Machel, Marcelino dos Santos and his wife, Armando Guebuza, Sergio Vieira, Wole Soyinka, Sheikh Ahmadou Diop, Andreas Shipanga, Baba, the Chinese ambassador, Frene Ginwalla, Boutros Ghali, the representatives of the Vietnamese National Liberation Front, Duma Nokwe ... On the terrace of the New Africa Hotel I had the privilege of shaking Dr Livingstone's hand.

In its final report the participants described colonialism as a complex system made up of more than just political and economic exploitation, and claimed that its effects lingered on even after the withdrawal of the imperialist masters. A more virulent form existed culturally – cutting up indigenous thought-worlds and languages through artificial borders; imposing on the people foreign languages, cultural forms and religions; assimilating a small local élite, thus severing it from the population as also from the élites and the masses of other colonies; disparaging indigenous culture, relegating it to a subculture. The loss of national identity led to the suppression of a colonized people's creative functions.

It was observed that local cultures and their artefacts were deliberately plundered, and history was deformed to make it compatible with the colonial phenomenon. It was felt that the masters' imposed culture was more materialist, that it was backed by a socially divisive religion, that it propagated an entire system of new values.

Colonialism, it was agreed, violently interrupted the evolution of indigenous cultures, and deprived humanity for centuries of the Third World's contribution to universal culture. The masses, less tainted than others by the colonialist impact, remained the guardians of homegrown culture, even if that was largely oral.

It was clear that the Third World still suffered from more or less dehumanizing forms of cultural domination – ranging from the extreme example of South Africa, through the Portuguese-dominated territories, through more subtle and complicated shapes of internal colonialism and neo-colonialism to the degrading situation of American Blacks.

The task of the developing world was seen as the acquisition and the development of the means of people's liberation, including that of their cultural energies . . . in a spirit of renovating the traditional heritage whilst eliminating retrograde or oppressive aspects . . . adapted to modern needs . . . within the framework of national construction . . . and evolving the sense of identification of oppressed peoples all over the world. It was recognized that certain tribalist characteristics had to be done away with without thereby shrivelling the roots of the artist.

It was considered essential that new societies be promulgated as bases for new cultures and that these could not be brought about without the total and active participation of local artists – indispensable as long as the community's goals were not clearly manifest within the newly created frameworks.

The meeting defined the new artist as someone with a sharpened conscience and a profound attachment to his people, a researcher in his own community, an interpreter of that society to itself and to the outside world, an intermediary, receiving from and not just giving to the people, an integral part of his or her community, of its aspirations, reclamations, economic objectives, its cause and its struggles.

The meeting thought that the language or the *form* of expression was extremely important, even if the *contents* of the artist's message remained primordial . . . Thus the importance of African languages was underlined, and it was deemed desirable that these should replace the colonizer's language in communication and artistic creation so as to: speed up the development of national consciousness and the realization of cultural potentialities; activate the fight against analphabetism; struggle against psychological and moral traumas; promote economic and social development and the interaction of the continent's peoples; obtain the adoption of one common language for the whole of Africa.

Still, the participants reckoned, spoken languages ought to be transformed into written ones; notice had to be taken of the fact that Africa was not yet entirely free and that national languages had to be used wherever possible as liberation instruments; the African languages had to be selected (or preferred) to promote a forming of linguistic macro-units, prefiguring the creation of larger African groupings, a necessary step along the road to uniting the continent.

How we dreamed, and what weird loops fate had in mind for

some of the people I met then! Some returned 'home' to ministerial posts; others went on to prison or to meet Big Mammy Death, the ultimate colonizer; still others became the victims of internal power struggles or sank into oblivion with hardly a bubble of gaseous commitment translated into writing; one at least turned his coat and went to share the crumbs from the master's dishes . . . The final report was quietly shelved by Unesco . . .

[ii]

Politics certainly would not merit even the slightest energy were it not justified by a cultural project.

Aimé Césaire

If one were to paint the picture of Human Rights in the Third World it would be macabre indeed. True, there has been the formidable period of decolonization. But then reality shows us that it was in most instances a process of independence in name only; on the political maps of school books the territories changed colour, but nearly everywhere the colonial governors were replaced by captive native élites, and economic dependence deepened. Of what use is independence if you lack the means of giving satisfaction to the wishes of the people for a decent life, for the right to dignity, education, creating? And how could the 'national' authorities be responsive to their peoples when their role was to be that of conveyor belts for capitalists or colonial interests? How could corruption then be avoided? And what could they do to avoid being despised by their own? Worse, in some cases – witness the Nkomati and Lusaka agreements – we saw a resurgent colonialism.

Abroad, in the metropolitan countries, there has been a revival of colonialist sentiments coupled to a disaffection with so-called Third Worldism (*tiers-mondisme*). In France, where the Old Right had been reaffirming its presence in new brown-shirted shapes, the cudgels were taken up by the 'new philosophers' – penitents and *transfuges* from the New Left of the late sixties. This 'new realism' was expressed in their indifference to the catastrophes of the Third World, and in a revalorization of 'European' values and interests accompanied by a re-evaluation of all internationalist commitments.

The intellectual, concerning the Third World, does not blame himself for having sinned through cowardice or being blind or ignorant (although his ignorance was often abysmal). His only self-reproach is for having been excessively generous due to an 'idealism' which, as we know, is a sign of youth.

Antenne No. 4, January 1985: a Parisian newsletter

These protagonists of 'pragmatic liberalism' and of 'scientific strategies', in their efforts to 'demystify' history, claimed that the ex-colonial powers had no debts to the ex-colonies neither moral nor, especially, material. Simultaneously they launched an all-out attack against the averred *tiers-mondistes* (formally during a colloquium of 23 and 24 January 1985, organized in the Senate in Paris by an upstart formation calling themselves the *Fondation Liberté sans Frontières*, on the theme of 'Le Tiers-Mondisme en Question'). They taxed the *tiers-mondistes* with having a narrow 'economicist' vision of the world, ascribing economic causes to all phenomena. In this view food shortages would be the fault of the world economic system dominated by the industrial powers. Third Worldists, they said, apply a diagnostic deformed by catastrophism which locks the people of the 'South' in the role of victims and makes of the 'North' a fortress of egotism, cynicism and wealth. Furthermore, they said, it is a one-way analysis of the origins of underdevelopment: the West plundering the Third World, the deterioration of exchange terms, the grinding power of multinationals, the breakdown of 'green revolutions', the development of export crops to the detriment of staple food . . .

These analyses (of the Third Worldists) were then supposed to lead to the putting forward of a number of solutions: a new world economic order, similarly a new world order for information, the scrapping of foreign debts, self-centred development – that is, independent of world markets, the introduction of 'appropriate' or assimilable technology . . . More precisely the Third Worldists were assumed to be asking for a price regulation of basic foodstuffs and raw materials, for the introduction of fair exchange rates, for the wipe-out of crippling debts, for a break in the Western news agencies' monopoly on information, for the creation of pro-development information services, for the valorization of social and economic rights as opposed to so-called 'formal' freedom.

Third Worldists, we were told, indulge in an astigmatic reading of the problems. Not only did they home in on Western democracies as their favoured targets, but they insisted on seeing Western expansionism depriving the Third World of all responsibility for its own history in an insidiously paternalist fashion. They, the Third Worldists, were said to insist upon government changes that destroyed the few existent formal liberties and foisted on the people an economic and social regression diametrically opposed to supposed 'true freedom'.

The 'new realists' then produced a long list of Third Worldist boobs and flubs, from the Khmer Rouge's Kampuchea through Ethiopia to the Miskitos of Nicaragua. Plus, it was said, the fact that excessively Rightist governments could at least be brought to their senses if not to heel – quite the opposite was the case of Left dictatorships. Look at Portugal, Spain, Bolivia, Somoza's Nicaragua, the Central African Republic, South A— (oops!).

It is true that these honourable opponents were ably abetted by the popular media. In the name of 'freedom of information' we were engulfed by sensationalism. Can we be surprised that the implicit themes of the Right make headway – such as our supposed ethnic superiority – when we see only the miserably starved profile of Africa? How are we to oppose the view that the Third World is a bottomless pit of beggary, that those gooks are unwilling to and incapable of taking care of themselves? How then resist the conclusion that we can help only through charity, through the tear-jerking racket of the Press (soothing our consciences), and that we are justified in using aid to strengthen our own interests? How can we then not look upon the people from the Third World as inferior and superfluous?

It is true too that we never analysed the motives and the effects of development aid thoroughly enough. Nor did we look at the political contents and the historical justification of Third Worldism. Foreign aid has never been without self-interest. It was a way of preserving a certain past, made up of privileges and power, and of buying a future – be it political (even, or particularly, via culture) or economic. Besides, the Third World is an arena for East–West conflicts: development aid is a weapon and a manifestation of this struggle for influence . . .

But under the pretext of purging Third Worldism (freed from residual guilt, putting Western interests first, taking care of the endangered minorities – a long shot away from a compassionate European élan, which supported peoples' rights, internationalism, liberation movements), a concerted and sustained attack is launched against the Left's positions and options. In comparing that which bears no comparison, in showing up our naïveté – ever so easy! – in accusing us of being soft on repressive governments grown from the gun barrels of liberation struggles, they are attempting to discredit and limit the Left's impact in Europe. The roll-back again. From Marxism, the opium of some intellectuals, especially in its Sovietist and Leftist derivations, we have gone on to the cocaine of liberalism. Hence the thinking and the doing flowing from generosity, tolerance and international solidarity must be bludgeoned, and a *Lebensraum* established for the Right pretending to be moderate, liberal and pragmatic.

Of course it constitutes a monstrous evacuation of history, ridiculing or obfuscating our true principles when it comes to aid; of course their act, attractively moderate and enticingly non-dogmatic and 'realistic', barely hides the harsh realities of racism and xenophobia; of course they caricaturize our Third World commitments.

And yet there is a fair amount of truth in their criticism. It is true that we stuck our noses into affairs that were none of our business, that many of us projected our impotence and our local marginalism on to a romantic, potentially revolutionary 'elsewhere'. It is true that our Third Worldism sometimes sprouted from sclerotic thinking. True too that our development aid only too often was conceived of and practised in terms of zones of influence, of access to raw materials, of the establishment of markets. True also that we were paternalistic in our attitudes, jaded by our disappointments (due, essentially, to our false readings), and that we weren't rigorous enough in our insistence upon justice in the Third World.

Whereas it is true that the debate can be 'de-doctrinized', only a blind fool could expect political reflection to be 'de-ideologized'.

Justice is not a Western prerogative. Force doesn't constitute a moral right. The essential is not elsewhere. You do not refashion history. You mustn't fall into the trap of opposing public or people's rights to individual ones. It is incumbent upon us to *think through* the complexities of these apparent contradictions. There cannot be a real contradiction between personal freedom and common freedom because that would imply the untenable notion that the first freedom arrogates to itself the right and the power to restrict the second.

Freedom doesn't exist in its pure form. It is invented, thought up and through, constructed, won, controlled, safeguarded. Above all a freedom is articulated by a right that cannot exist unless it has the possibility of being exercised, unless it has the *means* to be, and unless it is instructed by a knowledge of accountability.

It is not all that strange that our choices should be queried and that we should interrogate ourselves: let's not forget that our ill-famed crisis, this socio-political mutation, is at heart a contraction of humanism.

Third Worldism, expressed *inter alia* as development aid, will always take its cue from a power relationship. That's the set-up. Its contents, as far as we're concerned, should be the expansion of political consciousness.

247

End Notes

Boris Souvarine (in his *Ecrits 1925–1939*, p. 131, Editions Denoël) said:

> If bourgeois practice, itself the product of historical contradictions, gave a peculiar meaning to the words freedom and democracy, it is not for us to reject their implied contents in Socialist thinking, despite the embarrassment of using a vocabulary that cannot be renewed at will. The opposition wasn't capable of interpreting the democratic aspirations of the proletariat, even while it claimed to be democratic in too restrictive a way ... We agree with Rosa Luxemburg that Communist dictatorship is defined by *the way democracy is practised*, not by its *abolition*.

The above remarks, adapted here from the original French, I made on 26 January 1985, at the Sorbonne, at a colloquium organized by Socialist Human Rights on the theme of: 'For a New Society: Defence, Adaptation and Extension of Human Rights'.

[iii]

And on to the writer and his predicament, by way of some citations. I would say, for instance, that the present position and stance of the whitish South African 'intellectual' is in no way unique in history. Marko Fondse, in writing about Mayakovsky, said that pre-revolutionary literature in Tsarist Russia stood out against the background of social circumstances like 'a lilac flag on a mud barge'.

And in pre-war Germany Walter Benjamin wrote thus about the poems of Kästner (who was a spokesman for the *Neue Sächlichkeit* School):

> Finally house and rent remains the rope on which the well-to-do class leads the sobbing poet ...
>
> Their function is to bring forth in politics cliques instead of parties, in literature fashions instead of schools, in the economy representatives instead of producers ...
>
> One has never made oneself so comfortable in an uncomfortable situation ...
>
> To change the political struggle from the need to take decisions into a consumer product – that is the latest hit of this literature ...
>
> Early on the poets already learned this remarkable variation on despair: the worried feeble-mindedness ...
>
> They speak to the sombreness of the satisfied who cannot spend all his money on his stomach ...

End Notes

Certainly the noise in these poems is more fart than revolution. Since time immemorial constipation and melancholy went hand in hand . . .

Much nearer to us – Andrei Almaric writing from the USSR to Kuznetsov, the writer who had admitted collaborating with the authorities so that he might flee to the West:

You speak all the time of freedom, but of external freedom, the freedom around us, and you say nothing of the inner freedom, that is the freedom according to which the authorities can do much to a man, but by which they are powerless to deprive him of his moral values . . .

I preferred in general not to send my verses and plays to Soviet publishing houses rather than mutilate them in the hope that my name would appear in print . . .

I was given no choice – you seem to be saying, and this sounds like a justification not only for yourself but for the whole of the Soviet creative intelligentsia – or at least for that liberal part of it to which you belong. It sometimes appears to me that the Soviet creative intelligentsia – that is, people accustomed to thinking one thing, saying another and doing a third – is as a whole an even more unpleasant phenomenon than the regime that formed it. Hypocrisy, acceptance of things as they are foisted on it, has become so much a part of it that it considers any attempt to act honourably as either a crafty provocation or madness . . .

But it is always better to be silent than to utter falsehoods, better to refuse to publish any of your books than to put out something which is completely contrary to what you had written in the beginning . . . better to refuse a press conference than to declare publicly that there exists in our country creative freedom.

Amen.

Notes from
a Political Discussion Paper *p.66*

Looking now at this paper, which was written probably towards the end of 1972 since it reviews the events of a year, for the attention of some comrades, I am struck by the fact that the components of our 'problem' remain nearly exactly the same. And yet we feel that the situation has evolved, which it certainly has. The struggle is a long one and although one may be discouraged because the liberation, in the meantime, of neighbouring territories did not bring in its wake our liberation any closer, one must also be proud that the spirit of resistance has survived despite the most ferocious repression, that the isolation of White South Africa is stronger now than it was then (despite their military sorties over the borders), that political consciousness is firmer and more widespread than at any other period of our history (except perhaps the early sixties), that the traditional colonialist powers no longer form one united bloc of support to their Albo foremen down South.

As for the reading: it is interesting to see that some of the portents were realized – the Bantustans became 'independent' (Transkei, the first one, in 1984); South Africa did become an exporting power . . . selling arms far and wide (with no mean amount of support from Israel); there was a break in the ranks of the rulers, etc. . . . Did the liberation movement, meaning the ANC, take the lead in unifying opposition groups? Sadly no. It seems to be willing to work through a 'united front', but its insistence upon operational and ideological control has deepened the rift with Black Consciousness groups.

It was, as indicated in the title, intended as a discussion paper, and thus not really reasoned out.

Random Remarks on Freedom and Exile *p.71*

This writing dates, I think, from 1972. There are a few papers which I now have difficulty situating. This is one. *Conflict and Literature in South Africa* is another. There is a third, not included in this volume (much of the stuff is repetitive as it is), but from which I will quote at some length in this note. It must have been written during the same period.

These papers, I rather suspect, were written for Dutch and Flemish-speaking Belgian audiences. *Conflict and Literature* I've had to translate back into English from the published Dutch (in an anthology called *Verzen van Verzet*). It may have been a text that I'd addressed to my Flemish colleagues. The third piece of writing, passages of which will follow here, I now think was the subject of a talk I gave at some gathering in Groningen. The subject must have been 'Literary Commitment and the Liberation Struggle' (I have lost the original title). In any event it will be clear that the concerns expressed repeatedly move very much over the same ground. And that my intention is always to take a position rather than to expose the reader/listener to snippets of objective information! Somewhere in there was a poem, written by a South African – I can't remember who – that I'd like to share:

> Beasts are preying on our land:
> not stately elephant
> or elegant leopard,
> part of nature's pattern,
> but homecooked, sundried
> closecropped
> skinscrubbed
> chinchucking
> churchgoing
> monomanic
> misanthropes

In shaping his future, in transforming communities, man is changing himself, his own nature – for his nature is the total sum of his experiences, his place and role in society, his links and relationships to other people, the modes of production of his class, their power and the relationship of that class to others. He is the instrument and the subject of change . . . Man transforms and is being transformed and so on.

The reality of what and who we are consists of ever-changing contradictions, but underlying that realization is the concept (and the principle) of the unity of opposites – and dare I say the interdependence of opposites?

Nothing is eternal except transformation. Nothing is static except movement.

Or, as someone once said: Everything is relative except that which is absolute (and that too depends . . .) Does that mean then that one must renounce and lay oneself down, become a breathing corpse? No, of course not. The Zen master, Dogen, stated: 'In life you should identify yourself with the living, in death with the dead.'

I do not believe that things are simply in a perpetual flux and ebb, that that which is good the one day will be bad the next and vice versa. On the contrary, there is a dynamic evolution which contains jumps and advances in quality according to an ever-ascending spiral. Struggles reach certain levels, contradictions are seemingly resolved and new ones created. In this universe the tension between the two opposites of a contradiction is the force that allows societies to progress. It can thus be said that to progress, imbalance, conflict, struggle and tension are necessary. It is good that there is resistance to the present South African regime both inside and outside the country – and literary opposition can be one of its foci – because it is this resistance only that can put the whole of South Africa on the road to progress.

As in war the offensive and the defensive, advance and retreat, strength and weakness, victory and defeat are as many pairs of contradictory phenomena, which, under certain circumstances, can mutually transform each other.

Literary opposition – an expression of commitment – is a facet of what we generally refer to as culture.

The value of culture as an element of resistance to foreign domination lies in the fact that it is the vigorous expression, on the ideological or idealistic level, of the material and historical reality of the dominated people. Culture is the fruit of the history of a people and at the same time it can determine that history by the negative or positive influences it may exercise on the relationship between man and his milieu or between groups of the same society or between different societies . . . Culture can insure the continuity of history while indicating also the perspectives for evolution and progress of the community.

How should culture be seen in the struggle for liberation in Africa? What does one mean by 'commitment'?

Obviously for me, and I am sure for many other writers too, commitment means to be effectively on the side of those who fight for justice, for equal opportunities, for a fair distribution of power: in fact, for power to the people. I am with those who struggle against discrimination and exploitation and dehumanization. 'Commitment', or motivation rather, will be different for us depending on whether we are of the rulers or of those who are ruled and oppressed. For instance, for me as a privileged White the struggle is against those who humiliate and shame me by their exercise of brutal and brutalizing power – justified only by a pale skin (or 'European' culture if you wish). A Black writer will surely wish to expose the indignities suffered by his people and express his commitment to their quest for power.

Commitment is not a static component of one's literary luggage, nor is it abstract or paying lip service only; commitment is a vital link to a cause and to a people concerned by that cause, it is a coming alive to the possibilities outside one's limited consciousness, one's tortured soul, the ivory tower; it is a way of becoming involved with change and undergoing change too; it is a means of inserting oneself in the struggle.

But I cannot convince my friends of this by words alone. There must be a break, a decision, a point of departure. I must get tied to the struggle by my own experience, my own concrete participation. It is while walking that I learn how to walk.

The question of commitment is of particular importance in the Third World. The temptation is big for the writer from a conquered or subject people to become alienated from his background. More often than not he will express himself in the tongue of the colonizer – and, since no language is devoid of value connotations and a cultural colouring, he may well be addressing an audience consisting only of the same colonizers. He has become a product of the masters' 'civilizing mission'. Or he may be squabbling violently with the intermediaries between him and the boss – fighting in the forecourt where he was permitted to penetrate, but he will never be allowed to go any deeper into the heart of the house, and now he is fighting with a violence which is the measure of his alienation and frustration. His resistance is token and self-destructive.

History has shown us that it may be relatively easy, under certain circumstances, for the foreigner to impose his domination on a defeated people. But, whatever the material aspects of this domination may be, it can be maintained only by the permanent and organized repression of the cultural life of the subjected groups . . . As long as there exists a part of that people safeguarding a cultural life, just as long foreign domination will not be assured of its perpetuation. At any given moment, depending on internal and external factors, which will determine society's evolution, cultural resistance may flare up anew in other forms[?] – political or economic or armed struggle – so as to combat the dominators more completely.

The foreign occupier thus has one of two choices (as Cabral pointed out): either to eliminate the population of a given country to prevent the possibilities of cultural resistance, or to try to harmonize political and economic exploitation with the cultural identity of the oppressed people.

The first option obviously nullifies the prize and the object of foreign domination: the captive people. The second hypothesis is impossible also. It is not possible, for ever, to 'harmonize' economic and political domination of a people. In an attempt to flee this dilemma of cultural resistance the colonizers have persistently come up with theories that more or less crudely embody racism, justifying the maintained control of the indigenous peoples.

We have seen (and are still seeing) two such theories in operation

in Southern Africa. The one was the Portuguese variant of progressive assimilation of the colonized – based on a denial of African
culture – perhaps best summed up in the absurd words of Salazar
when he said: 'Africa does not exist.' We know how unworkable
that ploy turned out to be. The other is the theory of so-called
Apartheid, created, applied and developed on the basis of economic
and political domination of the peoples of Southern Africa by a
racist minority. This cruel exploitation of the labour of the African
masses locked up cynically in the largest concentration camp ever
known to mankind, this practice of Apartheid will fall apart too.

How can one then be an African writer and not be committed –
either to the preservation of some of the beauty and the pride of the
people, or to the struggle for change? To be an African writer and
not be in opposition would denote a betrayal of all humanity. It
would mean that one is a kept dog.

How do the authorities suppress literary opposition in the country?

When a whole nation is oppressed and can be liberated only
nationally, the characteristic of control is the negation of any historical
evolution of the dispossessed by usurping, in a violent way, their
freedom to develop the productive forces. In any given society the
development *niveau* of productive forces and the kind of social
utilization of these, determine the modes of production. This level
of productiveness is the true and permanent transforming agent of
history. Apartheid regulates the development of productive forces
for the benefit of a certain power system, to the advantage of those
who profit, exclusively, from those structures. This is true as well for
culture where, for example, we have Separate 'Bantu' Education, or
where we encounter the promotion of folklore as opposed to socially
conscious popular art . . .[1] Literary opposition must be repressed
because it reflects social conscience and because it can identify at
every evolutionary step of a society searching for means of survival
and progress the dynamic syntheses for the resolution of these
conflicts. Freedom of expression is denied the majority because the
means to freedom are not permitted to exist.

We are ruled by a panoply of laws, which can be, and are, invoked
to do away with opposition – from Censorship to the Group Areas
Act, which make interaction (theatre, readings) difficult, to the Pass

---

[1] Inferior and restricted education for Blacks is still, now in 1985, one of the
most detested and combated traits of Apartheid. And it is no surprise that
South Africa never developed a really indigenous cinematographic industry.

System, to the Law on Terrorism. Writers often end up in gaol or banned, not, ostensibly, for what they'd written, but for some other 'political' crime – that is, being involved in the struggle for freedom.

I ought to point out in passing that we should be alert when evaluating that which is happening down South at present. What is apparently dolled up as 'change' is only a rearrangement to preserve and to extend power. Writers have been imprisoned, banned and exiled for as long as we can remember. And this continues despite the more liberal and accommodating façade presented to the outside world. Among the young Black intellectuals detained recently, and still kept in prison without being charged, there are also writers.[1]

Could it be different? Can the White in power also participate in the transformation and not just *be* changed? I don't think he can for as long as he retains the power control that he has at the moment. Years of exerting and condoning oppression and discrimination, of self-brutalization brought about by the albocentricity that must be one of the most poisonous roots of imperialism, have made the Whites suspicious and loaded them down with complexes . . .

What forms does literary opposition take inside the country?

There are the popular and nearly spontaneous expressions of resistance, particularly as reflected through the freedom songs; there is opposition expressed via the theatre (an excellent example is that of the Serpent Players from Port Elizabeth with their plays describing and living the agony and the absurdity of Black existence in South Africa); there are also various attempts at street or guerrilla theatre by both Black and White.

Then there's a form of literary resistance, which has attracted quite some attention abroad: that coming from young White writers. This opposition is deemed important because of the function ascribed to Afrikaans literature within Afrikaner society. (The opposition is aimed at new censorship laws; I believe anti-censorship writers' organizations were created to defend the authors' interests.) The revolt arouses interest obviously because it reflects dissent among the ruling classes.

A promising form of literary opposition seems, to my mind, the attempt made by Blacks to publish and spread their own work. It

[1]Remember that this was written in 1973. We are twelve years further down the road. *Plus ça change, plus ça reste la même chose.*

indicates their starting to rely on their own strength by forging the means of communication.

I have left aside the major manifestations of literary opposition – the novels known to you – to concentrate on the new swords, the shiny new tongues one hears of and reads about, the revival (or the new spurt) of Black Poetry . . .

What form does literary opposition outside take?

By dissecting the rotten mess of South African society, the pain and the disgust of poverty and rootlessness and family break-up and violence and impotence – writers abroad amplify, and probably nourish also, cultural resistance in the country. They are the ladder between the dead and the living. They furthermore try to sever the cultural umbilical cord linking White South Africa to Europe particularly – this cord that at times serves as an excuse for strengthening those who are in power . . .

We should be aware of the class nature of culture . . . In Africa there is a complex number of levels of culture, changing from one town to another, from rural areas to urban slums, from one linguistic unit to another, from peasant to mineworker to half-assimilated intellectual. A liberation movement must know that the society that it represents, whatever the material conditions, will carry and create culture. A liberation movement must understand the popular or mass nature of culture, which cannot be dependent on some sector alone of that society.

Militant consciousness midwived by intellectuals only – that is, not defined by and attached to other forms of struggle – runs the risk of becoming a refuge, evacuating the ground where power is disputed and sounding off in directions where it cannot threaten the oppressors. Consciousness must not just become a means of venting frustration (objectively collaborating with the dominant minority by playing into their hands) but it ought to be a way of transformation. Neither must it be allowed to become just a merchant value, backed and exploited by the liberals, with the people's poets bought and sold and drooled over. That will be grist to the mill of capitalism, eventually emasculating the hard voices.

Cabral defined The Objectives of a Cultural Resistance thus:

> The development of a *popular culture* and of all indigenous posi-
> tive cultural values.
> The development of a *national culture* based on history and the
> liberation struggle itself.
> A constant increase in the political and moral conscience and

consciousness of people of all social categories, as well as patriotism, the spirit of sacrifice and devotion to the cause of independence, of justice and progress.

The development of a *scientific culture*, technical and technological, compatible with the demands of progress.

The development, based on a critical assimilation of human conquests in the fields of art, science, literature, etc., of a *universal culture* so as to be perfectly integrated in the present world and in the perspectives of its evolution.

Unceasing and generalized increase in the sentiments of humanism, of solidarity, of respect and sincere devotion to the human being.

Conflict and Literature in South Africa *p.77*

Dated December 1974. Having lost the original I had to translate this from the Dutch. (See note to *Random Remarks on Freedom and Exile*, p.250.)

The one area of pronunciamentos that I'd like to return to is that, subtitled (3) in the text, concerning the English-language White South African authors. I was clearly talking through my prejudiced hat there.

Our South African literature has been immensely enriched by the books of Nadine Gordimer, Laurens van der Post, Guy Butler, Sheila Roberts, David Livingstone, Athol Fugard, J. M. Coetzee . . . to name but a few. But even at the time of writing the paper I surely must have had a more nuanced view of work already existing then of Alan Paton, Nadine Gordimer and the older H. C. Bosman! If you scratch a bit you will find that my ill-formed attitudes reflect another cultural complex – that of the 'Afrikaner' towards the 'Englishman'.

There are historical roots to this animosity. There is also, for the Afrikaner, a barely camouflaged sense of unease and inferiority towards his English compatriot: it is provoked by the feeling of being part of a small, embattled cultural group as opposed to the world culture of English. And the contributions of English South Africans are then obfuscated by the brutal simplification of seeing the situation as a stark Boer-Black conflict only with the English South Africans as 'grafted-on foreigners'.

It is not only unfair, it is also untrue and therefore unwise. White English writing is doing as much, if not more, to open up areas of understanding of our predicament, and in so doing it is altering our perceptions and thus contributing to the solutions of the problems. Not only has the perceived position of some of them – as 'sensitive outsiders' or 'captives of privilege' – given rise to exceptionally fine writing, but many more are now participating as full-blooded South Africans of native stock (even if curiously marked, as we all are in some way or another).

Pierre Mesnard's Story *p.87*

Translated from Afrikaans. Printed in *Rapport*, 12 January 1983.

Borges was given his *Légion d'honneur* by President Mitterrand in the Elysée Palace. When I went up to congratulate him he asked me softly to describe to him what the medal pinned to his lapel looked like. He listened intently.

Freedom *p.91*

First presented as a small address during the reception of the Jan Campert literary prize during January 1983. Written in the train going to The Hague where the reception took place in the town hall, and where for the first time after such a long absence I could again greet some of the finest people in the world: Eva and Rutger, Laurens and Frieda, Adriaan, Gerrit, Martin and Connie, Aad . . .

Published, February 1983, as the first of a series of articles I agreed to do for *Rapport*, a Johannesburg Sunday newspaper. Translated from Afrikaans.

Paris *p.94*

This exercise in name-dropping, translated from Afrikaans, appeared in *Rapport* on 13 March 1983.

End Notes

The Writer and Responsibility *p.98*

A paper delivered to the Dutch section of PEN in the Flemish Cultural Centre, Amsterdam, 9 April 1983. A few months earlier a meeting with South African writers had taken place in Holland. I had been unable to attend. It was proposed then that all future cultural contacts with South Africa should be under the auspices of ANC. I could not agree – not because I'm against the ANC, but because I find pernicious *any* political control of the arts and literature.

I wonder – since I'm French now, would my writing in Afrikaans and publishing in South Africa get me on to the United Nations Special Apartheid Committee's blacklist?

W.F. Hermans is a distinguished and excellent Dutch writer who went on official invitation to South Africa despite repeated demands that he should not do so. He supports, or let us say, 'understands', the White regime. He did not take along his wife, a lady from Surinam, fearing racist incidents.

Keep Clear of the Mad *p.107*

Translated from Afrikaans. Printed in *Rapport*, 24 April 1983.

Berlin *p.111*

Translated from Afrikaans. Appeared in *Rapport*, 29 May 1985.

On our last night in Berlin there was a party in a bookshop. Two writers, a German and a Turk, came to blows. The Turk had accused the avowedly liberal German author of being a Fascist . . . Why? 'Because you people always want to *study* us, our culture, our books. You think you have the *right* to come and *dissect* us. You *steal* us. We are "interesting" objects!'

I was impressed by the sturdy and hefty German doors, wash-basins and taps. At the airport, when arriving, you see big posters of wanted terrorists. The faces of those who had been captured, killed or 'suicided', are cut out. An eerie impression. I had the feeling that Berlin must be an incestuous city. Racism seems to be widely spread and dour there, not just the work, as is the case here in Paris, of the anti-social police or some pot-bellied and frustrated crackpots.

9 June 1983 *p.116*

First read, in Afrikaans, at the Rotterdam 'Poetry International', 12 June 1983. Published by *Rapport*. Published, in the Dutch translation of Adriaan van Dis, by Van Gennep Publishers in their yearbook.

A Festival of Poetry in Rotterdam *p.119*

Published in Afrikaans, in *Rapport* of 28 July 1983. Dedicated to Martin Mooij, the guardian knight of poetry.

My Dear Unlikely Reader *p.125*

Written in Afrikaans, on the rooftop of the house of an old friend called Ashoop, in Rome. Published in *Rapport*, 21 August 1983. Ashoop was dying at the time.

'The likely reader' is an arcane South African legal concept, used in censorship cases. The sheep in the street.

We had gone to Italy (we were on our way to Palermo) so that I could complete work on *True Confessions of an Albino Terrorist*. Gaol was foremost in my mind; I was reliving the experiences of seven years. The same material was to fill many of the prison-book pages. I was still a coiled spring.

The Professor Barnard I refer to is the famous heart surgeon, staunch supporter and apologist of the South African government. Dennis Goldberg, recently released after more than twenty years of a life sentence, was a co-defendant in Mandela's trial. *Boop* is prison slang for 'prison'. A rand is worth around five French francs.

End Notes

Palermo *p.130*

Translated from Afrikaans. Published in *Rapport*, 18 September 1983.

We spent nearly two marvellous months in Palermo, working and living in one of the poorest quarters. A mafioso's car was headed off one night by a rival gang and he was executed by a shot between the eyes on our doorstep. His little boy, who had been in the car with him, ran up the road to the Fire Brigade station and howled: 'They've killed my father!' I'd heard the muted crack and went down (women were not allowed on the street). The police weren't interested in potential witnesses; they moved the sullen spectators along.

from Notes of Bird *p.135*

Extracts from a small book published (with the kind assistance of Meulenhoff Publishers, Amsterdam) on the occasion of an exhibition of paintings and drawings made since my return from Greyness, at Galerie Espace, Amsterdam, March 1984.

Fumbling Reflections on the Freedom of the Word and the Responsibility of the Author *p.142*

At the time of the Galerie Espace exhibition of my works, during March 1984, I wrote and delivered this paper at the Maison Descartes – the French cultural centre in Amsterdam. Jean Galard (author of *Orphée, Mort des beaux-arts* and *La Beauté du geste*) was at that point the director of the institute. Later that evening we had a fine meal in those refined surroundings, with some dear and close friends, and Noordhoek Hecht produced a crumpled note from his pocket from which he made a touching speech.

The text has been translated from the original French.

Upon Hearing about the Hertzog Prize *p.147*

Written in Afrikaans on Friday, 27 April 1984. Released to the South African press and published in part or *in extenso* by several newspapers.

The Hertzog Prize is probably the most prestigious literary award for Afrikaans literature. It is awarded once a year – in turn for poetry, prose and plays – by a jury appointed by the South African Academy for Arts and Sciences. This culturally powerful and ethnically exclusive organization groups the White élite Establishment. Writing in Afrikaans but being a *volksverraaier* (a traitor to the people), I had had my run-ins with the Academy over the years. Tch tch.

Professor T. T. Cloete, prominent academic and poet, during the early seventies wrote a secret report for the security police and the Broederbond in which he tried to prove why and how my writings and the writings of André Brink are subversive, 'breaking down standards, destroying the people's notion of colour (meaning awareness of ethnic categories), and softening them up for communism'. The Broederbond (League of Brothers) is a semi-secret Afrikaner 'cultural' organization to which all the White Nationalist politicians and local dignitaries belong.

Dead Locust Rumours
and Language as
the Random Thoughts of Camels *p.150*

For a three-day period during August 1984 a number of poets, poetry editors and publishers and festival organizers were gathered by the Dutch Unesco delegation under the chairmanship of Adriaan van der Staay (cultural advisor to H.M. the Queen of The Netherlands) at Muiden castle not far from Amsterdam. Among the participants there were old and new friends – Yehuda Amichai, Edoardo Sanguineti, Hans-Magnus Enzensberger, Michael Krüger, Michel Déguy, Peter Taylor, poets from Hungary and Yugoslavia . . . We discussed ways and means of better co-ordinating the translation, publication and production of poetry.

It was pleasantly hot. We dined off the ancient plates in the beautifully preserved castle. Most of the paintings on the walls visually illustrated verbal puns. On the last day we went sailing on the inland sea (Muiden was not only a Renaissance culture centre but also a fortress guarding the port); someone played the accordion and sang, the sun was ensnared by the sails and the ropes, and Edoardo took off his shirt.

Poetry is *p.156*

It can be boring to listen to the long statements people feel called upon to make about poetry. But in nearly every speech there was embedded some attempt at defining poetry. I jotted them down. This was the result. A truly communal effort.

the rabbit hunt *p.158*

This poem, originally in Afrikaans, describing a scene during an uprising in a Black township, was first published in *Rapport*, September 1984.

Letter to a Figure in Manet's *Olympia p.160*

Translated from the French. It has appeared in the 'Le Musée imaginaire' series of *Le Nouvel Observateur*, Paris. Ka'afir is an African poet, a friend.

Angel *p.162*

From a workbook; written during the autumn of 1984. Angel is my brother.

A Reading of the Present Situation
in South Africa, Autumn 1984 *p.167*

Written for the December 1984 number of *Les Temps modernes* in Paris.

In the light of recent events (July 1985) my reading of the Botha Government's scope for initiative may have been erroneous. The unexpected extent and intensity of internal unrest and foreign reaction to the state of emergency could well have stymied some of their projects. The ANC, after its recent national congress somewhere in Zambia, seems to be in a stronger position now. Its flag is seen ever more often in the country; even the red banner has reappeared here and there.

Desmond Mpilo Tutu *p.181*

Written for *De Volkskrant* in Holland. It appeared during January 1985.

I met Bishop Tutu for the first time when he came to Paris during May 1985 to attend the International Human Rights Conference organized by the French government. I was privileged to observe a very touching scene the day he left to return to South Africa. We were saying goodbye in a small salon in the conference building. Dom Helder Camara, small and slight in his cassock, walked in to take leave of Tutu. They met halfway across the room under the central chandelier and I heard one of them (which one?) say softly: 'Please bless me.' And then, for about a minute, they struggled because they couldn't decide who was to bless whom – as one sank to the floor the other would pull him to his feet again. It looked like a contest in humility. Eventually they were both on their knees facing one another, their hands clasped, their two heads touching, and for a few long minutes they murmuringly prayed together, oblivious of people passing along the passage and gawking at the door, oblivious too of the roar of Paris traffic outside. They got up, had their heads bent together some more – two martyred continents meeting – embraced, and left separately: Tutu to go and preside with raised arms at the innumerable burial services of our young ones assassinated by the police and to save some supposed collaborators from the anger of the crowds.

End Notes

On the Ethics of Resistance as a Writer in a
Totalitarian State *p.184*

The above paper was written in New York at the beginning of
February 1985, and first read to an audience at the New York
University. More or less the same version was read a few weeks
later in the African Studies Department of the University of California, Los Angeles.

In my shuffling verbal run-up to the delivery I tried to point out a
few discrepancies (it was only fair to do so): that I really had no way
of knowing whom I was addressing. Was I preaching to the converted? Was I shouldering an open door? Wasn't I perhaps just
telling people what they wanted to hear? Was I, through my mouth-
ings, pretending that reality is an image? *Is* reality an image?

Maybe I wasn't even really addressing the question. (You could
have asked me my opinion on the quantum theory and I would
have ended up condemning the South African minority regime.)

I did however try to warn the listeners/readers beforehand. It was
clear that I could not speak on behalf of anyone, that I'm neither
leader nor representative; I said that I was, partially, aware of the
corruption of suffering; that I wanted them to take what I had to
offer as one man's penpoint of view obviously formed and deformed
by personal experiences but as obviously also by 'the situation'. I
knew that they'd find my utterings shot through with paradoxes,
just like this tortoise-shield called 'my life'. Fair-minded and
standing up straight I then avowed to having, at the time (but when
then?), no snugly fitting ideology in my possession that could
silhouette the sense of it all and reconcile the contradictions. I even
waved my paws.

Then I went ahead and slightly spoiled the oratorical (or oracular)
effect by proclaiming that I was quite happy to be thus sloshing
about in uncertainties and that I hoped they'd be happy too. After
all (I told the audience): you are no sheep and neither, I hope, am
I . . . Leave aside then the untenable contention that clarity should
be a sheep-like attribute.

Usually I would thereupon attempt covering my bet by returning
to the theme of cultural confusion (the unknown I facing the
unknowable thou), highlighting the mind blindness that ensues.
And at last I would state the Breytenbach Law: A public speaker is
someone who has the knack of spinning out noise to amply fill
(amplify . . .) the allotted conference time.

It is all about the moving mind. What else is the mind but

movement, a moving consciousness from perception to impression? And life a long process of losing touch. Like shrivelling in the shell.

I Write *p.195*

Written in French for a special publication of the Parisian *Libération* on the subject of writing. Published during March 1985.

Can Reform Still Obviate Revolution? *p.196*

Written, April 1985, for the *Los Angeles Times*. Published also in the July number of a South African magazine called *Leadership*.

A few months later, while I'm writing this (July), the internal situation has deteriorated so much that Botha has been obliged to proclaim, for the first time since Sharpeville twenty-five years ago, a state of emergency. Meanwhile the number of victims killed in the townships has climbed dramatically; South African army saboteurs were caught trying to blow up American oil installations at Cabinda in northern Angola (after officially pretending that all troops had been withdrawn from that territory), and their soldiers raided Gaborone – mining houses and killing fifteen 'terrorists' (as usual women and kids and an odd tourist). We had been in Botswana a little more than a year earlier just as President Masire returned from pleading with Washington to intercede with the Reagan Administration's protégés on Botswana's behalf. Gaborone is a small sleepy town, entirely vulnerable to the big and brave South African soldiers.

Although the fast-developing events made my paper irrelevant, I think some parts of the analysis still valid. Despite mounting domestic pressure, and despite their being embarrassed by their South African allies, America still refuses to let go of their pre-established long-term plans in Southern Africa. Larry Eagleburger, President of Kissinger Associates (a so-called risk-analysis consulting firm) in a *Leadership* interview put it this way:

> I had thought that for most of the past four years, the authorities in America and South Africa had understood that by working reasonably and co-operatively together we could shape history. I would hate to see that lost and a blind eye turned to the future. The future has to be managed and it has to be managed now, not when it comes. It

would be a tragedy for both of us if we lost what we have built up at great effort and some political cost in both countries over the past four years.

Well, the bad news for Mr Eagleburger and other imperialists of his kind is that the Africans have decided to shape and manage their own future.

In Europe France was the first to break ranks with its reactionary Common Market partners and announce the imposition of sanctions on renegade White South Africa. These sanctions were largely symbolic, but to the honour of the Fabius Government it must be said that it took the lead in asking for similar measures to be adopted by the UN Security Council and in so doing forced out into the open White South Africa's real bankers and supporters: Britain and West Germany. Greed and racism were not going to be denied easily.

How long before the message gets through? A long time ago, before 1961, Chief Albert Luthuli, then the leader of the ANC, wrote:

> We painfully encourage the world to ostracize South Africa so long as she is unrepentant, and on our part we must be ever diligent in exposing the implications and effects of Apartheid. The situation calls for more effective action by the United Nations and its member nations ... to get South Africa to mend her ways ... the hour demands of us all to redouble our efforts in arresting the anti-democratic tide in our country and everywhere.

So much for the major issues. But in fact, thinking about the patterns I tried to identify in this article, I realized that our understanding of the evolving situation is very often built up from peripheral impressions.

Watch out for the soft signals. Be sure to track the movements from the corner of the eye. Truth is a tic. Some titbits of information, awash in a tide of words, can be indicative. They slip through, they are as nothing in themselves, but in passing they take on the importance of a revelation or a confirmation. For instance: I read in the press (January 1985) about this KGB fish who defected to the West, to Federal Germany. It appears that the turnabout had occurred some months earlier, but that it was kept secret till now. It is said that he had the rank of colonel, that he gave information about the structure of the KGB, and that he fingered important honourable correspondents growing turnips in Western Europe. The important point, for me, is that he is now living on a farm somewhere in South Africa.

Several reflections arise. Making his defection known so long after the event can be understood only in terms of an unfolding game. The Western services must be manipulating the contents and the timing of the announcement to strengthen their disinformation tactics. And then – hiding in South Africa! How eloquently the nature and the extent of their collaboration with South Africa's DNS (Directorate of National Security) is shown up. You don't perhaps think he's just an innocent immigrant down there, left in peace to work his turnip patch?

Take another instance: during 1985 the United States was, for the first time, to extend military aid to Mozambique. A million dollars in material and $150,000 spent on the training of Mozambican forces. The implications? How unthinkable that the world's sheriff could be called upon and willing to help a 'Marxist' regime! Thus then the results of 'the roll-back of Communism' launched by South Africa on America's behalf and highlighted by the Nkomati Accords. The subjugation of Mozambique is to be consecrated and consummated. Control will be tightened. How many ANC operatives will ever be able to slip through a country whose soldiers are American-trained and assisted by American 'instructors'? (Meanwhile the US Congress has made the unblocking of the aid dependent on the number of Soviet advisers in that country being reduced to fifty. It has also voted to lift restrictions on aid and succour to Unita in Angola.)

A last example, just because it's so perfectly absurd – enough to knock you off your chair with fits of hilarious weeping . . . Jacques D., loyal Party hack, lecturer at the Central School, guardian of orthodoxy, having led a life sucked smooth by non-thinking 'thinking' obedience, by obsequy . . . puts a bullet through that shivering mass of shame and ache and quirks called brain. *Aggornia-mento*. Remember, this happened at a time when the Party was in disarray, slipping down the poles, overtaken – even in the ranks of the dwindling working class – by the extreme rightist National Front! Remember too that the Party was just then moving towards a new *Congrès* with those holding the reins trying to stem the challenge to their leadership or even a real review of policies . . . The dead militant (or the deceased human) left a suicide note. The last ever. Under no circumstances was his act to be seen as political. He reaffirms his support for the Leader. And ends with: *Vive le 25e Congrès!*

Fuck thy fine face, O Death!

End Notes

Black on White *p.201*

A reiteration of familiar conundrums and pat positions: as if I have
to keep reading the riot act to myself lest the reality of my commitment and my involvement start crumbling under my feet (if you
permit the mixed metaphor). Rather too one-eyed when looking at
the liberals, their usefulness. Tougher, more left-wing writers, or
'cultural workers' as the euphemism goes, will disagree; they feel
that they are already part of a *national* consciousness and they
submit without questioning to majority leadership – some of them
paid dearly for their convictions. Liberals, ennobled by living the
contradictions of the land, may feel that their own brand of digni-
fied outrage – given their credibility, their exemplary courage and
their obvious reasonableness – has a better long-term chance of
modifying the attitudes of the people who matter. Both camps will
see me as a trouble-maker, a nihilist, an untrustworthy ally, quite
deluded (though the writing, some will hasten to add, is not
necessarily all bad), a muddled thinker, 'just a poet, you know . . .',
even a potentially dangerous amateur meddler.

Written during May 1985. Published, in a shortened version, by
Die Suid-Afrikaan, a Cape Town journal 'of independent opinion'.

A Letter from Exile, to Don Espejuelo *p.207*

Written during the month of May 1985 somewhere in northern
Spain, as a contribution to the two-day Human Rights Conference
(Carrefour International des Droits de l'Homme et des Libertés)
which took place in Paris on 30 and 31 May. Excerpts were published
in the Parisian daily, *La Croix*, during the week prior to the conference.

At about the same time I happened across the following quotations,
printed in another newspaper:

Et puis, n'est-ce misérable, cette existence sans famille . . .

Rimbaud, Harrar, 4 August 1888

Nous, qui nous passons passablement bien de patrie ainsi que de
famille . . .

Vincent van Gogh, August 1888

End Notes

A Letter to Winnie Mandela *p.213*

On 18 July 1985, Nelson Mandela celebrated his 67th birthday. The country was in uproar, had been in continuous turmoil for nearly a year. A few days later Botha announced a state of emergency – probably pushed over the brink by the recommendations of Johan Coetzee, the mad fanatic wielding power as the Commissioner of Police. One of the ensuing results was a universal condemnation of the Whites' policies (but did they care? could it deflect them?). And *the whole world* (plus the United States of America) asked for the release of Nelson Mandela. Maybe his liberation is on the cards . . . It would be an inexpensive 'peace gesture' for Botha to make. Maybe – with a concerted push and with a bit of luck – by the time this book is published, Mandela will be free!

The text was written to serve as a preface for a re-edition of the collected writings of Nelson Mandela, in French, by Editions de Minuit, Paris.

Dear David *p.216*

A Letter addressed to David R., a youngish down-and-outer met in New York. Because he didn't believe me when I claimed to be a writer.

Early Morning *p.223*

Written, while tired and sick of clowning in public, on the train from Brussels to Paris. Holding out the promise of a quiet future. A desperate wish.

Breytenbach by Espejuelo: The Interview *p.225*

As the heading indicated – an interview which took place in Paris on a cold day, with clouds scudding through the skies. A transcript of the interview was made by Marie Ngo. Don Espejuelo was in a vicious frame of mind.